MUMBAI A

Gabriel Khan is a journalist and writer based in Mumbai.

S. Hussain Zaidi is a Mumbai-based journalist, a veteran of investigative, crime and terror reporting in the media. He has worked for the *Asian Age*, *Mumbai Mirror*, *Mid-Day*, and *Indian Express*. His previous books include best-sellers like *Black Friday*, *Mafia Queens of Mumbai*, *Dongri to Dubai* and *Byculla to Bangkok*. He is also associate producer for the HBO movie, *Terror in Mumbai*, based on the 26/11 terror strikes. He lives with his family in Mumbai.

Mumbai Avengers

S. Hussain Zaidi
with
Gabriel Khan

HarperCollins *Publishers* India

First published in India in 2015 by
HarperCollins *Publishers* India

Copyright © S. Hussain Zaidi 2015

P-ISBN: 978-93-5136-368-2
E-ISBN: 978-93-5136-369-9

2 4 6 8 10 9 7 5 3 1

Gabriel Khan and S. Hussain Zaidi assert the moral right
to be identified as the authors of this work.

This is a work of fiction and all characters and incidents described in this book
are the product of the author's imagination. Any resemblance to actual persons,
living or dead, is entirely coincidental.

All rights reserved. No part of this publication may be reproduced,
stored in a retrieval system, or transmitted, in any form or by any means,
electronic, mechanical, photocopying, recording or otherwise,
without the prior permission of the publishers.

HarperCollins *Publishers*
A-75, Sector 57, Noida, Uttar Pradesh 201301, India
1 London Bridge Street, London, SE1 9GF, United Kingdom
Hazelton Lanes, 55 Avenue Road, Suite 2900, Toronto, Ontario M5R 3L2
and 1995 Markham Road, Scarborough, Ontario M1B 5M8, Canada
25 Ryde Road, Pymble, Sydney, NSW 2073, Australia
195 Broadway, New York, NY 10007, USA

Typeset in 10.5/14.5 Electra LT Std
By Saanvi Graphics Noida

Printed and bound at
Thomson Press (India) Ltd

For Shabana, Farida, Fatema and Narjis — the four
points of my life compass

Foreword

I've been attracted to films since childhood, especially those that deal with contemporary times and events that have changed the course of history. Many films in Hollywood do this brilliantly; they pick up events from the past and make parallel moving narratives that have some connect to it.

S. Hussain Zaidi is a writer who needs no introduction. He's known to churn out one best-seller after another and this book has all the elements, despite of it being his first foray into fictional writing inspired by true events. Hussain takes real events and retells them in print, which makes for a compelling read. This time, he has stepped out on another mission and skilfully blended fact and fiction to produce an adept, gritty thriller.

As it happened, Hussain and I were discussing another idea for a possible project, when he brought up the tentative idea of *Mumbai Avengers*. What he offered me was really exciting to turn into a film. It was right up my alley. It clicked with me instantly, since I've been a documentary film-maker as well, and have researched extensively in the genre relating to terrorism – be it in Kashmir or Afghanistan. I have also made three feature films

(*Kabul Express*, *New York* and *Ek Tha Tiger*), which in varying degrees, pertain to similar subjects. I lapped up Hussain's idea in the blink of an eye.

What made his plot more interesting is that it is a fine blend of fact and fiction, or as publishers put it, 'faction'. Hussain took factual instances and expanded on them wonderfully to form a rather interesting narrative, something which is plausible enough to happen in real life as well. I place a certain confidence in the facts Hussain states, since he is known to be diligent in the background and research for his books. His work has always attracted me, one of the reasons being his cinematic style of writing. That was a major asset he brought to the table in my collaboration with him.

Another aspect that really attracted me to the idea was its backdrop – India after 26/11. Not much has been done in print or film with 26/11, and even today, that red letter day is a provocative and disturbing reminder to every Indian. Many aspects of the horrific attacks are still unresolved. We are still grappling with many questions, and wondering why nothing of note is happening about them. I felt that if you could use a backdrop such as this, and provide a sense of catharsis to Indians, there would be some form of closure, even if in a parallel, fictional world. For instance, the killing of Osama bin Laden in Abbotabad provided a perfect sense of closure for Americans after 9/11. In this book and in my film, Hussain and I have tried to recreate that similar feeling for our countrymen.

Of course, there are differences in my screenplay and in Hussain's narrative that unfolds in the following pages. There are some things that work well in literature but perhaps not in cinema, and vice versa. Moreover, even though the seed of the idea has come from Hussain's book, we have both taken separate routes to reach the same finish line. This has also been done so that neither the book nor the film loses its novelty. I'm sure both our approaches to the same idea will leave you thrilled and entertained.

All in all, what Hussain brought to me was an extremely exciting package and it didn't take me more than a second to grab it. It shouldn't for you, either.

—**Kabir Khan**

Author's Note

Mumbai Avengers has been a sentiment, a dream and an ambition, especially in the post-26/11 scenario. It irks me that our cunning neighbours have always had an upper hand in proxy wars and that our government has often manifested its chronic impotence.

'We are in an age of asymmetrical war. No longer do vast armies of ill-trained conscripts confront each other in huge and, hopefully, decisive battles,' writes Nigel Cawthorne in his investigative book *Warrior Elite*. 'What is required are small forces of highly trained fighters.' In other words, a phenomenon which is accurately interpreted by the US, Israel, China—and even Pakistan—but not by India, which is among the most threatened nations in the world.

This book was brewing within me for years but it was only when I met Kabir Khan informally, and we got talking about stories, that it got the much needed impetus.

Mumbai Avengers became possible only due to the dedicated and selfless contribution from some of my friends. As always, doing research for a book and writing it turned into a journey that led to profound discoveries along the way.

The biggest contribution came from my friend, Additional Commissioner of Police Brijesh Singh, who is much younger than me, but whose expertise, skill sets and magnificent understanding of the world are refreshingly exhilarating. Had it not been for him, the book would never have come into existence. I am also thankful to him for reading the manuscript overnight and making several corrections.

Two young and creatively gifted protégés ensured that the book got off beyond the thinking pad – Aditya Iyengar, who was involved at the beginning, and Bilal Siddiqui, who stepped in to fill his shoes. Without their contribution, the book would never have seen the light of day.

Nashik Police Commissioner Kulwant Kumar Sarangal shared his ideas about how one could enter Pakistan. He gave me several hours of his precious time and explained to me the intricacies of espionage operations – pearls of wisdom which are spread through the book.

Apart from the police, S.P.S. Basra from the coast guard was also very helpful. He explained to me the treacherous waters that lay between Karachi and Mumbai.

Retired colonel Mahendra Pratap Choudhary helped me immensely with his profound knowledge of explosives and weaponry. A couple of meetings with him and I felt like an Ayatollah on arms and ammunition. Thank you, Choudhary sahib.

Some intrepid journalists also chipped in with their help. Ateeq Shaikh, special correspondent at DNA and Sagnik Choudhary at *Indian Express* were among those who helped provide touches of realism to the story. Ateeq's contacts with the coast guard and fishermen in Mumbai formed the basis for the final escape plan of the *Avengers*. Sagnik dug into the *Indian Express* archives to trace the famous story of the victory of Muslim commandoes on the treacherous peaks of Kargil. Sonia Thomas who recently graduated from St. Xavier's, helped me in the transcription of certain chapters.

Then there were those who agreed to read the manuscript and point out any factual errors in the story. Mrs Anjali Kale-Singh took time to read and draw my attention to a few gaffes. I must thank Major General (Rtd), Sayed Javed Jafri, who not only read the book but also made several corrections. I owe a major debt of gratitude to Jaspinder Singh Kang, who read the whole story and vetted certain sensitive portions.

Mr Rakesh Maria was the first person to read the first complete draft and give me an endorsement. I cannot thank him enough for his highly encouraging testimonial that adorns the cover of the book.

I must also thank my editor at HarperCollins India, Karthika V.K., a good friend more than just my publisher. Her consistent motivation and inspiration kept me on my toes and encouraged me to write better. My young friend, Mohsin Rizvi, slogged tirelessly to put together the cover of the book and Bonita Vaz helped us arrive at the perfect design.

My list cannot be complete unless I mention Sajid Nadiadwala, whose interest in the story resulted in the writing of this book. Ashoo Naik, the Tom Cruise of my life — remember *Jerry Maguire?* — was another driving force. Thanks, Ashoo.

The cherry on the cake has been my association with film-maker Kabir Khan. His insights into international espionage and storytelling were a revelation.

Prologue

24 January 2013 – Joint Parliamentary Committee meet.

The giant screen lit up and after a brief flicker, the images of three men, heavily bearded but without moustaches, flashed onto it.

All the people in the room knew who the three men were. They hated them, loathed them, but it was an impotent hate. They could do nothing about it.

The man standing in front of the screen, his back to them, spoke without turning around. 'When do we get justice?'

He looked like a grizzled, middle-aged man. Retired Lt Gen. Sayed Ali Waris was actually a few weeks over fifty-eight, with close-cropped hair, a perennial frown and bushy eyebrows, a strong jaw set below thin lips and fierce, flashing eyes. A faded, razor-sharp scar ran down his right cheek to his jaw. He seemed extremely fit and stood erect, his shoulders broad. It was clear, even to the undiscerning, that he'd had military training; nobody could mistake him for anything else, even in civilian clothes.

As Waris turned around, his audience unconsciously straightened up in their chairs, and grew more attentive. When the hero of Operation Blue Star and Kargil spoke, everyone listened, without exception. But as he glared at the assembly, there was only one thing on everyone's mind: why was he showing them pictures of these wanted terrorists, who were out of their reach and therefore old news?

Waris's deep voice cut across the room clearly, though he spoke in a tone scarcely above a whisper. He pointed at the three faces one by one. 'Look carefully at the screen, please. The first man is Sabahuddin Umavi, also known as Chachu. He trained the ten terrorists who attacked Mumbai on 26 November five years ago. He was their supreme commander, and he was the one who operationalized their mission.'

There were nods all around — they knew who he was.

'Next. Mehmood Azhar. Again, a very well-known face. He was the terrorist we were forced to release during the IC-814 hijacking. God alone knows how many attacks he has orchestrated or contributed to.'

Again, everyone nodded, though clearly wondering where this was going.

'Finally, Wajid Mir. The handler of the ten terrorists. He coordinated with them throughout the attack, and kept speaking to them directly via satellite phones. You have heard his voice in the recordings we obtained of the conversation between the terrorists at Nariman House and their handlers.'

The Lieutenant General paused to make sure he had everyone's undivided attention.

'All of you know what these men have done. What they're capable of. So I ask you again: when do we get justice?'

A woman sitting in the second row spoke. 'What do you mean by justice, sir? We have registered a case against them in a Pakistani court. There are charge sheets against these people. Isn't it clear to everyone? Of course we are pressing for justice! Our government is doing its best.'

Waris smiled grimly. When he replied, his voice was bitter. 'Oh, politics!' he spat. 'Is this your sense of justice, which you announce to the whole world? These men are still alive, and for all purposes, they're still free. Ask the people if they think that's justice. Go and ask the woman who lost her husband and only child in the attack. Talk to the man who saw his entire family die in front of his eyes, but has survived and is now reduced to a wheelchair existence. Go and talk to the families of all the 166 people who were shattered in one night. Go tell those people what your sense of justice is. Have you even spoken with any of them? I have.'

A man standing at the back of the room said, 'What do you mean by justice? How else can we get justice besides doing what we are doing now?'

Waris looked at him. 'Tell me something. In our ... quest for progress, what are we doing? Aren't we constantly emulating the developed nations? We look at the Americans and the Europeans and the lives of all those who live in powerful, developed countries, and all we want is to do what they do, live our lives like them. We ape them so much that we become empty carbon copies of them. Anyway, that's another matter. But have I said anything wrong? Don't we use them as models for ourselves?'

There was silence. No one knew how to answer this maverick army man's question put to them in this uncomfortably direct manner.

'We try to imitate these countries that have made their mark on the world. So I ask you – what do you think of America's sense of justice? Osama Bin Laden killed 3,000 of their people. How did the US reply? They declared war and turned a whole country upside down in search of that one man. No matter what the world said or how they labelled them. They didn't stop, didn't balk at anything until they got their revenge. Think of Saddam Hussein. He was alive and procuring weapons of mass destruction, which the US felt was a threat to them. So they sent their entire army in search of those weapons. Even when they didn't find any, did they stop? No! They didn't rest until they found the dictator and hanged him in full public view. *That* is their sense of justice, and everyone knows it.'

There was a stirring in the room. Nobody said a word, however, despite the fact that most of India's might was concentrated in that room.

The twenty-one people present were all part of a Joint Parliamentary Committee (JPC) instituted by the prime minister of India as was suggested by the chief of the Intelligence Bureau (IB). The JPC had been constituted to figure out what to do with the National Counter-Terrorism Centre (NCTC), and to present it in a good light. Unfortunately, since the idea had been conceived, the NCTC had met with a whole host of troubles, including jurisdiction and turf issues, and the chief ministers of several states were openly opposed to the idea.

The JPC comprised four members from the ruling party and seven from the opposition parties, as well as the chiefs of the IB, the Indian Army, Research and Analysis Wing (RAW), the Navy and National Technical Research Organization (NTRO). There were also a couple of retired military officers and Lt Gen. Sayed Ali Waris was one of them, earning his place because of his extraordinary services to the country. They had met a number of times to discuss how to combat the constant threat of terrorist attacks, but every time the discussions had been directionless and had not brought any clarity. In fact, this was the first time the matter had been put to them so succinctly – and so blatantly.

Lt Gen. Waris continued, 'There is no point in setting up agency after agency unless we have a clear will to decimate the menace of terrorism. After the Kargil war, we established the NTRO. After the 26/11 attack, we established the NIA. Now we want the NCTC. But what's the point of all these agencies if we can't use them to neutralize the threat?'

Nobody dared to interrupt, listening in nearly horrified fascination, almost knowing what the Lt Gen. was going to say next.

'I say, we follow the US example. Since we ape them in every other way, we should do so in this matter too. Our sense of justice should be the same. To kill these three people in whatever way possible. The government of India needs to devise a way. We have to—'

He was interrupted by the IB chief. 'But we are a democracy!' the man spluttered, enraged. 'We know what the US thinks of democracy. It's bullshit. We can't be like that!'

Waris was unperturbed. 'Check your facts, sir. The US isn't the only country that does exactly what it wants so as to protect its citizens. Think of Israel. What happened after those athletes were killed at the Munich Olympics? They eliminated each and every person responsible. They're a democracy; in fact, their democracy is closer to ours than the American system. So why can't we do the same thing? That's what justice is. Our citizens should know that whoever attacks us on Indian soil will be brought to book in whatever manner possible. If we can't do it officially, let's do it unofficially, off the books.'

The IB chief looked as if he was about to explode. He was joined in this sentiment by the RAW and army chiefs. It was becoming increasingly clear that most of them were completely against the idea.

'I know it's a war on terror,' said the army chief. 'But what you're suggesting is blatantly against everything we believe! For God's sake, man, we signed the Geneva convention!'

The retired army man looked at him quizzically. 'So are you suggesting we do nothing? Let them go scot-free? Should we let our country become a killing field?'

'I don't know, but we can't do this!' shouted the home secretary. 'I can tell you right here and right now, I will never support an act of retribution like this. We aren't like America. They can get away with whatever they want to, but we can't. And as far as Israel is concerned, you know the situation. They have to survive in the Middle East, and to do so, they have to protect themselves. But we can't!'

The general nodded. He had expected protest. But this was worse than he'd anticipated; they were all against him. He tried another tack. 'Very well, sir. If you keep talking about bringing them to justice but not killing them, let's do that. Let's bring those bastards back to India. The Mossad did that. They went to Argentina and brought Adolf Eichmann back to Israel. He was tried and hung. See? They didn't kill the Nazi, they brought him all the way from Argentina to Israel.'

Now the protesters were silent.

'This is why you won't find any terror attacks in Israel. This is why you will never see another 9/11 happening in the US. They will do the unthinkable, the unimaginable, to bring their enemies to justice. As for us, we keep getting bombed, because we are soft. We keep giving the world the impression that if anyone wants to screw us, we're right here, come and do what you will with us.'

He saw that he had disturbed them. Good. That was the idea. But he had anticipated less resistance. They knew him, knew he was capable, competent. Few were as skilled as he was at strategizing, and he was a genius at planning missions. They knew that he must have worked on the idea before putting it to them, and that he was perfectly capable of carrying out the mission—to either kill or kidnap the three men—successfully.

But despite knowing all this, they were against him. Except the Opposition party members. 'Incompetent fucks,' thought the general. 'They're just supporting me because they think they have to contradict the government. This isn't about government or politics, you fools. This is about our right to protect ourselves.'

Just then, his phone beeped. Frowning, he took it out, and at just that moment the door burst open and a man rushed in. He went over to the home minister and began to whisper frantically in his ear. The home minister's face grew pale and his eyes widened. Involuntarily, he looked over at the general, who was smiling grimly, as he pocketed his cell phone.

Everyone looked expectantly at the minister when his lackey stood back, but it was Waris who spoke.

'So, Daniel Bradley has been given a thirty-five-year sentence. In a luxurious five-star jail. AND THERE'S NOT A DAMN THING WE CAN DO ABOUT IT.'

There was a ripple of shock all through the room. The home minister stared at Waris, unable to say anything.

'So you see, minister, you sit here and talk about justice, but Bradley will spend the rest of his life in a nice jail, gorging himself, working out, maybe even playing golf. Thirty- five years, and the sentence may be reduced later, or he may even be out on parole sooner.'

Slowly, the army man walked over to the home minister's table, placed his fists on it and leaned forward.

'This man was the reason 26/11 happened. He was the one who caused so much mayhem in Mumbai, and he will still be out there. And our people, our widows and orphans, will still be weeping here.'

Straightening to his full six feet two inches, Waris looked around. 'You call this justice?' he snarled. 'Headley too needs to die.'

Without another word, he turned and strode out the door.

1

1 July 2013
Istanbul, 2 p.m.

Ordinarily, a raan is supposed to nourish the person who eats it. But the raan that was to be the highlight of this evening was different. It was designed to bring death.

'That was a fruitful meeting,' thought Sabahuddin Umavi, one of the masterminds behind the 26 November terror attack in Mumbai nearly five years ago. Umavi was a Ghazi, a stalwart of Islam, one who had despatched hundreds of Indian infidels to hell. The 26/11 carnage was the jewel in his jihadi crown.

And at that moment, Umavi was over the moon. Now was the time to celebrate!

Only a few minutes earlier, he had struck a deal with a Saudi Arabian organization that had enabled him to pocket half a million dollars. He could use the money to spread the spectre of mayhem and bloodshed across India: his lifelong goal. 'I'm on my way to eternal glory,' he thought, imagining life in a huge castle in Paradise, with thousands of nubile virgins at his disposal.

Umavi rubbed his hands in excitement as he paced the room, restless despite his victory and impatient to kickstart the celebrations. It had been a long time since he'd had raan, and this seemed like the perfect occasion to relish it. It was also fitting that he had struck the deal here in Istanbul, the home of that dish. The hotel he had checked into, the Marmara Taksim, was one of the biggest and the best, and their food and hospitality were world-famous. He had ordered several other delicacies as well, but his mouth watered in anticipation of the Royal Marmara Raan, even as his mind salivated at the havoc he would soon wreak.

In a room a couple of floors above his, two men sat listening very hard.

They could easily get into Umavi's room through the air-conditioning vent, but that would defeat the entire purpose of their being there. They knew his room's layout, how many men he had, and where they were stationed in the neighbouring room, how fit they were, their curriculum vitae of violence. That was why they had bugged the room just before Umavi had checked in.

Now, as Umavi made the call to room service, the two men heaved a collective sigh of relief. Things were going according to plan. They knew what they had to do.

One of them, a towering hulk of a man with an intimidating scowl and an even more intimidating moustache, clicked open his briefcase. He took out a small box, smaller than his palm, and looked at it suspiciously. 'You really think this will work?'

The other man was busy changing into a garish yellow suit with a pink tie and alligator green shoes.

He glanced over and said, 'Yes, it'll work. Ray said it would.'

The first man opened the box and sniffed at the white powder inside. 'Smells fine,' he grunted. He gingerly touched a finger to the stuff and tasted it. 'Tastes fine too, just like dry fruit.'

'It is dry fruit. That's the idea.' The second man had finished dressing. He took a South-East Asian karambit knife from his suitcase, and tucked the curved edge of its claw into his belt, at the back. He then surveyed himself in the mirror and nodded, satisfied with his look. 'I'm ready.'

'All right, let's go.'

The two of them walked out of their suite, avoiding the lift and climbing down two flights of stairs. They were now on Umavi's floor.

'You go to the other end. I'll keep watch here,' said the bigger man, who was clearly the leader.

His colleague nodded and strolled away to position himself just outside one of the floor's lifts.

Their mission was clear. They had to wait for the room service trolley to arrive, spike the raan while distracting the waiter, and return to their room without attracting attention. They had to do it all without making the waiter suspicious, and without being spotted by the guards in the room next to Umavi's, who had kept their door wide open. 'Shit, I hope this works,' the man in the yellow suit muttered under his breath as he walked on.

There were two lifts on the floor, one at either end, and he had to take his post at the other one; this was till they figured out which way the waiter would come. They had their cell phones ready in their hands. When one of them spotted room service, he would signal to the other.

They didn't have to wait long.

In just under half an hour, the smaller man's phone vibrated. His colleague had spotted the target.

He pocketed his phone and walked towards the other lift. As he turned the corner, he saw the waiter pushing his trolley forward, a bored expression on his face. There were several dishes on the trolley, draped with a white cloth, all of them covered with large dome plate covers; the one in the centre was the biggest and therefore the one with the raan, he knew immediately.

A few paces behind the waiter, he saw his leader walking quietly, his shoes silent on the carpeted corridor. It was now or never.

The waiter saw the man in the yellow suit approaching him and quickly assumed a more pleasant expression. He manoeuvred the trolley to one side, to let the guest pass. But the man in the yellow suit had other things in mind.

He stopped directly in front of the trolley, looking at the waiter, and slowly smiled. The waiter knew that smile, and knew what was coming. He slowed to a stop too. 'Good afternoon, sir.'

The man strolled to the waiter's side and stopped a few inches away. 'Good afternoon. Where are you going?'

'Delivering an order, sir.'

'Ah.' The man touched the waiter's elbow gently, then slid his hand down his side and behind.

'Maybe you could delay that order for a few minutes?'

The waiter knew he couldn't offend a guest, not without losing his job. 'That's very kind of you, sir. But I'm afraid I can't delay. The gentleman who ordered this is a very important—'

'Yes, yes,' said the man smoothly. 'I understand. But let me take a quick look at you. I haven't seen such a fine specimen in a long time.'

He gently prised the waiter's hands off the trolley, and grasped one of his hands. With the other, he gently turned him around, his hand still caressing the waiter's behind.

'You seem quite stiff. But that's a spectacular arse you have, my friend. Why cover it clothes.'

The waiter grew flustered, and tried to gently discourage the man. In the process, he completely missed what was happening behind him.

The first man had stayed directly behind the waiter during the exchange, out of his line of sight. The moment the waiter's back was turned, he lifted the biggest lid without a sound, opened the small box in his hand, and sprinkled the powder it contained all over the raan, over and around the meat, as well as the gravy. Then he replaced the lid, pocketed the box, and moved back behind the waiter.

The instant the man in the yellow suit saw that his colleague's work was done, he smiled again, as if giving in to the waiter's protests. 'All right, my friend. But do visit me when you can. I'd like to get to know you a little better. Room 512.'

'I shall certainly see to it that you get what you want, sir,' said the waiter, straightening his coat and turning back to the trolley, not seeing the first man at all. 'Goodbye, sir.'

The smaller man winked and strolled away. The waiter trotted off. He'd grown used to this by now. Most of the Saudi Arabians who stayed at the hotel seemed to like his physique and lusted after him.

The two men met again in their room upstairs. 'Well, that was a bloody convincing show you put on. Sure you're not gay?'

His colleague grinned. 'Definitely not. My girlfriend can testify to that,' he said, starting to change back into the drab black suit he'd been wearing.

'Hmph. Anyway, what happens when the fellow gets to Room 512?'

'Someone's going to get a shock for sure,' said the smaller man, chuckling.

His leader grunted again. He took the box out of his pocket and fingered it, looking troubled. 'That raan was at least a kilo. Ray gave me twenty grams. I hope this thing works.'

'It's concentrated. It'll work.'

The two men then positioned themselves next to the telephone, this time more anxiously than before.

Downstairs, the waiter had just reached Umavi's room, but before he could knock, he encountered two burly men. Through the open door, they'd seen the waiter walk up and rushed over to check for discrepancies. One of them lifted the lid of every dish, checked the seals of the water bottles and lifted the white cloth to check the trolley, while the other patted down the waiter. Finally, when they were satisfied, they nodded.

Umavi's ears perked up when he heard the knock. 'Yeah?'

'Room service, sir.'

'Come in.'

The door opened and the waiter walked in, pushing the trolley. Umavi looked at his guards over his shoulder, questioningly, and they nodded to him. He nodded back as they closed the door, and turned his attention to the waiter, who was now unloading the dishes onto the dining table and pointing them out as he did. 'This is the raan, sir, and the biryani, and the naan, and your dessert.'

After making sure he had arranged everything properly, the waiter looked up at Umavi. 'Enjoy your meal, sir.'

'Wait.'

The waiter turned back and faced Umavi. 'Is there anything else I can do, sir?'

Umavi stared at him for a full minute, during which the waiter squirmed with discomfort. At last he said, 'Take a spoon.'

Surprised, the waiter hesitated, then picked up a spoon from the platter.

'Now taste the curry. Not the raan, the curry.'

'But sir, I'm not supposed to have that. It's for you!' protested the waiter.

'I know. I don't care. Taste the curry.'

'But sir, waiters shouldn't eat the guests' food, and—'

'Shut up, you fool,' hissed Umavi. 'Your rules are for your other guests. I'm not like them. Now taste the fucking curry or I'll make sure you're fired by this evening.'

The waiter had protested enough. Slowly, he dipped the spoon into the curry and savoured it. There was no telling what guests might ask for, but this was a first.

'Now have a tomato.'

The waiter picked up a piece of tomato from the raan and stuffed it into his mouth. He chewed it quickly, wanting to get out of the room and away from its eccentric occupant as soon as he could.

Umavi watched the man like a hawk, alert for any strange movement from him. But the waiter seemed fine. He didn't become breathless, didn't collapse to the floor, nothing. He waited until the man had gulped down the whole mouthful and then stood watching him for another minute. Then, when nothing happened, he waved his hand. 'All right. Now you can go.'

'Yes, sir. Thank you, sir.'

Umavi watched the man hasten to the door and rush out. As the door closed, he rubbed his hands in glee. It was safe.

Being a wanted man in several countries had made Umavi deeply cautious. Even in his satisfaction at having brokered a good deal, he refused to let his guard down. But this time at least, it seemed his fears had been groundless.

Sitting down at the table, he grasped the knife and cut himself a big piece of the raan. If he could, he would finish the whole thing; otherwise his guards could eat the rest.

Like a true Muslim, he began his meal with 'Bismillahir Rehmanir Rahim', but he rushed through the customary pre-meal prayer and broke off a piece as soon as he could manage. He stuffed it into his mouth and started chewing, eyes half closed, savouring the juicy morsel, the pure, unadulterated taste of it, remembering the last time he had raan, and realizing that this was infinitely tastier. But a part of his mind was still on the meeting he had had that morning. As he swallowed the first morsel, a strange signal went off in his brain, but he ignored it.

He started chewing on a second mouthful, and suddenly a thought occurred to him. Why would they want to give him half a million dollars when they had never actually met him?

He'd had this thought before, and had contemplated it from every angle he could think of, finally dismissing it as a blessing from Allah. But now, something didn't seem right.

He swallowed the second mouthful.

The men he had met were from Saudi Arabia, or so they had said. Their paperwork had proven this. They said they were very happy with the work Umavi was doing. But how had they known about him in the first place? This was another question he had thought of earlier, but this time, it seemed more urgent.

As he bit into the third piece of raan, he began to feel a bit breathless. When he swallowed, the food seemed to be stuck in his throat. Then suddenly, he started to choke.

Alarm bells were now ringing in his mind: who were these guys who had come out of the blue and wanted to give him money and, more importantly, what was their real purpose?

By now, he couldn't breathe at all. His head was starting to hurt from the lack of oxygen, and a blanket of darkness seemed to be descending in front of his eyes.

He spied the jug of water on the table and lurched forward, trying to grab it. But his body felt heavy and he fell to the floor, clutching at the table. His hand caught the big dish of raan and it fell to the floor beside him, making no noise on the carpeted floor.

His body was failing fast and he couldn't find the strength to move his ninety-six kilo frame – but his mind, panic-stricken as it was, was still racing. He realized that the meeting had been a sham, and that the men he had met had done this to him. But what had they done? The waiter had been fine, so it couldn't be poison and yet, he could feel his life ebbing. His heart was beating wildly and he felt as if someone was strangling him. He struggled to get to the water, knowing all the while that he wouldn't make it. He couldn't move at all now, and there was no way he could alert his guards outside.

Those men had killed him! But how? How had they done it? What was happening to him?

All at once, he saw a crowd of faces in front of him. Bleeding, crying, wailing, crippled people. These were the dead, the victims of his actions. But why were they crowding around him now? To escort him to his final destination?

Then, through the crowds of the dead, his hallucinating eyes watched as a monstrous giant appeared. His eyes were red, blazing with anger, and his contorted face was the embodiment of rage.

But a black blanket began to envelope his vision. Finally, the darkness in front of Umavi's eyes was complete. His body stopped twitching. His final, thwarted attempt at breathing failed. In his suite on the ninth floor of the Marmara Taksim, the great warrior Umavi died, knowing who had killed him but unable to save himself.

In the room two floors above, the two men got up. Their highly sensitive bugs had just informed them that Umavi had collapsed. Earlier they had planted a listening device outside the window, hanging by a thin thread not visible to the naked eye. The bug was supposed to relay the slightest of sounds in the room, including a shuffling of papers.

The taller man knelt beneath the AC duct and the shorter man climbed on his shoulders to reach it. He clung to the ceiling for a moment, then forced himself up through the opening. The taller man followed, though it was slightly more difficult for him. Especially since he could hear footsteps approaching. By the time they had dropped silently onto the floor of Umavi's room from the AC duct above, Umavi was stone dead, the veins in his throat standing out, his hands clawing at his chest, eyes bulging from a red face.

As the smaller man watched, his colleague silently went to the centre table in the living-room area, picked up a bowl of hazelnuts, and emptied more than half of them into his pocket. Then he brought it down on the dining table.

Within a few minutes, they were ready to get out. 'Quick! His guards will be here any moment!'

The smaller man held out a muscular arm, and the tall man held it firmly. He mustered up all his strength and pulled his colleague up until his free hand could reach the ceiling. The tall man heard the footsteps right outside the door, and in one swift motion got into the duct. The door opened and the plastic covering of the air duct closed simultaneously. The two of them left the same way they had come, as silently as before.

'That was a close shave,' the tall man whispered. 'Now let's get the hell out of here!'

Umavi's death was discovered barely an hour later, when the waiter came back to collect the dishes and found his body sprawled on the floor, food splattered all around him. His cries brought in the bodyguards, but they knew it was too late. They threatened the waiter, who was trembling in fright, and found out how Umavi had forced him into tasting the raan curry. Unbelieving, one of the guards knelt and cautiously licked a sliver of the raan, then put it into his mouth, chewed and swallowed it. Nothing happened, which left them totally bewildered.

The hotel authorities went into a tizzy upon discovering one of their guests had died. The body was taken to the local hospital, where a reluctant doctor was forced by the two bodyguards into venturing his opinion that the victim might have died from an allergic reaction. The hotel employee who was with them conveyed this information to his seniors and soon, news of the death and its probable cause had spread, subject to official confirmation.

This was what the two men heard as they stood at the front desk half an hour later, waiting to check out. Umavi had died a natural death, brought on by a severe allergy. The post mortem had confirmed that it was a hazelnut allergy, and the hotel authorities also stated that the bowl of hazelnuts in his room was half empty.

The smaller man was chatting with the concierge as he drew up the paperwork for their check-out. 'But why the hell did he have the hazelnuts? He must've known he was allergic.'

The concierge, a small portly man with a harried expression, shook his head. 'God only knows, sir. Maybe he didn't know he had the allergy.'

The smaller man also shook his head, thanked the concierge as he pocketed the slip, assured him they would have a safe flight back home, and left. Around them, the commotion was rapidly escalating.

The mission was a success. The two men had been tense throughout, as this was a new method of killing for them. In a career that collectively spanned more than four decades, they had faced many combat situations, killed men with guns and knives and tanks and bombs. They were skilled in delivering death, but they had never used such a gentle method—something that they had both been highly sceptical about—as a means of killing. The innocuous hazelnut powder, which they had tasted themselves, killed their target in less than a minute.

The moment the two men exited the building, the bigger man took out his cell phone and dialled a number. It was answered on the first ring. 'Yes?'

'The groom has left to meet the bride, sir.'

'Mubarak. Let's have the wedding celebrations here.'

'Yes, sir,' said the man and hung up. His colleague signalled for a cab and minutes later, they were on their way to the Ataturk International Airport, where a Turkish Airlines flight would take them to New Delhi.

Sitting in his study inside his Delhi home, Lt Gen. Sayed Ali Waris struck Umavi's name off a list in his diary. There were two names left.

The army man smiled to himself. The odyssey of retribution had begun.

2

2 February 2013

It was a lazy Sunday morning, just warm enough for people to stroll out and bask in the sun. Amritsar's usually freezing winters seemed to be on their way to becoming a thing of the past, thanks to global warming and the resultant rise in the earth's temperature. Not that people here really cared—it was just another thing to adapt to, in their view.

But when the lazy peace of their day was disturbed by the roar of a motorcycle, people stared at the miscreant astride it, some curious, some annoyed. The rider was massively built, with a bushy beard and eyebrows obscuring most of his face, leaving only a fierce pair of eyes visible. He weaved his way through the obstacle course of men and machines with obvious expertise, sometimes shouting when a particularly obstinate individual refused to move out of his way. Most of the men he passed assumed he was on his way to the rally and was late. They could have been right.

Deputy Superintendent of Police Iqbal Singh Kang was late, but he wasn't going to the rally. He was on his way to see the man who would be speaking at the rally – to try and stop him.

It hadn't been planned as a big rally initially. A few local leaders were slated to stop by and mutter a few words into the microphone to an audience that would probably not even touch 500. Which was why the ground they'd chosen was a small one. But then, it was suddenly announced that Ranjit Raina would be present at the rally, and the local partymen and netas went berserk. From a tiny ground they moved the rally to the Ranjit Avenue Ground, off Ajnala Road, and the anticipated audience swelled to an easy 20,000. After all, it wasn't every day that the prime-minister-in-waiting addressed a rally and few would want to miss a man who was known for his fiery, charismatic oratory.

Indeed, Ranjit's impulsive remarks sometimes sparked controversies and even furores, such as when he'd quipped just a few days ago that nearly seventy per cent of Punjabis were addicted to drugs like opium. Swati Raina, his mother and the supremo of the ruling National Democratic Party (NDP), had disapproved of her son's remark. Rumour was that she had instructed him to visit Amritsar to make amends for the grief he had caused the Punjabi populace. The Sikhs had always been a patriotic race and had contributed vastly to the freedom struggle and post-Independence wars. As they were also one-time NDP loyalists, Mrs Raina knew she could not afford to alienate them; this sort of a remark should not have been made by a potential prime ministerial candidate. Ranjit's trip was intended therefore as more placatory than campaign-oriented (the elections were to be held the following year).

The sudden announcement that Ranjit would attend the Amritsar rally wasn't sudden enough, though. Ample time was given to a group that hadn't been active in years to prepare a crude welcome for him. Kang had found out about it just ten minutes ago, which meant that he had very little time, if any at all, to stop Ranjit from receiving that welcome.

Kang had just entered his gym for a muscle-blasting workout when he saw his informant Bashir looking at him from the other end of the gym. Bashir was a failed bodybuilder and one of Kang's most prized informants. The price he demanded was unique: he would challenge Kang to deadlifts and the officer would have to lose publicly. Once he had, Bashir would give him the tip. Even though Kang could easily have defeated Bashir, he knew the information he got in return for losing would be accurate. Today was no different.

'Raina is getting married today,' Bashir said in an undertone to him, just after he had 'won'.

That was enough for Kang. He was on his bike in the next ten seconds.

He drove crazily through the narrow streets, not caring if he knocked someone down – though he knew that with his training guiding his reflexes, he would never hit anyone. The men in the Special Task Force might not be the most talked about security force in the country, but they were as well trained as any other officers.

As he turned a corner, Kang's digital wristwatch beeped. It was 10 a.m. Ranjit's rally was expected to start in half an hour, and he was a punctual man who was never late for anything, be it rally, a meeting or a doctor's appointment. Kang knew that he would leave for the ground with his security any moment now. He revved his bike and drove harder, yelling at people to get out of his way. His voice held a slight note of panic now.

Three corners and six minutes later, he sighted his destination and knew he was almost out of time. Three cars and a few police motorcycles were lined up outside the bungalow and there were security officers milling around. As Kang approached, there was a slight stir of activity, and he realized that Ranjit must have left the bungalow; there he was, walking towards his car.

Horn at full blast and shouting at the top of his lungs, Kang drove straight towards the cars. He saw the alarm in the eyes of the security officers. At once, they raised their assault rifles and pistols – but relaxed upon identifying him. Had it been a civilian approaching in that manner, they wouldn't have hesitated to shoot, but Kang was in standard STF uniform. He was one of them. So, for the moment they held their fire, although they remained on alert.

Kang knew this and decided not to push his luck any further. A little distance from the cars, he screeched to a halt and dismounted. Not bothering to keep the bike upright, he let it fall and approached the men, staring down a dozen barrels.

He kept his eyes on the unit chief in front of him — the inspector general was the only man who hadn't unsheathed his pistol. 'Stop right there. You are not supposed to be part of this set up. What do you want?' Mukhtar Singh Dhillon was composed, but the note of warning in his voice was unmistakable.

'Sir, my name is Iqbal, Chandigarh STF. I have an urgent input and I need to speak to Mr Raina immediately.'

'I thought as much. Why?'

'Sir, I don't want to explain out here in the open. But I need to see him urgently.'

'Everyone wants to see him urgently. Why—'

'Sir, we don't have time!' screamed Kang. 'It's a matter of life and death!'

The chief remained unfazed. 'Please control yourself, Officer. Shouting won't solve anything. What do you mean by life and death? We have adequate protection in place. The Special Protection Group, the Punjab Police, and you can see that chopper hovering over us. What are you afraid of?'

Kang could see a knot of men moving toward the cars and realized Ranjit was on his way.

Kang took a deep breath to steady himself. 'Sir, I'm begging you. I have important information that Ranjit sir needs to know. I found out just this morning. Sir, I cannot let him go to that rally. It's dangerous. No security is foolproof. What if there's a Trojan horse? Please, you have to trust me!' By the time he'd finished, Kang was shouting again.

There was a slight commotion behind the chief and suddenly Ranjit Raina walked into the fray, followed closely by five anxious bodyguards. True to form, he'd ignored his security cordon and walked out into the open.

'Sir, what—' the chief started to say, but was cut short.

'I'm all right, Singh. With so many of you to guard me, I'm quite safe, I should think.' He smiled at the chief and then turned and looked curiously at Kang. 'What is it, officer? Was it you shouting?'

'Yes sir. Please don't go to the rally,' Kang said urgently. 'I beg you not to go. It isn't safe.'

Ranjit frowned. 'What do you mean, not safe?'

'I mean, sir, that your life will be in danger if you go to that rally.'

'Really?' Ranjit threw back his head and laughed. 'My life in danger? Officer, let me tell you something. My life is always in danger. I know that. These men around me know that. But I refuse to let that scare me. Both my grandmother and my father were assassinated, and if it's my fate to die in the same way, I will. But I won't cower like a frightened rabbit behind lines and lines of bodyguards, you understand?'

'But sir,' pleaded Kang. 'I have concrete information that there is a threat to your life!'

'What's your name?'

'Kang, sir. Iqbal Singh Kang.'

'Well, Kang, I get this information every day. Every time I go to a rally or a meeting or out anywhere, I get concrete information, just like yours, that I will die. Does that mean I should stop going out at all?'

'But sir—'

'Enough.' Ranjit held up his hand. 'Thank you for your concern, Kang, I appreciate it. But I'm going to that rally now.'

He turned and started to walk back to his car.

Kang couldn't control himself anymore. Before anyone realized what he was doing, he strode forward and stood in front of Ranjit, blocking his way.

A frown appeared on Raina's face and he looked at IG Dhillon, who immediately yelled at Kang. 'Officer, this is gross insubordination! Get out of the way at once or I'll have you suspended right now!'

Kang refused to budge.

Dhillon clicked his fingers at his men and six of them came forward, muscles flexing as they holstered their weapons with the intention of hauling him away.

They underestimated him. Kang was a 110-kilo behemoth who stood six and a half feet tall. He was also a professional wrestler with several gold medals under his belt.

The six men trying to drag him away found this out the hard way. Despite their efforts, Kang stood unmoved, yelling all the while for Ranjit to stay. Two more men came forward, and the odds shifted slightly in their favour.

Suddenly Raina held up his hand and walked forward. The men paused and stood still, huffing.

'I'll ignore this misbehaviour, Kang,' he said, 'because I can see you really believe you're right. I won't press charges against you. I know you're concerned, but watch yourself and don't cross the line. Now, I'm already ten minutes late. Since you're so convinced that I'm in danger, you can travel in the car with me and see for yourself how most of these threats are just hoaxes.'

'But sir—' started IG Dhillon, only to be interrupted.

'Please, I'm late. Let's get moving.'

'I'm against Kang travelling with you, sir,' said Dhillon firmly.

'Point taken, Singh. Can we go now?'

With that, Ranjit strode towards his car and got in, followed by Kang. The three cars and a host of accompanying officers on motorcycles rode off in a cloud of dust.

The Ranjit Avenue ground was massive, but the security forces were used to covering large areas. Under normal circumstances, the local cops would have been enough, but since Ranjit Raina himself was going to be present, nothing had been left to chance. After all, with someone like him, it was impossible to be too careful. The man was known to recklessly shove his guards aside and mingle freely with the public, making him a security official's nightmare. He often declared that he was a people's person, that he refused to hide behind a ring of bodyguards.

All the big guns had been called in: the Special Protection Group, the Punjab Anti-Terrorist Squad (ATS), RAW, local police, Special Branch. Everyone had arrived to make sure it was safe. Sniper patrol was in place, dog squads had sniffed around, and all paraphernalia had been checked and double checked. There were no loopholes. Not that they could see, at any rate.

They were wrong. This was proved within a matter of minutes.

Raina had been delayed by a good twenty-five minutes, and instead of arriving at the podium at exactly 10.30 a.m., he reached the flower-bedecked gate at 10.55 a.m.

He was greeted by a welcoming party, all carrying huge garlands. Raina kept accepting the garlands, letting them accumulate and then removing them and handing them to his aides, as was his wont at every rally. He greeted the women party workers with a folded namaste, a bright smile on his face throughout.

Behind him, Kang seemed to have been lost in the crowd, but he was watching everything like a hawk, his eyes darting here and there. The car park was too far, so that ruled out a car bomb. All the entrances had high-tech metal detectors, so a human bomb couldn't sneak in either. Then where?

Raina was the target, not the public. His informant had told him that much. Ranjit had moved past the entrance and, till he reached the stage, he would be surrounded by people. That left the makeshift corridor to the stage as the only possibility. The corridor was around sixty yards long, and ended at the steps up to the dais.

As Raina stepped into the cordoned off area of the corridor, all the while waving at the cheering crowd, Kang's heart began thumping loudly. It was all too familiar. It was as if the old failure had taken place just now.

Three white Ambassadors halted near the VIP portico of the secretariat. Within minutes, Chief Minister Beant Singh emerged from his second-floor office, dressed in a spotless white kurta pajama, and began moving towards his car. There was a bit of jostling as his security staff struggled to keep bystanders at bay.

Kang, eighteen years younger and brimming with enthusiasm, was waiting outside on his motorbike. He couldn't enter the secretariat with the vehicle until the CM had left.

He parked the bike outside and was strolling towards the gate when he saw a figure moving purposefully towards the CM. The man was dressed in standard police uniform, but something about his movements seemed wrong. He didn't seem to have the loitering gait typical of someone who had come with an application to the secretariat. He also appeared unconcerned about his surroundings, which was unnatural given that he was a cop near the CM's security cordon. But most importantly, his movements suggested a purpose, a deliberate mission.

Suddenly, Kang realized what he was seeing. The uniformed man was no policeman. He wanted to scream and alert Beant Singh's men – but then he saw something that made his blood run cold. The man was only a few feet from the CM, and his hand was moving towards his pocket. He was a human bomb.

Kang froze. His voice was trapped in his throat, his hands and legs seemed to have turned to lead. The distance between him and the minister was less than thirty metres, but there were too many men between them. A part of Kang's brain told him that he should use his amazing strength to push everyone aside and rush to save the CM. That was his duty – to protect the country that he loved, the state, his land, his people. And his chief minister, the man who had single-handedly tamed terrorism in the state.

Before Kang could pull himself out of his frozen state, there was a massive explosion right in front of him, and he was thrown back like a toy. A dark pall of smoke engulfed everything. Then, as the shock wave cleared the building, there was a deathly silence. Kang was lying on a heap of bicycles; all around him people were rushing about, screaming, wailing and calling for help, but he couldn't hear them.

As hearing slowly returned to his temporarily deafened ears, Kang knew that the CM was dead – and that he could have saved him if he had acted in time.

That was eighteen years ago.

Suddenly, Kang was assailed with the same feeling he'd had then. Something was not right. Raina had almost reached the steps that led to the podium and Kang knew it was now or never. He rushed up to him.

'Sir, stop!'

Ranjit turned and gave Kang an exasperated look. 'Not again, officer!'

Kang refused to budge. Irritated now, Ranjit turned to his security and was going to ask them to lead Kang away when it happened.

The blast ripped through the dais, blowing it to smithereens. Nearly twenty feet away from the stage, Raina was thrown back by the impact of the blast, fetching up against the fence.

The debris from the explosion and the shock wave from the blast hit several cars parked behind the stage, including those of Ranjit's entourage, shattering their windows and triggering their alarm systems. The audience was thrown into a panic, running in all directions through the cloud of dust, and the noise from the cars' alarms only added to the chaos.

The sound of the explosion had deafened Ranjit temporarily, and as he struggled to get to his feet, he could hear only faint screams from the crowd around him. Within seconds, his security cordon had got to him and whisked him away to his car, leaving behind many questions about the so-called tight security that had been organized.

A total of five men had been killed, all of them junior party workers who had either been sitting in front of the stage, handling the sound system, or standing on the stage. Twenty-four others were injured, six of them critically. As his brain slowly started to function, Ranjit realized that the delay caused by stopping to talk to Kang had most definitely saved his life.

He tugged at the sleeve of one of his bodyguards. 'Kang,' he croaked. 'I want to see Kang.'

3

RAW HQ, Lodhi Road, New Delhi
3 February 2013

He was sporting a blue turban, dark shades and a thick, bushy beard. Clearly, more than anything else, the point was to be unidentifiable and inscrutable.

He had given his name as Balbir Singh Sandhu, spokesperson for the Babbar Khalsa International group. The BBC had been showing runs and re-runs of the tape since morning, wherein the Sikh terrorist group had claimed responsibility for the explosion in Amritsar.

'The idea was not to kill Raina. It was just a warning bugle. Whoever insults the Khalsa will be dealt with severely. So Raina and all his friends in the Indian government should take note of this.We are alive, aware and ready to strike.'

Suresh Kumar Yadav, alias Sky, was watching the BBC telecast in his office. He was said to be the second best thing to have happened to RAW, after the founding director, R.N. Kao.

India's premier spy agency had been established after consistent intelligence failures in Pakistan and China. Kao, then deputy director of the Intelligence Bureau, had given its blueprint to Indira Gandhi and in 1968, the agency was established and given responsibility for strategic external intelligence in all forms. RAW was the only agency in India not accountable to the people of India or even the Parliament, reporting directly to the prime minister of India; much like Mossad in Israel. Ably supported by the National Technical Research Organization (NTRO), RAW was thus exempted from the Right to Information Act, and its director designated as Secretary, Research. Raised along the lines of the American Central Intelligence Agency (CIA), critics had accused it of having the potential to become another KGB-like monolith. However, stalwarts like Kao had more than once proved the merit of such a structure.

Within a few years of its establishment, the agency had disclosed Pakistan's frantic efforts towards uranium enrichment at Kahuta, the site for Khan's Research Laboratories, a nuclear weapon testing facility. Pakistan was developing high-range fissile material production and was producing highly enriched uranium (HEU), which RAW agents established was of weapon grade when they tested hair samples near the testing site. However, further penetration was thwarted when Prime Minister Morarji Desai boasted to the then President of Pakistan, Zia ul Haq, that India knew all about Kahuta and the work going on there. The ISI eliminated every single Indian asset in Pakistan it could find related to Kahuta.

In fact, politicians had consistently undermined the work carried out by RAW. The now infamous Gujral doctrine was another example. During his ten-month stint as the Indian prime minister, Inder Kumar Gujral had shut down the special intelligence operations of RAW in Pakistan, causing a major setback to the agency in intelligence gathering.

The chiefs of the spy agency were chosen from the Indian Foreign Services, Indian Police and even the Indian Postal Services. However, Sky was from an army background. It was the army man in him that had heard the intense emotional plea of his fellow army officer, Sayed Ali Waris, at the JPC meet. As was his wont, Waris had sounded logical and unemotional, but Sky knew the frustration and anger raging beneath. He had opposed Ali and shown his aversion to what he was advocating, but he knew that his friend was right.

Sky was accountable to the highest office in the country and being at the helm of RAW meant that he had to act with utmost responsibility. Therefore, even though he'd known that Ali Waris was right in pushing for a revenge mission, he knew he couldn't sanction it based on his own instinct alone. The RAW chief of India couldn't act on impulse.

The screaming Sardar on the telly was now replaced by two intelligence experts specializing in South East Asian affairs. Sky switched off the TV and turned to his officers, who were watching the broadcast with him for the strike. Until then, only the Indian news channels had been crying themselves hoarse about it. But when a channel like the BBC got involved, and when the Khalsa fellow had given an 'interview', they knew it was no hoax.

'Sir, I'm telling you. The ISI's signature was all over the blast,' said the first officer. He pushed a file towards Sky. 'The bomb was a crude, improvised explosive device, concealed in the hollow of the amplifiers on the stage. The explosive charge, fuse, circuitry and initiation system—everything points next door.'

'Any arrests so far?' asked Sky.

'The local police have picked up some suspects. DSP Iqbal Kang has emerged a hero of sorts. They're saying it's because of him that Raina is still alive,' said the other officer.

Sky was silent for a minute, lost in thought. Then he looked around at the others and said, 'Very well, gentlemen. Thank you for your report. Now, if you'll excuse me, I need to make a few calls.'

As soon as the door closed, he picked up his phone and dialled a number. It was answered almost immediately. 'Ali? You busy?'

'What do you think, Sky?' replied Lieutenant General Ali Waris on the other end. 'I was hoping I would be, but you didn't seem too intent on letting me shield our asses.'

'All right, old man, take it easy,' Sky said soothingly. 'What you proposed at that meeting caught us all by surprise. You didn't really think we'd agree immediately, did you?'

'Well, what do you want? And who're you calling an old man?'

Sky chuckled. 'Not you, old boy, that's for sure. Anyway, I need to talk to you.'

'So talk to me.'

'Not here, not now. Can you come over to my place this evening?'

There was a pause before Waris replied. 'Fine. I'll be there at eight.'

At exactly 7.58 p.m., Sky's doorbell rang. The moment Sky opened the door, Waris noticed his host's furrowed brow. He waited until Sky led him to the study, and then came straight to the point.

'What's on your mind, Sky?'

The RAW chief didn't answer immediately. He stared blankly out of the window into the darkness of his lawn.

After years of service with Sky, Waris knew better than to interrupt his friend. He sat back in his chair quietly and waited.

Abandoning any pretence at small talk, Sky asked, 'Ali, what do you know about K2?'

'What, the mountain? It's high.'

Sky gave him a dirty look.

'Oh, you mean the Iranian mullahs – what are their names, Khomeini and Khameini? Iranian warlords who fucked America before UBL took over from them. You getting nostalgic in your old age, Sky?'

Despite his state of mind, Sky chuckled. 'Come on, you old bastard. Seriously, what do you know?'

Waris shrugged.

'Not much, really. The only K2 I know is code for the Khalistanis and Kashmiris. But—' He stopped as he saw the expression on his friend's face.

'That's the one I'm talking about,' said Sky.

'But they're long gone! We wiped them out ages ago! They slunk away when they realized we were too powerful for them!'

'I know we decided that, my friend,' said Sky, nodding sadly. 'I'm going to disappoint you. K2 is active right now.'

There was a stony silence. Waris felt his heart pound against his ribcage.

Back in 1971, Zia ul Haq had mounted a diabolical campaign to bring Kashmiri militants and Khalistani terrorists together. Neither on their own could cause a dent in the might of the Indian Army, but he felt a combined onslaught would be far more difficult to repel.

Then began a series of hijackings and notorious plane landings in Pakistan. Khalistanis began addressing the media from Pakistan and badmouthing the Indian government. All this and the Kanishka bombing had caused massive setbacks to the Indian government in their fight against militancy, though India was ultimately successful in eliminating the K2 threat. Waris was among those who had believed this. Until now.

'Confirmed?'

'Absolutely. I guess you haven't seen the afternoon news,' Sky said, sitting back in his chair.

'No, I haven't. I was with my daughter.'

'Babbar Khalsa has taken responsibility for the Amritsar blast.'

Waris's eyes widened. 'Khalsa? Where the hell did they come from?'

'No idea. Apparently, they called the BBC in London. The usual stuff, you know – we could have killed Ranjit if we wanted to; next time he won't be lucky, that kind of thing.'

'Yeah, that's the tune these fuckers play when their plan fails. As if they could kill someone like Raina so easily.'

Sky half-smiled at Waris and shook his head. 'Ali, that's the problem,' he said seriously, getting up to pace the room. 'Raina would have roasted in that blast. My man was there, he told me Raina's alive only because of bloody luck. An STF fellow got wind of the attack and tried to warn Raina. Delayed him by twenty-five minutes.'

Waris understood immediately. 'And the bomb was on timer! Raina's alive because he was late to the rally!'

Sky nodded. 'Exactly. Ali, we had no idea. These bastards are everywhere, and I believe them when they say we won't be so lucky the next time.'

Waris looked at his friend questioningly. 'But isn't that what I said to you fellows that day? We'll never be safe until we get these fuckers.'

'I know. But the situation is more dire than you think. Recently, we unearthed a secret tunnel in Sialkot that opened into the Samba region of the national highway. I'm sure you've heard of it. Then some of my men reported that around fifteen men are being trained in Aksa for a suicide attack to take place in Jammu's Doda district. Now there's this blast in Amritsar, where my officers tell me that the IED's design is identical to the ISI's handiwork. On top of that, the Khalsa has resurfaced, meaning that there's got to be some kind of an alliance that's been resurrected.'

He stopped and returned to his chair. 'Ali, the meaning is very clear. Things are going to get very messy, very soon, unless we can do something to stop it.'

'So you've reconsidered my proposal?'

Sky sighed and rang for his manservant, who appeared promptly. 'Want something to drink? Scotch?'

'Strong black coffee, no sugar.' Sky nodded at the man, who withdrew silently.

Sky looked back at his friend. 'You're still the same, Ali. I still remember how you took a mug of coffee and climbed onto that jeep's bonnet in Drass, while the shelling was still on.'

Waris chuckled. 'Yeah, God knows what possessed me to do that. But it worked, didn't it?'

'Worked?' said Sky. 'Of course it worked! Nobody dared to shoot you! You lucky bastard!'

'Yeah? Who're you calling lucky? What about the time you were refused your first deputation to RAW? We met in Srinagar on the frozen Dal Lake, remember?'

Sky chuckled, reminiscing. 'I remember we drove right into the middle of the lake and stopped there!'

'Exactly. Of all the damned places to catch a drink! You and I, sitting in the middle of a frozen lake, you with your Scotch and I with my coffee, and God knows how many snipers hidden all around. It's a bloody miracle we weren't shot!'

'True. We're a pair of very lucky fellows, Ali.'

'Luck's got nothing to do with it, Sky. I've always told you that. It's easy to be brave when you're hiding behind a clutch of AK-56s. You need balls of steel to be a real man, like you and I. And these Pakistanis have not learnt the aleph, bey, tey of bravery,' said Waris, grinning, knowing his friend would appreciate his use of the Urdu alphabet.

Sky's manservant entered with a tray bearing a pot of coffee, two mugs, two glasses and a decanter of whiskey. He deposited the tray on the table, bowed reverentially to Waris and went back out.

'Yes, well, it's that damned bravery of yours that got you into trouble,' said Sky, pouring out his friend's coffee and then a stiff Scotch for himself. 'You should move on, Ali, and find peace in the good things of life.'

He grew serious then. 'Look, you almost caused an international scandal by marching your brigade across the LoC. They could have court-martialled you for it, but your track record saved you. You can't do that this time, Ali. You can't dance into the fray in your usual manner, wanting to die a warrior's death. Too much is riding on this.'

'I don't want to die in my bed, Sky. That's not a bad thing to want, is it?'

They were both silent for a while, each lost in his own

thoughts and poison, one muddy brown, the other golden. Then Waris said, 'Let's stop beating around the bush, Sky. Why am I here?'

Sky stared at him for a long moment, taking his time. He then said, 'Remember that plan you told us about at the meeting?'

'Yes.'

'Please go ahead with it. I'll back you with resources, but that's it. Beyond that, you're on your own.'

Waris stared at him, 'Credit me with some intelligence, Sky. I understand the issue of plausible deniability.'

'It can't get back to me, Ali. You have full independence in choosing your team, right from wet works commandoes to tech support, no questions asked. You can call me only in exceptional circumstances, when you're in totally deep shit. But I'm telling you again, Ali. It can't get back to me. For me, this conversation never happened.'

'I know what you're saying, Sky. Inshallah, this will never come back to you. With me, you don't have to watch your back.'

Sky sighed and leaned back. 'Ali, I do know. And that's why I called you over.'

Ali looked up and smiled. 'Is that so? I thought you called me to have your blasted sarkari coffee!'

Sky grinned back. 'I thought you wanted to have grilled meat.'

'I used to like it, but now I think it's time I precipitated hell's fires to roast others in it.'

As he spoke, Waris's countenance underwent a total change. His hands formed into tight fists and his lips were pressed together. His eyes had a distant look, a look that would have shrivelled his enemies. For a moment, even Sky could not look into his friend's eyes.

'Good luck, Ali,' said Sky, smiling, knowing that now it was the enemies of Waris who would need all the luck in the world.

4

1999. Kargil. The war had all but been won. The Indian Army had neutralized resistance from Pakistani forces almost everywhere. Few remained who could withstand the might of the jawans. The fight that had begun in May continued till July, resulting in a decisive Indian victory and humiliation of the Pakistanis. At the end of the war, the Indians had lost over 527 soldiers, the Pakistanis 1063.

But there were some pitched battles that were never reported.

A vital link remained under Pakistani control: Point 5250, near the Khalubar ridge in the Batalik sub-sector. It was a plateau-like structure that afforded an almost unrestricted view of the surroundings for miles around. Even on a bad day, with below par viewing conditions, it would have been impossible to approach the ridge unseen, far less climb to the top and vanquish the enemy. There was a single road leading through the peak, but it was heavily manned and impossible to approach, as the narrow pass and the high ground around it meant that anyone trying to take that path would immediately be killed.

For days, the Indian Army tried to capture Point 5250. Artillery troops kept firing at the Pakistani forces at the top, occupying their attention while others climbed the walls of the plateau, trying to get to the top from where a more organized resistance could be put up. But every attempt failed, as the Pakistanis would immediately spot anyone scaling the ridge and gun them down. From their strategic height, they repulsed every attack, often just by hurling boulders down at the advancing army. Two entire battalions fell to the tactical advantage of the Pakistani soldiers.

Finally, the Indians gave up all hope of capturing the point. The enemy was too well positioned, it simply couldn't be done. Not by any conventional means of warfare, that is. Something different was needed, something foolproof, something that couldn't be achieved by ordinary infantry tactics.

Brigadier Ali Waris, sector brigade commander, had been watching from his headquarters a kilometre away. He had left his deputies to capture the peak while he marshalled the remainder of the forces to consolidate the Indian Army's victory. But finally, he realized that too many men had died pointlessly trying to overcome the unconquerable, using all the standard war tactics. It was time he intervened. Waris knew that wars are won only through strategy; if the enemy had an advantage, he would have to create one for himself. And he did just that.

Some time just before noon, on the fourth day of fighting, when the two forward battalions had finally given up attacking the peak and retreated several miles further back, the Brigadier walked into his camp. By evening he had drawn up a plan, a daring and highly risky one that would have to be executed in darkness. There would be two teams, both from his reserve battalion – one would climb behind the other. Leading the first team was his trusted man, Major Brijesh Singh, who handpicked his men, choosing them for specific qualities only they had. The man in charge of the second team was a young captain by the name of Vikrant Singh, who had proven himself to be a quick-witted and highly capable officer on the numerous patrolling assignments led by him in the brigade sector.

The first team would approach the plateau slowly, in the dead of night, and because of the darkness they could remain concealed until they started climbing the peak. After that though, the noise would alert the enemy. This was where Waris's genius came into play.

The first team up, led by Brijesh, would number around thirty. They were all heavily bearded Pathans dressed in Pathani suits, long kurtas and pajamas with rucksacks slung across their backs. On their heads were turbans or the knitted skull caps worn by Muslims. From the moment they started the climb, they shouted slogans of 'Naare-takbeer' and 'Allah-o-Akbar'. Brijesh had to practise very hard to correctly intone the Muslim war cries and sloganeering; for a Thakur from Pratapgarh, they were quite a mouthful. The Brigadier was gambling on the fact that the Pakistanis at the top would assume that these men were their own Muslim brethren, both because of their chant and how they were dressed, and wouldn't open fire. They would think that these were reinforcements for their own ranks, and allow Brijesh's team to climb all the way up.

Following Brijesh's team from behind would be Vikrant and his men. They too would be dressed in Muslim attire, but would climb quietly. The darkness would hide their identity effectively and Brijesh's team would keep the enemy busy until it was too late. And here was the second gamble: to keep Brijesh and his men from winning the peak, the Pakistani soldiers would call in reinforcements. But they wouldn't arrive immediately, certainly not in time to lend support. So the soldiers who were guarding the only path through the peak would leave their posts and join their fellow soldiers to defeat Brijesh. Once the way was clear, Vikrant and his men would attack from the rear, which the Pakistanis would by that time be powerless to defend.

All through the next day, the two teams readied themselves. They had to carry food and ammunition because it was impossible to predict how long they would have to keep up the fight, especially if reinforcements for the enemy arrived quickly.

As soon as darkness began to fall, they set off. By 10 p.m. they were at the base of the plateau and starting the climb. Soon the silence of the night was shattered by the false war cries and the scraping of the boots of twenty-six men as they climbed the face of the plateau, clinging to tiny handholds, ledges and assorted undergrowth.

Far below them, the second team took their own diversion and headed towards the path. Soon enough, they spotted the sentries prowling the area, and more than two dozen snipers perched high above, giving them full visual access to the valley. At that spot, they waited. They couldn't afford to show themselves until the soldiers on the road rushed to repel Brijesh's attack.

In the dead of night, the Pakistanis did exactly what the Brigadier had predicted — one by one, they began helping Brijesh's men in the final stages of ascent, pulling up the climbers as they reached the top, mistaking them for their own. No shots were fired. No boulders came hurtling down, aimed to crush the climbers.

But it was nearing morning by now, and Brijesh could see the slightest glimmer of light on the horizon. He realized that he couldn't wait any longer. As soon as twenty men were up on the peak beside him, he yelled without warning, '*Yalgaar!*'

Hearing Brijesh shout to his men to attack would have been warning enough, but his use of Urdu left the enemy uncertain. Before any of the Pakistanis could react, his men opened fire.

The front ranks of the Pakistani soldiers were cut down before they could offer any resistance at all, and Brijesh's team managed to get behind cover as they engaged the rest of the forces. However, both numerically and strategically stronger, the enemy retaliated once they gathered their wits. In the space of four hours, Brijesh lost three of his men, while the others grouped around him, firing constantly.

The instant the shots rang out from above, the second team became alert. Any time now, the soldiers below would abandon their posts; it was only a matter of time.

But time was against them. Even though the second team of Pakistanis was immediately alerted of the attack, none of them moved. Not a single man left his post, and the road remained as impenetrable as ever.

Throughout the day, shots rang out from the top of the peak. It was impossible to tell what was happening, or who was winning. All Vikrant and his men could do was wait grimly and impatiently.

The Brigadier had underestimated the Pakistanis. They didn't give ground and for the entire day they fought, every man to the last breath. Brijesh soon realized, as did his men, that things had gone horribly wrong. But none of them retreated a single step.

Night fell, but the shots didn't stop. At brief intervals, a gunshot would shatter the silence. But nothing changed. And the men guarding the road still didn't budge.

On the third day, when Brijesh's team had worn thin, with

only twelve of his men standing, they heard shouts from behind the enemy. Reinforcements had arrived at last. The captain of the team of soldiers barricading the road had sent a runner up to the peak, and decided to retaliate. Brijesh realized what had happened, and so did his men. With renewed vigour, they fought on.

Down below, Vikrant waited and watched. He maintained the holding position he had been ordered to, while Brijesh's men drew fire. Nearly the entire regiment had now left to reinforce their troops, and only four snipers had been left behind. Easy.

He selected three of his men, all brilliant marksmen. Together, the four of them marked their targets and, at a signal from Vikrant, fired. Every shot found its mark and the four snipers fell from their perches, stone dead even before they hit the ground. The path was theirs. Leaving six of his men to guard the post, Vikrant and his men charged up the peak, not a minute too soon.

As the Pakistanis heard them approach, their cries of victory turned to dismay.

'Ya Ali madad!' cried Vikrant as he dove into the fray, firing left and right, every shot finding its mark. His men shouted in chorus, 'Ya Aliiiii madaddddd!' The dark night rang with screams and gunshots. This was pure battleground. Waris had used religion to turn the tide against his enemies.

Brijesh and Vikrant's heroics proved too much for the Pakistanis. Within a matter of hours, the peak was theirs. Except for one casualty, all of Vikrant's men were alive, and the twelve remaining men on Brijesh's team, and Brijesh himself, were alive too — exhausted beyond belief, but alive.

Waris's gambit had paid off. He set off now with two companies drawn from his battalions, determined to push the advantage and move deeper into enemy territory, to capture it before the Pakistanis could launch another attack. The apparently indefatigable Peak 5250 had been captured – but not without a final setback. As the two teams settled down for the evening, Vikrant's men lined up in front—any reinforcements would come from there, and Brijesh's exhausted team had fought for three whole days—while Brijesh watched the rear.

Even the best of men have their weaknesses, and Brijesh let his guard down for a few minutes; the Muslim jawans had expressed a desire to offer namaz to express gratitude to the almighty.

Brijesh knew that it was these men who had saved the day for the country, and they were entitled to kiss their motherland with their foreheads.

It was this moment of weakness that the enemy was waiting for.

Somehow, enemy soldiers managed to sneak around the camp and attacked them from behind. Brijesh was caught unprepared, and even as he scrambled up with his weapon in hand, he watched as his men were cut down in front of him. Vikrant and his men joined the battle almost immediately, but they were exhausted and too few in number.

It was only because of the frenzied pace at which the Brigadier was driving his men that they arrived just then. Before the Pakistanis could take back the peak, the Indian soldiers fell upon them and averted the danger.

Of the fifty-two men who made the climb, Vikrant's team was left with only seven. And not one of the men in the first team survived, except for Brijesh. It wasn't his fault – after three days of continuous fighting, he was barely able to stand. But there, in that makeshift tent, Waris knew he was looking at a broken man.

It had been almost a decade and a half but Brijesh still awoke at night with his clothes and bedsheets drenched in sweat. The same old dream haunted him: of Pakistanis charging towards his men as they prostrated on the ground, oblivious to the attack, while he watched in horror from a distance, helpless.

Brijesh had spoken to counsellors and therapists, but none could help him. He still couldn't sleep properly. Even the strongest of sedatives failed to tranquilize him.

He had opted for a desk job and spent years at the Immigration desk in Attari post, still haunted by his vivid dreams of losing his men.

Waris had kept in touch with Brijesh. He knew only too well that no amount of therapy, counselling or sedatives could help a warrior overcome his demons. Brijesh would be healed only through a similar mission.

The moment Sky gave the go-ahead, Waris knew that Brijesh would head his crack team.

5

Sayed Ali Waris had been recruited into the Indian Army in 1971. His grandfather, Sayed Mohammad Hasan, had fought in World War I and his father, Sayed Mustafa Husain, had retired as a colonel in the Indian Army. Waris's three uncles and several of his cousins were still in the army. His grandfather and father were known to be legends in their own right. This illustrious and patriotic lineage accorded Ali Waris a meritorious position in the army.

Hailing from Barabanki near Lucknow, Waris rose to become a role model for most of the army and policemen in all of Uttar Pradesh. At the time of Partition, his grandfather refused to go to Pakistan. For his clan, India was one of the most sacred places on the planet.

Waris disliked what he thought of as the treachery and duplicity of Pakistan. While New Delhi was initiating bus diplomacy with Islamabad, the Pakistani army was slowly infiltrating Kargil and Kashmir. Brigadier Waris had been part of the convoy that had taken that bus trip with Prime Minister Atal Bihari Vajpayee, to be greeted in Lahore by the Pakistani premier Nawaz Sharif.

After a first glance at Nawaz Sharif and Pervez Musharraf, Waris took his friend Sky aside and told him, 'I don't trust either of these men. They could be really harmful to India.' Kargil proved that Waris's fears were not unfounded.

Waris almost caused an international scandal when he took his brigade across the Line of Control in Pakistan, in response. Given the length of the border and its porous nature, it was possible to walk across. 'I want to tell Musharraf that warriors don't hide and backstab; they take to the battlefield like men. Let him send his best men. We will send ours. Kashmir can be settled here and now.'

His misadventure could have cost him a court martial. Only his pedigree and the PM's direct intervention saved the day. He was quietly shunted to a desk job at RAW. He had served at RAW earlier and the experience came in handy in his second stint. In his second coming, he quietly bided his time until he retired.

A widower, Waris never remarried. His daughter Vibha had moved to the US after marriage and he lived alone.

His Kargil wounds had been opened afresh by the 26/11 attack. He knew that diplomacy was often a sham, that nothing could be achieved through lobbying. He believed in the justice system of Israel, where an attack on a Jewish person anywhere in the world was tantamount to an attack on the State of Israel and retribution would be sought.

Five years after the attack in Mumbai, he realized that his government was still trying to get the conspirators out of Pakistan and that they were not willing to cooperate. He decided to take matters into his own hands and dispense justice. He was not an army man anymore and did not have to take orders from anyone. He just needed a few intelligent and dedicated soldiers to deliver justice to the victims of 26/11.

Brijesh and Vikrant were both obvious choices for his Justice League. While Sky managed to get immediate sanctions for both, Brijesh took a lot of convincing. He finally gave in when Waris told him, 'This may be your only chance to redeem yourself and take revenge for your martyred team.'

Brijesh's eyes showed the spark that had been missing for so many years as he finally relented.

A professor of anthropology, Brijesh had initially joined the Indian Army by sheer accident. But once he got in, he forgot his academic background and showed an amazing passion for intelligence work. The transformation was surprising. The man was a paratrooper, comfortable with any gun and skilled in close combat martial arts; his fitness level was that of an Olympic athlete, which is why he had been chosen for that dangerous Kargil mission of Peak 5250.

Vikrant Singh had been biding his time with the Border Security Force (BSF) and proved to be a revelation. The G

Branch of BSF, which is its intelligence wing, had been facing major strife as most of its top honchos were reeling under corruption charges. With most of his bosses facing an inquiry for cooking up actionable intelligence, Vikrant had been given additional charge of the branch. He had not only spruced it up, he had made them look much better than military intelligence.

When the Bangladeshi army had begun killing Indian jawans, Vikrant had sent a subtle message to them. One night he slyly crossed the border, planted explosives in the arsenal of the Bangla army, and blew it to smithereens. 'It could have been an entire battalion instead of an arms depot,' Vikrant conveyed to his counterpart in Bangladesh. After that incident, the BSF began to call him One Man Battalion.

Vikrant's promotion to the post of commandant relieved him of his duties at BSF, and he was asked to report to Ali Waris immediately.

Waris was setting up the biggest mission of his life, against astronomical odds. He needed good, solid men, men whom he could trust without question. Brijesh and Vikrant were those men.

The three of them sat quietly in the General's study, not speaking, reliving without words the anguish that the Kargil victory had brought with it.

The door opened and Iqbal Kang walked in.

'So this is the man,' thought Waris, as he scrutinized Kang from head to toe. 'Looks like a strong character, has clearly gone through a lot.'

Aloud he said, 'Come in, Mr Kang. Take a seat. Please excuse me if I don't say anything more, I'd rather wait for the final members of our team to arrive. I dislike repeating myself.'

Kang nodded equably and sat down on a chair in one corner of the room.

It wasn't a large room. One side of the wall was lined with tall, barred windows, and in front of it was an enormous table, behind which sat Lt Gen. Waris. The other three walls were lined with bookcases, reaching right up to the ceiling. A flat TV was set into a groove in one of them, and was soundlessly flashing a news channel.

The table was in a corner to the right of the door, which was set into the wall between two bookcases. It opened into the room in such a way that anyone coming in wouldn't see the table until he'd closed the door behind him.

There was a potted plant to the right of the table, and Vikrant sat on the chair next to it, reading a newspaper. Brijesh was sitting on one of the three chairs facing the table. With the exception of Vikrant, they were all watching the news silently.

Finally the door opened again and two people walked in. One of them was a slight man with a balding head, thick glasses resting on his nose and a nervous look on his face.

The other person was a woman who they knew was in her late thirties but looked considerably younger. She was wearing a dark grey pencil skirt that accentuated her curves and showed off her shapely legs, and the white shirt she wore fit her snugly, its top two buttons open to reveal a little more cleavage than was necessary. The effect she had on most men was electrifying, and she knew it. She also knew that the effect was lost on everyone in the room except for Iqbal and the man she had come in with.

Waris stood up and looked her up and down. 'Is it really necessary to dress so provocatively, Ms Borges?'

The woman was unfazed. 'Not really, sir,' she said. 'But then, how I dress shouldn't matter, should it? It's my work that has got me here.' Her voice was honey, heavy and alluring, but it also possessed an air of command.

He looked at her appraisingly, then nodded. 'True.'

He sat down and signalled for the others to take their seats. 'I'll introduce everyone in turn. This is Laila Borges. She's our tech expert. Her companion is Subhrata Ray. He's a biotechnologist, geneticist and computer systems expert. They are both on loan from NTRO.'

He pointed at Vikrant. 'He's an army major, and has also served with the BSF. And this is Iqbal Kang. He's from the Punjab Special Task Force. And this is Brijesh Singh, retired colonel.'

Laila looked at Vikrant. 'Isn't he too young for this, sir?'

'He may look young, Ms Borges, but I assure you, I've seen his work and what he's capable of, and he's the best field agent I know. Is there anything else?'

'Yes,' said Laila. She turned to Brijesh. 'I know the colonel. Again, I'm wondering at your choices, General. If I'm not mistaken, Colonel Singh took voluntary retirement from the army after being found unfit for duty.'

Till then, Brijesh had sat silently, eyes on the floor. But Laila's words struck him like a whip. His eyes flashed, and he turned and looked her full in the eye. 'You may be eminently qualified, madam, but have you ever lost an entire team and been unable to save them? Have you ever watched them die in front of you, knowing their deaths were because of you?' He spoke quietly and firmly, but there was an immense sadness in his voice.

Laila was taken aback. 'I–I–I'm sorry. I didn't—'

'It doesn't matter,' interrupted Waris. 'I know Brijesh is capable and he's my first choice for what we're about to do.'

Kang cleared his throat and spoke. 'Sir, what are we here for?'

Waris smiled grimly. 'Retribution, Mr Kang. It's time to strike back.'

6

28 April 2013

'The deaths have to look natural.'

There were puzzled looks all around at Waris's statement. Only Brijesh sat expressionless, staring at a spot on the wall.

Kang leaned forward in his seat. 'All of them, sir?'

'Yes.'

'But sir,' said Laila, a troubled look on her face. 'That will complicate matters immensely.'

Waris nodded. 'I'm sure it will, Ms Borges. But that's the way it has to be.'

Vikrant spoke up. 'Correct me if I'm wrong, sir, but these are India's enemies, and we're going to kill them. But if they appear to have died of natural causes, how will that get the message across?'

The others nodded in agreement. 'A clean shot or a garrotte will show them we mean business,' said Kang. 'We're just as deadly as anyone else, and we can do it.'

'I understand your concern, Kang. And I'm not doubting any

one's abilities. You are among the best, which is why you've been chosen for this mission.'

Kang shifted uneasily in his seat. 'Thank you for your confidence, sir. But I don't think you're aware—'

'About your background? Transferring you from the Chandigarh STF, which was your home base, was a punishment. I know everything, Kang.'

Before Kang could reply, Laila broke in. 'What do you mean, punishment?' She eyed Kang quizzically. 'What did you do?'

'It wasn't what he did, it's what he didn't do,' said Waris. 'Mr Kang here was present at the time of Beant Singh's assassination. He was charged with dereliction of duty.'

The attention in the room shifted, as everyone first looked at Kang, and then back at Waris. Brijesh stared at Kang, a fierce light in his eyes.

'Mr Kang was at the top of his class. He was assigned to the Punjab chief minister for protection duty. Then departmental rivalry got him shunted out of the protection unit. But he was at the spot when the assassination was carried out.'

'I was just outside the secretariat,' said Kang mechanically, in a low voice. 'The perimeter was secure. The CM was walking towards his car, and as he was getting in, I saw a man in a police uniform walking towards him. I should have shouted an alert. But I couldn't take my eyes away from him. It all happened too fast. And then …' His voice trailed off.

'I did some background research,' said Waris gently. 'Your son had been taken very ill the night before. It is possible that you were already distracted.'

'I froze, sir. It had never happened to me before. I was the only one who knew what was going on, but I froze. And the minister was killed.'

Waris got up, walked over to Kang and placed a hand on his shoulder. 'I know what you're going through, Kang. But what happened that day has got nothing to do with my choosing you for this mission. You're a good soldier, I know that. And you're clearly capable, since we all know you saved the prime minister designate from certain death. That's why you're here. You're loyal, obviously quite fearless, you've proved that you can overcome the past, and that's what I need.'

Waris glanced at Brijesh as he spoke, but the younger man's face was inscrutable. Waris knew that of all of them, Brijesh understood exactly what Kang was going through. He hoped his words would have some effect on Brijesh and bring him out of his own private hell.

'That's what I need from all of you,' Waris said, straightening up. 'You know your enemy, and I know you want to wipe them off the face of this earth as much as I do. I need your cooperation, your expertise and experience.'

'But sir,' said Laila. 'None of this explains why we can't simply shoot them dead.'

Waris went back to his desk and sat down. 'We don't exist, gentlemen. As far as our colleagues and compatriots are concerned, we are not here. We won't have support from anyone, not the government, nor any of the agencies. It is only us, a rogue team, if you want to call it that. We cannot let this get back to India. It is a private mission and not a government-sponsored hit job.'

There was a chorus of protests. But Waris quietened them with a raised hand and continued to speak. 'I know. I understand your indignation. Unfortunately, this is the way it has to be. We are a peaceful, democratic nation, and the world knows us as such. We cannot take the law into our own hands;

these people, even though they're terrorists, need a fair trial in the eyes of the law. But I say we don't give them that. Just as there was no sense or justice in the case of the hundreds and thousands they have killed, these terrorists don't deserve our justice. This is war, and if the enemy can intrude on our land and kill our innocent citizens, why can't we do the same? After all, everything's fair in love and war.'

'But sir,' said Vikrant, 'how are we different from them then? If we too ignore all the rules and laws, if we too kill whoever we want, don't we become the same as them?'

'No, Vikrant, we don't. They're violating every principle in the book, so why can't we? The difference is that they are killing innocents. We will kill the guilty. And it's because of our standing in the world that we can't show everyone that we are the ones who killed them. That's why the deaths have to look natural.'

Finally, Brijesh spoke. 'And how do we plan to do that, sir?'

Waris smiled and waved at the small man who till now had been quietly observing the proceedings. 'I believe,' he said, 'that Mr Ray is more qualified to answer that question.'

Ray grinned and got up. 'Sir, with your permission, I'd like to use your desk.'

Waris waved his assent.

Ray walked over to the desk and plonked his backpack down on it. He took out a thin laptop and switched it on. There were no logos on it, and upon Vikrant's questioning look, he said, 'Oh, this is a laptop I built. I didn't like any of the ones on the market. They weren't, shall we say, efficient enough, and didn't have any of the designs I wanted.'

He jabbed at the trackpad and a few keys, then suddenly closed the lid. Nothing happened for a second, then the opaque cover of the lid lit up, and a shape formed in the air just above it. Ray was using the laptop as a holographic projector, and instead of a wall or a screen, he was projecting the images in the air.

The others were suitably impressed.

'I've prepared a small presentation using the data Lt Gen. Waris provided me. Observe, please.'

He clicked a small pen in his hand, and five images appeared above the laptop. 'These are your targets. First, Sabahuddin Umavi: 26/11 mastermind. Second, Wajid Mir: recruiter, trainer and strategist of Lashkar. Third, Damien Bradley: white American, all-round recon man. Fourth, Mahmoud Azhar: fugitive, terrorist. Fifth, Haaris Saeed: the man in charge, the brains behind Lashkar.'

'Our objective,' said Waris quietly, 'is to eliminate each of these men. With them gone, the Lashkar-e-Toiba will be directionless without a leader. That's a step in the direction we want to take – to make India safer. Umavi was the mastermind. He's our first target.'

Ray went on, unperturbed by the interruption, 'There are several ways in which this can be done. For example, you can attack the target and hold his head underwater. Autopsy will reveal drowning as the cause of death.'

Vikrant shook his head. 'Difficult. Impossible if there are people around.'

'Then there is the customary push from high above. The target will fall to his death.'

'It'll be difficult to ensure that the target is at an elevation. Do you have anything practical?'

Far from being discouraged, Ray seemed to liven up at the challenge. 'Well, what about a staged car accident?'

'And where would we get the equipment and men necessary to do that?' asked Laila, icily.

'That's easy,' scoffed Ray. 'It was difficult, back when Yugoslav president Slobodan Milosevic or even Princess Diana were killed. You needed men, expensive equipment, bribes and God knows what else. Today I can arrange for a software malfunction of the car. It's easy, all I need to do is to get close enough for wireless access of the car's onboard computer. I can simply disengage the brakes. Done!'

He looked around, beaming. They'd all been impressed by his holographic trick, but now they were looking at him with newfound respect.

'That does have possibilities, Ray,' said Waris. 'What else?'

Ray looked crestfallen. 'So we won't be using that? There are other variations too. If he's in a lift, I can cut out its brakes, drop it down like a brick. It'll just be a malfunction!'

'We might, my dear fellow,' said Vikrant, chuckling. 'Depends on the situation.'

Ray nodded. 'Agreed. Then there's the anthrax hit. Carry a pellet with anthrax in your gun chamber, wait until the target is clear and fire the pellet. It should pass close to his face so he inhales, and he's a dead man. The biggest problem is that it has to be fired from close quarters and the bullet has to necessarily explode close to his face. It's difficult to monitor the bullet movement and the target's location in such conditions.'

'Intriguing,' said Kang, a gleam in his eye.

'But problematic,' said Waris. 'The bullet will be lodged somewhere and can be discovered; if there is anyone else close by, the anthrax will get them too, and anthrax poisoning itself can be detected.'

'Well then, it looks like the best way we can do it without attracting attention is poison,' said Ray.

Kang cleared his throat. 'Poison?' he said, eyebrows raised. 'What kind of poison?'

'Oh, there are thousands of them, take your pick. My favourite is the umbrella shot. You know, the CIA's weapon in the seventies? The Bulgarian dissident, George what's-his-name, Markov, I think, was killed with a ricin pellet fired from an umbrella gun. Killed him in minutes.'

'And where exactly do you think we'll get the opportunity to use your umbrella gun?'

'Well, ahem, that's up to you. I'm just listing possibilities.'

'What else?'

'Well, for a time, the frozen poison dart was quite popular. There's speculation that JFK was killed in that manner. The entire poison mixture is shaped into a tiny dart, maybe mixed with some analgesic, and kept in the chamber at high pressure or a low temperature. Fire it at the target, it pierces the skin, dissolves and mixes with the bloodstream. Death in seconds, and no trace except for the puncture wound.'

'And won't they find that?'

'Not if they're not looking for it. They'll assume the death was due to natural causes and won't even look for a tiny red dot.'

'What about the poisons themselves?'

'Well, ricin is a good one. I'm sure all of you know about cyanide. Then there's arsenic, scopolamine, thallium—'

'Can they be traced?' said Laila.

'I suppose some of them can—'

'Then they're no good. What about poisons that can't be traced?'

'Well, you have your standard muscle relaxants. Not necessarily poison, since administered in extremely low doses. But a high enough dosage will paralyse and kill. There are some drugs that can do that.'

'That's more like it!' exclaimed Kang.

'Yes. Then there's something that I've only heard of, but it's extremely effective. You know how your heart pumps in a set rhythm? When that rhythm is disrupted for a brief period, it's called arrhythmia. Prolonged arrhythmia is fatal. So you aim at the target's chest and fire a microwave beam containing extremely low frequency signals given off by the heart. It puts the heart in a chaotic state, and you have a heart attack!'

Waris nodded. 'That is an interesting piece of information, Ray. However, Umavi is in extremely good shape. He's muscular, athletic and most importantly, he gets a check-up every month. If he dies of a heart attack, it'll definitely be suspicious.'

'Yes,' said Brjesh. 'Umavi can't have a heart attack, and all your poisons will induce something of the sort.'

Now Ray looked faintly anxious. 'Well then, gentlemen, I'm stumped.'

'Ray,' said Waris, grimly. 'You're here because you're the best, because you're never stumped. That's why I wanted you and nobody else. Can't you give us anything else?'

Ray was silent for a minute. Then he said, 'There might be something, but I cannot guarantee results, sir.'

'Agreed. Out with it.'

Ray looked around. 'I'm sure you're aware that we are made up of strands of DNA. Deoxyribonucleic acid. It's a sort of gene pool, if you want to think of it that way. All of us have unique —'

'Ray, I think all of us are acquainted with basic biology.'

'Yes, sir. Just checking,' said Ray hurriedly. 'Now, all DNA has anomalies, weaknesses. We don't know most of them because, frankly, our technology isn't that advanced yet. But if I could get a strand of the target's DNA, I could run some tests, see if there is a specific genetic defect or weakness or anomaly in him. If there is, we can exploit it. But I'm warning you, it's a long shot.'

'And how exactly do you propose we get Umavi's DNA?' exclaimed Kang. 'Do you expect us to simply saunter over and ask him for it?'

'There's no need to be so dramatic, Kang,' said Laila. 'It can be done.'

'But how?'

'We do it ourselves here, as training for our IB candidates. They're all given a target and told to find out everything they can about him: background, history, family, medical records, everything, all in just forty-eight hours. So they tail the fellow for a while and then visit his house, posing as a polio census executive. Then they ask him or his wife all kinds of questions and get all the details. Simple.'

'I've heard of this,' said Vikrant. 'The CIA do it too. Call up some poor chap and tell them to answer a survey or something, ask some dumb questions like, do they read *Playboy* or do they use condoms or vibrators, and then slip the important questions in between.'

'What happens if they refuse to answer?' smiled Waris, persisting for the benefit of his team though he was sold.

'Well, they tell them they'll get a free one-year subscription to *Playboy* if they complete the survey,' grinned Vikrant. 'Who's going to say no to that?'

'Indeed. But I don't see us being able to replicate either of those methods in Pakistan.'

'Sir, do you remember the plutonium mission?' asked Brijesh.

'Ah yes, I seem to remember something,' Waris replied, frowning. 'Remind us, Brijesh.'

'It was in the 1980s. We were worried that Pakistan was becoming nuclear capable. The IB had to know how pure their plutonium was, what grade they were using. There was no way we could find out. So they activated an IB asset and instructed him to monitor a barber's shop close to the nuclear plant. The fellow stole the hair from the barber's bin and smuggled it out to India in a doll's tummy. The IB got the plutonium grade by examining the strand of hair.'

Ray's eyes were gleaming. 'Can you get me Umavi's hair? I don't need much, just a couple of strands.'

'It can be arranged,' said Waris. 'I'll make a few calls, see what I can do.' He picked up his cell phone from the desk and started walking towards the door when Ray called after him.

'Mind you, sir, I'm not saying I'll find anything.'

'I know. But then again, you might find something.'

'You always said the sky's the limit for you, Sky. No harm in becoming a barber for a change.'

'Very funny.'

'Well, you heard what I told you. Do you have someone in Pakistan?'

'I have quite a few someones, Ali.'

'Today is Wednesday. These mullah types get their beards and moustaches trimmed on Fridays – get me a few hairs.'

'That's in two days. You'll get your hair in four.'

This time it was raining, well past midnight. The team huddled together in Waris's study, which was cold despite the warmth emanating from the heater.

They were talking in low voices, outlining the risks of various methods, activating their networks across the country, listening to information as it poured in from all quarters.

Suddenly the door burst open and Ray came running in, shouting and waving a piece of paper in the air.

'I've got it, sir! I've found it!'

Waris asked quizically, 'What have you found, Ray?'

'Exactly what I was hoping to find, sir! It was a real piece of luck, I can tell you that much.' Ray was almost dancing in his excitement.

'All right, all right, calm down. What did you find?'

'Allergy, sir!'

'Allergy?'

'You know how we're all allergic to something?'

'Nonsense,' said Kang. 'I'm not allergic to anything!'

Ray clicked his tongue in exasperation. 'But that's exactly the point, Kang! Everybody is allergic to something. It's just that you don't know what it is. And if it's a rare one, it's impossible to tell, unless you know what you're looking for.'

'What are you allergic to?' said Laila, smirking.

'Fish. But—'

'You're allergic to fish?' laughed Kang. 'A Bengali allergic to fish? Now, that's funny!'

'Not at all. There are many Bengalis who are allergic to fish. Well, not fish but a certain secretion from—'

'Ray,' thundered Waris. 'Get to the point, please!'

'Sorry, sir,' Ray said, without any sign of contrition. 'As I was saying, DNA mapping can give an idea of the substance the individual is allergic to. Administer that same substance to the target, he'll fall dead. Autopsy will reveal death by severe allergic reaction. Simple! Nobody will imagine for a second that it could have been an assassination!'

'What is he allergic to?'

'I analysed the DNA from all possible angles and it was only by a piece of luck that I did the test.'

'Control your excitement, Ray. What's he allergic to?'

'Hazelnuts, sir!'

'Hazelnuts?' said Kang incredulously. 'That's not uncommon! Surely he knows?'

Ray shook his head vigorously. 'I had full access to everything we know about Umavi. We have his medical records too.'

'How?' said Vikrant, surprised.

'I hacked into his doctor's computer,' said Laila. 'I got details of quite a few men before they discovered my attack. And before you ask, no, they don't know who hacked into their system. All they know was that it was an attack from Moscow.'

'Impressive, Ms Borges,' said Waris.

'Yes, well,' Ray butted in. 'The doctor mentioned his allergy to pineapple, but nothing else. So we can safely assume the man's never had hazelnuts in his life, otherwise he'd have known. All we have to do is take him some place where there are hazelnuts, administer a small but lethal dose, and we're done.'

Brijesh looked at Waris. 'So what now, sir?'

Waris stood up. His fierce eyes blazed at them. 'I think Iran, Afghanistan, Turkmenistan and Turkey are the countries which use hazelnuts in almost everything.'

'We can't just invite him to Iran or Afghanistan,' said Vikrant.

'Turkmenistan is too difficult to operate in,' Brijesh said.

'Istanbul is the best place,' concluded Waris.

'Then let's arrange a meeting between Umavi and his maker in Istanbul,' said Borges, her excitement evident on her face.

7

Umavi had just finished his prayers and was folding his prayer rug when he heard a respectful knock on his door. His assistant entered. He wore the same elated expression as Umavi, but wasn't able to control his emotions as well as his superior.

This quality was the one flaw that Umavi perceived in his loyal assistant, Abdul Qadir Qandahari. Maybe it wasn't even his fault; it wasn't as if he wore his heart on his sleeve, the fellow just had a very expressive face. But there was no one Umavi would rather have by his side than Qandahari. The man was indispensable. Also, he assisted Umavi in a special way that nobody else knew about.

In a world of constantly progressing technology, Umavi was an uncomfortable fit. He didn't like the new age fad of complete digitization and still preferred a letter delivered by the hand of his personal messenger over an email.

Few knew about Umavi's discomfort with technology; it would be foolish to expose the fact that a senior Lashkar-e-Toiba member had a weakness. Qandahari was, however, the most tech savvy recruit Umavi had trained. So, as Umavi took Qandahari under his wing, in addition to guarding Umavi, brainstorming with him and advising him, Qandahari also provided the digital touch to Umavi's analogue brain.

Given his immense usefulness, an expressive face was something Umavi gladly overlooked.

Umavi was a disciplined, fastidious man and Qandahari knew it. He watched as Umavi folded his prayer rug and neatly deposited it in its bag before walking forward and kissing his right hand.

Umavi smiled and embraced his assistant. When they'd disengaged, Qandahari looked at his senior with shining eyes and asked, 'So are we going through with it?'

Umavi's smile was answer enough and his reply confirmed it. 'They have asked for a numbered account. The money will be transferred to us next Friday, after namaz-e-jummah.'

Qandahari still couldn't believe it. It was a gift from Allah and had come quite out of the blue. The email had arrived on his smartphone only a couple of weeks ago, from Rabeta Bank. He knew of the bank, of course; he had a few friends in Saudi Arabia who held accounts there. He had on occasion received promotional emails from many such banks and usually deleted them almost immediately. No point in letting spam clog up your inbox. But a few words in the email had caught his eye and he decided to read through it. Before he'd finished, he realized this was no ordinary email. He would have to take it to Umavi.

His senior had reacted exactly as he'd thought he would – with scepticism and disbelief, but hopeful nevertheless.

'And they just want to give it to us?' he said, squinting at the printout of the email Qandahari had brought him.

'That's what they're saying.'

'Who are they?'

Qandahari cleared his throat. Naturally, he'd done his homework before bringing it to Umavi.

'They call themselves Ansar-ul-Ikhwan-ul-Muslimeen.'

'Hmm. Helpers of the Muslim Brethren. Interesting, but there are dozens of groups like that, which are actually composed of CIA spies.'

'I know, Ameer. According to the email, they represent a wing of the Saudi government. I did some digging around on the internet, but I couldn't find anything. So I wrote back to them.'

'You sent them a letter? By whose hand did you send it?'

'Not a letter, Ameer. I replied to their email.'

Umavi clicked his tongue in exasperation. 'How many times have I told you not to expose yourself like that? How do you know your mail won't be intercepted?'

'No, Ameer, my email is safe. I sent it using our 128-bit encryption protocol, they won't be able to break it.'

'Sir, I've broken the encryption.'

Brijesh looked calmly at Laila, who was standing in front of him. 'Are you sure?'

'Positive, sir.' Normally it would be impossible to break a 128-bit encryption, but Ray had designed the programme well.

They were at a safe house in Delhi, in a small apartment in Chittaranjan Park. It would be their temporary command centre, as setting up base in Lt Gen. Waris's house was unsafe. He was known to live alone and only his daughter visited him at times, so the constant coming and going of five others would certainly arouse curiosity, if not suspicion. They had decided that for every mission, they would set up their command centre in a different place, so that there were minimum chances of being flagged.

Once they had established the means by which Umavi could be eliminated, they had to figure out how to get him to go to Istanbul.

A number of theories were discussed and rejected, before a chance reaction by Vikrant gave Ray an inspiration; Vikrant had jabbed at his phone's touchscreen irritably before jamming it back into his pocket.

'What happened?' Brijesh asked Vikrant.

'Nothing, just these blasted promo emails. I keep getting them.'

'Why don't you just—'

Whatever Laila was going to say was lost as Ray suddenly stood up, his eyes alight. 'That's it! That's how we can do it!'

Waris narrowed his eyes. 'Explain, Ray.'

'Well, sir, we can use the phishing trick, only this time, we'll introduce a covert software in the email. Have any of you heard of XSS?'

Everyone except Laila shook their heads.

'XSS means cross-site scripting. It's a type of computer security vulnerability through which we can bypass access controls on websites. We can use non-persistent XSS to automatically render a malicious script and—'

Kang put up his hand. 'Stop, stop! Speak normally, will you? I can't understand anything you're saying!'

Ray looked around at the pained expressions on everyone's faces and shifted gears. 'All right, forget what it is. I'll tell you what we can do. I'm sure you know that we have entire lists of email addresses these terrorists use. Can we get those lists?'

Laila nodded. 'That can be arranged.'

'Perfect. We'll scan for Umavi's email address. Then we'll send them an email, which will have a URL in it. Once they click that URL, they'll be taken to a page that will contain my hidden script, which will immediately start running. Alternatively, if they reply to the email, my code will start running. Now this code will introduce a software, a kind of Trojan horse, into their system. You can think of it as a kind of malware, one that collects all the data and sends it to us covertly.'

'That's all very good, Ray,' said Waris. 'But how does that get them to Istanbul?'

'Well, you said Brijesh and Vikrant will promise a donation, right?'

'Yes. They'll pose as Bangladeshis sending money to help the Lashkar's cause.'

'And how will that money be transmitted?'

'We won't actually be sending any money, Ray,' said Waris frostily.

'I understand, sir, but it will appear to be through a bank, right?'

'Certainly not. These kinds of transactions are always done in person first, before any money exchanges hands.'

'Let me suggest something, sir. Let's use Rabeta Bank as an example. I'll clone the bank's website. Then, when Umavi replies to my email, we can send him pages of transactions that we have apparently made, using the bank's web pages that I've cloned. I'll keep my script hidden in these pages, and we can give them access to view several of these transactions—'

'To show them that we've done it before?' asked Vikrant, who was following Ray's words intently.

'Exactly! That will give them confidence that you are genuine. Once that is done, you can ask them to come to Istanbul for a meeting.'

'It won't be that easy,' Brijesh said thoughtfully. 'We'll have to get him to choose Istanbul himself.'

Umavi scanned through the documents Qandahari had given him. He could scarcely believe what he was reading.

'And this is everything they've donated?' he said incredulously.

'No, Ameer,' said Qandahari. 'This is only what they've donated in the last two years.'

That was even more surprising. The group that called itself Ansar-ul-Ikhwan-ul-Muslimeen was apparently very generous, but more importantly, it seemed to believe in the same things Umavi did. The documents showed millions of dollars donated to charities that cared for orphans in Iraq, provided aid to the Palestine Liberation Organization, and helped displaced Afghani children. There were transaction records, receipts and documents validating every single donation. And it had all been done without anyone's knowledge.

According to the email that Qandahari had replied to, the Ansar-ul-Ikhwan-ul-Muslimeen didn't want their name to be displayed anywhere for several reasons. For one, it would immediately put them on the CIA's radar and would adversely affect international politics and diplomacy. Umavi understood and agreed with this, because if there was a breakdown in current diplomatic relations, Lashkar would be the first outfit the Americans would target.

Secondly, the Ansar-ul-Ikhwan-ul-Muslimeen believed that nobody else needed to know who was donating and to whom. Again, this touched a chord in Umavi.

'Qadir, I like these fellows and the secrecy they seem to believe in. If they really are who they say they are, I think they might actually want to do something for ummah. After all, that is what Islamic charity and zakat is all about; when you give with the right hand, the left should not know.'

'I agree, Ameer. And they've said they believe in our cause, in jihad. They too want to see India crushed, the arrogant West brought down from its throne. I think they're quite sincere.'

'Well, if you're right, Allah has just made a provision for the next two years of jihad. We needn't worry about how to sustain ourselves and our boys.'

'Al-ham-du lillah!' cried Qandahari, his epiglottis constricting as the words tumbled out from the depths of his throat.

'And you must consider what they want to give us. People give us fifty thousand rupees, one lakh or two lakhs, but these people are willing to give us two million dollars! Half a million every six months.'

Qandahari grew sober. 'That is something I've been wondering about, Ameer. They want us to furnish them with details of how we would spend that money. Why should we do that?'

Umavi got up slowly and walked to the window. The sun was just setting over Lahore, and his window offered a beautiful view of the city. It had been over six decades since Partition but Lahore still retained its rustic charm, unspoilt and uncorrupted by the vertical development and real estate rush. The skyline of the city remained pristinely authentic. Umavi had chosen the flat specifically for the view, saying that it calmed him and helped him think.

Without turning around, he said, 'I was worried about that too, when you came to me with their proposal yesterday. But I've thought about it and I think it's only fair. After all, since they're giving us so much money, it stands to reason that they want to see the results, don't you think?'

'But do you believe them?'

'Yes,' said Umavi, turning around and walking back to the table. 'But only after I saw these documents. And you've shown me their transactions. The records of the money they sent to the PLO's Yatama organization, the Mujahideen-Iraq and Madrasatul Muslimeen in Afghanistan. We went through them indirectly, through the bank's website, which means that they must be genuine.'

'So now, shall we meet them?'

'I'm not going to meet them, Qadir. You are.'

Kang was frowning. 'Who the hell is this Qandahari fellow? I thought we were dealing with Umavi.'

'We are,' said Ray. 'Qandahari is Umavi's assistant. Umavi won't meet us himself, he's sending his crony instead. He's obviously a smart man.'

'I thought money always works with these bastards,' grumbled Kang.

'Apparently not. Umavi is clearly an idealist, he won't be swayed by money, only by ideology,' said Waris. 'Vikrant, you're well versed in Urdu, right?'

Vikrant nodded. 'Indeed, sir.'

'Good. Ray, we need Vikrant's voice to sound different. Do you have anything?'

'Of course. I have a voice changer.'

'Good. I want Vikrant's voice to be unrecognizable.'

'Easily done, sir,' said Ray, and started clicking away at his computer.

'Vikrant, I want you to talk to this Qandahari fellow and convince him that you won't do business with a faceless organization. Insist that you want to meet the man at the top. Don't name Umavi. Tell them that your organization's president and a high-ranking representative of Rabeta Bank will personally be present at the meeting, and they won't meet just anyone. It has to be someone higher up. That should get Umavi out of his lair.'

'He's a cautious man, sir,' said Vikrant.

'I know. I believe he won't meet you the first time. It'll either be a no-show or he'll give you the runaround. But he'll come. I know he will. And once he decides on the location, Kang and Laila will be on recon. They'll give you and Brijesh the layout.'

As it turned out, the Ansar-ul-Ikhwan-ul-Muslimeen refused to meet with Qandahari. They wanted someone higher up. Naturally, this made Umavi highly suspicious. At any other time, he would have immediately cut off all contact and gone into hiding for a few days just to be safe. But this was two million dollars! And the background check, the bank – everything looked solid. Maybe, just maybe, these guys were genuine. But Umavi wasn't going to take a chance. He relayed his instructions to Qandahari, who then asked the Ansar-ul-Ikhwan-ul-Muslimeen for a meeting via satellite phone or VoIP. But again, they refused. They wanted to meet in person.

'Your leader's reluctance is most confusing. We are beginning to assume he might not need our donation after all.'

Qandahari almost panicked when he read the two-line email. But it gave Umavi the encouragement he needed; finally, he agreed to a meeting.

According to the Ansar-ul-Ikhwan-ul-Muslimeen's wishes, the meeting had to be held in a neutral location and not in Saudi Arabia, for obvious reasons. They left it to Umavi to decide, and after a lot of deliberation, he agreed to meet them at a private location in Istanbul, a neutral place where they could safely assume the CIA wouldn't be watching them. The venue – a five-star hotel in Taksim Square, overlooking the Bosphorus, built on the highest of Istanbul's seven hills, was called the Marmara Taksim.

Qandahari wanted to book a presidential suite, believing that it would go with Umavi's stature. He was surprised when Umavi shook his head.

'No. Think, Qadir, don't be stupid. The best place to hide a tree is in the jungle. If I book a presidential suite, I'll instantly attract a lot of attention. Everyone will want to find out who I am, it's natural human instinct. I don't want to stick out. Book me a normal room, I'd rather mix with the populace as a commoner.'

Umavi smiled at Qandahari's doubtful look. 'It'll also serve another purpose. It will show our friends from the Ansar-ul-Ikhwan-ul-Muslimeen that our cause is jihad, not earthly pleasures: we have a spartan lifestyle and don't splurge on ourselves. That will encourage them to donate more generously in the future.'

Impressed with his master's reasoning, Qandahari thought to himself, not for the first time, that not for nothing was Umavi the head of the Lashkar-e-Toiba.

The man with whom Qandahari spoke was courteous – speaking chaste Urdu, but with a Bengali accent, as most of his Bangladeshi friends did – and quite firm. The top men in their organization were going to be present at the meeting, and they wanted the same from Lashkar. Initially, when Qandahari told them about Umavi, that he was the man behind the 26/11 attack in Mumbai, and that he was the brilliant mastermind of the Lashkar, they seemed suitably impressed, but they didn't think that he was high enough in the outfit. Qandahari explained to them about Umavi's role, his planning and strategizing capabilities, and that he was the one who had trained the ten 26/11 mujahideen in Pakistan and had personally overseen their departure for Mumbai. Finally, they agreed.

'Shahid Latif, our president, and Sajjad Khan, the manager of Rabeta Bank's headquarters in Mymensingh, will be arriving from Bangladesh,' the man told Qandahari. 'They have instructed me to inform you that we are also prepared to aid any other organizations you name.'

When Qandahari relayed this information to Umavi, the Lashkar head immediately shook his head. 'We should ensure that all the aid comes our way. Why should others benefit from this? Who else knows the true meaning of jihad? Who else is devoted to Allah like us? Others might even be tempted if they get such large amounts of money. No, we are the only ones who must get the aid. We will never misuse any funds earmarked for Allah's service.'

Amjad walked into the lobby of the Marmara Taksim and looked around. It was just past noon, and there weren't many people. He didn't know what the two men from Ansar-ul-Ikhwan-ul-Muslimeen would look like, but he was confident that he would be able to identify them.

His faith in himself was well placed. Of the twenty-odd people in the lobby, some were chatting, alone or in groups, and others were reading magazines and newspapers, no doubt waiting for someone to arrive. Only two were not talking. Amjad noticed them on one of the sofas, wearing drab grey suits, briefcases at their feet, sitting erect, with a military air of command. He had no doubt they were Latif and Khan.

But his orders were clear. He wasn't to engage them, or talk to them; on no account was he to let them know he was there. Not for some time, anyway. He would watch them surreptitiously from a point where they couldn't see him, and relay what he was seeing to Umavi and Qandahari, in their room a few floors up. It was not the most exciting of assignments, but Umavi had chosen Amjad precisely because of this; he was one of the most patient men he knew. He would wait for as long as was required, which could be very long, if Umavi had his way.

Nearly an hour dragged by, but none of the three men in the lobby moved. Amjad noted that the two men were sitting in exactly the same posture as before, throughout; not moving, not talking.

When they'd been waiting for nearly two hours, Umavi called Amjad's cell phone. 'All right. You know what to do.'

'Yes, Ameer.'

Amjad hung up and dialled the number of the hotel reception, and asked to speak to Mr Shahid Latif, who was waiting in the lobby. In a few seconds, the hotel speakers crackled and a sexy female voice informed Mr Shahid Latif, waiting in the lobby, that he had a call.

One of the men got up and went to the lobby phone. Amjad waited until he heard the hello from the other end and said, 'Salaam alaikum, Mr Latif. My name is Amjad. My master Ameer Umavi would like to extend his deepest apology to you for not being able to be present. He suddenly took ill last night, a case of food poisoning, and his flight to Istanbul had to be cancelled. He shall be arriving tomorrow, and has asked me to kindly consider another meeting, same time, same place.'

There was a pause at the other end. Amjad watched the man on the phone, himself concealed by a large potted plant. Then the man spoke. 'I understand. Please give him my best wishes. We pray he will get better soon.'

'Thank you, Mr Latif. Once again, our deepest apologies.'

'It's all right. Salaam alaikum ware hmatullah.'

The line was disconnected.

The man walked back to his colleague and shook his head. Amjad heard him say, 'He's not coming. Let's go back to our room.'

The two of them moved towards the elevators. As they waited, Amjad wandered up behind them, looking like any other guest. He nodded at them amicably. In the lift, he waited until they had pressed the button for the eleventh floor, and then pressed the twelfth.

At the eleventh floor, the two men got off, and just before the door closed, Amjad slipped out too. He followed them to their room, satisfied himself that nothing appeared out of the ordinary, and went back to report to Umavi.

A similar scene played out the next day, only this time it was Qandahari, and Umavi made them wait for nearly three hours. When he finally got the signal from his master, Qandahari walked towards the two men slowly. He was quite astonished at their iron discipline, the way they sat there without moving or talking.

When he reached them, Qandahari assumed his most apologetic face. 'Salaam alaikum. My name is Qandahari.'

The shorter man looked at him and replied in perfect Urdu, 'Alaikum salaam. I am Shahid Latif, and this is my colleague Sajjad Khan. How is Mr Umavi?'

'I'm honoured to meet you, gentlemen. I am ashamed to be the bearer of bad news for you, but the illness that afflicted Ameer Umavi has claimed the life of another. It is due to this death in the family that Ameer will be unable to meet you today. Please accept our humblest apologies.'

For a moment, the two men were silent. Then the shorter man spoke again. 'It is indeed unfortunate to hear this bad news. Please convey our condolences to Mr Umavi. Shall we postpone the meeting then?'

Qandahari nodded. 'Yes, sir. Ameer is taking tonight's flight out, and he will be here in time for our meeting tomorrow. Please do pardon the inconvenience.'

The man raised his hand. 'It's all right. But I hope Mr Umavi will have the … understanding to meet us tomorrow.'

'He will, Mr Latif, he will. I promise you. Can I offer you something in the meantime? Some food or beverages?'

'That is quite unnecessary. Fi Amanillah, Mr Qandahari.'

'Fi Amanillah, Mr Latif. We shall meet tomorrow.'

The two men nodded and strode away.

On the eleventh floor, Amjad was waiting in disguise at a little distance from the elevator doors. He followed the two men to their room. Nothing seemed to be out of order.

Umavi was satisfied. The next day, exactly at noon, Qandahari brought the two men to his room.

After the initial pleasantries were exchanged, Umavi apologized for not meeting them earlier. 'It was unavoidable, gentlemen. You have my gratitude for being so patient.'

Latif smiled. 'We are patient men, Mr Umavi,' he said smoothly. 'And we appreciate the trouble and the risk you took. If we were in your position, we too would have taken similar precautions and made sure the man we were going to meet didn't turn out to be something else.'

Umavi's eyes widened, then he smiled.

That had been two hours ago. The two men had just left, and Umavi was feeling elated. It had worked! They were genuine. He had just made the biggest deal of his life, and now the Lashkar wouldn't have to worry about funds for at least two years!

He looked at Qandahari's shining eyes and realized they had to celebrate.

'What should we do now, Ameer?'

'We should thank Allah. The Quran says if we thank Allah, our bounties will be increased manifold. Then we should celebrate.'

'Zaroor Inshallah. How would you like to celebrate, Ameer?'

'Awwallutta'amba'ad al-kalam. First let's have food and then we can talk.'

'Shall I order something?'

'Call room service. I want to know what the best dish here is. Order two, one to your room and one to mine. We can order some dessert and juice and after that, kahawa.'

Within minutes, two royal marmara raans were ordered.

The Bangladeshi duo in their eleventh-floor room listened to the order being placed. They were ready for their real mission now.

8

Brigadier Arif Jan Afridi

A booming gunshot and the ringing in the ears that followed. That's all it had taken to turn his world upside down. That had been over forty years ago, but he still remembered his ears going numb as he ran in the direction of the shot, right into his father's study. He had been the first to arrive at the scene, to find his father slumped on the carpet, face down, a gun in his limp hand and blood gushing out from his temple and spreading towards the door. In his haste, he failed to notice that he had stepped in the puddle. Since that day, he had seen a lot of blood, but this was one instance he would never forget or recover from. It had haunted him for four whole decades.

Lt Gen. Yusuf Jan Afridi shot himself in the head soon after he had signed the Instrument of Surrender in the Bangladesh Liberation War. The document was signed on 16 December 1971 by Lt Gen. A.K. Niazi and Y.J. Afridi on Pakistan's behalf, giving up the half of Pakistan known as East Pakistan until then.

Lt Gen. Afridi was at the forefront of the opposition to the separation of East Pakistan, and he was ready to fight to his last breath to keep that chunk of land under Pakistani's control, where it belonged. But after the Indians had arrested 93,000

Pakistani soldiers, making them the largest contingent of POWs—larger than those at the end of World War II—and had strategically foiled all attempts of the Pakistani army, Lt Gen. Niazi and Afridi had no option but to sign the Instrument of Surrender with the Indian and Bangla army at Ramna Race Course, Dhaka (then Dacca).

Afridi returned home in a pensive mood, refused to eat anything, hugged his son and after one final look, kissed him gently on the forehead and quietly walked towards his study. He left behind only a note, saying, 'My beloved Arif Jan, I could not live with this humiliation. But I love you now and shall love you forever – General Abbu'.

Arif Jan, who was only ten years old, re-read the letter again and again for years thereafter. Its frayed remains continued to inhabit his wallet, like a talisman, a statement of purpose, a cause. He had fondly called his father General Abbu. General Abbu was his biggest hero, even bigger than Quaid-e-Azam, M.A. Jinnah.

Every morning he looked at General Abbu's picture before he started his day and every night he looked at it before switching off the lights. He joined the army and rose steadily through the ranks. He had only one mission in life: to avenge his father's humiliation and teach a lesson to those arrogant Indians. They had been dishonest to deny Kashmir to Pakistan, and had subsequently taken away East Pakistan too. They would pay for it, he promised himself.

Brigadier Arif Jan Afridi became the Pakistan army's ace weapon against India. He became the mastermind behind the militant infiltration into Kashmir and caused havoc in the country. His ingenious handling of the proxy war got him a fast-track to the Inter Services Intelligence (ISI). Every army, intelligence and government organization wanted Afridi on their team. The man was known for his innovative ideas and brilliant, painstakingly drawn up schemes that unsettled his rivals.

Among the Pakistani intelligence agencies, which included the Federal Intelligence Agency (FIA), Naval Intelligence, Military Intelligence and Defence Intelligence of Pakistan, the ISI has long been considered the most influential and resourceful organization. In fact, it is widely claimed that the ISI is regarded as the largest intelligence agency in the world in terms of sheer staff strength. No one even knows the official number of people employed by the agency, though according to one account, there may be over 10,000 people on its payroll, excluding informants, moles and general assets strewn around the globe.

After successfully running assets in Kashmir and Punjab, with stints in the FIA and Military Intelligence, Afridi had been given charge of the ISI's main division, Joint Intelligence X. The department coordinated with all other departments in the agency. Gathering, collating, structuring and processing intelligence and information from all other departments, JIX prepared the intelligence report for the director general of the ISI and subsequently, the president.

Afridi had wanted to personally run Daniel Bradley and participate in the 26/11 operations in Mumbai but departmental politics had kept him out. He had now begun working with Chinese intelligence agencies. Afridi found Chinese intelligence to be much smarter, sharper and more efficient than the much hyped CIA, though he had friends in Langley as well. The Chinese, of course, were more than matched by the Mossad of Israel or the UK's MI6.

What Afridi liked about the Chinese was the basis of their alliance with Pakistan – thwarting India. They had been the first to refuse to recognize Bangladesh as a separate nation. It took years and a long process of diplomatic lobbying by the Indians for them to finally give in. Unsurprisingly, since the time Afridi joined the Pakistani army, he had begun working closely with them. It was with their help that the ISI had notched up consistent successes in north-east India.

Major John Hu Wang had one of the shrewdest brains in the intelligence world. Wang's ideologies were clear: Arunachal Pradesh and Ladakh belonged to China, Pakistan was welcome to keep the rest. Both Wang and Afridi had made inroads into India.

Even if Afridi could not participate in managing 26/11, he decided to continue with his private war against India. Within a couple of years of the Mumbai attacks, Afridi and Wang worked together to plant a Chinese research vessel disguised as a fishing trawler off the coast of Little Andaman. It collected sensitive data until it was detected by Indian naval intelligence and had to be withdrawn. They began working on reclaiming the posts in Ladakh. In fact, they got their troops into Ladakh, and also blatantly violated the airspace before the Indians began making a fuss about the incursion.

Neither Pakistan nor China would relent. 'Indians don't have their brains and spines in the right places,' Wang said, with a crooked smile. They were determined to persist with their Ladakhi adventure, while the Indians continued to crib about the violation of air space.

Afridi was seemingly happy with his life. His mission to hurt India was well on track. He was so dedicated to it that he refused to get married or have a normal family life, declaring them to be distractions. For days, he would be off planning a secret mission. This time though, Afridi returned to his head office in Islamabad to rather unexpected news. 'Sabahuddin Umavi found dead in his room in Royal Marmara in Istanbul. PM report says he died due to food allergy.'

Afridi was shocked. Umavi and he had recently met at a gathering in Karachi and he had seemed hale and hearty. When they were introduced, Umavi had told him, 'Pakistan needs men like you at the helm. Only then can we win this war against the infidels. They have everything – money, guns, manpower; all we have is our dedication and that's all we need.'

Afridi had taken him aside and congratulated him on his success in Mumbai. 'We are planning an equally big push in Delhi and south India. Let us sit together and plan the operation.'

Umavi had agreed immediately, but mentioned the paucity of funds. Afridi had promised to look into the finances for any campaign that they would jointly launch against India. But now, he had lost his newfound ally.

Something about Umavi's death didn't sit right with Afridi. Had he planned to travel to Istanbul? He had not mentioned any impending business in Turkey. What had taken him there so urgently?

Afridi picked up the intercom and called his aide de camp, Major Sarfaraz Rashid. Rashid was not an army man. He had no grounding as an intelligence officer. Hired through the Federal Public Service Commission (FPSC) of Pakistan and primarily an academician and a linguist, Rashid had never fired a weapon in his life. Unlike his boss, he had something of a soft corner for India and loved Hindi movies and songs. A big fan of Dilip Kumar and Mohammad Rafi, in his free time he could be found downloading music and audio clips of film dialogues from Indian websites.

'Ji, farmaiyye,' he said, stepping into the cabin. The AC was motoring away at full blast on the lowest setting – sixteen degrees – and it was almost freezing.

Afridi was smoking a cigar and looking out of his window. His face wore a dull, expressionless look and his eyes weren't nearly as bright as usual. It was enough to worry Rashid. 'Rashid, my friend,' Afridi began calmly enough, before exploding, 'how the fuck did we miss Maulana Umavi's death? Why was I not informed about his trip to Turkey? Did he take the required permission? I thought he was well protected.'

'Sir, I will check …' Rashid almost stammered.

'Don't check, get me his man Friday, ask him to fly down now. I want to see him before the end of the day. Is that understood?'

Rashid nodded limply.

9

Everyone's knock is unique, a somewhat limited manifestation of one's personality. This was something Waris believed, and so he knew it was Laila who was seeking an audience with him.

'Come in, Ms Borges.'

Laila walked in and said 'Sir, something's not right.'

'Could you be a bit more specific, Ms Borges?'

'That's the problem. I can't. Call it a gut feeling, but there's something about Bradley that doesn't seem quite right.'

Waris indicated the chair opposite him. 'Explain.'

He leaned back in his chair, elbows on the armrests and fingers steepled in front of him. It was his favourite position for tackling a problem.

Laila sat down.

They were in Mumbai, in a small flat a few minutes walk from Turbhe railway station. The area was peaceful, inhabited bachelors who worked for the IT companies and BPOs housed nearby, away from the thoroughfare of the metropolis. It had been easy for Vikrant to get exactly the sort of flat they needed: secluded, large and peaceful, with not too many people around. Nobody would notice their comings and goings.

Immediately after their first mission turned out to be a success, Waris had ordered them to vacate the flat in Delhi and find another command centre, preferably in another city. 'The more mobile we are, lesser the chances of anyone pinning us down,' he said. The others agreed unanimously.

Now, a week later, Laila sat in front of Waris and tried to put into words what was on her mind.

'Well sir, you know how we have so many forms of communication. The most important form, however, is not what we say, but what we *don't* say. Non-verbal communication, body language, whatever you want to call it.'

Waris nodded. 'I know. I also know that you're especially gifted in reading these signs.'

'How can you know that, sir?' asked Laila, surprised. 'It's not in my profile.'

'There are a lot of things that aren't on our profiles, Ms Borges. What I know comes from word-of-mouth.'

Laila shook her head. 'I can't imagine who could've told you that.'

Waris sighed. He'd made the slip, and now it was clear that he would have to give Laila some answers.Otherwise she might go digging and find out about the one man who could not be identified on any account, the man who sat in the RAW chief's chair. 'Who assigned you to me?'

'The order document was unmarked, sir. Signatory classified. All I know is that someone at the top of my organization recommended me to you.'

'You're right. Well, Ms Borges, the same benefactor who made sure you were assigned to me also told me of your many qualities, which I was made to understand would prove invaluable in carrying out our mission. It's the same individual who has provided us with the resources you're using and seeing around you.'

Laila nodded. 'I suspected as much, sir.'

Ali Waris inclined his head. 'I know that all of you on this mission are of the highest calibre. I know that if you look really hard, you might just find out who our benefactor is. But I would like to request you not to attempt it. He has taken a massive risk in agreeing to help us, and if he is found out, it will be devastating for both him and our country. Please respect his wishes and don't delve deeper into what needs to be kept secret. I give you my word that he is one of the biggest patriots India has ever had.'

After a long pause, during which he could see her struggling to accept his request, she nodded. 'I understand, sir. I'll intimate the others too.'

'Thank you. Now, you were telling me about Bradley.'

'Yes, sir. As you know, I've been hacking into the US federal system for a while now. Since my activity is completely non-attacking, I've been able to bypass many of their securities.

'I isolated the prison logs and data files, and accessed the Chicago prison system. I also downloaded the interrogation recordings they have of Bradley. I've been studying them—'

'Ms Borges, I must congratulate you!' said Waris, impressed. 'I read in your progress report that you had got into their system, but I didn't know you'd got this far! The US cyber security system is quite difficult to break into, I'm told.'

'It is, sir,' said Laila, ignoring the compliment as usual. 'But I did manage to get every video recording of Bradley I could find before their threat detection system kicked in.'

'And—'

'Before you ask, sir, they won't be able to trace my signal.'

'Good. So what's the problem?'

Laila looked a troubled. 'I don't really know how to explain it. Call it a gut feeling.'

'I'm very open to gut feelings, Ms Borges. I respect them enormously. But you'll have to do a little more than that in such a situation.'

After a pause, she said, 'Imagine you have a clone. An identical clone made of you when you were fifteen. Then both you and he were placed in different parts of the world, where you grew up without any contact with each other. Do you think you'd still be similar?'

Waris shook his head. 'No. We might still look alike, but we'd be a product of our surroundings and experiences.'

'And you'd behave differently?'

'I suppose so.'

'Well, that's the feeling I'm getting. It's almost as if someone else is posing as Bradley, and has conditioned himself to looking, behaving and doing everything like him.'

'And he looks exactly the same?'

'I'm telling you. It *is* him, just – just not him.'

'Hmm. Most unhelpful, Ms Borges,' said Waris, frowning. This was not looking good. Laila was the best in her area of expertise, which was all about hacking and obtaining information from any computer system in the world, as well as working in the field as tech support and background operator. She wasn't an authority on behavioural sciences or psychology.

Then again, she was a valued NTRO analyst, which meant that she would surely have had *some* training in the area.

'I'll try and be more coherent in my analysis next time, sir.'

'Good. You have time, we aren't after Bradley yet. Now, have any of you found out where we can ambush our dear Wajid Mir?'

It had taken them hardly any time to pinpoint Wajid Mir, thanks to the software Ray had installed in Qandahari's system, almost as an afterthought. They hadn't expected much from it initially, as they knew the LeT's highest echelons would never commit to digital memory any information that might be compromised by hackers. So it was mostly about the kind of emails Qandahari received – which couldn't possibly amount to much since all major decisions were handled by his master Umavi – and the browsing history on Qandahari's system, which might give them a vague idea of what was on his mind. They knew he would be cautious enough to not save his passwords anywhere on his system in a way that they could be found, but as long as his entire flow of data, both via download and upload, was being monitored, there was a distinct possibility that he would use his passwords at some time, which would immediately give them access as well. The only glitch in this plan would occur if Qandahari changed his passwords frequently, and Laila had assured them he would, given his tech-savvy nature and the paranoia of his organization.

All of this meant that the A-Team, as they had come to call themselves jokingly, had access to information which might or might not prove to be useful. As far as their mission was concerned, the entire setup on Qandahari's system would become irrelevant once they had disposed of Umavi but, as Ray said, 'You never know when you might need to tap into it again.'

It was Ray who had begun to refer to them as the A-Team: A for Ali Waris. Initially, as was the case with anything he said that didn't have to do with his work, he wasn't taken seriously at all.

'A-Team? Really?' was Kang's incredulous reaction.

'Just because Ali Waris sir bears some faint resemblance to Liam Neeson, we do not become A-Team,' said Laila. 'Maybe get Bradley Cooper to join us too?'

'Why, Laila!' said Vikrant, smiling teasingly at her. 'I had no idea you were such a diehard Hollywood fan!'

'Why Hollywood?' asked Ray. 'Actually, when I named it A-Team, I wanted to make a mathematical equation of A+RB2+VK. A for Ali, RB2 for Ray, Borges and Brijesh and VK ...'

But he never got to complete the equation.

'Oh, shut up!' snapped Brijesh. 'Come on, you guys, don't get him started or he'll bore us to bits!'

Ray looked indignant. 'Hey, I never bore—'

'No, no, of course not,' said Vikrant soothingly.

'You're a storehouse of interesting titbits, man!' Kang chipped in.

'Hmph. Well, you guys should know. This is retribution! We are on a mission of vengeance, to right the wrong done to our country—'

'Our mission is *not* one of vengeance, Ray.'

Ray swivelled around to see their leader standing at the door.

The army man looked at his team, sitting in a semi-circle: Kang with a newspaper in his hand, Brijesh upright in his chair, Ray and Laila with their laptops on their knees and Vikrant lounging on a sofa, balancing his karambit knife on the tip of his finger. They all snapped to attention when they saw Waris.

'We *are* seeking vengeance, yes. We *are* punishing those who have committed crimes against us. But our mission is not just to get revenge. Fundamentally, our mission is one of justice. To bring justice to those who have been wronged.'

He looked at each of them in turn, frowning fiercely. Ray opened his mouth, clearly about to apologize, when the frown suddenly disappeared and a twinkle appeared in Waris's eyes.

'Then again,' he smiled, 'the A-Team seems to be quite an apt name. We are alpha in every sense of the word.'

Going by the content of the emails Qandahari was exchanging with others in the LeT, it was clear that his master's death had caused quite a flurry. But none of the communiqués suggested that any suspicion had been aroused within the LeT's ranks. This impression was aided by the testimonial of Umavi's doctor. He had confirmed to the LeT that it was impossible to have known of Umavi's allergy for hazelnuts beforehand, but that it wasn't an uncommon allergy, and the autopsy report of Umavi's death was conclusive – Umavi had died of a severe allergic reaction and not as a result of an assassination.

Under Waris's direction, Ray had sent one final email to Qandahari after Umavi's death had hit the news. Ansar-ul-Ikhwan-ul-Muslimeen had forwarded its condolences to Qandahari and the Lashkar-e-Toiba, and said that Umavi's death had made them cautious; they were withdrawing their donation for the moment. Once the leadership of the organization had been decided and settled upon, Qandahari could contact them once again.

Qandahari's reply held a frantic plea for the Ansar-ul-Ikhwan-ul-Muslimeen to reconsider, but it elicited no response. For now, the A-Team had closed off that avenue, and without raising any suspicions.

Meanwhile, the LeT's loss had precipitated a chain reaction among the leaders of Lashkar. The death of one of their top comrades, even if accidental, had left them in a precarious state. Once Qandahari had briefed them on the Ansar-ul-Ikhwan-ul-Muslimeen donation, they realized that a replacement had to be found immediately. Unfortunately, at the time, Lashkar's top brass was scattered across the globe. Flying in for a meeting to Pakistan was out of the question, as almost every security agency in the world, from the CIA to the Mossad, kept a close eye on the comings and goings in Pakistan. Therefore the meeting had to be somewhere outside.

This was all that Laila had been able to glean from monitoring Qandahari's system.

It was frustrating for everyone. They knew that one or more of their targets would soon be meeting in one place, and it could provide them with the perfect opportunity to set up an ambush. Moreover, it was a safe bet that this would be the only time that the Lashkar leaders would be out in the open, stripped of the invulnerability of their base in Pakistan.

But Waris knew better than to yell and rant at his team. They were giving their best, and it would be foolish and probably even detrimental to their morale, if he vented his frustration on them. So he let them be, each working their own angles to try and find a way in. But nearly two weeks went by, and the opportunity eluded them. The pressure was getting to the team, tempers were becoming frayed, and their training was the only thing that kept arguments from breaking out and cracking their confidence.

The breakthrough came early in the morning on the seventeenth day after the Ansar-ul-Ikhwan-ul-Muslimeen had cut off contact with Qandahari. Laila had finished her night shift, sifting constantly through reams of data coming in on Qandahari's system. She had been trying all night to replicate Ray's programme and place it covertly in one of Lashkar's internal servers by using Qandahari's access, but had found no success so far. Vikrant saw her out to the front door, watching her retreating figure appreciatively and marvelling at the near perfect curves. Then, with a sigh, he went back to his station for the transition watch before Ray took over.

In less than two minutes, he found the opportunity.

It was an email from Ateeq, private aide to Wajid Mir, to Qandahari. The subject line was in Urdu, and it said, 'Seratul Mustaqeem'. *The righteous path of jihad.*

Had it been Laila or Ray, they would have dismissed the email as mere promotional material for jihad and what they called the 'insane ramblings of mad preachers'. But Vikrant was fluent in Urdu and interested in Islam. He was one of those who held the view that Islam in its true form was a peaceful religion, and peace was what the Quran actually taught. Because of this, he was always interested in the points of view of radicals and extremists, and would read through their preaching when he found the time. Right now, he had nothing but time on his hands.

The first part of the email was standard stuff, containing a discourse on how infidels were always mistreating Islam and that they should be killed and made to burn in hell. It was clearly Ateeq's private, personal viewpoint, which he was sharing with Qandahari. But at the end of the email, there were a few lines that nearly stopped Vikrant's breath for a second.

'WM *majlis daurane Mushrekeen – muqaabla Sitambar mein, zaroori intezaamaat farahaam karein* (During the encounter between Christian forces in September, make necessary arrangements for the WM summit).'

Decoded the sentence read: 'Wajid Mir to hold a meeting during Australia-England match in September, make necessary preparations.'

Vikrant rushed to inform Waris, whom he found at his computer, writing an email to his daughter.

'Sir, it's 3 a.m.!' said Vikrant.

Waris turned to look at him. 'After my wife's death, Vibha is all I have,' he said. 'And she expects me to be in constant touch with her. I realized I had not written to her for a long time. But tell me why you thought it was necessary to come knocking at my door now. What is it that cannot wait till morning?'

'Sir, I think Wajid will be in England in September!'

Waris sat up straight. 'How the hell are you so sure?'

Vikrant explained about the chance email and Wajid's planned meeting during the Australia-England match; the next such match would be the ODI at Edgbaston on 11 September.

'Wajid thinks it was a clever decision to choose such a place to meet, where none of our leaders will be spotted among so many others like us; Edgbaston is a small town with a huge Asian immigrant population. It also has the second biggest stadium after Lords.'

As Vikrant concluded, Waris became pensive.

'What is it, sir?' Vikrant asked

'How will you spot Wajid in a crowd of 25,000 people and kill him without getting caught?' asked Ali Waris, abandoning his half-written email. 'Call for everyone to assemble.'

10

'It's got to be the match, I'm telling you!' said Brijesh, thumping his fist on the table emphatically.

'I agree,' said Vikrant, steadying the swaying table. 'It would seem like the perfect cover for them.'

'But it's completely out in the open!' cried Ray. 'From what we know of these men, they would never expose themselves to such a situation, especially one that poses such a huge security risk!'

'I understand what you're saying, Ray. But Brijesh sir and I have met these men. We've formed a good idea of what they're like. And I'm telling you, they would want to be in a crowd where it'll be impossible to spot them. That would give them far more security than several bodyguards standing outside hotel rooms, believe me.'

Laila was frowning at her laptop screen. 'You might be wrong, Vikrant,' she said.

The 42-inch plasma screen on the wall came to life as it interfaced with Laila's computer. Wajid Mir's face flashed on the screen on the left, while his profile and several details and personal habits scrolled upwards to the right.

'Look at his profile. He has never come out in the open. He has not been outside Pakistan for God knows how long, so he won't be comfortable wherever he goes. The more exposed he is, the less secure he's bound to feel. Inside a cricket ground, he will be completely out in the open. It goes against his profile, he won't take that risk.'

Vikrant was silent as he considered the information on the screen. Laila continued, 'Also, think of the logistics. This is an Australia-England match, which means there will be close to 25,000 people at the ground, and that means there will be a huge security cordon there. These guys won't be able to simply walk to a deserted area for a meeting, they'll be spotted immediately.'

Brijesh shook his head. 'Laila, do us a favour and get your head out of your ass. You're forgetting Vikrant and I have met these people. Nothing, and I mean *nothing*, can match first-hand experience, certainly not your fancy gadgets and technology. I don't care what your profiler says, they're going to meet at the match.'

Laila stared at him for a long second, then inclined her head, her face inscrutable.

At that moment, the door opened and Kang and Waris walked in. They were both sweating, but looked refreshed and cheerful.

'How was the exercise, sir?' asked Vikrant.

Waris grunted as he sat down. 'I'm an old man now, Vikrant,' he said ruefully. 'But it helps me stay young and fit.'

'Wrestling with Kang will certainly keep you fit, sir,' said Ray, still a little awed at their leader's physical prowess.

The scientist had initially scoffed when he'd found out that Waris had decided to wrestle with Kang every other day.

'Come on, he's an old man now! And look at Kang here. He looks like he can take over from where Schwarzenegger left off! I bet you a hundred bucks Kang throws him in twenty seconds.'

'You're on, mister!' Vikrant had said, his eyes gleaming mischievously. 'Laila, are you in?'

'You mean, am I excited that you barbarians are betting on pitting your testosterone against each other?' she had offered, then sighed. 'Fine. I bet against Ray.'

Brijesh had also bet on Waris.

Kang, who had been listening intently, leaned forward and said, 'Count me in too.'

'Wait a minute!' Ray protested. 'How can he—'

'Sure, Kang. What'll it be?' Vikrant said, shushing Ray with a look.

'I'm betting against me. The chief is in quite good shape.'

'You mean you won't be able to take him down in twenty seconds?' Ray asked disbelievingly.

'I don't know. We'll see.'

As it turned out, it took Kang more than a minute to throw Ali Waris. Ray refrained from betting after that, but his respect for the others on the team seemed to have increased, especially seeing Waris's own commitment mirrored in them.

Now, refreshed as he was from his exercise with Kang, Waris immediately noticed the tension in the room. Turning to Brijesh, he said, 'Update please, Brijesh.'

'Yes, sir. As you know, Wajid Mir is definitely going to be in the UK sometime between the tenth and seventeenth of

September. We haven't managed to get any more information than that from the remaining data from Qandahari's system.'

Ali Waris nodded. 'In fact, I believe this Ateeq fellow made an error in writing that line in his email. Don't ever forget, these Lashkar fellows are very cunning and cautious. They wouldn't put something like this in writing anywhere—'

'—which must be why there's no other mention of the trip!' finished Ray.

'Exactly. Continue, Brijesh.'

'Well, sir, we're in disagreement about the venue for the meeting. Vikrant and I believe that they will choose the place in such a way that they can melt into the surroundings. They will get the ideal opportunity at the Edgbaston cricket ground in Birmingham on 11 September.'

'It's the perfect cover,' said Vikrant quietly.

Waris glanced at the plasma screen with Wajid Mir's face plastered on it, and turned to Laila. 'And you disagree with them?'

'Yes, sir,' she said. 'According to his profile, Wajid Mir would never expose himself in this manner. It is too open, too much of a security risk for him.'

'Hmm.'

Everyone waited, as Waris walked over to the window and looked out over the garden maintained by the housing society.

Identifying the meeting venue correctly wasn't the hardest part, he knew. The more difficult bit would come later, when they would have to identify Wajid Mir among the thousands of brown-skinned individuals present.

From what he knew of Wajid Mir and his associates, the Edgbaston ground stood out as the most likely venue. Not only would they be automatically hidden, lost in the crowd, but they would also get to enjoy a charged match between Australia and England. 'Would they pass up that opportunity?' thought Waris, and shook his head. Not a chance!

Having made up his mind, he turned back to the others, who were waiting patiently. 'They'll be at the ground. It's the best opportunity they have.'

'Acknowledged, sir,' said Laila, and turned off the huge screen. 'But now we have a problem.'

Waris nodded. 'I know. We'll have to identify him.'

'Exactly, sir. I don't see how we can solve that problem. Plus his profile suggests he's a master of disguise. That makes our mission doubly difficult.'

'Maybe,' said Vikrant, 'Daddy can help.'

It hadn't taken the team long to figure out that they were being backed by someone. No matter how ingenious Waris was, it would have been impossible for him to procure the resources they had access to. But their chief had refused to reveal who it was, and they respected his decision. They only called him Daddy.

'Indeed, Vikrant,' said Waris. 'My thought as well.'

'Finally, a challenge!'

'What, you're so comfortable now that you need challenges? Sky, there's something wrong with you for sure, I'm telling you.'

'Well, whatever's wrong with me has got you too, Ali.'

'Yeah, it always did. Listen, can you get me that intel?'

'Like I said, Ali, this is going to be a challenge.'

'Why? You helped out the last time.'

There was a pause at the other end of the line. Waris could imagine the RAW chief sitting in his office in Delhi, taking off his spectacles and pinching the bridge of his nose, a sign that he was thinking hard.

'The last time was in India, old friend. What you're asking from me now brings the London guys into the picture.'

Waris laughed. 'Well, Sky, you being you, I'm sure you've got some men there.'

Sky chuckled. 'Of course, why would you think otherwise? But seriously, give me a couple of days. This is an international matter. I'll have to move carefully.'

'Fine, but don't dawdle, Sky. We don't have much time. Our friend will travel to London any time beginning next fortnight. We can't miss him.'

'I may know of something else that can help. I'll get back to you tomorrow. By the way, are you getting your usual coffee there?'

'Yes, but it's not the same. I can't quite figure out why. Must be some Chinese shit.'

'I've told you this a million times, Ali. Let me send across a bottle of Scotch for you. You'll see it'll help with—'

'Fuck you,' grunted Waris, and hung up while the RAW chief was still laughing at the other end.

The team assembled again the following night, at half past ten.

Waris went to his chair, behind the only desk in the room, and waited until the others had arranged themselves in front of him. Then he spoke.

'Daddy did it.'

'All right!' exclaimed Vikrant.

Waris put up his hand. 'But there's a catch. We're not going to be alone in this mission. There will be some backing from the lower levels of MI6.'

'MI6?' said Kang, looking troubled. 'But won't that complicate the whole thing?'

It was Laila who replied. 'It will, but it can't be helped. Whether it's the match or anywhere else, since we're going to be in the UK, it will be under MI6's jurisdiction. We really won't be able to avoid that.'

'Correct,' said Waris, nodding. 'And since we can't avoid them, we might as well collaborate with them. But that's not all. I'll leave Ray here to explain the rest.'

Ray got up importantly and took centre stage. 'Has any of you heard about terahertz?'

As was usually the case when Ray asked such a question, everyone except Laila looked blank. 'I've heard of it vaguely,' said Laila. 'It's used in body scanners and the sort, isn't it?'

Ray nodded. 'Yes. Terahertz is a kind of electromagnetic radiation, a sub-millimetre wave. Its frequency lies between microwaves and infrared light waves. It's a fairly new avenue of research, but currently there are some full body scanners that implement terahertz frequencies.'

'Why?' asked Kang. 'What's wrong with what we already have?'

'Well, terahertz appears to have more penetrating power than the millimetre wave scanners and backscatter X-ray machines that are used now. They can be tweaked to detect many materials and substances that the others can't, by combining the current conventional imaging technique with spectral identification. Conventional scanners can sometimes miss them if they are.

concealed properly. But these materials leave a kind of spectral fingerprint in the terahertz range. And since terahertz radiation can penetrate fibres and plastics, it can be used to detect those materials.'

'But you're saying this is very new?' said Vikrant.

'Yes. There's a lot of ongoing research in this field. And,' he glanced at Waris, who nodded to him, 'one of these areas of research is going to be very useful to us.'

Everyone's attention was focused on Ray as he continued.

'A certain technology is being developed, using which the genetic makeup of the cells of the human body can be detected. What this means,' he continued hurriedly, before the others lost interest in his technical explanation, 'is that if you have a few of my cells and know my DNA structure, you can identify me anywhere using this technology, no matter how I disguise myself, or even if I get plastic surgery and look completely different.'

Kang let out a loud whistle. 'But that means anyone can be identified anywhere!'

'Exactly. Now, just as those materials leave a spectral footprint in the terahertz range, our DNA will also leave behind a trail. It won't be visible using just terahertz radiation, but if that radiation frequency can somehow be boosted, all we'll need to have is a profile of an individual's DNA to identify him virtually anywhere.'

'But who—'

It was Waris who answered. 'Mossad. Who else?'

There was a stunned silence. Finally Vikrant broke it.

'Sir, am I to understand that we're going to have to work with not only MI6 but Mossad as well?'

'Unfortunately, major, we don't have an option. Ray, if you would care to continue?'

'Yes, sir. Mossad claims to have developed a microchip that can be installed on any scanner in the world. That's the technology I told you about. They're calling it the T-Ray Profiler. They've used computational genomics to identify individual genes, which they feed into the Profiler. So there is a T-Ray profile for an individual stored on the chip, containing genetic information, and it will be quickly analysed and matched with input data. Now the chief has just told me—' Ray broke off, and again glanced at Waris.

'Daddy has provided us with a contact within Mossad. They don't care how we use it, or on whom we use it. But according to our contact, they have only just readied the technology, they haven't tested it fully yet. They've done it in the lab, and on some unsuspecting Israeli citizens too, no doubt. But they haven't field tested it yet, not when the stakes are high.'

'And we're going to be the guinea pigs?' said Brijesh.

'Well, not us, no,' said Ray with a sly smile. 'Wajid Mir will be.'

'But how the hell will we get his profile?' said Kang.

'You're forgetting, Kang,' Waris said, 'that this is Mossad we're dealing with. They already have Mir's profile. It's just a matter of testing it, and that has fallen to us. Mutual cooperation, people. They give us the technology we need and we run the test that they need.'

'But how will it work?' asked Laila.

'That's where MI6 comes in. Brijesh, Ray has been given the coordinates of our local contact in London. Get on to him. He'll put you in touch with MI6's man.'

'I have a question, sir,' said Kang, looking worried. 'Do we really want the MI6 to get involved? What if they find out Daddy's identity? Even we don't know who he is. But if MI6 gets into the fray, they might just find out who he is.'

'Don't worry, Kang. Our benefactor knows how to protect himself and his identity. Now, Ray, if you would explain the situation to them?'

It took just a day for the team to chalk out a plan. 'I've chosen well,' Waris thought to himself, as he reflected on how quickly they had strategized the entire mission.

Brijesh, Kang, Vikrant, Ray and Laila would arrive in London on 9 September. They would meet the local RAW contact in London, who would set up two temporary bases for them – one in London, the other in Birmingham.

Immediately after arrival, Brijesh and Kang's target would be the security station at Heathrow airport. Somehow, they had to get the T-Ray Profiler installed in the scanner there. Laila showed them how.

Usually, the computer chip of the airport's security scanner was taken for maintenance work every thirty days. However, in anticipation of a massive influx of foreigners and cricket enthusiasts for the Australia-England match on 11 September, every single piece of gadgetry at the airport was being monitored and taken for routine maintenance far more frequently, on Monday, Wednesday and Saturday. This schedule would leave no room for error at all, and would be continued until the match was over.

According to Laila, who had hacked into the scheduling

information, the scanner chips would be taken for maintenance to a separate location every time, notified to the transport team only an hour in advance. They would have to keep tabs on the transport team at all times, and ensure that between the conclusion of the maintenance and transport back to the airport for reinstallation, they put in their own addition, the several T-Ray Profilers that would be on loan to them from Mossad. RAW's local contact would work with MI6 in delaying the transport team long enough – once for Ray to install the Profiler, and once later, to get it back.

All this, however, meant that MI6 would want a piece of the pie, and Mossad might just turn out to be unwilling to share their technology. This realization almost led to the mission being aborted, but Waris once again got Sky involved. MI6 was promised separate and unrelated information that it had been asking the Indians for.

The next step was identifying when Wajid Mir would land at Heathrow. Here, the team was unanimous. He would certainly not come from Peshawar or any other part of Pakistan that was under suspicion of housing terrorist groups. That left only Islamabad and Lahore. So all flights to Heathrow from these two cities would have be monitored closely.

The means to eliminate the target was also unanimously agreed upon – a lethal dosage of a muscle relaxants. Ray had created a variant of the drug succinylcholine, a quick-acting, depolarizing paralytic muscle relaxant that causes almost instant loss of motor skills, but without inducing loss of consciousness or anaesthesia. Succinylcholine had been used in the assassination of top Hamas militant Mahmoud-al-Mabhouh and had been identified only after ten days.

Ray's tweaked version, a variant of succinylcholine, was more lethal. It was more dangerous in that it induced loss of consciousness and had a traceable life of just under three minutes. After those three minutes, it would dissolve into the bloodstream and become completely untraceable. The victim would appear to have fallen asleep and never woken up.

The disagreement came about when deciding on the target. While Vikrant and Laila felt that they should eliminate as many Lashkar targets as they could find, Brijesh, Kang and Ray disagreed. Their target was Wajid Mir, and that was their mission. Killing the others would also mean a higher risk of discovery. 'If only Wajid Mir dies of natural causes, it might be overlooked,' said Kang. 'But if all of them die in that manner, our cover will definitely be blown.'

'Yes, and we can't assume they're idiots,' said Brijesh. 'That's one mistake we *cannot* afford to make. If there's the slightest slip up at our end, you can be assured they'll come down on us like a ton of bricks.'

Vikrant and Laila were still unconvinced. According to them, the opportunity to eliminate an entire group of terrorist leaders was not to be passed up.

Finally, Waris intervened. 'I understand what you're saying, Vikrant, Laila. But we can't overreach. This is a very slippery slope we're on. If we start killing people indiscriminately, we are no better than them. Our targets are on our hitlist because they have been proven to be guilty and they've not been punished. We *had* to step in.'

He paused and looked around. 'Believe me, I want to,' he said quietly. 'But it would be too damned easy to go down that path. And that path, people, leads only to needless violence. There is a thin line between a warrior and terror monger. We don't want to cross that Lakshman Rekha. It would make *us* terrorists.'

Vikrant and Laila had nothing to say after that.

11

London

Intelligence agencies around the world are constantly updating and modernizing their arsenal to upstage their rivals. At any given time, their repertoire of tricks includes all sorts of ideas, from the brilliant to the bizarre and everything in between. Most of these games are part of shadow wars. If China raised 10,000 hackers as part of their Red Army to break into any computer system in the world, then Mossad has perfected the art of tracking their favourite targets, no matter where they are hiding.

After eliminating Osama bin Laden, the United States of America was convinced of the importance of personal touch to espionage. After decades of obsessing over technological surveillance, the country's clandestine services rediscovered the impeccability of 'humint': human intelligence.

According to an unconfirmed report, over 3,000 Mumbai cabbies are sleeping resources for mighty Uncle Sam. These cabbies are supposedly part of their 'War on Terror'. Their brief is simple: they are always positioned at particular pick-up points across the city. The cabbie is expected to listen for any kind of suspicious conversation between passengers or a lone traveller talking on the phone. This immediately gets reported to the officer assigned to collate and process information. Most of the time, it's a waste of precious man hours but there's always the possibility that you might hit paydirt.

The outside world thinks of Indians as unsophisticated in the field of espionage. But, as is the case with stereotypes (good and bad), the anomalies tend to undermine the stereotype. There was a very good reason that Sky was regarded in the same light as James Bond. In fact, Waris often addressed him as Abu Bond.

Waris knew that they could not let Wajid Mir disappear and get lost in Britain. It was necessary to keep tabs on Mir's location from the moment he set foot in London.

Sky was the one who came up with the idea. It was almost four months since British soldier Lee Rigby had been brutally hacked to death and beheaded by two men in Woolwich, South East London, in broad daylight. London's Metropolitan Police and citizens alike were still rattled by the attack. The MI5 were apprehensive about the possibility of a spate of attacks across the country.

Sky called his friend Alexander Perry, deputy director of MI5 and a strong opponent of Pakistan's hardline elements. He knew that he needed help from a top MI5 official who did not have any misplaced sympathy for Pakistan, and Perry was just the man.

Sky began with his customary greeting: 'Namaskar'.

Perry returned the greeting to the best of his ability, despite his thick British accent. 'Naam-osk … Naam-ask … Bloody hell! Good morning, Sky.'

Sky laughed aloud and said, 'You still need a lot of practice, Alex.'

'Yeah, I'll get on it immediately,' said Perry sarcastically.

Sky got straight to the point. 'Tabrez is coming to London.

He is a person of interest to us. We need to keep a watch on him and will require help from you.'

'Why should we help you? If his request for a visa has been cleared, it means he is deemed a law-abiding citizen,' Perry said. Then he added, 'Unless we have reasons to suspect him, it would be highly illegal for us to keep him under surveillance.'

'Of course, because the United Kingdom would never do a thing like that,' said Sky snarkily, adding, in a calmer and more sincere tone, 'I just want to tail him and keep an eye on him. Give us access to him and tell your boys not to throw a spanner in the works.'

'No funny business?' Perry asked half-heartedly. He did not particularly care about the man's fate.

'Well, I can't promise you anything, but I have heard he may be one of the people in charge of rounding up disenfranchised and disillusioned youths to take part in some brutal attacks, like the one that claimed Lee Rigby's life this year,' said Sky, stretching the truth but not exactly lying; he was using his famous sting-in-the-tale strategy. It was sure to get Perry's undivided attention.

There was a long silence. Then, with a resigned sigh, Perry said, 'Sky, you can courier the package to any destination.'

He immediately disconnected the line and smiled to himself. He had got what he wanted. He called Waris at once.

'*Vishwas teri shakti hai, sangharsh teri bhakti hai, tera karm hi teri vijay hai* (Confidence is your strength, struggle is your worship, your action is your victory).'

Waris replied, '*Aameen Summa Aameen* (Amen, again Amen)'.

He called his team and gave them the go-ahead.

The wheels were in motion.

Wajid Mir was dressed in his expensive Armani suit and carried a small briefcase in his hand. He cleared the immigration formalities at Heathrow and exited the airport, looking like one of the rich Asian men who arrived there regularly on business.

The weather was pleasant by London standards. June usually provides a welcome respite from the gloomy weather but this year it was proving to be a soggy month. A spotless black Mercedes Benz S-class stopped in front of the man. The chauffeur opened the car door and Mir entered the vehicle regally, as if obliging him.

As the luxury vehicle left the airport complex and pulled onto the motorway, an ordinary looking taxi began trailing it at a safe distance. One of the lessons Sky had learnt from the CIA was that any unmarked car that follows another can be spotted after three traffic signals; cabbies, however, are less likely to be spotted.

The cab was being driven by Kang, and seated behind him was Brijesh. They knew that Mir had a booking at the Grosvenor House Hotel. Mir's choice of hotel stemmed from the fact that he rather enjoyed the room service and the courtesy of the staff. The hotel management drew their staff from a pool of Polish girls and Turkish boys through a recruitment agency, and it seemed they were specifically trained to handle ill-mannered Asians who liked to be showered with attention.

Mir checked in with a passport that bore the name of Tabrez Alam and had been issued in Islamabad. He had twenty-four passports, including some with Christian names. Simply put, he was the most elusive operative in the world of terror. So far, none of the agencies had tracked him. He trusted no one and was always on his guard. He did not like anyone looking at him for longer than was strictly necessary. If they did, he immediately became suspicious – even if a pretty girl looked at him and smiled. Any member of the hotel staff who showed any extra bit of hospitality made him sceptical. He could never be caught off guard, which is why he had survived so long.

As Mir slid into a huge bathtub and relaxed, his thoughts wandered to his current mission.

Syria was on his mind. He was supposed to take a flight to Amman and then sneak into Damascus. Saudi Arabia had financed this project for Al Nusra, which had openly affiliated itself with ISIS. They were keen on overthrowing the Bashar Al-Assad government and establishing the caliphate. Things weren't going well for Assad as the entire West was opposed to his regime and he was finding it difficult to face the combined and multi-dimensional onslaught of his enemies with Israel, Al Qaeda, America and Saudi Arabia lining up against him. All he had was the covert support of Iran.

Then the tide had suddenly turned in his favour. As Russia stepped in to upbraid Israel and warn America, Assad's regime got a shot in the arm. Vladimir Putin dispatched Yakhont anti-ship cruise missiles to the region and was planning to send sophisticated S-300 anti-aircraft batteries and other ammunition.

Russia wished to play the same sort of role that France had in Algeria, which ensured that hardline radicals could not take over the government. The US on its part had plans to dismantle the Islamic state in Iraq and Syria – which involved some tacit cooperation with Assad – and for now, the Syrian president breathed a little easier.

All the top strategists, planners and commanders, including Wajid Mir, were summoned for an urgent meeting. He was supposed to enter Damascus through Jordan's border, and then put together a contingent that would launch a cohesive push and disrupt the supplies of Russian weaponry so that they did not reach Syria.

Russia is only a twenty-four-hour drive from Aleppo, Syria's northernmost metropolis. Having crushed a Muslim fundamentalist uprising in Chechnya and Dagestan at the turn of the century, and having stood up for a friendly Chechen state government in the aftermath, Moscow remained wary of the spread of radical Muslim movements in nearby Levant. Over fifteen per cent of Syrians are Christians, many of them belonging to the Eastern Orthodox branch that has its roots in Russia itself. These Orthodox Christians, a key constituency for Putin, had opposed the overthrow of the secular Ba'athist government, seeing it as a protector.

Mir was slowly formulaing a strategy to counter the Russians' designs when a phone call disturbed him. It was Hamid, his man Friday in London. 'Salam Janaab. *Angrezi kutte tumhari boo soongh rahe hain.*' The British dogs are sniffing around for you. Mir froze. This was totally unexpected. He had the perfect cover: of a businessman about to set up distribution headquarters in London. His papers were in meticulous order. Nobody knew about his mission except his ISI handler, Brigadier Shamshad Khan.

He had to immediately leave the hotel and find his way to the safe house nearby, a flat in Hounslow. His only regret was that he didn't have the change to tip the young housekeeper. As he stepped out of the hotel, Hamid called again. 'Khan sahib had called, he wants you to avoid Hounslow and proceed to Southall instead.'

Mir got into the first cab he could find and stated his new destination. Southall, with its Pakistani and Punjabi population, would be better than Hounslow, which was a favourite with the young Indian techies. Crowded Southall, with its numerous Asian shops and groceries, would also offer more options to satiate Mir's various desires.

Mir was at once at home amidst restaurants and takeaways named Lahore Kabaabwala and Karachi ki Kadhai. Southall was a good hideout. Besides, the money shops were open for extended hours on holidays and weekends to facilitate the easy transfer of funds.

Mir did not know that his presence in Southall had made Brijesh and Vikrant's job much easier.

Over the next few days, women, food and wine kept Mir busy. Southall was like a homecoming for him and he indulged lavishly. This was the part of the trip where he was meant to relax and satiate his whims. He had to lie low for the next couple of days until his coordinators decided to get in touch with him. Then he would make his trip to the midlands for the cricket match at Edgbaston.

An Australia-England encounter is always exciting, especially when Australia is on tour. But Mir was going to the match to receive a crucial bit of information that would help him in his trip to Damascus. He didn't know the identity of the person who would give him the chip, except that he would be a fellow Pakistani who had spent years in Syria.

Meanwhile, Waris was still trying to figure out the reason for Mir's trip. If there was a terror plot brewing, the British anti-terror agencies would have some inkling of it. However, at this juncture, they thought it prudent not to interact with their British counterparts.

One option was to get Mir into a situation that would bring the police in. But the continuous vigil on Mir did not yield any unusual results. He was on a proper tourist visa, getting drunk in his flat while listening to Hindi songs, and the women visiting him belonged to a notorious but legal local club.

Finally, the army officers decided to maintain a watch on Mir by turns and in disguise. They knew they would have to wait patiently and bide their time until the match on 11 September.

Their temporary cover for being in the stadium had already been provided to them. They just had to look for an opportunity to strike. Kang was supposed to provide backup, Vikrant was supposed to play the part of a waiter, and Brijesh had been given a cleaner's job.

The relatively relaxed security measures at the entrance did not surprise them. Scotland Yard was known to sanitize through various other means and at different levels. After the 7/7 bombing, they had prevented several terror attacks by close surveillance and pointed intelligence inputs, unlike anything that India had managed.

But this was not the time to reflect on the structural defects of many Indian intelligence. Mir may not be a trained agent but his physical prowess matched his sharp mind. The Indian trio was ready to strike, but the question was: were they ready for Mir?

12

Birmingham

The midland city of Birmingham is the second most populous in Britain and home to a sizeable south Asian population. Starting off as a manufacturing and engineering hub, the city soon became home to numerous British cultural movements, including two of England's oldest football clubs, and it was this sport that took precedence over all others. If Lord's was where visiting teams generally began their England tours, Edgbaston was traditionally where they came to be annihilated in the swinging conditions and on the seaming track. It seemed Mir's fate was to be somewhat similar today.

The atmosphere at Edgbaston was reputed to be the most hostile in England for visiting teams. At a ground whose official capacity was 25,000, there had been instances when over 32,000 spectators had watched a match. Today was one such day.

After all, this was among the most keenly fought contests in the history of cricket. With the five-match series tilted 1-0 in Australia's favour, this match—the third in the series—was one England needed to win, to keep alive their chances of winning the series. A loss for Australia would not be quite as disastrous, but their momentum would take a hit.

Despite the typically English weather – rainy, overcast, cold and windy – the atmosphere was electric,with smiling painted faces and flags fluttering in the stands. This was one of those days when the Aussies and the English would rediscover their rabid rivalry and let loose at each other. It was a shame that when the game finally got underway after a seemingly never-ending delay due to the rain, only fifteen overs of play were possible before the fixture had to be abandoned.

Amidst the numerous south Asian faces in the crowd, one small group in the VIP enclosure of the West Stand caught the eye of Brijesh and his cohorts. Built only a couple of years ago at the site of the previous William Ansell Stand, the West Stand had two large tiers of seating. Apart from an Edgbaston suite, it had a 750-seat banqueting and exhibition space whose bright blue presence was a distinctive feature of both the inside and the outside of the ground.

The group inside the suite was made up of slickly clad men in impeccably tailored suits, smoking cigars and drinking Coke in elegant glasses that were better suited for something more potent. Wajid Mir and his entourage could easily have been mistaken for corporate bigwigs or powerful business magnates, engrossed in their laptops and spreadsheets. They seemed to be talking very animatedly and intensely, barely bothered about the fact that the players had fled to the pavilion for the umpteenth time that day.

As they sat watching, Brijesh and his group looked far less glamorous than the 'businessmen'. Two of the three were in waistcoats, holding trays, and the third was in a white shirt and sported a cap with a local cleaning agency's logo. The trio were in the Wyatt Stand, which consisted of a single tier of seating beneath two rows of executive boxes. The stand also included two pitch-view restaurants: the Marston's Suite and the Executive Suite.

'He doesn't seem to be talking too much,' Vikrant said. 'Hasn't even had much of his Coke.'

'How much of the xypamide did you drop in it?' Brijesh asked, adjusting his cap.

'Enough to make him want to rush to the loo.'

'Should've put more,' Kang butted in. This was Kang's first outdoor assignment. Although he did not have much of a role, Waris had wanted him on the team. 'For orientation and as a warm up for the next assignment,' he had said.

Kang was nervous to begin with, but when he saw Brijesh and Vikrant behaving as if they were on a picnic, his anxiety dissipated and he calmed down.

Earlier, Vikrant had surreptitiously dropped xypamide into a Coke glass when he had gone into Mir's stand as a waiter. Mir was a man of many acquired tastes and ideas, and one of these was that lemon enhanced the flavour of everything. He always had Coke with a wedge of lemon in it. This had made Vikrant's task even simpler; he spiked the lemon wedge, saturating it with xypamide beforehand.

Xypamide is a diuretic that is used across the world by athletes and body builders who are on regular steroids; it flushes out the remnants of dope through excessive urine.

The team wanted Mir to make frequent trips to the washrooms, so that he could be cornered. Supposing the toilet was busy and they could not get access to him, they needed for there to be a second time to get him.

'Put more?' snorted Vikrant. 'So that he overdoses right there and chokes on his own vomit.'

'Okay,' Brijesh interjected. 'Let's go to our designated posts. I'll be in the hallway, you go back to the bar. As soon as you see him getting up, let me know through the earpiece.'

'If I want you out of there, I'll say "going down legside" and if the coast is clear, I'll say "daylight between bat and pad"', added Brijesh.

He picked up the metal broomstick and sanitizing liquid and walked out, away from the balcony. Vikrant and Kang moved away from each other, and Vikrant shot another look at Mir's entourage; the man of the hour was sipping luxuriously on his Coke.

'Hey pal,' an English patron summoned Vikrant. 'Get me a beer!'

'Yes sir,' Vikrant smiled. With the match providing very little entertainment, the ticket-buying public had to find other ways to entertain themselves. He walked to the bar and got the man a beer, then trudged out to the balcony and watched the crowd enjoying their day out, even as the players returned to the pavilion for another rain break. After a cursory look at some of the interesting faces in the crowd, his attention shifted back to the West Stand enclosure. He was taken aback by what he saw. Rather, by what he didn't see. Wajid Mir's single-seater sofa was vacant.

He had walked out sometime between when the Englishman had called him over and right now – a window of eight and a half minutes. The other men seemed to have stopped talking so animatedly, now that Mir was gone. They watched the attendants desperately mopping the soggy field, in vain.

Vikrant's eyes fell on Mir's glass. It was empty.

'Brijesh, target approaching the toilet. I repeat, target approaching the toilet!' Vikrant said into his watch. To an onlooker, it would appear he was muttering about being late after having seen the time on his watch.

'Copy that,' Brijesh said, as he swept the floor. 'I saw him coming twenty seconds ago. He's walking into the washroom.'

Brijesh followed Mir till the washroom door and was about to follow him in, when he felt a strong hand land on his shoulder. Mir had already gone inside. Brijesh took a second to get his story straight in his mind, before turning to face whoever had stopped him in his tracks.

'Do you mind telling me why you're stopping me from doing my work?' He said belligerently to Mir's heavily built, lightly bearded guard. 'Unless you want to do my job of cleaning the loo, I suggest you get your hand off my shoulder.'

The guard eased his grip and gently pushed him aside to show that he was still in charge. Brijesh opened the door and walked in but the washroom was empty. He walked hurriedly to the urinals, and saw none of them were being used. His mind began to race. Had Mir's security guard found some way of signalling to his boss that he was being tracked and had he then made his exit? No, that was impossible. The windows of this particular loo were sealed and double-glazed. There was no way he could have climbed out.

Then it hit him. Wajid Mir was a staunch Muslim and like other staunch Muslims, he sat down to pee. He was an Orthodox jihadi who did not mind having a flute or two of champagne, but he would always urinate squatting. Brijesh heard the flush and continued with his charade of cleaning the floor.

Mir walked out, zipping up his trousers. He was startled for a moment to see Brijesh, sweeping the floor nonchalantly. Mir went to the wash basin and turned the tap on. He washed his hands and then bent slightly, cupping his hands with water to splash on his face.

Suddenly he appeared to have felt the urge to urinate again and contemplated stepping into the cubicle – then decided against it as the need was not yet urgent. In that moment, he did not pay attention to Brijesh, who had now left the broom to one side and stood behind him.

He looked up momentarily and saw the half-smiling face of Brijesh in the mirror behind him. Startled, he opened his mouth but before he could turn or scream, Brijesh forced his hand over it and in one swift motion, pushed the syringe into his neck with the precision of a surgeon and injected the entire vial of succinylcholine into him. The drug would kill him within half a minute.

'To Allah we belong, and to Him is our return,' Brijesh whispered. 'Isn't that what Muslims say when someone is dying? Unfortunately, you never belonged to Allah but to the army of Satan. You will only burn in hell.' Brijesh's words seemed to fall on deaf ears as a dazed Mir stumbled around, a hand on his neck, unable to fathom what had just happened. He struggled to stand straight and tried his best to focus on the face of his assailant. All he could see was a boot heading to his chest, kicking him back into a cubicle. He landed straight on the commode and slumped.

The Jihadi warrior had directed the 26/11 attack from the control room and issued instructions to the attackers, giving them step-by-step directions. He had asked his men to destroy the plasma televisions and computers in the Taj Mahal Hotel, and to shoot the Jewish couple in the Chabad house, giving precise instructions all the time. He'd also asked his men to tie the Improvised Explosive Devices (IED) to the bodies of the dead Jews. This sadistic planner of the 26/11 attacks who had thought of the most nefarious ways in which to target Indians, was now unable to think, leave alone stand, straight.

Brijesh closed the door to the cubicle and walked out of the loo. The guard was standing in the corner, puffing on a cigarette and watching the match. He didn't notice a smiling Brijesh slipping past him.

Brijesh tried to speak into the earphone but realized that in the struggle with Mir, it must have got damaged; Vikrant could not hear him. It was vital that he inform Vikrant and Kang that the deed was done, before Mir's dead body was discovered and a manhunt was launched in the stadium. As temporary staff, Vikrant and Brijesh would be among the first suspects.

Desperate moments call for desperate measures. Brijesh pulled out his cellphone and made to dial Vikrant's number, waiting till the crowd had something to cheer for. A call for a Mexican Wave was enough to keep the dwindling crowd entertained.

When Vikrant answered, all he could hear was the sound of breathing, no words.

Brijesh was thinking ahead to what was next for the team. First off, the SIM cards had to be destroyed, after a couple of red herring calls to Israel. The second thing to do was to get the hell out of Edgbaston, to get to Birmingham's international airport and fly back to Mumbai via Dubai. It seemed simple enough. As long as no one did anything stupid.

13

Meanwhile, on the other side of the world, Nawaz Sharif had been in power for nearly three months and well entrenched in Pakistani politics. His resounding victory was bad news for the ISI and army, because the latter had been responsible for overthrowing him in 1999 and the former had done nothing to stop the coup. Sharif took his oath on 5 June 2013 and made two major announcements: a move towards improving ties with India and the prosecution of former president General Pervez Musharraf.

While his intentions against a former army chief caused anxiety in army quarters, the intended friendship caused a major setback for the ISI's director, Zaheerul Islam, and made Arif Afridi sick to the pit of his stomach. Not that it would necessarily make things any more difficult for cross-border action; it was the idea of the head of state wanting to make friends with the enemy that was nauseating.

Soon after assuming office, Sharif held a meeting with the army top brass and the senior-most ISI hawks. The army and intelligence bigwigs had already strategized before the meeting and had decided to keep the brief simple for the PM: you focus on politics and we concentrate on our powerplays.

After that fairly simple bureaucratic procedure, Afridi went back to his plans. He was scheduled to meet Major John Hu Wang in Singapore. They had decided that they would always meet at neutral locations to avoid any suspicion, and if at all they had to meet in their respective countries, they became part of the visiting diplomatic delegations. During a warm and friendly chat, Wang and Afridi agreed to send more men into India for reconnaissance purposes. While Wang wanted to use the borders of Ladakh, Afridi suggested that they enter through the northeastern borders of Nepal or through 24 Parganas in West Bengal. It was a well chalked-out plan which optimized their chances of catching India off-guard.

Afridi was very pleased with the result of the meeting as he arrived at Changi International Airport. His dream of hitting back at India and causing it to implode from within seemed to be coming to fruition one piece at a time. Pakistan would go on to dominate India, he had long convinced himself. India would be chastened for splitting Pakistan into two and the world powers would prevail upon India to return Kashmir. Old mistakes could be rectified.

His thoughts were interrupted rudely by the vibration of his cell phone on the car's dashboard. He looked at the phone and saw that the number began with '+44'.

He answered the phone curtly, 'Yes.'

But the caller surprised him. 'Sir, Wajid Mir was found dead in the stadium toilet. Preliminary reports have ruled out foul play and suggested he had a heart attack.' Afridi could not believe that a man with Wajid's fitness levels could die of a heart attack. Where had his guards been? Hadn't someone tried to resuscitate him? Why had he not been rushed to the hospital?

'Sir, he was declared dead on arrival.'

Afridi was fuming. This clearly carried the stench of an Indian conspiracy. He refused to believe that it was a natural or coincidental death. Wajid Mir had been killed. Cleverly, but killed nonetheless. Just how had they caused the heart attack?

Had his food or drink been spiked? Had they used some sort of tazer? How were these Indians managing to eliminate important assets? First Umavi, now Mir.

Afridi reached his headquarters and immediately sought a meeting with the director.

Once inside the cabin, he began at once. 'Sir, they've bumped off Wajid Mir.'

Zaheer was one of the shrewdest of chiefs the ISI had. The man had no personal life, no children, no vices and no political affiliations. Despite his unflinching and uncompromising dedication to his work, he was pragmatic in his approach to the future annihilation of India.

Zaheer removed his glasses, leaned back in his leather chair and looked at Afridi.

'Arif, we are not the official protectors of these people. They don't consult us before flying off to such places. We are not even given enough time to conduct a recce and find out if it's safe to travel.'

'Sir, we should not allow any of them to leave the country without our clearance.'

'I'll ensure the message reaches their handlers.' Zaheer seemed to be relieved that Afridi had backed down. After all, how many of these people could the ISI babysit? There was also the question of plausible deniability. How would the ISI continue to play its favourite card if they had their fingers in so many pies?

As Afridi pushed his chair aside and rose to take his leave, he said to Zaheer, 'There is one more thing ... I need your approval to launch an offensive against the Indians. We need to go after them before they inflict any more damage. Arif, I thought you had some big operations coming up in Kashmir and Assam.'

'Sir, those are already in the works and they will keep progressing while I focus on this investigation.'

'Arif, I think your expertise is needed in Kashmir, this can be handled by any army Major.'

'Sir, with due respect, no one can do this with as much precision and focus as I can. I have an added motivation to succeed,' Afridi said, his voice cold.

'Careful, Arif. Your emotions could blind you someday,' warned Zaheer. There was no reasoning with a man so emotionally invested in something. 'Let me think about it. Give me the report on Kashmir and Assam and I'll see what I can do. For now, this meeting is over.'

Zaheer opened a file. Afridi saluted, turned and stormed out of the office. The director had asked him to make a report, but he'd said nothing about not probing the deaths and establishing the Indian hand in the killings. He could easily do both. As he walked down the corridor away from the director's office, he reached for his cell phone again and called one of his many go-to guys in the UK.

'The bodyguard. Has he been debriefed?' As it turned out, the bodyguard had been having a smoke and watching the match, until a patron who had entered the toilet rushed out in a panic.

'That incompetent oaf,' snarled Afridi. 'Get me CCTV footage of that toilet from the moment Wajid entered, right to the point when he was carried out.' He hung up.

14

Aberdeen Street, Hong Kong

The stench of alcohol filled the room where a hazy cloud of smoke swirled, but none of that bothered the half-American-half-Australian Jacob Aiden, as he read through the ten-page document. By now, he was used to the cramped room and besides, it was a small price to pay for his 'offences'. According to him, and a growing support base across the world, he was no villain; he was a revolutionary. He was responsible for a new awakening in the world. There were people who cursed him and people who thanked him and protested for his freedom. Jacob Aiden, once stereotypical teen hacker, had grown into a full-blown pain in the ass for governments worldwide.

He had started an explosive website, *www.stoolpigeon.com* in 2008, but the government paid no heed to it and considered it to be just another bombastic attempt by yet another hacker. But the tables had turned, and how. A year ago, Aiden had played whistleblower as he always did, with his tiny team of six – with one difference. This time, it was big. Aiden revealed, through documents he had obtained 'anonymously', that a Chinese spy of the MSS had been shot dead by a CIA agent whilst on an operation. The spy had been off the radar and the MSS (Ministry of State Security) had had no idea as to where he was, until the documents exposing the great American cover-up popped up randomly one evening on the whistleblower's site.

There was a huge media frenzy, which led to Jacob Aiden escaping America and seeking asylum in China. The MSS then set him up in Hong Kong, in a safe house at Taishan, a coastal city in the Southern Guangdong province. Plots to assassinate the forty-two-year-old whistleblower had been hatched by various governments ever since. But nobody knew his exact location, save for the top officials of the MSS.

Aiden got up from his couch and opened the window, letting the stale smell out. He ran his fingers through his long peroxide blond hair and scratched his three-day-old stubble. He hadn't bathed for a couple of days and his body odour had begun to irritate him. He squinted at the documents in his hand and re-read them. Then turned and picked up the phone, which lay next to an unfinished bowl of pork noodles. He looked at the phone for a while. *How do I play this? This is a potential gold mine.* He dialled a number he had memorized. It rang for a while before it was answered.

'Squealer here,' Aiden said. 'Are we secure?'

'What the fuck, man. It's three in the morning!'

'This is important stuff, Nianzu. It can't wait.'

'Well, what is it about?'

'A document I printed out, from an anonymous Star-Spangled source in the agency.'

'I'll see you in the morning. At eight. The usual place.'

Aiden placed the phone back on the receiver. He walked hurriedly to the bathroom, stripped, stood under the shower and turned it on. The warm water fell on him softly. He closed his eyes. *This is my chance to get back at America. This is truly unbelievable. The hypocrisy of that country is unbelievable. This time it will be different. This time I won't expose them publicly.*

He stepped out of the shower, dripping. He ran his hand through his thin blond hair and moved it away from his face. Looking in the mirror, he shrugged and decided against shaving off his beard.

He dried himself, pulled out a pair of boxer shorts from his drawer and put them on. Then he pulled out a pair of rugged jeans and a plain black Armani T-shirt. He put them on, then pulled out an Armani jacket, dropping it on the couch. He opened the small refrigerator, took a can of beer and sat on the edge of the bed with the document again.

He had to understand the repercussions of this fully. There were two distinct choices in dealing with the piece of information he had in his hands. Some righteous CIA agent had silently leaked it to his partner, Rob Jackson, who was naturally startled by the singular piece of information the document conveyed. If it had contained any other kind of information, Rob would have probably uploaded it on their website. But he was wary of its volatile nature. He had to clear it with Aiden before uploading it. This little bit of intelligence could tear down the relations between the United States and rest of the world.

Aiden's first choice was to leak the information on his website, like he had done on numerous occasions, and then sit back with a bowl of popcorn and watch the world crumble. The second was one he had never tried before. He would send the document to none other than the government of the country that the United States was fucking over. What they did with it was their choice.

The Forest Bird Café, Hong Kong

8 a.m.

Jacob Aiden sat at his little table within the cosy confines of the Forest Bird Café. He had ordered himself a strong espresso. It was now two minutes past eight. His friend from the MSS and 'baby-sitter' Nianzu Cheng hadn't arrived yet. Over the past year, Aiden and Cheng had grown pretty close. Cheng admired Aiden's work, but he had been told to keep a strict watch over him and not let him rock the boat too much.

There was an agreement between the MSS and Aiden, that he would have to pass along any document that he wished to upload. In return, they would give him refuge in Hong Kong and deny his existence in the country. Besides, since Hong Kong itself wasn't under the jurisdiction of China, they would be able to control him more easily. Aiden willingly complied, and he hadn't leaked any documents in a while. But today, he was about to break the jinx, he thought, as he watched Nianzu Chen open the café's glass door and walk in briskly.

'You're late, Nianzu.'

'I hadn't heard from you in a while, Aiden. I liked those days.'

'I got this document from Rob last evening.' Aiden handed it over to Nianzu.

Nianzu looked at it, leaned back in his chair and read it quietly, taking the time to let each word register. He mouthed the words softly to himself, reading every sentence twice. With every word he read, Aiden's heart raced faster. Nianzu folded the document and handed it back to Aiden silently.

After a few seconds, he summed it up with one word: 'Bastards!'

'Exactly,' Aiden said. 'I'm not going to sit on this document, Nianzu.'

'How sure are you about this?'

'A CIA operative sent it to Rob,' he said. 'He revealed his identity as well. But that I'm not going to tell you. In fact, Rob hasn't even told me. He destroyed any evidence of the name after reading it.'

'So, it's authentic?'

'Every bit of it,' Aiden replied.

'How do you want to handle it? You know the repercussions, right?'

'Of course,' Aiden said. They paused briefly, as the waiter served them coffee. Aiden nodded at him, then continued.

'I don't want to put this up in the public domain, though.'

'What do you want to do then?'

'I need your help, Nianzu. You know I could leak this to the press. But that's pretty much the same as putting it up on my website.'

'So, what is it you want to do?'

'It's also risky, you know. If I leak this, it'll be traced back to me for sure. And that will make them want me dead even more.'

'Again, so what do you want to do?'

'Send it to the Indian government,' Aiden said quietly.

Nianzu closed his eyes and leaned back. It sounded preposterous. But ... it would still be less damaging than allowing the information to go public. It might ease relations between India and China. *Besides, if we are lucky enough, we can even palm off Aiden to the Indians, in exchange. He'll be their headache then.*

'I know a man at RAW,' Nianzu said. 'But the Indian agency is a joke. They'll do nothing about it. I'm pretty sure of that. Also, I don't want to give it away so cheaply.'

'What do you intend to do?'

Cheng smiled. 'I intend to trade you to them for the information. India is a nice place to live, Aiden.'

'You're a bastard, you know.'

'I know,' he said. 'But I'm saving your ass as well. You've been here for over a year. And the last time I checked, the Americans knew you were in Hong Kong.'

Aiden was silent for a while. He knew it was true. If they figured out his exact location in Hong Kong, he would be a sitting duck for the Americans in no time.

'I think you should try and speak to them first, before jumping to any conclusions.' Aiden said, handing over a pen drive.

'There is a folder on this,' he continued. 'We can upload it anonymously on a peer-to-peer sharing site. The document is stored along with a decoy, a little known Swedish art film.'

'Pornography?'

'Just as a decoy. It's good to know we share the same taste in art, though.' They laughed softly.

'All you have to do, Nianzu, is give me the permission to upload this file. And then tip off the Indian agencies. What they do with it is where the fun lies.'

Nianzu handed the pen drive back to Aiden.

'I'll let you know when you can upload it.'

A-Team Base, New Delhi

So far, it had been just another day in the tech chamber for Ray. He scratched his curly hair as he sat, downing yet another cup of coffee. He was reviewing the modus operandi of the team's future executions. So far, so good. What worried him was the way they planned to take Bradley out. It would be getting into a highly secure Chicago cell which was no joke, even if the assassins were of the calibre of Brijesh and Vikrant.

It was nearing two in the afternoon and Ray hadn't had his lunch yet. He looked at the numerous computer screens and switched off the one right in front of him. He then slid his chair closer to the one on the left. The screen flashed the notification of an email and his eyes narrowed in curiosity. This system was meant only for very important messages. It was also the system that had a highly secure connection and sent and received encrypted messages from various intelligence agencies around the world. Ray clicked on the email.

'We have something that might interest you, and of course benefit you. We have the actual location of DB. Reply with a "yes" if you're interested. I'll give you 12 hours – a friend from the MSS.'

It took Ray a few seconds to understand who 'DB' was. He cursed softly under his breath and ran to look for Sky. Before that, he locked the door of the room and slipped the key into his pocket.

Minutes later, Sky walked into the room and bent over the computer. He read the message thrice. 'DB' was undoubtedly Daniel Bradley.

'Reply immediately, Ray.'

'Are you sure, sir? I mean, I know it's not a hoax. But this popping up now seems too coincidental. And in our profession, we don't believe in coincidence.'

'I almost feel relieved,' Sky said. 'I didn't want to send the team into Chicago. We all know their prospects of coming out clean are bleak.'

'How do you know Bradley isn't in any place even more dangerous, then?' Ray quipped.

'I don't,' Sky said sardonically. 'That's why I want you to reply.'

Ray shrugged, leaned over the computer, and typed in his brief reply. He rolled a chair over and dropped himself into it. Sky turned around and looked at him inquisitively.

'Where do you think Bradley actually is?'

'I can't say for sure, sir. I mean, we always knew he wasn't in that jail,' Ray's voice trailed off. 'But if I were to guess, I think he'd be somewhere in Cuba.'

'Possibly,' Sky said. 'That, or he's hiding deep in the US. Logistically though, it might be easier to take him down if he's in Cuba.'

Sky had hardly completed his sentence when the screen of the computer started flashing with an audio call. Ray looked at Sky, who nodded. Ray accepted the call.

'I take it you're interested in the information we possess, Sky.'

Sky was slightly surprised that the voice on the other end knew who he was. 'Since you know my name, it would be kind of you to tell me yours,' Sky replied.

'Your name is no secret. Besides, I call you as a friend. We have information that you will find useful.'

'You haven't told me your name yet,' Sky said.

'What's in a name?' the voice replied. 'Anyway, let's cut to the chase. We know where he is, thanks to one of the most infamous of whistleblowers.'

'How certain are you of the intel?'

'A hundred per cent. I will forward you a CIA document if you agree to my conditions.'

'I thought we were friends,' Sky replied.

'And friends do each other favours.'

'What do you want?' Sky asked. 'If it's reasonable, we'll comply.'

'I want you to give refuge to the said whistleblower,' came the reply. 'Here's a hint. He's half-Australian.'

There was a long pause. Ray looked at Sky, his mouth open. Sky's face didn't betray his thoughts.

'I'll need time to decide,' Sky said.

'You have ten seconds,' replied the caller.

'These kinds of decisions call for time. You're working for a government agency just like I am.'

'Five,' came the response.

Sky shook his head and Ray looked on, amazed. Sky remembered Waris's conviction the first time he had proposed the idea. He remembered the memorials he had attended for the victims of 26/11. He was *this* close to finding out where one of the perpetrators lived. He imagined making life easier for the team that had set out to eliminate the terrorists. He imagined all of this in four seconds.

'I cannot guarantee asylum to Aiden, I need clearance from the Ministry of Home Affairs,' Sky said.

There was total silence at the other end. Sky and Ray both thought the line had gone dead.

Cheng was thinking. He knew that Aiden was keen on releasing the information. He couldn't sit on it.

'I need your word that you will respond soon on Aiden. You can hide him in India or wherever you like, anywhere in the world. But soon,' he said, at last.

Sky said, 'I can give you an assurance, not a promise.' He could tell that Cheng was more keen on sharing the information than he was to acquire it.

'He is in Uppland, Stockholm,' Cheng said.

'Thank you,' Sky said. 'We'll keep our end of the bargain. Soon enough.'

Within seconds the screen flashed, indicating the delivery of a new mail, with an attachment. Ray opened the attachment and they both began reading it. Their eyes widened with disbelief. The classified document revealed a sordid tale of American double standards.

America had an understanding with Bradley that soon after sentencing, he would receive a new identity. He was far too valuable an intelligence asset to be simply given up to India, and needed to be safely relocated. Under a witness protection programme, he was to be moved to a place of his choice in Europe. However, he would be on his own. Bradley had chosen Stockholm. The document ran ten pages long, and had plenty of details of communication between various department heads. It also revealed that Bradley had already shifted to the secret location in April – within three months of the verdict.

Sky didn't wait to read the rest of the document. He needed to call Waris and alert him before his team left to recce the Chicago State Penitentiary.

15

Stockholm

March was a good time to be in Stockholm, particularly around Lake Mälaren, where a gentle breeze skimmed its surface. The lake itself is the third largest in Sweden and is bound by the provinces of Uppland, Södermanland, Närke and Västmanland. According to Norse mythology, Lake Mälaren was created by the goddess Gefjon when she tricked Gylfi, the Swedish king of Gylfaginning. But the task at hand required a different sort of trickery – the more sinister sort.

The weather at this time of year was the kind that dragged Indian travellers out to Europe and the spot was perfect for a tourist. But, among the recent army of foreigners who had seemingly taken over Stockholm, at least four were not here to soak in the scenery of the visually stunning Scandinavian city. It was also no coincidence that all four were Indians and that they were all staying together in a little suite in an ordinary looking motel off Uppland. Most importantly, the motel—Hotel Fjord— was inconspicuous. Perfect for the team's purpose.

'So, if our intel is accurate, this is where Bradley should be located,' Laila said, her immaculately manicured fingernail circling the map. She tapped a spot on it. 'One of these little cottages in Uppland.'

'I'm pretty certain our information is solid. All we need is to zoom in on the bastard,' Vikrant said. 'It's time we nailed him for good.'

Brijesh remained silent, and then with a quick gesture, asked Laila to push the laptop towards him. He began typing, lost in his own thoughts, clearly planning four steps ahead. Kang walked into the room with a large pot of coffee and four styrofoam cups. He sat down next to Brijesh and looked momentarily startled when he saw the screen. Eventually, this gave way to a pursing of lips and a narrowing of eyes.

'I hate to break this to you, Brijesh,' said Vikrant, 'but this is probably not the best time to be surfing for nude pictures.'

Brijesh ignored the wisecrack and quickly spun the laptop around so the rest could have a look at his grand plan. 'This is what we need,' he declared triumphantly. Laila stared incredulously at the screen. 'Go on,' said Vikrant warily, adding with a wry smile, 'I'm not sure Laila is into women, though.'

'Shut up, you pervert,' Laila snapped. 'What nonsense is this, Brijesh? We haven't come to Stockholm for you to spend time with prostitutes.'

'Why not? We can have some fun on the job!' Kang grinned. 'We deserve it, don't we?'

'That's enough, guys,' Brijesh said, sticking a pin in the conversation while it still remained in the realms of decency. 'We will be visiting these bordells, but not for the services they offer.'

'Bordells?' Kang asked.

'That's what brothels are called here,' Brijesh said. 'It's no secret that our friend Bradley is quite fond of the ladies.'

There was a slight pause, during which Brijesh filled his cup with coffee. He took a sip and continued, 'We need to go and describe him to the owners of the brothels. Maybe pay them off a bit. Also, maybe, just maybe, there is a chance that Bradley has some favourite ladies in there. And I won't be surprised if they're Moroccan.'

'Why Moroccan?' Kang asked.

'Bradley has a special liking for Moroccan girls. Didn't you glean that from the statement he gave the NIA?' Vikrant chipped in. 'Also, his fourth official wife, Ayesha O Talha, told the FBI that he loved Moroccan girls. Not to mention that TV interview where that Indian actor … What was his name?'

'Erm … I can't remember but anyway, the actor also revealed Bradley's preference for Moroccans,' Brijesh said.

'Moroccan women, Iranian women, Brazilian women … How does it matter? It's not as if you're going to find a Moroccan woman to lead you to—' Laila paused as she began to put the pieces together. It was a long shot, but at the same time, there was a distinct possibility that Bradley could be located through this network.

'Well, in that case, looking at these semi-naked women is justified,' Kang said, as he pulled the computer closer.

'There may not be too many Moroccan hookers,' Laila said. 'I think we should get a list of all those in the Uppland area.'

Kang nodded, with a slightly mischievous grin.

'Okay, Kang, get to assembling the list immediately. But remember, we are professionals. I hope I don't need to elaborate on that fact.'

They chuckled.

'I'll accompany him,' Vikrant added, 'just to make sure he stays professional.'

Brijesh finished his coffee and crushed the cup. He stood up and looked at Laila.

'Maybe, if they list all the names, I can have a crack at the various women,' she told him.

'Yes, they may be more at ease giving you the information,' he replied. 'Just list all the bordells in the vicinity so that our bravehearts can go about their Himalayan task with ease.'

Laila smiled and turned the laptop towards her. She cringed for a flicker of a second, and then got started.

Brijesh woke up later than usual. He had wanted to nap for an hour and hit the sack at around 5 p.m. He realized he had been sleeping for hours and it was now close to sunset. He jumped out of bed, and put on a black T-shirt that was lying on the couch. He scratched his stubbled chin, and then looked at the tiny alarm clock. It was 7.30 pm. Poking his head out of the room, he realized he was alone.

He strolled leisurely to the toilet, took his toothbrush and squeezed a generous amount of toothpaste onto it. As he held the ready-to-use toothbrush in one hand, he looked at himself in the mirror and ran his fingertips across the grizzly stubble on his cheeks. This was no way for a soldier to look, especially not a soldier who was on a mission of this nature. What would happen after this operation was complete, he wondered, as the movement of his toothbrush against his teeth became more vigorous.

He walked out of the bathroom, the foamy toothbrush in his mouth, and thought about life on the run, after the operation. After all, if the Pakistanis were able to put two and two together, it was likely they would be on the team's trail till the end of time, he reasoned. Brijesh made his way into the living area of the unkempt suite and walked past the clutter towards the large window. The team's suite was on the first level of the motel.

The logic was that if they found themselves in a situation where exiting via the main door was no longer an option, they could make their way out through that first-floor window which wasn't high enough to cause serious injury. But that could work both ways. Defenestrating a combatant from their suite would not have a fatal or possibly even serious effect on him/her. They would just have to hope that the enemy did not find their way to the team's hotel suite.

He continued to stare out into the distance as he let these thoughts wash over him, breaking his concentration only when he saw Laila jogging towards the motel. In her white tank-top and trackpants, she jogged with the grace of a gazelle and the rhythm of a derby racehorse. Watching her make her way towards the hotel, he felt mesmerized.

Brijesh walked back to the bathroom and spat a mouthful of foam into the sink before rinsing out his mouth. As he sprayed a burst of shaving foam onto his hand and prepared to rub it on his face, he heard the door click.

'I'm coming in! I hope you're decent,' Laila announced cautiously from the door of the bedroom.

'I'm always decent,' Brijesh fired back jokingly, as he spread the shaving foam evenly over his cheeks. 'Good jog?' he asked.

'It was energizing. Gave me the chance to take in the local sights and also stay fit,' she smiled, as she appeared at the door of the bathroom, drenched in sweat. 'Unlike some people,' she said wryly, before adding, 'you know, this is a lovely place. You should get out and see it sometime.'

Brijesh could not help but notice her perfectly toned body, the lithe arms that were both feminine and muscular and the long athletic legs. Beads of sweat trickled down her hairline, her jaw and her neck. Her hair was tied up in a high ponytail. Brijesh looked back in the mirror as he ran the razor down his cheek in a straight line.

'I need to use the shower,' Laila said, her cheeks reddening under Brijesh's glance; he made no attempt to hide the fact that he was admiring her.

'The bathroom will be all yours in ten minutes. Unless, of course, you want it immediately,' he joked.

She laughed nervously.

'Irresistible as that offer is,' she said, 'we have more important matters to deal with.'

'We sure do,' Brijesh smiled, as he resumed shaving. 'Where are the boys?'

'Being boys, I presume. At the bordells.'

Brijesh washed his face, then rubbed it with a towel. He vacated the bathroom as Laila walked in.

'So, how many brothels are we hitting in total?'

'Six,' she said. 'The two of them left after I went for my jog.'

'Moroccan women,' Brijesh said. 'Let's hope there aren't many. It will certainly make our job easier.'

'Getting lazy?' Laila teased.

'No,' Brijesh said.

'Then?'

'They're supposed to be irresistible. It's better if we have to speak to fewer of them. I'm tired of being reminded that this isn't the time,' he said with an exaggerated frown on his face, before getting serious and adding, 'Also, the fewer people we speak to, the fewer people know we are here.'

Laila nodded, then closed the door on Brijesh.

The time for joking was at an end.

Kang and Vikrant walked into the sixth lane of the red light district of Uppland that evening. Though aware of the gravity of the situation, the two were playing the part of a couple of lads out in town and walked around enjoying the sights and sounds of the area – much as Laila had done earlier in the day, but in a very different setting. The environment here was less crass and overt than that of the notorious red light districts back home in India. A customer was less likely to be intimidated or hassled for being a pervert on these streets. Here, a customer was just that: someone looking for a business transaction.

The girls looked seductively at Vikrant and Kang, as they walked into the brothel. Vikrant avoided their gaze, but Kang seemed to enjoy the attention. Kang knew he wasn't exactly Adonis, and he knew that these women would leer at the Hunchback of Notre Dame had he wobbled in, but he basked in their gaze nevertheless.

'Remember, discretion and vigilance,' Vikrant said to Kang, before adding, 'and most importantly, keep it in your pants.'

'I'm only watching. *Dekhne ke toh paise nahi lagte,*' Kang laughed.

'All right, but pay attention. This is where the bordell mamma operates from,' Vikrant warned.

'Welcome, gentlemen. How may I help you?' There was something close to mockery in the voice that greeted them.

The bordell mamma was sitting on a sofa, next to a girl who was smoking a cigarette.

'Yes, ma'am,' Kang said. 'We would like to hire your services—'

'It's odd you would want my services,' the slightly elderly woman scoffed. 'I thought I had some pretty fine girls here.'

As Kang went red, Vikrant interjected, 'What he meant was, we are here to seek your help, ma'am.'

'What kind of help? You do know that we aren't a tourist help-desk, yes?'

'We would like to spend some time with a Moroccan woman,' Vikrant said politely and then grinned. 'There's nothing like a Moroccan woman.'

'Well,' she said. 'You are out of luck then, gentlemen. I only have one girl of Moroccan descent working for me and she is busy. It's difficult to find them in these parts.'

There was a brief silence. Kang looked at Vikrant for a solution.

'We'll just meet her then,' Vikrant said. 'Something's better than nothing, isn't it?'

'I'm afraid you can't meet her,' the lady said. 'As I said, she's busy and not here at the moment. You can hire her later, of course.'

'Oh, where is she?' Kang asked nonchalantly.

'Somewhere in Uppland. Regular customer. Foreigners can't get enough of her,' the lady replied carelessly, then added suspiciously, 'What's it to you anyway? You're not a couple of stalkers, are you?'

'Oh no,' Vikrant laughed. 'We just want to know when we can meet her.'

'Later tonight,' the lady replied. 'And just so you know, Nadia doesn't meet two men at one time.'

That's okay, Vikrant thought. She's going to meet a woman anyway.

'All right,' Kang said. 'I'll be meeting Nadia then.'

'First,' Vikrant added.

'First,' Kang repeated as he bid the woman adieu.

As they left, the woman picked up her phone, dialled a number she had dialled many times before, and said, 'Where is Nadia?'

16

'You're in big trouble, Nadia,' she said gruffly, the phone pressed against her puffy face. 'You forgot to sign out when you went to meet your client. How am I supposed to know where you are? By the way, some Asian fellows were looking for you. Hello?' Nadia seemed to have hung up before she could finish.

'So she's meeting a regular customer somewhere in Uppland,' Brijesh muttered when Vikrant detailed the conversation that had taken place earlier that day. 'It doesn't take a genius to work out who that is.'

Kang nodded and glanced at his wristwatch. 'It's almost eight,' he announced. 'She should be here at any moment.' Kang couldn't stop himself from imagining what she must look like, what she must sound like and indeed, what she must smell like. It wasn't within the mission parameters or else he would have also allowed himself to imagine what she ...

The doorbell buzzed loudly, causing Kang to come crashing down from his little daydream. Brijesh stood up, gestured to Kang to follow him and went into the other room. Vikrant opened the door and looked at Nadia. He had the sharpest of reflexes, but

Nadia's beauty made him freeze. Had she pulled out a knife and stabbed him, he would have just stood there and taken it.

She wore a red scarf around her neck. Her hair was shoulder-length and chestnut brown, her nose was narrow and well sculpted. Her cheeks held a slightly artificial red blush and her lips were full and red. Her aroma, whether natural or accentuated by Chanel, was intoxicating. She wore a short black dress that revealed neither too much nor too little. There was an inescapable touch of class to her sex appeal; she was no garden variety hooker. That said, the inches of skin that she did reveal were golden and smooth.

'I believe we have an appointment,' she said softly. There was no need to say anymore. She had an economy with words that took Vikrant's breath away.

He nodded, still unable to speak, and opened the door fully to let her in. Nadia walked in leisurely, but with the elegance of a supermodel. She dropped her little red purse, and the scarf next to it. That was when she saw Laila sitting at the opposite end of the room. She seemed ever-so-slightly disgruntled at the idea of another female presence. Laila stared back at her. It seemed to Vikrant that Laila too was bewitched.

'Is she going to be joining us as well?' Nadia asked Vikrant, warmly enough to seem concerned but coldly enough to speak about Laila in the third person, as if she wasn't sitting right there.

'Well, yes.'

'Just so you know, I generally prefer working alone. I'm far better when I'm the only woman in the room,' she offered, caressing each word with her tongue before letting it leave her lips.

'I'm sure you are,' Vikrant said, smiling.

'Nadia,' Laila gestured to her to sit down. 'Make yourself comfortable.'

'You do know you're wasting your money,' Nadia said. 'I'm on a clock.'

'Go ahead, Vikrant.' Laila smiled sardonically. 'Break the poor girl's heart. Tell her what she's here for.'

Nadia's eyes widened a notch and she slowly sat upright. She looked up at Vikrant as he pulled up a chair and sat opposite her.

'As much as I'd love to,' Vikrant said, 'I can't sleep with you.'

'Oh,' Nadia said. 'That's okay, I've met men with such issues before.'

Laila stifled a giggle.

'No.' Vikrant shook his head and smiled. 'It's not that. It's just that we want something else from you. Inform—'

'I'm going to interrupt you right there.' Laila stood up and walked towards Nadia. She sat right next to her, relaxing on the sofa. 'Do you value your life, Nadia?' Nadia looked startled. She twitched awkwardly and was about to get up, when Laila put her hand gently on hers.

'I don't know who you people are, or what you want. Please let me go.'

'Do you value your life?'

'Yes.'

'How would you feel if one day, you're spending time with your family and for no fault of yours, a man barges in and shoots them dead in front of your eyes?'

Nadia remained silent.

'And after he shoots them, he turns his gun on you and fires. In that little moment,' Laila said, 'that tiny little moment between the time he shot someone you love and the time he shoots you – do you have any idea how you would feel in that moment?'

'No,' Nadia said, softly. 'W … what is this about?'

Laila gestured to Vikrant for his phone. Vikrant unlocked it, fidgeted with it for a couple of seconds and passed it to her. She looked at it and held the screen against her thigh.

'What do you know about the terror attacks of 26 November 2008 in India?'

'I … I read about it,' Nadia stuttered.

'And what did you read about it?' Laila pressed further.

'A group of Pakistanis attacked Mumbai and killed a lot of people,' Nadia mumbled.

'And would you happen to know who planned these attacks?' Laila fired back.

Nadia looked clueless. 'Pakistan?'

Kang grinned to himself and muttered under his breath, 'Typical. Fucking Western media.'

Laila held the phone up, a few inches from Nadia's face. Her jaw dropped and it was clear she was shocked from the way she clutched her stomach.

'That's Michael! The American who lives in Uppland.'

'Yes,' Laila said. 'He is one of those who planned the attacks.'

'And his name isn't Michael,' Vikrant added helpfully. 'He's a terrorist.'

'Yes,' Laila said. 'That's about the gist of it.'

Nadia remained silent for what seemed an eternity.

Then she began to cry. Her head in her hands. 'Are you sure it's the same man?' she asked.

'This is for your own safety, Nadia. Your phone is probably tapped. Your life could be in danger,' Laila said gently.

Nadia remained silent for a moment. Then she looked up morosely through mascara-streaked eyes and hastily excused herself. 'I have to go now.'

Laila waited for her to make her exit before saying softly, 'The bait's out there. The fish is biting. All that's left is to reel it in.'

She should be here by now, the man thought, as he paced up and down. He made the bed and went over to the sofa. He picked up the television remote and turned it on. He skipped through channels and stopped on CNN International as he caught a glimpse of that strangely familiar visual – the burning dome. The images of Umavi and Wajid Mir flashed on the screen, interspersed with footage of the Taj Mahal Hotel in Mumbai, ablaze during the 26/11 attacks. Apparently, the two deaths seemed completely disconnected and were purely coincidental. The only thing that linked the two men was the attack of 26 November.

The man felt a sudden surge of panic. *Should I call? Should I find out what's happening? No. Fuck, no. The entire world thinks I'm in prison. I've been told I can never make that call.*

Vikrant and Laila watched from their car as they tailed Nadia from a distance as she drove slowly up the gravel path leading to Bradley's plush accommodation. She pulled over to the side of the road. Brijesh leaned forward from the backseat and quietly asked, 'You think she bought it?' He got his answer as Nadia's car roared back to life and peeled away from the side of the road. She apparently decided against visiting Bradley that night.

The doorbell rang.

'Finally,' said Bradley as he threw open the door, only to find Brijesh's fist heading straight for his nose. He turned his head and the punch glanced his cheek rather than catching him flush in the face. But that brief distraction was enough for Vikrant to jump at Bradley and slip a plastic bag over his head. He wrapped it tightly around his throat, suffocating him. Bradley thrashed about wildly, knocking over a vase and a wine glass. Eventually, he was subdued and his thrashing became less frantic. Brijesh grabbed his legs as Vikrant kept a tight grip around his throat.

A few minutes were all it took before Bradley eventually passed out and his body went limp.

'Are you sure he's unconscious?' asked Kang as he walked over to take a look.

'We need to be certain,' said Vikrant as he picked up the vase and placed it on the table. 'And make it look like our man died naturally.'

'Let's take him out to the lake and drop him in. Make it look like he drowned while fishing,' Brijesh said.

Vikrant and Kang nodded.

After loading him into the boot of their vehicle, they drove for ten minutes to the nearby lake, where Bradley's rented boat was moored. Vikrant and Brijesh hauled the body into the boat like it was a sack of potatoes and then got in themselves, carrying along their snorkeling gear. Vikrant began rowing towards the middle of the lake where it was deepest.

'This looks like a good spot,' said Brijesh as he began propping Bradley up to roll him over the side of the boat. All of a sudden, the seemingly lifeless body of Bradley kicked out at Brijesh, then jumped into the icy cold water.

Brijesh and Vikrant dived in after Bradley. The duo was far too strong and fit for Bradley to take on by himself. But he put up a fierce resistance, struggling like a fish on a hook, and managed to pull Vikrant's snorkel clean off his face. A breathless Vikrant had to rush to the surface, gasping for air. It was now only Brijesh versus Bradley. He did not want to have to strangle Bradley as it would show up in the autopsy. And that would not do at all. It had to look like an accident. Bradley was supposed to die from water filling up in his lungs.

As they wrestled underwater, Bradley's struggle slowly waned, and so did Brijesh's strength but Bradley managed to launch one last attack. He reached for Brijesh's crotch and grabbed him. The searing pain blinded Brijesh, who momentarily let go of Bradley. As Bradley was about to emerge from the water, however, Brijesh managed to wrap his arms around his ankles with the last reserves of his strength – just enough to keep Bradley from the surface.

Bradley's limbs began to thrash about in a desperate effort to shake off Brijesh. In the melee, he managed to free a leg, and as it flailed about, it connected with Brijesh's chin. The disorienting effect of that kick was enough to give Bradley the time he needed to escape and he began swimming upwards in a desperate attempt to scale that last foot of water before he could breathe again.

With his head inches below the surface, he suddenly felt Vikrant's muscular arms around his neck, pulling him back, down into the water.

That was when Bradley seemed to give up at last. His vital organs were shutting down one after another; his body was being deprived of precious oxygen, and his heart rate began slowing down. His arms waved slowly underwater one last time, as both his attackers held him down.

And then he stopped moving.

Brijesh and Vikrant released him and he slowly began to sink to the bottom of the lake.

He descended slowly, his fingers frozen in place and curled in agony, his eyes wide open.

17

Islamabad

The sound of heavy shoes hitting a leather belt, punctuated by loud grunts, was acutely audible in the air-conditioned room.

Two well-built men had sprung to attention and were looking at the slimmer but extremely fit man in his early fifties, running on the treadmill. The men knew their boss did not need any help from them, but out of habit, they always sprang to attention.

It spoke volumes about Afridi's fitness that at this age he could run at the speed of fifteen kilometres per hour for twenty minutes straight. It was part of his daily routine to complete his mandatory quota of five kilometres before entering the pool and swimming another kilometre. He was the centrepoint of awe and admiration for most army cadets, who couldn't match his dedication to fitness. At the age of fifty, Afridi had the physique of a twenty-five-year-old, easily matching the athletic resilience of an Olympian.

He had yet to recover from the setback of Wajid's mysterious heart attack in a toilet at Edgbaston, when he heard of Daniel Bradley's drowning accident in Stockholm.

Sometimes, providing information on a need-to-know basis is a self-defeating policy. Wajid's trip had been cleared by his handler, Brigadier Shamshad Baig who was in the agency purely for of his sycophantic abilities, no merit to his dismal track record. If Afridi had been aware of Wajid's travel plans he would not have allowed him to go, regardless of the importance of the mission. Bradley's death was a glaring failure in comparison, caused by the complacency and overconfidence of the Americans.

Afridi finished his last lap in the pool lazily, a near perfect plan in his head. Many a conquest in intra-departmental rivalry within the ISI circles or against India had been plotted while running and swimming.

This time too, he had come up with a plan, and this time it would not be rejected by the director.

Afridi began by launching a full-scale investigation into the three killings.

He summoned Rashid, his chief analyst, and issued a barrage of instructions.

'Rashid, leave for Istanbul immediately. Speak to the local police, hotel authorities, and the doctor who conducted Umavi's autopsy. Take whoever you wish to along, use whatever resources, pull as many strings as you can. In two days, I need a complete report on my table.'

Rashid was on his feet immediately.

Afridi continued, 'Get someone to speak to Umavi's man Friday ... what is his name ...'

Rashid said, 'Abdul Qadir Qandahari.'

'Haan, the same. Let me have the whole interrogation report,' Afridi said.

'Sure, sir, I'll get it for you.'

Afridi then focused on the second death. Brigadier Baig would be a little harder to handle.

Within a few minutes, the Brigadier was in his office.

'I believe Mir had your blessings before he left for London,' Afridi began, without any preamble.

Baig swallowed hard and said, 'Yes, he made the request a few weeks before his departure. We conducted a thorough recce and sensitized our men in the UK. Only after we got a green signal from our people did we clear his trip to London.'

Afridi wanted to erupt. But he knew this was not the time.

'Since Wajid was found dead in such an unflattering manner, I am sure you understand that your men did not do their fucking sensitization well. Can you personally look into the matter to and find out what went wrong?' Afridi asked through gritted teeth.

Baig did not like this conversation, which was slowly turning into an interrogation. 'We were alert and took great care with Mir; he was our best asset. We did not let our guard down for a moment,' Baig said, displeasure in his tone.

Afridi said, 'As you can see, your care and alertness were not enough. His killers not only kept track of his movements but knew exactly when he was due for a leak. They killed him in a crowded stadium with 25,000 people.'

Baig was flustered but he did not give up easily. He ventured with confidence, 'When we realized that MI6 was on his trail and he was being watched, we lost no time in asking him to change his residence from Grosvenor House hotel. We did not even allow him to go to our safe house at Hounslow, but asked him to choose the maze of Southhall.'

'Then you become complacent. Why didn't you order him to return to Lahore immediately?' Afridi had begun to lose patience now.

'Sir, we tried, but he was adamant on proceeding to Amman,' Baig said, realizing that he was fighting a losing battle.

'Would you mind leaving for London on the first available flight and meet me in two days, with your complete assessment of what went wrong?' Afridi said, his steely gaze boring into Baig's eyes.

The Brigadier realized there was no point in prolonging this fight. Afridi had good connections with the director and the army chief; he could make his life miserable.

'Inshallah sir, there will not be any mistakes this time.' Baig rose, saluted and left the room.

Afridi sat back, satisfied with himself. But he still had the third case to think about.

Bradley's death was even more mysterious than Umavi's and Mir's. He was a convicted felon according to the American justice system. The US courts had sentenced him to thirty-five years of imprisonment. He was supposed to be serving time on US soil in a high-security jail. How had he been found dead in a lake in Stockholm?

It was preposterous to imagine that the Indians could have had anything to do with it. Was the CIA involved? Had the Swedish police helped them? He needed his friend John Hu Wang's insights into the whole sordid episode.

He picked up his phone and called him. 'Hey John, they say the Chinese are interested in Africa?'

'We are planning to give Africa a new future. But I'm sure you haven't called to express sympathy for Africa,' John Hu Wang said. 'Why do I sense worry in your voice?'

'Come and show me Africa and your projects,' Afridi said.

'Okay my friend, we will meet in Dubai and then we can proceed further,' Wang replied.

'The usual location,' Afridi said, matter-of-factly.

They signed off with the usual pleasantries.

Afridi knew that Chinese intelligence, once invoked against the Indians, would definitely help snare those who had perpetrated this mayhem.

Once they furnish the damning evidence, the director will have to sanction some sort of response to India.

18

Dubai

At 829.8 metres, the Burj-al-Khalifa is the tallest man-made structure in the world. Built to accommodate a maximum of 35,000 guests, the imposing steel and glass structure was designed as a modern take on Islamic architecture and is considered by many to be the jewel of the city.

Afridi knocked on the door of the Ambassador Suite at the Armani Hotel Dubai, sitting pretty in the towering Burj-al-Khalifa. He saw Wang enjoying a steaming cup of his favourite green tea. The big smile on his face as he got up from his plush chair, and his firm handshake, were indicative of the army man's persona. Afridi knew that this younger but shrewder spy had the answers to all of his queries – those worrying little details that had bothered him since Umavi's killing in Istanbul.

It was only the second time that Afridi had come to this huge suite. It was booked in the name of a Chinese diplomat and Wang used it as his office whenever he was in town. Through the glass walls the tall buildings below look like soldiers standing to attention before a gigantic general.

'Mr Afridi, I must tell you that our Indian friends have plans for you,' said a beaming Wang.

'And what makes you so sure of this in two days?' asked an incredulous Afridi.

'This is the era of cyber warfare. These days, a mouse and keyboard are the most powerful weapons of war, and what's more, they have unlimited ammo. Bigger and better things can be achieved in a jiffy – what used to take months, and at times years, to find out. You know a whole country can be brought to its knees in a few minutes, and for that you don't have to fly planes into towers.'

Afridi was aware of the exploits of Pakistani hackers and how they had defaced various websites of the Indian government and left their imprint. In fact, he also knew that Pakistani hackers, most of whom were barely in their teens, had caused havoc on Indian defence sites; the Indian techies had taken weeks to restore them. One particular hacker group had defaced over 300 Indian websites.

Elsewhere, a handful of Ukrainian hackers using scores of computers had shut down the country of Estonia for four days in April and May 2007. The online assault had been triggered by a seemingly inconsequential political decision by the Estonian government on 27 April 2007: to move a Soviet World War II memorial from downtown Tallinn. This sparked furious protests from the Russian government and rioting among Estonia's ethnic Russian minority, followed by four days of chaos in cyberspace. Estonian authorities traced the so-called denial of service attacks to Russia, and suggested they had been orchestrated by the Kremlin.

However, it was later established that they had been unleashed by Ukrainian hackers who were widely regarded as the deadliest in the cyber world.

The Chinese spy agency – Ministry of State Security (MSS) – had raised a huge group of over 10,000 hackers and trained them for cyber armageddon. Known as the Red Army, their clear mandate was to monitor the Dalai Lama, Tibet, Taiwan and, most importantly, India. The hackers first accessed other people's computers through zombie applications – malicious software that overrides security measures or creates an entry point. Once hackers gain control over so-called zombie computers, they can network them together to form cyber armies, or botnets. This either results in denial of service or pilferage of information.

It was this Red Army and their Ukrainian pals who managed to penetrate Indian systems and, subsequently, Ray and Laila's communications, to unearth Waris's team's plans. 'We were watching the Indians for a long time, especially since they began planning to set up their National Centre for Counter Terrorism (NCTC). It was in the last few weeks that we managed to make a breakthrough and found an interesting piece of information that would be useful for you,' Wang said.

Afridi was all ears.

'What information is it?' he asked impatiently.

'Lieutenant Ali Waris has planned an important operation which is named BMW–UH–Car Series,' Wang said, with relish.

'Fucking BMW car series?'

'Yes, our boys thought like that, but then we managed to crack it with a little bit of patience and persistence,' Wang said.

'You have my attention,' Afridi said.

'B is Bradley, M is Mehmood Azhar, W is Wajid Mir, U is Umavi and H is for Haaris Saeed. The last time we checked, they had started discussing the remaining HW, since they have already taken care of B, M and U,' Wang said with a devilish grin.

Afridi was numb with disbelief. How and when had the Indians managed to muster up the courage to take on the Lashkar-e-Toiba stalwarts? It was so unlike them.

'What about Bradley? How was he found in a Stockholm lake?' he asked.

'Bradley was transferred to the American Witness Protection Programme. He was given a new identity and relocated to Europe. The FBI wanted to place him in Lisbon but he preferred Stockholm because he wasn't too fond of the Portuguese ladies,' Wang explained.

'You mean the Indians got wind of Bradley's stay in Stockholm and then got to him?' asked Afridi incredulously. Wang nodded. Of course, he wasn't going to let on that it was the Chinese who had tipped off the Indians about Bradley's hideout.

Afridi rose and shook hands with Wang, thanking him profusely. Rashid and Brigadier Baig were due to join him in a few minutes. The restaurant was almost empty. The usual lunch hour patrons were yet to troop in, and the three Pakistani men could not have found more privacy than in this secluded corner of the hotel's premiere restaurant.

'Wajid was on his way to Syria to help the Free Syrian Army (FSA) plan their confrontation, aided by Russian supplies. The last man who went into the washroom after him was an Asian, probably an Indian. He was a temporary worker, never seen after that. We've managed to get a CCTV grab of him entering the loo,' Brigadier Shamshad Baig said.

'RAW operative,' Afridi added.

'Actually, we checked our database but couldn't find a match for his image,' said the Brigadier.

'But he seems to resemble a major in the Indian Army, Brijesh Singh. He looks a lot like the man we met in the lobby of Hotel Marmara Taksim in Istanbul,' offered Rashid.

'But the most intriguing part is that when we checked the call data records of people in the area, we found that there were three prepaid UK numbers which had never been used earlier but were used immediately after the killing. A particular number in Haifa, Israel was dialled. The SIM cards were apparently destroyed after a brief conversation with the Israeli contacts,' the Brigadier said.

'That means that Mossad and the Indians are working together in this operation,' Rashid added.

Afridi's brooding eyes had narrowed to slits.

'We were aware that the Indians and Israelis were close, but the idea that they would collaborate so closely to eliminate our assets is unimaginable,' he said.

'Sir, I beg to differ. The Israeli hand seems absolutely plausible. Wajid Mir was the man who choreographed the killing at the Jewish Outreach Centre in Mumbai. He issued instructions pertaining to the killing of the Rabbi. It's quite likely that the Israelis wanted to help the Indians with this operation with limited involvement,' said the Brigadier.

'Yes, I see.' Afridi had to concede.

'Sir, another thing. Wajid Mir was injected with the same muscle relaxant, succinylcholine, that was used in the Shaikh Mahbouh killing in Dubai, which was orchestrated by Mossad,' the Brigadier continued.

'Okay Rashid, tell me what you found out,' Afridi said turning to his analyst.

'Sir, some Ansarul Ikhwanul Muslimeen had fixed to meet Umavi in Istanbul with the purpose of donating two million dollars to his charity over two years. Umavi did not want to go but when his assistant, Qandahari, gave them a clean chit, he agreed to meet them in Istanbul.' Rashid then added, 'The IP address of the computer used to contact Umavi was traced to a computer in New Delhi. It was all part of a popular phishing technique, to lure Umavi in.'

'Fuck these greedy mullahs. Why are they so hungry for worldly riches and comforts?' Afridi erupted. 'Any idea if his trip was cleared by someone from the agency?'

'Sir, I'll have to check with his handler,' the Brigadier said, nervous again.

'And how did he die?'

'I interviewed the doctor personally and also pressured the Turkish National police. They had to conduct two autopsies on him to establish that he died of a rare hazelnut allergy,' Rashid said.

'Hazelnut allergy?' Afridi and the Brigadier chorused, in disbelief.

'Was he aware of this?' Afridi asked.

'No sir, the allergy was not known to anyone. We interviewed over eighty people, including his wives, children, friends, relatives …' Rashid said.

'Then how the fuck did the Indians know about this hidden allergy when even his family and friends didn't?' asked Afridi.

There was silence.

They finished their meal without any further conversation. But it was clear in Afridi's mind that the next move would be his.

'You will make a detailed report for me so that I can debrief the director,' he told the two men.

He began walking towards the lift. This project BMW-HU, or whatever was left of it, called for his total and immediate attention. He could put other initiatives on the backburner but this had to be dealt with as a top priority. He needed to not only save H and W but also finish the Indians involved in this. And it had to begin with the man behind this operation—this Ali Waris—and end with Brijesh Singh and company. Waris was spared when he had shown the temerity to cross the LoC after Kargil. But it had been a mistake to think that the invasion had been the cause of his funeral.

Now, Afridi would begin to write the script for Waris's actual funeral.

19

Jeddah

There are very few people in this world who can tolerate the prospect of being outsmarted. Lt Gen. Sayed Ali Waris was not among them. He had been caught off guard by the ISI and it was galling to a man of his experience and expertise that he hadn't been able to foresee this. He was used to seeing things coming from a long way off, and foiling them. That was his special skill. He simply had no experience in being upstaged in this manner.

It had started with a seemingly innocuous article in the Pakistani firebrand newspaper, *Nawai Waqt*, which reported that Maulana Mahmood Azhar would not be allowed to go for Umrah this year owing to a security threat. The government had opposed the idea of his travelling to Saudi Arabia, it said. This mushroomed into a story for various news channels and the English press went to town in its inimitably shrill manner, reporting how the government had proactively stepped in to protect an eminent member of the clergy of Pakistan. The next day, however, Azhar lambasted the government, saying that nobody could stop him from travelling to Saudi Arabia. He was, after all, visiting the abode of God, considered to be the safest sanctuary according to Islamic belief, and if he wasn't safe there, then he was never meant to be safe. He refused to comment further and his spokesperson stated that he would be ridiculed by his enemies if he acknowledged this particular threat to his life. He was, after all, Mahmood Azhar.

The Lieutenant General's team saw this as the perfect opportunity to strike. The only glitch—and to call it a glitch would be euphemistic at best—was that Saudi Arabia was like a jungle in the midst of modern civilization. It was difficult for non-Muslims to enter and move around without raising any eyebrows. After a long discussion, they settled on Jeddah as the location for their rendezvous with him.

'We have to kill him in Jeddah,' Brijesh declared. 'If he manages to cross over, any further attempts on his life would be pointless.'

'He won't cross over,' Vikrant said boisterously. 'Except in a box ...'

'So how do you propose we about it?' Waris directed the question at Brijesh.

'Well, we certainly can't sprinkle powdered hazelnut on his raan,' grinned the affable Kang. He always had time for a bit of light-hearted comic relief, no matter how grave the situation.

'You don't say?' Laila rolled her eyes.

'Nor can we use succinylcholine again, after Mir. What are our options?' Vikrant asked Waris, as he scribbled illegibly on a notepad.

'Well, it has to look natural. Not that the ISI won't know it's us, but they can't tie it to us if we make it look natural,' Waris reasoned.

'I guess we'll settle for a consumable poison then,' Vikrant said. 'Cyanide? Arsenic?'

'No, not arsenic. Cyanide will do just fine,' Laila said. 'It's easier to handle and, in its powdered form, is easy to carry around.'

'But we can't get access to his food this time,' Waris said.

There was a brief silence. Vikrant got up and moved to the window that looked out into the street, which was bathed in neon lights. After a few minutes, he pulled himself away from the window and said, with grim determination, 'Let's inflict some physical harm. Stab him with a blade. We'll take the chance of getting caught.'

His idea floated past the others, unheard. Vikrant was an incredibly smart man, but he was given to the occasional impulsive urge.

Then Brijesh slammed the table with his hand. 'I've got it!' He stood up. 'These fellows still use those pieces of wood to brush, right? *Datoon*, if I'm not mistaken.'

'*Miswak*,' Kang corrected him.

'Powdered cyanide sprinkled on his *miswak* will be …' Brijesh trailed off. He didn't need to say any more. Every head in the room nodded.

'Yes,' Waris agreed. 'Just remember, it should not pop up in the post-mortem reports.'

'We'll just have to haul our asses back to India before it does,' Laila smiled.

'But who will do the spiking?' Kang asked, stroking his long beard.

'The answer, my friend, lies in your hands. Quite literally.' Brijesh allowed himself a smile.

Kang's confusion was plain to all as he turned his hands over and examined them. Everyone, including Waris, burst out laughing.

'I meant your beard, Kang. Nobody will bother questioning you. They'll think you're one of them.'

'And your Urdu is well above average,' Waris said.

'It's not at their level, sir. Besides, my Arabic isn't exactly fluent,' said Kang matter-of-factly.

'You don't need to bother too much about that, Kang. It's your appearance that is key here,' Brijesh said.

Suddenly, Kang's eyes shut tight as he placed his hand behind his head and said, 'Kesha.'

Everyone looked at him, puzzled.

'My long hair, how will I hide it? I can't wear my turban, after all.'

'You can part your hair in the middle and leave it loose. It's a Sufi thing to do, having long, untamed tresses. Hazrat Mohammad – peace be upon him – and his progeny had long hair,' said Waris.

'You can trim it a bit if you wish. The revered gurus sacrificed their heads and their young children. So why can't you sacrifice a bit of your hair?' asked Brijesh.

'That settles it. Kang will take the lead on this mission and the rest of us will just have to play our parts,' Waris concluded, as Kang nodded.

Laila looked at him and grinned. 'Let me get my kohl and trim your beard. I'll be playing the role of a make-up artist!'

'Yes, all right, Laila,' said Waris, a little dismissively, before turning to Vikrant. 'You will organize all the documents Kang needs.'

'And so, please meet Maulana Iqbal Zafar *Kangi*!' Brijesh grinned, as they went about their different tasks.

Maulana Mahmood Azhar was scheduled to travel to Saudi Arabia in the holy month of Ramzan, for umrah – a minor pilgrimage. After a little of research, the team knew exactly where he planned to stay and with how many men. The Al Bastan Hotel on Palestine Street was no Burj Khalifa, that much was certain. But what it lacked in opulent modern luxury, it made up for with a rich and elegant feel. Stepping through the doors of this, one of the oldest hotels in Jeddah, felt like stepping into a time capsule, away from the breakneck speed of life in the twenty-first century. Rather appropriately, this would be the Maulana's temporary residence, offering him the sort of temporal setting that matched his mindset. Also, the eighty-two-room hotel boasted a prayer room that met his requirements. Azhar and his entourage had booked the entire sixth floor.

Kang was to occupy a room right above Azhar's, and Vikrant and Brijesh, posing as a journalist and a businessman respectively, were to stay two floors below him. If shit hit the roof, they had to be ready to extract Kang as soon as possible.

Kang was given a Bangladeshi passport, but was posing as a Pathan who originated from Lahore and had settled in Bangladesh. That would explain his thick Punjabi accent.

On that fateful day, there was a commotion late in the evening.

'Naaretaqbeer!' came the call. 'Allah o Akbar!' the crowd chanted.

'Target has arrived. Awaiting visual confirmation,' Brijesh told Kang and Vikrant.

'Copy that,' Vikrant replied. He came down to the lobby within the next two minutes, and saw Brijesh reading a newspaper in the corner. The lobby was swarming with faces covered with thick beards and flowing robes.

The cynosure of all eyes was a bespectacled man with a gentle yet wily smile. He was waving while getting the top of his forehead and the back of his hand kissed by his loyalists. His entourage was trying to shield him, but he stopped them and allowed his devoted followers to continue with their extravagant greetings. For devout Muslims this might be a spiritual scene, but for those not familiar with the practice, it bordered on the obscene.

'Target is headed towards his room,' Brijesh said into his transmitting device, pleased that the team's research had provided accurate results.

Kang asked, 'How many men does he have with him?'

'Thirteen, to my knowledge,' Brijesh replied. 'All of them are likely to travel with him. But on the plus side, they are all staying on separate floors, save for a couple, who are on the same floor as him.'

'That's enough for today, boys. We'll have to get to work when he's away. Once we get a better idea of his habits,' Brijesh said, as he got up and tossed the newspaper on the couch. He walked up the staircase and met Vikrant.

'We're halfway there, Vikrant. Mumbai is this close to being avenged.'

'*India* is this close to being avenged,' Vikrant corrected him.

Every minute that passed seemed like an eternity. The target was within kicking distance and yet, the team had to wait for the right moment to strike.

Hours passed and much later in the evening a commotion in the lobby caught Vikrant's attention. The target was leaving with his entourage. Vikrant went up to a bearded man, who was trying to catch a glimpse of Azhar.

'Who's that man?' Vikrant inquired. 'He seems to have quite a few followers.'

'And rightly so,' the bearded man smiled. 'He is Allah's gift to us. We are his followers.'

'You'll have to forgive me, brother,' Vikrant said respectfully. 'Would you mind telling me who he is?'

'Maulana Mahmood Azhar. He is leaving now to address his followers,' the man said, as he began to walk away. 'I'd better get going. Ma assalaam.'

'Khudahafiz,' Vikrant said.

The man looked at him with a strange expression in his eyes.

Vikrant raised his voice several notches: 'Khudahafiz, Maulana Mahmood Azhar. Khudahafiz.' He muttered under his breath, 'And I mean every word of it.'

Vikrant rushed back to Kang's room and nodded at Brijesh and Kang. Their target had been identified, now it was time to move in on him. Kang and Brijesh began to arm themselves. Brijesh pushed his gun into a holster below his armpit, and put on a waistcoat. Kang, meanwhile, gently caressed his little box of powdered cyanide with the tip of his index finger as he began moving towards the door.

They headed for the staircase, on their way to Azhar's floor. Their heels clicked as they walked down the staircase; softly enough to avoid raising an alarm, but loud enough not to sound like they were sneaking anywhere.

'Remember, Kang,' Brijesh instructed him. 'Once you're in, you're on your own. We can only cover the floors above and below.'

'There's one guard right outside his door,' Vikrant said. 'Brijesh and I will stage a scene and get him out of the way. That's when you sneak in.'

They reached Azhar's floor, where a bearded guard stood right outside his room door. Big, burly and brutish looking. The perfect security guard to protect someone as sought after as Azhar, Kang reasoned, before quickly moving aside into a blind spot. He waited for a while to see if he had inadvertently attracted the guard's attention. But the large man seemed to have a limited sense of awareness about his surroundings and Kang gave the other two the go-ahead.

Vikrant and Brijesh burst out of the stairwell and walked down the corridor towards the guard, talking in loud and hostile voices.

'You FUCKED me over, you bastard!' Brijesh yelled at Vikrant. 'I trusted you with all my money, hoping this business would flourish!'

'And what do you think I've done? Absconded with the money?' Vikrant argued back. 'I'm RIGHT HERE, ASSHOLE! I lost money too!'

They caught the guard's eye. He looked at them warily.

'I don't give a FUCK! I want all my money BACK!' Brijesh ranted, grabbing Vikrant's collar aggressively.

'DON'T TOUCH ME,' Vikrant yelled as he threw a wild, inaccurate punch at Brijesh's chest. Brijesh fell backwards. The guard had seen enough. He rushed over to them, trying to break up the fight as Kang sneaked in from behind and walked towards the room. By now, Brijesh had recovered.

'Is there a problem here?' the guard said, as he stood between them. 'If there is, sort it out elsewhere.'

'You bet your ass there's a problem, mister. Imagine putting a million dollars into a dud business. Have you seen a million dollars? Do you even know how many zeroes there are in a million?' Brijesh yelled at the guard, who grew red in the face.

'This is the last chance I'm giving you to walk away,' he said sternly.

'Last chance or you'll do what?' asked Brijesh. The guard lurched forward with the intention of grabbing the man who had just spoken to him so insolently – when everything suddenly went dark. Moments before blacking out, the guard had seen a blur from the corner of his eye. The blur bore some resemblance to Vikrant's foot as it flew through the air and connected squarely with the guard's large head. He crumpled to the floor like a gunny bag of potatoes and lay there motionless. Lights out!

Vikrant and Brijesh dragged the man's body to one side of the corridor. Vikrant positioned it in a space where he would attract the least attention, while Brijesh made sure the coast was clear. They had bought Kang enough time to have begun his mission in Azhar's room. The rest was upto him. Vikrant began to pull the guard towards the staircase, and watching him struggle to move the heavy gorilla of a man – he probably weighed 100 kg, they conjectured – Brijesh joined in to help. They pulled him down the stairs and, in the process, eventually lost sight of the door. Reaching for the edge of the floor carpet, Vikrant ripped it off and rolled the guard over it, wrapping him up in its folds in the process.

Meanwhile, Kang had made his way into Azhar's bathroom and found three units of *miswak* with minimal effort. It seemed almost too easy, but then he reasoned that *miswak* wasn't exactly something that a person would hide. He spread a generous amount of cyanide over all the pieces. Then he returned them to their original position, looked around to see if he had left any clues and made his exit, closing the bathroom door carefully behind him.

As he stepped out of the bathroom, he took a moment to address a nagging feeling at the back of his head like he'd forgotten something. He had covered each stick with cyanide, and made sure to wipe off his fingerprints, and he hadn't messed with the bathroom curtains or doormat. There wasn't anything else he was meant to do, was there?

And that's when Kang felt a powerful thud at the base of his skull. Had it been another man, who wasn't blessed with a skull as thick as Kang's, he would have passed out at once. But Kang countered the blistering numbness and, only slightly disoriented, turned and threw an expansive righthook – and hit nothing but air. He could barely see his opponent, his vision still blurry and his ears ringing from the blow to the back of his head.

He braced himself too late against a punch to the chest. The unidentified assailant then unleashed a stinging kick to Kang's solar plexus. That was enough to make him collapse to the floor, much as the guard had done. The only difference was that Kang was still conscious. He felt a sudden flurry of kicks to his ribs and his head. Even in his groggy state, he realized that there was obviously more than one hostile in the room. A second later, Iqbal Kang had been rendered unconscious by a kick between the eyes.

A man watched the action blow-by-blow on a little LED screen. *I've got you now, you bastard.* It was just a matter of time before he had Kang spitting out a confession in a bid to save his own life. He had seen many men blurt out secrets, hoping to be granted a new lease of life. And if they didn't die while being tortured, he always extracted their secrets and then put the little squealers out of their misery. It was the only humane thing to do. *This man would be no different.*

Just then, the screen showed two other men running up the corridor and kicking the door open. Two men he had never seen before. He froze and stared silently at them, hoping to get a clear view of their faces. Something with which to identify these violent, good-for-nothing mother …

And then, they turned and looked right into the camera without knowing it. One of the men was shouting an order furiously into the phone. The other one ran towards the staircase. Finally, Arif Afridi had some faces to work with. He grinned as he turned his eyes away from the LED screen. He had not only thrown a spanner into the works of these Indian agents, he had gained the upper hand.

'Yes, Brijesh! I can see the car,' Laila yelled into her phone, as she got behind the wheel of her rented SUV. 'I'm going to tail them. Just stay on the line and get a car of your own as soon as possible.'

She sped off, shifting gears and driving as fast as she could. The only thing going at a quicker speed than her car was the pounding of her heart. The game had just changed.

20

'Your bastard father,' Kang spat out – along with a mixture of blood, saliva and fragments of tooth. Clearly, being pummelled unconscious had no effect on his defiant spirit. One of the two men restraining him in the back of a speeding, unmarked black SUV grabbed him by the throat, while a third man punched him in the abdomen and asked the same question for the fourth time.

'Who sent you?' This time, Kang said nothing, winded after the last punch.

The mission to eliminate Maulana Mahmood Azhar was a colossal failure. It had been a failure because they failed to take out their target, and because a team member had been captured and was going to be interrogated, probably beaten, possibly broken – but definitely killed.

Kang had blacked out on the floor of the hotel room and had no idea who these men were. What he knew for sure was that this man in the group, the interrogator, was definitely in charge, while the goons restraining him were the muscle. And the man behind the wheel was the driver.

Without warning, the interrogator slapped Kang right across the face, leaving his cheek stinging.

'This is the last time I am going to ask you this question,' he said and added, 'then, I will start cutting off parts of your body.' The man grinned as he brandished a rusty cleaver. The cleaver came to settle on Kang's cheek with the sharp edge resting on his ear.

'So … Who sent you?'

'Maybe I was wrong … It was your real father,' said Kang matter-of-factly, unconcerned about the sharp blade against his face.

'You asked for it, you son-of-a-bitch,' said the interrogator, as he pulled Kang's left ear outwards and readied the cleaver to chop it off.

Kang clenched his fists, gritted his teeth and prepared for the pain that was about to surge through him.

'Stop fucking around, and keep him intact,' the driver of the SUV turned back and said derisively. 'If you turn him over to the boss without an ear, you'd better be ready to chop your own off and hand it over.'

Clearly, it wasn't the interrogator but the driver who was in charge. Kang allowed himself to breathe again. The spilling of his blood had been delayed for now. But for how long?

The tyres screeched as Laila hit the brakes, narrowly avoiding an oncoming vehicle as she hurtled the wrong way on a one-way lane in an effort to cut off the SUV in which Kang was being held captive.

'What are you doing, Laila? Do you have a visual?' Brijesh's voice screamed out of the speaker on Laila's cell phone.

'No visual. But I haven't lost him,' she said, as she craned her neck to look down the narrow lane to ensure that there were no more oncoming vehicles.

She was accompanied by Rizwan Bashir, a local asset cultivated by Waris five years earlier. After a careful and rigorous screening process filled with multiple background checks and interrogations, Waris had decided that he was just the man to keep in reserve for a situation like this. A banker by day, Rizwan had been told that he would be contacted should the need arise – and his knowledge of the streets of Jeddah was just what was needed for this mission. In fact, it was he who suggested they take this 'short cut' to intercept the SUV.

Laila's reading of the onboard GPS system led her to believe that he had a point – if she went up this one-way street, she would be able to intercept the other vehicle before it had the opportunity to turn off into any lane. Their plans hinged heavily on the hope that the other SUV would not take a U-turn and give them the slip.

Brijesh knew she was gambling and that this was a high-stake gamble. She had to be allowed to work calmly and in peace, so he signed off with a simple 'Keep me posted and stay safe'.

Laila burst out of the lane and onto the main road, having safely managed to drive the wrong way up a one-way street. She looked left and then whipped her head around to the right, but there was no sign of the black SUV. Unless it was travelling at a speed in excess of 180 km per hour, she calculated, there was no way it could have passed her.

Rizwan confirmed this by saying, 'There's no possibility of them having gone ahead of us. Turn back.'

This meant one of two things: either the car had gone off the road or a deft U-turn had taken the SUV beyond their reach.

Laila drove out onto the main road to retrace the black vehicle's movements. Her eyes scanned the road, but to no avail. And that was when her phone began to ring again. She answered it immediately and regretted her decision milliseconds later. 'Did you find him, Laila?' came Brijesh's concerned voice. Her silence spoke volumes. 'What is the status? Rizwan?' There was no response.

'Oh shit!' screamed Laila, as she finally spotted the black SUV.

'What happened? Did you find them?'

The vehicle was parked on the side of the road.

Laila reached into the glove compartment for a pistol as she pulled over. Her field experience was very limited, but she had no choice. 'Cover me,' said Rizwan, as he jumped out of the vehicle with a sidearm of his own, and headed for the parked car.

Cautiously, he crossed the fairly busy street and walked up to the SUV, his gun raised and ready to fire. Laila looked on, her gun primed and ready to take out anyone who jumped out of the black car. Looking around the side to see if he could sneak a peek into the car via the wing mirror, Rizwan noticed that the front door was slightly open.

'What is the status, Laila?' Brijesh's voice enquired again.

'They've parked at the side of the road and Rizwan has gone to investigate. I'm covering h-'

A blinding flash of white light and a loud explosion made Laila's blood run cold. Their failure had just turned into a massive clusterfuck.

'It was a trap!' She screamed in panic, struggling to regain her composure.

It was a low-intensity explosion that caused superficial damage to a passing vehicle, but was enough to gut the SUV from within. Rizwan must have triggered it by opening the door. She sprinted across the street without a care for the speeding traffic, hurdled over the divider on the road and ran towards the SUV. Then the possibility of a second bomb made her stop in her tracks and walk around to take a look from a safe distance. The two-bomb strategy was a common one among terrorists. The first is always a low-intensity one to cause panic and draw in the crowds. The second is the lethal high-intensity explosion.

She saw Rizwan's charred torso, motionless behind the smouldering black SUV. The rest of his body lay in a crumpled, bloodied heap around five metres away.

Not only had they given her the slip, but that bomb had probably been meant for her, she thought.

'We've lost Rizwan, Brijesh! And we've lost Kang,' she said, as she returned to her SUV and picked up the phone. There was no doubt any more, the enemy had fired its opening shot and they had hit their target. Now, with the explosion, the local authorities were bound to be involved and with the team's cover virtually blown, the last thing they needed was for the Jeddah police to be swarming all over. Their dislike for Indians was well documented. It was time to run.

This wasn't the first setback Brijesh had suffered and it wouldn't be the last.

'Head back to the rendezvous spot, Laila,' he said quietly. 'I'll deal with this.'

Arif Afridi paced up and down the corridor on the eighth floor of a little apartment complex in the city. Finally, he had a bit of luck going his way. One of the Indians had been captured and two others had been dragged out of the shadows of anonymity. As he paced, a battery of intelligence officers across the world were running a series of facial recognition programmes to identify the two men.

This was just one more debt of gratitude Afridi owed his cyber connections. After all, they had been instrumental in giving him the information that his own informants and agency were clueless about. The quest for screen grabs from Stockholm and Birmingham had been fruitless. But his meeting with Major John Hu Wang had made all the difference.

Because of the CCTV grabs taken from the camera outside the toilets at Edgbaston, they had been able to get a look at Brijesh from behind. Wang's computer army did the rest. They pulled up a list of visitors to Bradley's residence from the CIA database, and used it to check Nadia's client list from the bordell mamma's computer. It was interesting that the last people to meet Nadia, before she became Bradley's final visitor, happened to be Indians. Using the CCTV footage from the bordello, in conjunction with facial recognition software, they were able to correlate the faces with a group that included a man whose build almost exactly matched that of the cleaner at Edgbaston.

Tracking the men's movements across the world became simple, as their fake passports carried real pictures. All Afridi needed was confirmation that these were the same men, and he got it when Vikrant and Brijesh looked into the camera after Kang had been picked up. Life was good again, as far as Afridi was concerned.

Brijesh and Vikrant arrived moments after Laila had fled the scene of the explosion. Vikrant pulled their inconspicuous dark blue sedan over to the side of the road and Brijesh walked over to the smouldering black SUV. He shook his head as he bent to look at the remains of Rizwan and signalled to Vikrant, who was keeping a watchful eye on the surroundings.

'A low-intensity IED, there's no doubt about it,' said Brijesh, as Vikrant jogged up to him. 'And the aim was to limit the damage to the person who opened the car door.'

'That doesn't tell us where they took Kang,' said an agitated Vikrant.

'We'll find him … We just need to find …'

'Need to find what?' asked Vikrant.

Pointing at a CCTV camera planted on the building wall across the street, Brijesh ran over to the sedan and reached for his cell phone. After a disastrous day, this was the first glimmer of luck.

'Hello? Yes, Laila, do you have your laptop handy? I need you to do something for me,' he said as he crossed the road quickly and looked at the little plaque below the CCTV camera

– Vigilant Security Systems. 'I want you to do your magic with this security agency's camera feeds and find me footage of what happened before you got to the scene. And make it quick. Every second we waste, Kang gets further and further out of reach.'

'Got what you need?' asked Vikrant as Brijesh ran back across the road and into the car.

'Not yet, but we need to be ready for when I do,' he said, as they got back into their vehicle.

They sat in silence, contemplating their next move and giving some thought to the very real possibility of having to continue the mission without their trusted companion. The ISI was undoubtedly onto them. But the Jeddah police might also have been given instructions to apprehend them. Leaving Jeddah was going to be no walk in the park, thought Brijesh. The phone rang just then and he snapped it up.

'Do you have it?'

Vikrant studied Brijesh's expression, but he knew he was looking at a man with one of the best poker faces in the business.

'Thank you, Laila. Stand by to track movements.'

Brijesh disconnected and turned to Vikrant. 'We're looking for a battered grey Toyota Camry. Find a place to take a U-turn and go back up the road while I track down the car.'

They began to drive and Vikrant took the phone to dial a number, only this time he was not talking to Laila – it was the Jeddah police.

'Yes, my name is Azmatul-Haq,' he said in perfect Arabic, 'and my grey Toyota Camry has been stolen.'

21

Kang's eyes opened to unfamiliar surroundings. He wasn't used to waking up in complete darkness – much less waking up with his arms tied behind his back, his legs tied to the chair and his face feeling like someone had used a jackhammer on it. His right eye was swollen to the point where a flesh-coloured bulge obscured his vision. His training had taught him to be aware of his surroundings, even in the dark, but there was no chance of that when most of his senses had been taken out of the equation.

His sense of smell, however, was still functional and he could smell a hint of dried blood in the stale, musty air. He rocked back and forth, hoping to make the chair topple over and in doing so, wriggle out of the ropes that bound him. At once, a door swung open and the light from outside nearly blinded him.

'Who's there?' he screamed, as his eyes began adjusting to the invasion of light.

No response.

'I said, who's th—' His enquiry was cut short by a hand clutching his throat, and he felt his chair being dragged from behind; its hind legs scraped along the bumpy floor, front legs in the air. After ten seconds of dragging, the chair came to a standstill once more and a bright light shone down like a spotlight on Kang's head.

For the first time, he could actually see his captors. Even though they wore balaclavas, the white hot rage emitting from their eyes was more than palpable. Realizing the futility of trying to interrogate his interrogators, he sat back and waited. The masked men stood around him, not speaking or attacking; just watching him wriggle to try and get loose – and then giving up the futile exercise.

Eventually, Kang lost patience.

'What the fuck do you want?' he snapped.

Just then, the door opened and in walked a sophisticated looking man with a slight build – slight compared to the men who had brought Kang to this place. But the malice he exuded dwarfed the rage in the eyes of his men.

He stopped for a minute to dust a tiny shred of lint off the sleeve of his blazer and looked back up.

'Have I taught you guys nothing about how to treat a guest?' he asked rhetorically, as he walked up to Kang and placed a hand on his shoulder. 'Did you have a pleasant journey, Maulana?' he asked with a mocking emphasis on the last word.

Kang struggled to get free. Who was this man? Was he a CIA operative? ISI? Or worse?

'Stop struggling!' the man barked at Kang. 'These ropes are stronger than your weak will!'

The venomous tone was Arif Afridi's signature style.

'Now, should we do this the hard way or the easy way?' he asked calmly, looking over at one of the masked men who was rifling through a set of what looked like dentist's tools.

Kang didn't utter a word. The silence was quickly shattered by a punch to his chin, courtesy one of Afridi's goons.

'The easy way or the hard way?' Afridi asked again, the mildest irritation in his voice.

Again there was silence. And the result was virtually identical, except that Kang, for the second time that evening, spat out another mouthful of saliva and blood.

Afridi signalled to his man to take a break, before turning to Kang. 'I don't think I need to tell you that my men have fists like steel. Fists that have developed over years of pounding bone to pulp. So I'm offering you the chance to cooperate with me and spare your face from turning into mincemeat.' Kang looked over at the man with the dentist's kit, who was examining some sort of diabolical cross between a pair of tongs and a knife.

'Oh, I see my associate's toys have your attention,' grinned Afridi. He took the hybrid tool from the masked man and held it up lightly. 'This one is a personal favourite of mine. It's just a shame that you'll become virtually useless after I use it on you. After all, what good are you without a tongue to tell me what I want to know?' Afridi clicked the contraption together, demonstrating just how it could rip a man's tongue out of his mouth.

'So what's the point of telling me all this when you're not going to use it?' asked Kang defiantly.

'I'm so glad you asked,' smiled Afridi, as he walked closer to Kang. 'You see, your tongue isn't the only thing I can yank out with this.' He tapped the instrument on Kang's thigh and walked back to put the device down on a table. 'For now, this will do,' he said, as he whipped a ceramic knife out of his pocket and stabbed it into Kang's thigh, slicing through muscle and sinew.

Kang screamed in pain as Afridi twisted the blade slightly and then pulled it out.

'What's the latest position?' asked Brijesh, as Vikrant drove cautiously along the street that had slowly become less and less busy.

'According to police radio dispatches, they're tracking the CCTV footage to find the car, but there's a gap in the footage for around 200 metres,' said Laila. She added, 'The car doesn't re-emerge in the footage taken from the camera after the gap.'

'So that's where we lost them. Vikrant, get us there on the double.' Brijesh sensed his opportunity and jumped at it.

After the complaint about a 'stolen' vehicle had been lodged, Laila had been tracking the police radio frequencies. Despite having nothing near the absolute CCTV coverage of a place like London, Jeddah had its fair share of cameras on the streets. The police had dipped into the surveillance tapes to track the vehicle and transmitted its last known location to its patrols. Eavesdropping on that conversation gave Laila an idea of where the cops were heading and ultimately, brought them closer to Kang.

As the car hurtled down the street towards the junction Laila had identified, Vikrant said, 'But what do we do if we get there and Kang …' He trailed off.

'We'll cross that bridge if we get there. For now, all we have is hope that Kang's resilience will save him,' said Brijesh.

After a few moments, they arrived at the CCTV camera where the car had disappeared. There were no major roads leading out from there; just a tiny lane. 'Take it,' said Brijesh, as he looked for any indication of the grey car's whereabouts. It was then that he noticed the glint of another camera a few hundred metres down the road.

'Pull over,' he said to Vikrant as he picked up the phone and dialled Laila again.

'I see a camera down this lane. Any word about it in the police radio communications?' he asked.

'The car didn't emerge out of that lane, Brijesh,' said Laila.

'All right, stay sharp.' He signed off and turned to Vikrant. 'That means they're in this area. You search the buildings on the left of the road and I'll scour the ones on the right. They're definitely here somewhere.'

'Or they've left in another car,' offered Vikrant, somewhat unhelpfully.

Brijesh grunted and set about the search.

Kang writhed in pain as Afridi stalked him slowly, like a predator circling his injured prey.

'I assume that by now, apart from your leg, we've also cut through the bullshit,' said Afridi. 'And that you're willing to tell me who planned this little adventure of yours. This game of cat-and-mouse. Clearly, it wasn't you.'

Kang's eyes smouldered fiercely, but he remained silent.

'What's all this worth?' asked Afridi, gradually beginning to lose his cool. 'You think your friends are going to come and find you? They've probably run away by now, with their tails between their legs.'

Afridi's irritation showed in his voice. 'Who are you doing all this for anyway? Your country? You think your country gives a shit about what happens to you? Or how many of your vital organs fail before you die? Or how many pieces you are chopped into?

'Why would your country care? When it's not busy bullying another, it's making the life of its own citizens a living hell. And this is the country you are fighting for? You think they are going to care about a worthless little speck like you?'

'You are partly correct,' said Kang, breaking his silence.

Afridi smiled, 'Ah! He speaks!'

'Yes. You are partly correct. No respect for other countries, no respect or care for its citizens. That part is correct. Except, that sounds more like Pakistan to me,' said Kang calmly, disguising the searing pain coursing up and down his leg.

Afridi looked at one of his goons and nodded. He obliged by smashing his fist into Kang's already swollen jaw. 'That was your final warning. There will be no more. I will simply start cutting off parts of your body,' said Afridi. 'I will give you one last chance to tell me who is responsible for these little tricks of yours. Who is pulling your strings?'

Kang chose to say no more.

'All right, we'll do things your way,' said Afridi, as he walked out of the room, prompting the guards to push Kang's chair forward, towards a table, and then tip it onto its front legs, so he was slumped face down on the table. Still tied to the chair, he was completely immobilised now. He didn't see Afridi enter the room with an electric power drill in his hand.

He heard the sound though, as it began to whir and before he knew it, it was burrowing a hole in his back. Shredded flesh and blood flew in all directions, as Kang let out a scream of agony. One of the guards turned away from the horrific scene, but Afridi remained steadfast, the blood and gore splattering all over his determined face. Blinded by the pain, Kang felt the drill make its way through the bone and screamed again – only this time it didn't sound human. It sounded like an animal in excruciating pain.

'Quick, over here!' said Vikrant to Brijesh, in a hushed tone. 'Did you hear that?'

Brijesh shook his head and ran over to Vikrant's side of the road.

'I definitely heard a scream,' Vikrant said, pointing at a building, 'and it came from in there.'

The pair entered the compound cautiously and looked around the car park for the grey car, but it was nowhere to be seen. 'The sound came from upstairs,' whispered Vikrant, sensing that his colleague did not want to move up the stairs unless they were absolutely sure the car was here.

'Fuck the car! That's probably—' Vikrant stopped talking as he saw Brijesh pull a dirty grey sheet off a parked vehicle. Sure enough, it was the car they were searching for. Without another word, they made their way into the building and entered the stairwell. Brijesh pulled out his cellphone and sent Laila a message with their GPS location and an order to arrange for immediate evacuation. She replied to say that she would arrive in ten minutes.

That's at least nine and a half minutes too long, thought Brijesh to himself, as the pair noiselessly made their way up the staircase to look for the source of the scream. He reached into his back pocket for a sidearm and checked its magazine. There had better be less than five people there, he thought, thumbing the remaining rounds in the cartridge before slamming it back into the gun.

They began to move up the stairwell, when out of nowhere, a door burst open. A comfortingly familiar, yet simultaneously alien looking blur ran at them, knocking Vikrant off his feet and smashing Brijesh into the wall. The latter aimed his gun at the blurry figure and then asked incredulously, 'Kang?'

Kang's bloodied face looked up at the duo, who wasted no time in running down the stairs with him and out onto the road, where they were greeted by the sound of screeching tyres. Vikrant helped Kang into the backseat as Brijesh hopped into the front passenger's seat.

'Drive!' he said, as he heard car doors slamming behind them.

The chase was on.

'We need to get to the Indian consulate on the double,' said Brijesh urgently, as Laila surged the car forward.

22

'That's right. A car accident,' said Brijesh calmly, barely belying the level of panic in the car.

'Let them in!' barked the security guard at the Indian consulate in Jeddah, as he motioned to his colleague in the control booth. The electronically controlled steel gate gently glided on its wheels and slid open, so Laila could drive them into the compound. A flock of paramedics, armed guards and volunteers gathered around the vehicle. Vikrant's door flew open as he hopped out and ran around to the other side to help the semi-conscious, blood-soaked Kang onto wheelchair brought out by the paramedics. As this was not a medical facility, there were obviously no stretchers and very little in terms of medical equipment.

The vice consul, a mild-mannered man of average height, with an elegantly parted and combed head of greying hair, walked briskly out of the main consulate building and onto the driveway. He had been briefed about the situation and its gravity was clearly emblazoned across his face. He walked over to Brijesh and held out his hand.

'Good evening, I'm the vice consul, Naveen Varma. What can I do for you?' he asked, as he shook Brijesh's hand politely, lines of tension etched across his forehead.

'Thank you for helping us. We need to have our friend patched up immediately, so we can return to India as soon as humanly possible,' said Brijesh, without beating about the bush.

'May I ask what actually happened to your friend?' asked the vice consul, looking at Kang as he was being wheeled into the consulate building with Vikrant and Laila following him.

'It was a car accident,' said Brijesh, with a straight face.

Both men knew this was far from the truth.

'A car accident?' said Naveen, as he looked Brijesh in the eye.

'That's right.'

A Mexican standoff.

'It wouldn't happen to have anything to do with the SUV explosion a few hours ago, would it?' asked the vice consul sternly.

'I'm afraid I cannot give you that information,' said Brijesh.

'Well, you will have to give me some information if you want me to help you and your friends return to India,' offered Naveen, a veteran at negotiations – both diplomatic and otherwise.

'I'm sorry, but all I can tell you is that there are some men who wish India harm, and by association, Indians,' said Brijesh.

Naveen mulled this over for a moment and asked, 'Are you with the government or do you work independently?'

Silence.

'Look, I have no problem turning you out on to the streets or even to the Jeddah police, considering they're handling the investigation of the car explosion,' said Naveen gently, but the threat in his words loud and clear.

Meanwhile, inside the consulate, one doctor was shining a tiny flashlight into Kang's eyes every time he regained consciousness, to see if he was responsive. Another doctor was stitching up the horrific cut in his thigh. Laila and Vikrant stood by with their arms crossed, willing their comrade to make a full, and—equally important—timely recovery.

'Can you hear me?' asked the doctor with the flashlight. 'How did this happen to you?'

'C-c-car accident,' mumbled Kang through clenched teeth, feeling every jab of the needle as it stitched up his wound. Stitching up a straight cut or even a crooked one is a fairly simple procedure as the aim is to pull the skin together, stop the bleeding and let the body heal itself. This was why the gash in Kang's thigh had taken hardly any time to stitch and patch up. The gaping cavity in his back, which was still spewing blood, was a different thing altogether. The hole was a safe distance from his spine, and the drilling had stopped a few centimetres away from his lung. That was the good news.

The wound was taking longer to fix because after getting past the shreds of sinew and muscle and picking out the shards of bone, the skin still had to be stitched together. Vikrant tried to pay attention and follow the procedure, but gave up quickly. All the adrenaline that had been pumping through his system for over an hour, had dissipated.

'This wound in your back, son,' said the doctor, trying to revive Kang, 'how did you get it?'

'Car accident,' came the reply.

'Were you driving? Were there others in the vehicle?' asked the doctor, as he struggled to keep Kang conscious.

'Car accident,' replied Kang under his breath, before reverting to a semi-catatonic state.

Despite the pain, Kang's training had not abandoned him. He had been briefed on the journey to the consulate and knew exactly what he was supposed to say. Brijesh and Vikrant had taken little time to formulate what they thought would be a plausible story and why the Indian consulate should provide help. Sadly, their version of events proved to be less credible than they had imagined, particularly in the eyes of the vice consul.

'I'm afraid you leave me with no choice,' sighed the vice consul, as calm as ever before he called out, 'Security!'

Brijesh watched two members of the security staff jog over to the two of them.

'All right, listen …' began Brijesh and almost immediately, Naveen waved the guards away.

Brijesh glared at the diplomat, then said, 'I can't tell you much, but whatever I can tell you, I certainly can't say it out here.'

The vice consul invited him into the building, where they could talk in private.

'No.' Brijesh shook his head. 'Do you have a garden or a backyard?'

Naveen nodded and led him down the left side of the building into a little backyard. They walked together silently, Brijesh thinking about how much he could disclose to Naveen. As they arrived in the backyard, Brijesh walked around to check for any suspicious overhanging branches or lamp posts that might contain a listening device of some sort. Satisfied with the results of his quick scan, he walked to the centre of the backyard.

'What are you doing?' asked the vice consul suspiciously.

'I may trust you, but I don't trust that the Indian consulate is free of bugs and audio surveillance,' said Brijesh.

'Okay. So what is it you want to tell me?' asked Naveen, unconcerned by Brijesh's scepticism.

Brijesh took a deep breath. 'We are a combination of undercover police officers from across India, trying desperately to stay incognito and find out who is responsible for the human trafficking of Indians. You are right, it wasn't a car accident that injured our friend. One of the people involved captured and tortured him. And now, we have to leave Jeddah to carry our findings home,' he said, virtually in one breath.

Naveen nodded and then made a quiet suggestion. 'You should have just stuck to the car accident angle instead of trying to sell me another pile of—'

Unfazed, Brijesh interrupted, 'The possible involvement of the ISI is why we are here and today that was confirmed. Who do you think caused that car explosion?'

The vice consul's eyes widened slightly as he scratched his chin.

'Now do you understand why I can't give you any more details?' asked Brijesh.

Naveen was unmoved. But he said, 'Let's go and check on your friend, because as soon as he is patched up, I want you on the first plane out of Jeddah.'

Brijesh didn't know whether this meant that the vice consul believed him or just wanted them out of his hair. But frankly, it didn't matter all that much, as long as Kang was ready to be moved.

The journey home was a surprisingly relaxed affair. The quartet sleepily yawned their way out of Delhi's Indira Gandhi International Airport, having been rushed onto a waiting Air India flight with minimal frisking or security checks. Once they landed, they walked over to the vehicle that was waiting for them. Kang's steps were a little more careful than usual; he did not want to flex his back muscles or stretch his taped-up quadricep muscle too much.

Something wasn't right in the team either. There had been an uneasy tension brewing between them ever since they had left the gates of the Indian consulate in Jeddah. They climbed into the vehicle and Brijesh—who would usually hold the door open for everyone—entered the car first and sat sullenly near the window as Kang sat in the front seat beside the driver. They remained quiet all the way back to HQ, where they would meet Waris and be debriefed. In fact, the only interaction between the teammates was when Laila offered everyone some chewing gum, and they all declined politely.

Kang was the last to enter the conference room where Waris was supposed to be meeting his lieutenants. Laila, Brijesh and Vikrant were already seated by the time Kang limped in and took a seat.

Brijesh got straight to it, at last. There had been no opportunity to talk en route.

'How did you escape?' he asked Kang unflinchingly.

'What do you mean? You were there when I escaped,' said Kang.

'I saw you running down the stairs,' corrected Brijesh. 'I have no idea how or why they let you get away.'

Kang stood up to face Brijesh.

Vikrant cautiously positioned himself between the two.

'I don't like what you're implying,' Kang said, anger in check.

Vikrant placed his hand on Kang's shoulder and said, 'No one is implying anything. Don't worry.'

Brushing Vikrant's hand aside and standing straight, despite the pain, Kang said defiantly, 'No, let him continue.'

'So just how did you get out?' Brijesh maintained his line of questioning.

'After drilling a hole in my back,' began Kang, pulling off his T-shirt. 'You know the gaping, fucking hole they made in my back with an electric drill?' he asked as he started ripping the bandages off his wound.

'Don't be so dramatic,' chided Brijesh, even as Laila jumped up to stop Kang from tearing off his bandages.

'After leaving me to bleed in the hope that I would give up information about all of you, one man came back to keep an eye on me,' Kang said sturdily. 'I used all my strength to back my chair into him and push him against the wall. Then I snapped my neck backwards to break his nose and knock him unconscious. The struggle had loosened my bounds and I was able to get out of the knots and make my way out before anyone could come and check. And that's when I ran into you.'

'Are you sure he was unconscious?' asked a clearly unconvinced Brijesh.

'NO! Because I was trying to run away!' raged Kang. 'Did you expect me to stop and check on him?'

'No, it's just that it all seems awfully convenient.'

'Be careful, Brijesh.'

'We also never got down to checking you for bugs or tracking devices.'

'Brijesh …'

Vikrant stepped in again. 'Calm down, guys. I'll scan him but then will the two of you settle down?'

'Nobody put any trackers or bugs on me,' said Kang. 'And I'll break the hands of anyone who dares to check me.'

'Please, let me give you a quick scan, just to settle this,' pleaded Vikrant, as Laila calibrated the signal scanner, which would be able to spot any device that emitted a signal – a vital characteristic of any tracking device.

Kang reluctantly agreed, but as Laila set about scanning him, his eyes bore a hole through Brijesh.

'He's clean, Brijesh,' announced Laila shortly. 'Now can we please drop this?'

'Then why did they just let you leave?' persisted Brijesh. 'The ISI is never so sloppy.'

Kang lunged at Brijesh.

'Are you calling me a traitor?' he screamed, as his arms scythed through the air, missing Brijesh narrowly.

Brijesh elbowed Kang in the chest to create a bit of space and avoid being cornered.

'Are you saying they let me leave because I spilled the beans?' asked Kang again, as he tried grabbing Brijesh by the throat.

Deflecting Kang's hand and retaliating with a swift jab to his ribs, the unflustered Brijesh said, 'I just want to know what deal you struck with them.'

That was enough for Kang, who threw a crushing punch, knocking the nimbler Brijesh off his feet and on to the floor. 'That's it. I don't need to put my life on the line and be questioned by the likes of you.'

Brijesh rubbed his chin and sat up, as Vikrant and Laila tried to defuse the situation, but in vain.

'You decide what you want out of this whole operation,' said Kang, as he picked his shirt off the floor. 'For me, the mission is over. Consider this my resignation.' As he reached the door, Kang turned around for one parting shot.

'You can question my strength, my tactics and my intelligence … After all, I did get captured. But you should never have questioned my integrity, you son–of–a–bitch,' he spat, turning back towards the door. As Kang's hand reached for the handle, the door opened and in walked Waris.

'Stop acting like a bunch of kids. That's exactly what those bastards want!' he said.

23

New Delhi, 31 May 2014

With Chinese and Pakistani agencies now hot on the heels of Waris's team and their operation exposed, it was going to be difficult for them to continue their clandestine activities. But Waris believed in providence and its strange ways of helping the righteous. He knew that dawn breaks only after the darkest hour. He waited for that divine signal.

And like the transformation of water to red wine by Jesus, Waris witnessed the colours of his government changing. He saw a wave of saffron taking hold of the Indian masses.

The new government's hardline stance with Pakistani mischief mongers and the prime minister's attitude towards its government—not to mention his retaliation to heavy shelling at the LoC—bolstered the morale and courage of Waris's men. The retired army officer and his team had never counted too much on government support. But one lurking insecurity was the chance of them being captured alive by the enemy. They knew they could be used as an excuse to embarrass India.

However, a tough government at the helm made a difference. A non-negotiating prime minister inspires and emboldens the soldiers to do better and crush the enemy with their entire might and confidence.

Waris decided that now was the chance to really get to his enemies.

Aware that the trauma Kang had suffered less than twenty-four hours ago—not to mention his decision to walk out—had made him more than a little cranky. Waris explained, 'We should definitely strike back, but we can't go after our targets directly as we've done so far.'

'They know we are after them, we won't be able to work as smoothly now. Of course, there will be restrictions on the movement of our friends Haaris Saeed and bigger hurdles for us,' Brijesh said.

'So are you saying that we abandon our mission halfway?' Vikrant asked, eyebrows raised.

'No, we will not abandon the mission at any cost. We'll kill them even if it means penetrating Pakistani boundaries to get them,' Brijesh said.

'Rein in your emotions, we'll get them all right. Even if they are hiding at the ends of the earth. But we need a bit of misdirection, deception ... Do you follow?' said Waris. He turned to Kang. 'I hope you will reconsider your decision to leave us. If you do, you'll join the team once they've set up the trap and drawn in the targets. I want you to stay in India and recuperate until then.'

Before Kang had a chance to protest that he was absolutely fine and ready to resume work at once, Vikrant placed his hand gently on the warrior's wounded shoulder and said, 'I agree, Kang. You need to rest and we need to find ways to take out our remaining targets undetected. Laila, I need updates on Azhar and Haaris Saeed.'

Brijesh walked over to Kang, and they exchanged glances. There was no need for words.

Laila had already grabbed her laptop, flipped open the screen and placed it elegantly on her knees. That image of elegance was shattered moments later when she started hammering at the keyboard, punctuating each command with a bout of curse words. 'What's wrong with this fucking thing?' she said irritably, as Vikrant came over to take a look. All he saw was gibberish.

'Ray, get in here!' Laila said into the intercom. 'Could you please access the D-server for me? I need real time updates on Azhar and Saeed.' Ray walked in with his laptop, placed it on a table and switched it on as the team huddled around. He fiddled with his spectacles and tried to restart his computer. 'I'm not sure what the problem is. Give me a second or two,' he said.

'It's the same gibberish,' confirmed Laila. Ray looked closer and declared gravely, 'That's not gibberish. It's an error message.'

Brijesh and Vikrant crossed their arms and looked at Ray, waiting for him to elaborate.

'Oh right, sorry,' sputtered the nervous analyst. 'An error message appears on the screen when a computer can't boot up its operating system.'

He tried to use a backdoor to access the data on his system but frustratingly for the team huddled around him, there seemed to be no representation of what he was typing onscreen. Vikrant nudged the analyst. 'What are you typing, genius? There's nothing showing up,' he said derisively.

'I've figured it out,' Ray announced triumphantly, lifting his fingers off the keyboard at last. 'The reason there's an operating system error is simply because there is no operating system on the computer.' He grinned at this quick diagnosis of the problem.

'You mean we've been fucking hacked and burned,' seethed a furious Laila.

'What do you mean, hacked and burned?' asked Waris.

'It means someone broke into our systems and erased them,' answered Ray.

'It's like a robber who breaks into a house and steals what he wants and then sets the house on fire to cover his tracks and destroy all evidence,' said Brijesh.

'There are no coding signatures or tell-tale signs or anything that indicates who it could be. Ukrainians, Syrians, Chinese, Americans – it could be anyone,' said Ray.

'Pakistanis?' offered Vikrant.

'Possible, but too sophisticated for the Pakistani hackers. Besides, there's the fact that their hacker groups are more interested in online vandalism – defacing foreign governments' websites, etc. The level of encryption we use on our servers is far more complex than that on government websites,' explained Ray. 'Also, I don't think the Pakistanis are at the level yet where they can break this encryption.'

'Without assistance,' added Brijesh.

'Excuse me?'

'They may not be able to break this encryption *without assistance*. But with assistance, let's say from the Chinese, surely they would be able to break into our servers?' asked Brijesh.

'In theory …'

'That's how they knew about our plans and were waiting for us at Jeddah,' Vikrant said, thinking aloud.

'Let's not forget that the Chinese helped us with Bradley's location. I really don't think they would want to screw both India and Pakistan over. But at the same time, playing us against each other is a win-win for the Chinese. Anyway, let's proceed with caution and reframe the next phase of our plan.' Waris spoke calmly. 'We have to assume that Kang's identity is known to them and so we can only reintroduce him much later in the plan. That works well for us, because he needs his wounds to heal.'

With the exception of Laila, who was busy typing on her iPad, the rest of the team nodded.

'Good. But that also means that we need another operative in the field. Ray, you will take Kang's place in the first phase,' declared Waris.

'… particularly now that security arrangements around Buddhist structures are being beefed up. In other news, a UNESCO team will be departing for Mansehra in Pakistan to participate in an archaeological dig to uncover an Ashoka pillar, believed to be nearly 2500 years old …' droned the inflection-free voice of the BBC World News anchor.

An archaeological dig to excavate the remains of an Ashoka pillar that had been discovered in Mansehra was an attractive proposition to the team for many reasons. The first was the obvious: it would give them a way to enter Pakistan. The other reason was that it would act as a perfect tool of misdirection, because if the ISI and other security agencies had their eyes on the dig, it gave the rest of the team a better chance of sneaking into the country undetected.

'It says here that the UNESCO team will be leaving from its Paris headquarters in eight days,' Laila read off her iPad.

Waris watched the screen, then turned to say, 'Vikrant and Brijesh will be the Bangladeshi members of the UNESCO dig. Being "Bangladeshi", it'll be easier for them to slip under the radar, while Ray and Laila can enter Pakistan as a couple, Ray in need of a kidney transplant.' Ray didn't need to say a word; the expression on his face betrayed his apprehension about suddenly having to turn into a field operative.

'Don't worry about it,' said Vikrant, as he playfully patted Ray on the shoulder. 'Laila is more than capable of looking after herself and you.' Laila narrowed her eyes at Vikrant, who continued, 'In any case, Brijesh and I won't be too far away.'

'I'm glad you're apprehensive,' said Waris. 'It's perfectly natural to be when you're about to be the bait. But before we push you out of your comfort zone, I want you to get hold of clean computers, encrypt them and use them from a different server to add Vikrant and Brijesh's names to the UNESCO dig list.'

He then looked over at Brijesh and Vikrant. 'Also, I want Ray to contact Sky's people and get on with the task of creating Bangladeshi passports and identities for Mushfiqur Mirza and Nasiruddin Rafique. You can decide who will be who.'

After a moment, Ray piped up, 'But what happens when they actually have to participate in the dig?'

'Use Wikipedia and learn a few terms. Use them liberally, without actually doing anything,' said Waris. Laila looked up from her tablet, where she was drawing up a list of the various tools and methods used by archaeologists.

'And what happens when they don't have any published articles or research papers among them? What if they are not known in archaeological circles? How will we even get Mushfique and Nasir on to the UNESCO list?' she asked.

'Let me handle that,' Waris said, 'and you take care of your end.'

'Why do we have to be part of the dig at all?' asked Kang. 'It will just be an additional headache.'

'An additional headache that will save us ten headaches down the road,' replied Brijesh.

'Speaking of headaches, you said something about a kidney transplant?' asked Ray.

'What do you know about "transplant tourism" in Pakistan?' asked Waris. 'The sale of kidneys is increasingly becoming a way for the poor to make money. After being convinced that they don't need both kidneys to live and that selling one kidney would make them a lot of money, they agree to the procedure. They are promised large sums of money, but are often duped, or worse, left with terrible infections, blood loss and in some cases, dead.' He continued, 'And why are kidneys such hot property?'

Ray didn't say a word. He knew he would hear the answer to the question.

'Because where there is this sort of supply, there must be some serious demand. And there is. People from across the world—'

'With the means to travel,' interrupted Brijesh.

'That's right. People from across the globe, who can afford the journey to Pakistan, buy kidneys relatively cheaply there, in the "kidney bazaar"', said Waris. 'Any questions?'

'Are we going there to sell or buy kidneys?' asked Laila through narrowed eyes.

'Buy, of course,' said Brijesh, swiftly.

'Thank God!' sighed Ray.

The plan would require Ray and Laila to pose as a rich couple flying into Karachi from Dubai. The backstory would be that a life of luxury and opulence had taken its toll on 'the husband', whose kidneys had stopped functioning. Doctors had recommended an immediate transplant and with his doting wife in tow, Ray was in Pakistan for just that. Locating a seller would not be difficult, Waris pointed out, as he handed Laila a printout with a list of four recommended kidney brokers from which to choose.

'You're probably wondering why I selected these guys. My first criterion was that the broker had to be a mid-level fellow; not too well-known and not too obscure. Secondly, he shouldn't have any obvious links to the ISI or the army. And finally, he should be located in a city that is convenient to us – Karachi. Why is it convenient? Because that is where a sizeable chunk of Muhajirs have settled down, and that could be good cover for us. In case of a crisis, we can lose ourselves among them. The Pakistan army and ISI will have a tough time tracing us,' explained Waris.

'Hang on a second,' said Vikrant.

Waris looked over at him. 'If we're going to this dig as Bangladeshis,' he said 'then we really should—'

'We should be fluent in Bengali,' said Brijesh, cutting him off.

'Yes,' nodded Vikrant.

Ray ventured, 'If you want, I know a man who could sit on the other end of the radio unit that you and Brijesh can wear in your ears, translate and give you real time responses to use in conversations. If that's all right.'

'That is unacceptable, Ray,' said Waris bluntly. 'What we need is for them to be reasonably capable of speaking in Bengali.'

'How the hell am I going to learn a new language overnight?' asked a shocked Vikrant.

'You will try,' said Waris firmly.

'It's not very difficult,' offered Ray helpfully.

'That's why you will teach them,' said Waris.

'What?' asked Ray, Vikrant and Brijesh in unison.

In a few hours, Brijesh and Vikrant were flipping through their brand new Bangladeshi passports, complete with photos in disguise. Men of the build and appearence of Brijesh and Vikrant would not blend in with a group of highly skilled archaeologists. In any case, wigs, fake beards, glasses and false teeth would be used to help the pair evade facial recognition programmes. Meanwhile, the wheels that would get the names of Mirza and Rafique on the UNESCO list had been set in motion. The only obstacles that remained were Kang's entry into Pakistan and the basic mastery of Bengali on the part of the two archaeologists.

Ray turned towards Brijesh and Vikrant. 'Say *aamar naam* … xyz.'

They both said in a chorus, '*Aamar naam xyz.*'

Ray restrained himself and said, 'Sir, in place of xyz you have to use your Bangladeshi name.'

'Oh, I was wondering why you were saying xyz after naam – what a strange language!' exclaimed Brijesh.

'It's not a strange language, it is the sweetest and most romantic language on earth,' Ray retorted.

'Of course we don't question that, we just have to absorb it's sweetness and understand the romance,' said Vikrant.

'A*amar naam* Mushfiq,' Brijesh said, and Ray nodded with approval.

'A*amar naam* Nasiruddin,' Vikrant joined the fray.

Ray went on to the next lesson.

'*Tomar naam ki?*' he said. And before they could make a mess of it, he explained, 'That means, what's your name?'

Both nodded, trying to mouth the question.

Ray then asked, '*Tumi kemon aacho?*'

Waris could see the two of them were struggling. Ray let out a small moan, no doubt feeling he had been saddled with the dumbest of students. The trio were sent off by Waris to a separate room, with a white board and other accessories. This was serious work.

Then Waris turned towards Kang, who had also been observing the mutilation of the Bengali language.

'You will be on the jatha that will go to Pakistan for Guru Nanak Dev's birth anniversary in November,' said Waris, adding, 'that will give you enough time to recuperate and it will keep you away from the ISI until the last phase.'

'And it will let me be myself – a Sikh,' added Kang, with more than a tinge of vindication in his voice.

24

Two communities have been the biggest victims of Partition in 1947: Shia Muslims and Sikhs, both minority groups. The Sikhs had suffered the most because their sacred places and religious shrines were also usurped by Pakistan. The holiest of Sikh shrines is in Nankana Sahib, the birthplace of their first guru, Guru Nanak, who was born in 1469 AD. The second holiest spot is the shrine of Guru Arjan Singh, the fifth guru, followed by that of Panja Sahib and others. But the Partition cruelly ensured that those shrines became a part of Pakistan.

This resulted in mindless violence, including trains returning to Amritsar with piles of Sikh corpses. The bloodshed continued for days. What should ideally have been managed and looked after by a Sikh council came under the control of the Pakistan Waqf Board.

Soon after assuming presidency in 1978, Zia ul Haq realized that he could exploit the Sikhs' devotion to further his own nefarious designs against India. In the eighties, he gave birth to K2 – Kashmir and Khalistan. The Sikhs were incited to rebel against the Indian government and seek an independent state of Khalistan, and thus began the hijacking of planes landing in Lahore. Here, the Khalistani terrorists were allowed to hold press conferences and spew venom against the Indian government's atrocities.

Later, Zia allowed the planes and passengers to return to India but the terrorists were granted amnesty and allowed to stay back in the Nankana Sahib precinct. Many Sikhs were misled and became a part of Pakistani machinations because they believed that they would get to spend their lives in this holy place, where they preferred to live and die.

Eventually, when the Indian government managed to crush the Khalistani movement, they ensured that Sikhs were allowed to visit these shrines on a regular basis. The Pakistani government also allowed them to do the same annually. The Shiromani Gurudwara Prabandhak Committee (SGPC) organizes four group visits called jathas every year – during Baisaikhi in March and the birth anniversaries of Maharaja Ranjit Singh, Guru Arjan Singh and of course, the birth anniversary of Guru Nanak, which is the biggest and largest jatha.

A jatha of over 4,000 pilgrims is organized every year on Guru Nanak Jayanti after it has been cleared by the Ministry of Home Affairs. These jathas include non-Sikhs as well. Thus the Indian government found a window of opportunity: they began sending 'messengers' to bring back information from post boxes or Indian sleeper assets, following clandestine meetings in Lahore's Anarkali market.

Until Inder Kumar Gujral became the prime minister and enforced his Gujral doctrine, RAW and military intelligence managed to ferret out significant actionable intelligence. But the Gujral doctrine had devastating effects on the Indian intelligence community operating within Pakistan. In exchange for an assurance that ISI officials would not work in India, Gujral dismantled RAW's architecture in Pakistan, as a result of which there are no agents posted there.

The absence of agents in Pakistan didn't perturb a man as irrepressible as Waris, who had long decided that if there were no agents there, he would ensure he put a few. Since the Jeddah fiasco in July, Waris had quietly been planning to penetrate Pakistan, to eliminate the brains behind 26/11. Finally, Kang had come to him with the idea of entering Pakistan as part of one of these jathas. Since they had already missed the July jatha which had left for the birth anniversary of Maharaja Ranjit Singh, they would try for the next on the occasion of Guru Nanak Jayanti, on 17 November.

While Brijesh, Vikrant and Laila were busy planning their foray into Pakistan through subterfuge and clever camouflage, Waris and Kang perfected their plans for the jatha visit to Nankana Sahib. They would leave for Lahore on 10 November, via the Wagah border special train.

When the team was ready and their roles clearly defined, Waris sought a meeting with his friend Sky to apprise him of their plans, together with his team. Even though Sky had all but disassociated himself from the team except for logistical support, Waris felt it necessary to keep him in the loop. After all, Sky needed to know what he would later be expected to profess no knowledge of. He arrived at their base, covertly and low-key, and the meeting began.

'All six of us will be in Pakistan at different times under various covers,' said Waris.

Sky was clearly taken aback at the audacity of having all six of the team in Pakistan.

'While Vikrant and Brijesh will travel to Islamabad via Dhaka as archaeologists and specialists, Laila and Ray will enter Pakistan via Dubai as Mr and Mrs Khalid Latif, who are US green card holders; Mr Latif has serious kidney issues.'

'Who is Khalid Latif?' Sky asked, though he had an inkling.

'Our Bangla bandhu Ray, with his frail look and emaciated face; he can pass off as a man on the verge of renal failure,' Waris said, with a chuckle.

'And since a single male can raise suspicion, his burkha-clad wife will give him company,' Laila added.

'After they have accomplished their mission in Mansehra, Vikrant and Brijesh will return via the Kashmir border, through the Uri sector. Since most of the Pakistani army and the ISI will concentrate on these two men on the run, we get enough leeway to do our work.'

'Why do you want to go to Pakistan?' Sky asked.

'For two reasons. I want to destroy the Lashkar headquarters, the Jamaat-ud-Daawa office in Muridke that sent us Kasab and his friends on 26/11. Also, I am sure of finding Haaris Saeed, the mastermind of the attacks, in the Muridke complex,' Waris said.

'You could get killed, sir,' said Kang.

'Oye Sardar, are you scared of dying?' asked Waris.

'No sir, not at all.'

'What's the plan?' Ray asked.

'You will give us technical support, while Laila, Kang and I will target Muridke,' said Waris.

'But how will you reach Muridke? It's difficult to blow up forty-three kilometres of the Lashkar complex. Even air-dropped bombs or American drones cannot have the desired impact,' Sky said.

'If an Indian reporter like Harinder Baweja can reach Muridke soon after 26/11 along with a video camera and a television channel can show footage of the complex, why can't we? Also, we don't want to target the whole complex; they also have a hospital, swimming pools, masjid, etc. We will only target the markaz, the training centre or school,' Waris summed up his plan.

'How will Laila contribute in the markaz?' Brijesh asked.

'Laila is my passport to the markaz. She will help us get in and out of Muridke. The Diwali celebrations will be organized by Kang and me,' Waris said.

'How do you get in and out of Pakistan?' Vikrant asked.

'Kang and I will go with the jatha to Nankana Sahib. Muridke is exactly 99 kilometres from there. If all goes well, we should be able to finish our job in the markaz and be back with the jatha in five to six hours,' said Waris.

'What about Mr and Mrs Khalid Latif?' Sky asked.

'Mr Latif will be booked into the special suite of the Sindh Institute of Urology Transplantation (SIUT) in Karachi, undergoing various tests as a prerequisite for a renal transplant and taking short naps in between. His wife can make a trip to her relatives in Lahore and back the same evening,' Waris said.

'We will return to the US via Dubai, postponing our transplant programme for later,' Laila finished.

'Things can go wrong, Ali; what is your back-up plan?' Sky said, with a hint of concern. He still hadn't recovered from Jeddah. None of them had.

'We could cross over from the Durand Line to enter Afghanistan via the Hindu Kush or we could become part of a smuggling caravan and move towards Balochistan to Iran, via the Sistan province ... There are several other possibilities,' said Waris, when suddenly Brijesh interrupted.

'Sir, things can always go horribly wrong, but we will improvize. Shift gears and tackle the situation with contingency plans. Just waiting, or hoping for things to be right won't help us,' he said.

'All right.' Sky made a placatory gesture, 'So what happens next?'

'Brijesh and Vikrant leave for Mansehra in a couple of days. Laila and Ray will leave for Dubai a week after that and take the flight to Karachi once they get a signal from me. Kang and I will board the special bus on 10 November as Jaspinder Singh Kang and Gurubaksh Singh,' Waris replied.

'How will we keep in touch?' Vikrant asked.

'Through WhatsApp, email and Terminal,' said Ray.

'Terminal?' asked Kang.

'It's a satellite phone. These days we get satphones which are highly advanced and can be used in remote areas. They don't need a cellular tower for signals. I would recommend Thuraya XT Dual. It can be hidden in your underwear and is a powerful satphone. If you wish, I can teach you guys to assemble in CKD condition,' Ray said.

'Please speak English, Ray,' Waris reprimanded him.

'I mean, "complete knock down" condition. I can also teach you guys how to dismantle it and then assemble it from CKD,' Ray said.

'Sky, we need at least three of these, one with each pair. To communicate among ourselves in case there is a change of plan.' Waris looked at his friend, who was already rising from his chair with a sombre face.

'You've got it, Waris,' Sky said. 'Just make sure you come back alive.'

The two men hugged briefly and Sky left, leaving the team to contemplate the enormity of the task ahead.

25

Apartment, New Delhi

Emperor Ashoka, dismayed by the destruction he had caused during the conquest of Kalinga, adopted Buddhism. Subsequently, he built numerous pillars bearing inscriptions detailing his new morality law. The Mansehra rock edicts in Pakistan are among the thirty-three inscriptions describing Buddhism and the concept of dharma.

'UNESCO is asking for NGOs to volunteer for the preservation of ancient rock edicts in Pakistan. The Department of Archaeology and Museums in Pakistan proposed that the edicts be recognized as World Heritage Sites in 2004. It seems that proposal has gone through now,' Brijesh said, pointing to the screen of his laptop.

'If we can pull this off, we have a good chance of entering Pakistan. But remember that it's close to Abottabad, where Bin Laden was hiding, and there is a military academy nearby,' he added.

'It shouldn't be too tough.' Laila said. 'I've been working on IDs and covers for the two of you. You need to have a look at the UNESCO applicant forms though.'

'Already have,' Brijesh said, as he spun the laptop around to face Laila, who was preparing an omelette for herself. 'Not too complex.'

Vikrant walked into the room, looking fresh after a hot shower.

'I've filled out my form already,' he said, as he pulled on a white vest.

Laila frowned at him. 'I thought I asked you not to do any such thing, Vikrant. Not until we have visas for your fake passports and all the other paperwork.'

'Nasiruddin Rafique.' He looked back at her. 'I know who I'm going to be. I've done my research and looked him up. He runs a small NGO in Dhaka, and there are no pictures of him on the net.'

'You had to provide an email ID, didn't you? His original is Nrafiq72@gmail.com,' she read from her laptop. 'I hope you haven't used that one.'

Vikrant sighed and lay down on the bed.

'Grant me some intelligence, will you? I've used the same ID under the Hotmail domain name. UNESCO will send the mails to the ID I've provided.'

'If you're so certain about this,' Laila said, 'help Brijesh set up his as well. His name, according to the cover, is Mushfiqur Rehman Mirza. He's your aide. The second in-charge. Nobody needs to talk to him.'

'Well,' Vikrant smiled wryly, 'that will be a nice change.'

Brijesh shrugged his shoulders. He pulled the laptop back towards himself, and typed something rapidly. Vikrant peeped over his shoulder and watched him fill out the UNESCO application form online. Laila began to eat her omelette, ignoring them.

'What story do we go to them with exactly?' Vikrant shot a quizzical glance at Laila, feigning ignorance to annoy her. 'Can we go over it again?'

Laila rolled her eyes and assumed an authoritative tone.

'I'm going to go over this from the top, guys. The two of you will pose as Bangladeshi archaeological volunteers who want to help preserve the Mansehra edicts. We – and by we, I mean you two – propose that with the help of our laser mapping technology, you will create three-dimensional models. The process will be cheap and will conserve the heritage sites of Mansehra. Of course, you have to sound as sincere as you can. That's a hard task in itself.'

Brijesh smiled. 'It sounds all right, but do we have the technology ready? In case they want a demo?'

'Of course,' she replied. 'Ray is working on a presentation. The technology isn't uncommon. You must insist that these edicts are under the constant threat of being destroyed by religious zealots. Don't come across as too jingoistic, though. And yes, we have procured two Bangladeshi sim cards for you guys, be ready to take calls from UNESCO.

'When will Ray be sending them?'

'Sometime this evening,' Laila replied. 'The IDs will also be ready by then. All you need to do now is to wait for UNESCO to get in touch with you. It should be like clockwork from there.'

'Clockwork from there,' Vikrant mimicked her. He laughed, and Laila realized he had been teasing her all along. The A-Team was rallying nicely; at last, their spirits were up, now that the new mission was in place.

'That's rather mature,' Laila said, pushing her plate aside. 'Now let's go check on Kang. He seems to be responding well to the medication.'

It was seven in the evening when Brijesh's secure phone began to buzz. He squinted at the number and looked at Laila.

'It's Ray,' he said, as he answered it. 'Tell me, Ray, what have you got for me?'

'I've sent a presentation to you, regarding the 3D reconstruction and mapping procedures. There is also a spreadsheet which will break down the cost of the entire procedure.'

'Surely you haven't called to tell me just that?'

'Of course not,' Ray replied. 'There's going to be a slight hitch. UNESCO has already received a proposal from a certain Singaporean firm that is, believe it or not, genuinely interested in reconstructing the edicts using the same technology.'

'Well, that's not good. How similar is their technology though?'

'Very. They're doing it for a cheaper price too, and the last I heard, they've already been signed on.'

Brijesh was silent for a moment. Then he sighed and said, 'Thanks, Ray. We'll see what we can do. Can you send in a dossier on the firm that has sent the proposal?'

'Already have,' Ray said.

'Thanks. Bye.' Brijesh disconnected the phone and turned to Laila. 'Check the inbox.'

'What's happened?'

Brijesh called Vikrant and explained the problem. They looked at the computer screen, at a picture of an Asian woman with long straight hair, in her mid-forties, who smiled disarmingly at them.

'Nicole Wong,' Vikrant said with a wry smile. 'So she's the one in charge of the reconstruction.'

'Yes, she is also the head of the NGO.'

Upon further research, they realized that Nicole Wong's father was a well-to-do entrepreneur who had started the NGO on his daughter's insistence.

'What next?' Laila asked. 'We can't conduct our reconnaissance any other way.'

There was silence, as Brijesh walked to the mini fridge and pulled out a can of Coke.

'Put Waris sir on the line,' he said. She nodded and dialled the number instantly.

'Hello,' Waris said wearily. 'This had better be important. You don't know how difficult it is to get sleep at my age.'

Brijesh kept his Coke aside and spoke softly into the phone. 'Sorry to have disturbed you, sir.'

'Well, go on.'

'There's a slight glitch in our plan. As you are aware, our cover was to infiltrate Mansehra as UNESCO volunteers and offer to reconstruct the Ashokan edicts with our technology.'

'Yes, so what's the problem?'

'A Singaporean agency has already offered to help them using the very same technology. And they're doing it for less.'

'Who runs it?'

'A certain Nicole Wong. Apparently, her father is a hotshot real-estate tycoon. And her LinkedIn profile shows that she has studied Eastern Asian history at Cambridge.'

'Wow,' Waris said. 'Someone is actually bothered about those edicts?'

'Clearly,' Brijesh said.

There was a brief pause. Brijesh sipped his Coke while Laila and Vikrant stared at the screen.

Waris eventually broke the silence. 'Hop onto the next flight to Singapore.'

Brijesh raised an eyebrow at Vikrant. Laila at once looked up the next available flights.

'Tomorrow early morning seems plausible, sir.'

'Vikrant, Brijesh, pack your bags. Laila, stay with Kang.'

And without another word, their leader disconnected the call.

Helipad Rooftop Bar, 6 Eu Tong Sen Street, Singapore

Vikrant and Brijesh had been tailing her for three days. Nicole Wong's life seemed ordinary. She left her house at eight in the morning for a jog and would be back by nine-thirty, after which, she sent her eight-year-old son off to school. She was a divorcee. She freshened up and refuelled herself for another ordinary day. She stepped out, and drove an electric blue Toyota Prius to her father's seven-storey real estate office, the top floor of which was used solely for her NGO and welfare activities. It was a Saturday and she wouldn't be long at the office. At seven in the evening she met a girlfriend and they headed out together. Brijesh and Vikrant tailed them in their black rented Honda sedan and took the elevator after them to the Helipad Rooftop Bar. Vikrant wore a sharp black blazer over a crisp white shirt. He ruffled his hair and opened a few buttons to show that he had just finished with a long day of tedious desk-work. Brijesh wore a casual blue jacket over a white T-shirt, with a pair of dark blue jeans. After looking around for a bit, they finally spotted Nicole, with a woman who looked roughly her age.

'Go work your charm.' Brijesh winked at Vikrant. 'On the right one, though.'

'We don't want any accidents.'

'Don't act suspicious.'

'You know what, Brij?'

'Don't ever call me that again.' Brijesh looked annoyed. 'And no, I don't know what.'

'We both need a date. And, clearly, the two of them need dates as well.'

'I don't think—'

'Come on,' Vikrant urged, smiling. 'Be a man. Besides, that way, there is no fear of the wrong one being swept away by my charm.'

Brijesh looked at him sternly, then nodded. They walked over to the two women, who seemed to be swapping stories over a plate of shrimp cocktail and flutes of champagne.

'Let me do the talking,' Vikrant told Brijesh in his ear. 'We use our real names and we are new in town, working at the Indian Bank on a short-term project.'

Brijesh nodded and walked towards the one he knew wasn't Nicole.

'Hey,' he said. 'I'm Brijesh. And you are?'

The woman hesitated for a moment as Vikrant walked up to Brijesh.

'Forgive my friend,' he said, looking at Nicole. 'He may have had a drink too many. He loses his way with words when he's with pretty women.'

'Michelle,' the other woman then replied with a smile, looking at Brijesh. 'And my friend here is Nicole.'

She had long jet-black hair and a seductive smile.

'I'm Vikrant,' Vikrant said, putting a confident hand out towards Nicole. 'Mind if I buy you a drink?'

The women looked slightly amused by the two Indian men popping up out of nowhere. They looked at each other and shrugged.

'Sure,' Nicole replied. Vikrant handed Brijesh his wallet with a display of nonchalance and sat beside Nicole. Brijesh walked over to the bar.

'So, what do the two of you do? Are you new in town?' she asked.

'Yeah,' Vikrant smiled, making eye contact. 'We are working on a short-term project at a bank. Heading back to our country in a couple of days, and we thought we'd soak in some Singaporean atmosphere before that.'

Brijesh walked back over with two glasses of the Helipad special mojitos. He placed one in front of Nicole and the other he gave to Michelle.

'I was just telling them about how we are new in town,' Vikrant said to Brijesh.

'Don't worry,' Michelle said. 'We'll make you feel at home, even if only for a night.'

'How about we continue the celebrations at our hotel then?' Vikrant said.

Nicole smiled and sipped her mojito.

'Why not?'

They split up in pairs and drove back to the Hilton hotel. Vikrant and Nicole took her car, while Brijesh and Michelle took the Honda. On the way, Nicole told him about what she did and how much she was enjoying working on the NGO's latest project, which had something to do with some edicts in Pakistan. Vikrant appeared to be disinterested but smiled politely through the journey.

Nicole couldn't keep her hands off him once they arrived at the hotel, and she started kissing him in the elevator on the way to the room.

Vikrant fumbled with the key card clumsily before he finally managed to open the door. She pushed him into the room authoritatively.

Vikrant had never slept with an older woman before. Well, there's always a first time, he thought to himself. She pulled his jacket off, and then his shirt. She pushed him on to the bed and admired his perfectly chiselled upper body. Without any hesitation, he reached for her and they made passionate love until they were both exhausted and beads of sweat had formed on Nicole's hairline.

'That was something,' Vikrant said as he got off the bed. 'Want another drink?'

'Yes, please,' she smiled. Vikrant poured her one and emptied into it the contents of a little sachet that sat hidden beside the bottle. She'll be pretty ill by tomorrow morning, he thought.

'You don't look like a banker,' she told him, as she scanned his muscular body in awe.

'You don't look like a social worker. More like a supermodel,' Vikrant smiled as he handed her the drink. She took two long sips and smiled.

'Tell me when you're ready again,' she said.

'I'm always ready,' Vikrant grinned.

The next morning, Nicole woke up in her own house. She was confused. She was wearing what she had worn the previous night and Michelle was fast asleep beside her. She looked at her phone and saw that it was one in the afternoon. She realized she hadn't dropped her son to school, but then it hit her that it was a Sunday. She looked around her and found a note. She squinted at it.

'You seemed in no condition to drive, but directed us to your house well. We had a great time last night. Your friend seemed out of it too, so we asked her to spend the night at your house. We hope to see you again some time soon. All the best with the Pakistani edicts you told us about. Regards, Vikrant and Brijesh.'

Another wild night out. She felt feverish and then, without warning, she vomited on the floor.

Islamabad

Vikrant had a rather uneasy flight from Singapore to Islamabad. He hadn't been able to catch any sleep and his conscience was bothering him. He had never carried out an operation that involved tricking a woman. He tried his best to get some rest, but sleep evaded him. There was a lot to be done in the days to come and he knew how much was at stake for him and his country.

When he got down at Islamabad under his Bangladeshi alias, the man at immigration seemed to be very interested in him. He asked him various questions about Bangladesh and UNESCO, then took his passport away for further verification. He came back smiling, apologized for the delay and wished him luck.

He made his way to the JW Marriott hotel where a suite on the eighth floor had been reserved under his false name. He unpacked, undressed and stood under the shower for a good half hour. Then he ordered himself tandoori chicken through room service. He waited for a while, and then brought out his laptop and placed a call to Brijesh.

Brijesh had boarded another flight and would have landed an hour before him. They didn't want to take the chance of being seen together publicly, especially after the failed attempt on Azhar that had left Kang severely injured.

'Yes,' Brijesh said as soon as he answered the phone. 'I'll come to your suite in an hour. I'm on the fifth floor.'

'Good,' Vikrant replied. 'We need to make the arrangements as soon as possible.'

'You go ahead and call the rent-a-car agency,' Brijesh said. 'Book one for yourself for the moment. I'm still trying to figure out how our stuff will reach us.'

They were close to the end of their most ambitious mission. Vikrant got up and stared out at Islamabad from his window. He picked up his cellphone and searched for a good service cab agency. He found one online and dialled the number.

'Salaam alaikum,' said a voice. 'Regent Taxi Service.'

'Alaikum salaam,' Vikrant replied. 'My name is Nasiruddin Rafique. I plan to go to Mansehra by road.'

'It won't be a problem, sir. What kind of car would you like?'

'I have some equipment to carry. I've been sent here by UNESCO on a project regarding the Mansehra edicts.'

'So you'll need an SUV?'

'Yes, please. And you'll be sending a driver with me, right?'

'Yes sir, of course. Will a Toyota SUV do?'

'Perfect. So we'll leave in the morning, day after tomorrow. I'll message you the details. I'm at the Marriott.'

'Inshallah, sir. I'll call tomorrow to confirm.'

'Khuda hafiz,' Vikrant said with a strong Bangladeshi accent.

The chicken had arrived, but Vikrant didn't feel like having it any more. He decided to lie down for a while, until Brijesh decided to visit him. Within a few moments, he drifted into a deep slumber.

'Sir, Vikrant plans to make his way to Mansehra in a rented car. Once he assesses the scenario, he'll signal for me to follow.'

'And what scenario is he assessing?' Waris asked Brijesh.

'He's going to meet the Pakistani personnel from the Museums department and explain the technicalities to them. In the interim, how do we get the equipment? I could disassemble them so they can fit into our so called "equipment cases".'

'Sounds good. The equipment is already on its way. A courier will come soon and deliver it to your hotel, just give me your room number,' Waris said. 'One thing; you might have to arrange for the grains,' he added.

'The equipment is already here! How did you …'

'I'll explain later. Keep me updated.'

'I will, sir. Thank you.'

Brijesh took a lift to Vikrant's floor. He looked ten years older than he was, he thought, looking in the mirror. There were wrinkles he had never seen before, his temples were greying and his eyes looked tired and soulless. To add to this, he had an unruly salt-and-pepper beard which he needed to maintain his Bangladeshi cover. He would have to shape it soon enough, or the folks at UNESCO might laugh at how he couldn't 'reconstruct' his hair but wanted to reconstruct a heritage site. He knocked at Vikrant's door.

Vikrant opened it, and without as much as acknowledging him, turned around and went back in. He wore a plain T-shirt and a pair of Nike track pants. His beard looked disastrous too, but he seemed to look the part more than Brijesh did.

'I'll be leaving the day after tomorrow in the morning,' Vikrant told Brijesh. 'What about the equipment?'

'It will be delivered to us tonight,' Brijesh replied as he picked up a piece of chicken that Vikrant hadn't eaten. 'I'll go over first and set everything up. You should get some rest. You look like shit.'

'This entire mission,' Vikrant said abruptly. 'It's emotionally draining. I look at ordinary people around us and wonder, can you and I ever lead a life like them?'

Brijesh sat silently.

'I've thought about it and I don't think so,' Vikrant continued. 'I mean, we were destined for this. This is our life. I can't imagine living it any differently. Even though I want a family, I'm not sure I'll be able to be there for them.'

Brijesh still didn't say anything. He just stared at the wall.

'It makes me stop and wonder,' Vikrant said. 'Will this ever end? Will there ever be peace? So that everyone can just live their own fucking lives?'

'It's a choice we made, Vikrant.'

'Don't get me wrong, brother. I'm not regretting any of this. If I could start my life all over again, I'd still choose the same road.'

'It's because of people like you and me that everyone else has a shot at normal life. And we aren't doing this for recognition.'

Vikrant smiled at Brijesh.

'So, what do you plan to do after this mission?'

'Try and lead a normal life,' Brijesh replied. 'Whatever that means. Unless, of course, duty calls.'

'My plans exactly,' Vikrant said.

'Look, the consignment is expected at my room anytime now. I'd better go and wait for the guy,' Brijesh said.

'Fabulous. The old man is so resourceful that sitting in Delhi he can get a sophisticated sniper gun delivered to us in our hotel room in Islamabad,' Vikrant muttered.

'We have to arrange for the bullets. He is only sending us the gun.' Brijesh smiled and started for the door.

'Vikrant,' he said suddenly, turning and looking at him. 'For what it's worth, we are each other's family. Now get some rest. There is work to do.'

26

Islamabad, 5:30 a.m.

'Salaam alaikum.' The driver flashed a toothy grin at Vikrant, as he helped him stuff his two heavy equipment bags into the boot. 'I am Abdul Hafeez.'

'Alaikum salaam, Abdul bhai,' Vikrant replied. 'I am Nasiruddin Rafique.'

'You look sleepy, sir. You can lie down at the back. It's quite a distance from here to Mansehra. Around two and a half hours.' Vikrant nodded and smiled. 'I slept well enough, bhai.' Abdul Hafeez shrugged his thin shoulders. He looked like a man in his mid-twenties. His beard was scanty and he wore a tight skullcap. He assumed his position in the driver's seat as Vikrant got in the back. He switched the air-conditioning on, muttered 'Bismillahir Rehmanir Rahim' and started the engine.

The roads weren't crowded at all and they sped up the clear stretches at a steady speed of seventy to eighty kilometres.

'Rafique bhai?' Hafeez turned and looked at Vikrant. 'Is it okay if I play music?'

'Of course.' Vikrant smiled back. 'What kind?'

'I have Salman bhai and Shah Rukh bhai's songs,' he grinned. 'Who do you like more?'

Vikrant sighed, having come from a land that constantly played the songs of these two Bollywood superstars. He replied, 'Any Nusrat Fateh Ali Khan?'

'Yes bhai, of course. Is he big in Bangladesh too?'

'He's big all over the world, Hafeez bhai.'

The man smiled and fiddled with a disc set, then finally pulled out a Nusrat Fateh Ali Khan compilation and slid it into the music player. The soulful music changed Vikrant's sombre mood. He hummed along to the pleasantly crackling voice of the maestro. Abdul Hafeez seemed to speed less; it was calming him down too.

'Which hotel will you be staying at, bhai?'

'Hotel Shamiana,' Vikrant replied. 'That's where the other members of the crew are.'

'Are you shooting a film?'

Vikrant laughed. 'No, Hafeez bhai. We aren't shooting a film. There are some historical writings on stone called the Ashokan edicts there. I'm part of an international organization called UNESCO.'

'So,' Abdul Hafeez said. 'You are going to film them?'

'Yes,' Vikrant said softly.

'Sounds interesting. How is it back in Bangladesh? From which part are you?'

'Dhaka,' Vikrant said, with an air of finality. Hafeez didn't ask anything else, taking the hint. Vikrant realized his tone had been a little rude and tried to make amends.

'Are you married, Hafeez bhai?'

'Yes,' the man replied. 'I have four children. What about you?'

Vikrant was thrown off guard.

'No,' he said immediately.

'Why not?'

'Haven't fallen in love with a woman who has returned the favour,' he half smiled.

'Well, we don't have the luxury of falling in love here. We marry who our parents get us married to.'

'Well, if it's any consolation, love is over rated.'

Abdul Hafeez shook his head and smiled. He went on to speak about his three sons and one daughter. How the sons went to madrassas and the daughter was made to do household chores. He spoke about how he knew the system was backward, but couldn't do anything about it. And then he touched upon the topic of terrorism, which was rampant in his beloved country.

He interrupted himself before getting carried away, when a small shanty came into view by the roadside. 'Do you want to stop at a dhaba for some breakfast?'

'Sure,' Vikrant replied. 'That would be nice.'

They parked the Toyota Innova outside the little dhaba, then walked in and sat on the low wooden plank which was meant to be a seat. Nobody was around, except two young boys and their father, who was clearly the owner of the dhaba.

'Where are we exactly?' Vikrant asked Hafeez.

'Just a little ahead of Abbottabad,' he replied. 'You know, where Osama was killed.'

Vikrant nodded silently. One of the young boys came up to ask what they'd like to eat.

'Beta, bring us five paneer parathas and two glasses of lassi,' Hafeez said to him, without consulting Vikrant. The boy went away. 'I hope you don't mind having what I ordered. It's delicious.'

Vikrant smiled to show his approval.

'So, all this while, when Osama was here, did the locals know his identity?', he asked.

'Of course,' Hafeez replied instantly. 'Everyone knew. In fact, we all laughed about the fact that our government denied all knowledge, considering they put him here.'

Vikrant was silent, then he asked Hafeez in a low tone, 'What do you think of people like Osama?'

Hafeez looked surprised at the question. He gazed outside the dhaba, towards the Innova. 'People treat him like a hero,' he said finally. 'According to them, he was the answer to the injustice the kafirs of the world meted out to us Muslims.'

'But what do you think about him?'

'I'm not too clear about it myself. Our religion never justified killing.'

'Exactly, Hafeez bhai. Personally, I think that because of Muslims like him, Muslims like you and I don't get a chance to lead a normal life.'

'Forget Osama,' Hafeez said. 'He is too difficult a man to understand. Some of his actions, I would like to think, are justified. But then, there are many that aren't.'

At this juncture, the little boy came running with two brass glasses brimming over with lassi. He ran back and returned with a plate of parathas dripping with butter.

'Well, here's a heart attack on a plate.'

They picked up a paratha each.

'Did you hear about Umavi's death?'

'Yes,' Vikrant replied. 'He died of an allergy.'

'Are you that naive? You think all it took to kill that devil were some hazelnuts?'

'Well,' Vikrant shrugged. 'I don't know much. What do you think?'

'Soon after his death, Wajid Mir died of a heart attack in a cricket stadium.'

Vikrant drank a mouthful of lassi.

'I think it's the Americans,' Hafeez whispered. 'They've killed the two of them. They think they're preventing another Osama in the making.'

'Well,' Vikrant said. 'They did make Osama after all.'

There was a brief silence, while both of them dug into their parathas and polished off the lassi. The dhaba owner had a satisfied smile on his face as he came up to them.

'Aur kuch, janaab?' he asked.

'Nahin, bhai,' Vikrant replied. 'Do you want to kill us?'

They laughed and Vikrant left several red Pakistani hundred-rupee notes on the table. He got up, but Hafeez continued to sit.

'Don't you want your change?'

'It's okay, Hafeez bhai. He has two children.'

'Shukriya,' the delighted dhaba owner said, clasping his sweaty hands. Vikrant smiled, put his arm around Hafeez's shoulders and walked back towards the car.

'It's interesting, isn't it? God's way of justice?' Hafeez asked introspectively, as they drove on. 'First He lets those men kill hundreds of innocent people, and then He gets them killed himself. What is He trying to prove?'

'I don't think that God should be blamed for killing these people, Hafeez bhai. Anyway, play that Salman Khan CD now. We need some frivolity to lighten us up.'

Soon, Salman's chartbusters rocked the car, putting an end to any serious conversation.

Later that afternoon, Vikrant checked into Hotel Shamiana. It was an ordinary looking, pale green building with its name painted in blue in both Urdu and English. It wasn't taller than three storeys but was said to be one of the best hotels in that part of Mansehra. The most expensive one here was Hotel Aashiana. Word had it that it was visited by the big shots of Mansehra. That's what Hafeez said anyway.

Vikrant unpacked his personal things and, with Hafeez's help, deposited the two huge bags of equipment on the carpeted floor. A strong scent of rose lingered in the air.

'So,' Hafeez said. 'When will you be needing me next?'

'I'll wait for my assistant,' Vikrant said. 'He'll turn up in the evening, inshallah. We'll take a couple of days here. What's your plan? Will you wait around with me, or will you come back when I call you?'

'It's up to you, bhai. But it would be better if I waited around, rather then going and coming back. I could find myself lodging somewhere in the vicinity. I do it all the time. Besides, I can drive you around whenever you need me. There's one hitch, though.'

'And what's that?' Vikrant looked up at him as he pulled out a plain polo T-shirt from his bag.

'We'll charge you rent for the car as per the number of days you spend here. And you'll have to pay for my lodging and food.'

Vikrant smiled. 'That's not a problem, Hafeez bhai. I'll go in for a shower now. Call me down when it's time for namaaz. You have my number.'

From his wallet he pulled out a 500-rupee note.

'Have something to eat.'

'Khuda hafiz,' Hafeez said with a smile.

'These are the specifications of the sniper,' Brijesh said, once he had checked into his room and invited Vikrant in. He put his laptop on, then opened up a file that Ray had forwarded to him on his secure ID. It had a picture of a firearm in all its glory.

'The McMillan TAC-50 Caliber sniper rifle.' Brijesh got up from his rather shaky chair and clasped his hands. 'This is the same rifle that Rob Furlong of the Canadian army used to execute a confirmed 2430 metre shot in Afghanistan. He set the world record for the longest successful tactical shot in combat.'

'Wow.' Vikrant was impressed. 'That is some distance.'

'Yes,' Brijesh said. 'Hopefully, we let Mr Furlong keep his record, and try to take the shot from a radius of anywhere between 1.5 and 2 km. Despite its power, the TAC-50 is surprisingly easy to shoot, according to Ray.'

'Why is that?'

'Some technical mumbo-jumbo about the sniper owing its proprietary design to the McMillan muzzle brake and geometry of stock. But here's the real problem.'

Brijesh sat on his haunches and unzipped his bag. He pulled out a large glossy map that explained the anatomy of the rifle and spread it out on the bed.

'There are fifteen basic parts, which we need to get right in order to hit the mark. Remember, we can't have more than one shot.'

'True,' Vikrant said. 'If we miss, he has plenty of time to get away before we get another shot in. Also, we need to keep in mind the dynamics of the environment. The speed of the wind and its direction will affect the bullet's trajectory.'

'Absolutely,' Brijesh said. 'When Azhar is addressing the rally, he will not be moving too much. We need to find a safe vantage point before that. It should not be too far away, nor too close. The closer we are, the greater our chances of getting caught. And then, there's always the technological uncertainty. What if we miss the shot because of faulty reassembling?'

'Hasn't Ray tested it to ensure that it's as efficient even after being broken down and reassembled?'

'This is a sniper rifle, Vikrant. Not a handgun. Besides, it's an anti-materiel sniper and can penetrate shields and brick walls. It's not meant to be subtle.'

'I still don't get your point,' Vikrant replied. 'You mean to say it won't be as effective if we reassemble it?'

'I can't say for sure,' Brijesh said. 'There's always a possibility of the accuracy wavering by approximately half a metre. That's what Ray said, anyway. But he had a solution.'

'Ray always has a solution,' Vikrant said, smiling nervously. 'They're usually silly.'

'Not this time, though. It does involve some collateral damage.'

'Innocent people?'

'No,' Brijesh said. 'The people who might be on stage with Azhar during the rally. We have no idea who they could be.'

'If they're on stage with him,' Vikrant replied, 'I couldn't care a fuck. Let's wipe them off the face of the earth.'

'Anyway, there's an explosive bullet called the Raufoss Mk 211,' Brijesh said. 'It's an anti-materiel projectile that causes a small explosion as soon as it hits the target. When Azhar is talking, he's bound to be wearing a bulletproof vest. This will make it look like a joke. Also, since it's a .50 calibre bullet, it has lesser chances of drifting and will give us a higher probability of getting a clean shot.'

Vikrant ran his hand through his unkempt hair, then smoothed his unruly beard.

'Where do we get these bullets?'

'They're of Norwegian make, apparently. But you can get something close to them at the hathyar mandi. For a price, of course.'

'I didn't know there was an arms bazaar in Mansehra.'

'Brother,' Brijesh laughed. 'We are in Pakistan. An arms bazaar here is the equivalent of a Starbucks in America.'

Vikrant laughed, then picked up the map.

'Well,' he said. 'The assembling will require some practice. Even for us. And we can assemble any short-range weapon blindfolded.'

'Yes,' Brijesh said. 'For now, I've made arrangements to visit the arms bazaar. It's not too difficult to get in if we grease the right palms.'

'Are you sure these backyard hacked munitions will give us what's required?'

'Not sure, but we can test them; they allow that there too.'

'Works well for us,' Vikrant chuckled. 'I hope Waris continues to be as generous with his funds after we are done with our mission. I'll take my wife to see the Sistine Chapel.'

'Since when do you have a wife?' Brijesh raised an eyebrow.

'I don't,' Vikrant said, with a straight face.

'Then how do you know she'll want to see the Sistine Chapel?'

'I don't,' he said. 'But I want to.'

'Well,' Brijesh smiled through his thick beard, 'for now we'll be visiting the hathyar mandi.'

Brijesh and Vikrant walked out of their hotel at seven-fifteen that evening, wearing plain kurtas and pajamas. They wore skullcaps and looked eerily similar. They had scarves wrapped around their necks, which they could use to hide their faces if required. They arrived at the arms bazaar a few minutes after eight. Walking was easier than having Hafeez with them. After all, what was the UNESCO doing buying expensive projectile weapons?

'Have you spoken to the guy from the Pakistani museum department?' Vikrant asked Brijesh.

'Yeah,' he replied. 'He's going to meet us at the foot of the edicts tomorrow. We'll proceed with him and he will "educate" us about them. After which, we explain what we plan to do with them.'

'I have no clue about the shit we'll feed him.'

'We'll improvise,' Brijesh replied. Suddenly, they heard a flurry of gunshots. Involuntarily, Vikrant's hand reached for the gun at his hip while Brijesh looked amused.

'We're nearing the bazaar,' he said with a half-smile. 'They have an open shooting range, where they can try out the guns.'

'Oh,' Vikrant said, embarrassed. 'Let's make this quick, anyway. I'm hungry.'

They walked towards the high gate, which was guarded by two pot-bellied security guards.

'What do you want to buy?' one of them asked Brijesh. The other one sized up Vikrant.

'Salaam alaikum. We are here to buy bullets,' Brijesh replied earnestly. 'For shikaar, bhaijaan. We are travelling to Alaska next week for a hunting competition.'

'Where's Alaska? Are you locals?'

'From Rawalpindi,' Brijesh replied with a smile.

'I'm afraid I can't allow you in.'

'Bhaijaan, this competition means a lot to us. We will win lots of money if we manage to get through. And for that, we need bullets to practice.'

'How much money will you win?'

'We don't know, but it's in dollars. Please, bhaijaan. We'll be indebted to you.'

'No need to be indebted,' the guard said with a grin. 'You can give me a token now itself.'

Brijesh looked at Vikrant, then fished out his wallet and handed the men two blue thousand-rupee notes each. Their eyes glittered. He kicked open the rickety gate without saying anything, and thy let the shikaaris enter right through.

Vikrant sputtered sardonically, 'Well, whether India or Pakistan, the slimy ones can always be bought!'

'Greed is universal,' said Brijesh.

They walked into a small, dimly lit tin enclosure. Two men were leaving with a plastic bag filled with tiny bullets.

The shopkeeper was clearly in a hurry. 'Salaam alaikum, what do you want?'

'Walaikum assalam. I want a .50 explosive bullet.'

The shopkeeper raised his eyebrows, then nodded. He got up and walked into the back of the shop. His hands were scarred and the shop smelled of smelt iron and gunpowder. There was another man sitting in the corner. He was bent with age and his beard was grey. Not much of his face could be seen, but his mouth was scarred.

'Salaam alaikum, chacha,' Vikrant said to him.

The old man nodded. He raised both his hands and indicated in a blessing. The shopkeeper came back inside.

'That's my Abbu,' he said. 'He can't speak. He was in the same business and, one day, while testing a weapon, a projectile pierced his mouth. He lost his tongue.'

Brijesh and Vikrant nodded silently. The shopkeeper placed a metal box on the ground in which there were three bullets.

'These are similar to the Raufoss of Norway,' he said, as he handed one to Vikrant and another to Brijesh. Similar in dimension to a Sheaffer pen. 'I have only three left.'

'We'll take them,' Vikrant said. 'How much?'

'Rs 5,000 per bullet,' the man said, expecting them to bargain. Instead, Vikrant took out his wallet and counted the money. There was an extra thousand-rupee note in the wad he handed over. The shopkeeper looked at Vikrant and Vikrant smiled at him.

'Khuda hafiz,' he said to the older man, as Brijesh walked out of the hut with the small tin box. Vikrant was about to leave, when he turned around and stopped.

'I also need three rounds for a regular Walther PPK, a tiny block of Semtex and three shotgun shells.'

The man nodded, went inside and brought out the bullets. Vikrant handed him another thousand-rupee note and left.

Brijesh looked questioningly at the plastic bag in Vikrant's hand.

'The C4 will be used to destroy the sniper. And the remaining bullets are to show the guards at the entrance what we've been shopping for. Just in case they ask. Hide the .50s in your pajamas and I'll hide the C4 in mine. If they do get nosey, they'll only see ordinary pistol rounds.'

'Well,' Brijesh said, as they walked towards the exit. 'If you blow up money like this, you won't be visiting the Sistine Chapel anytime soon.'

They laughed and rather surprisingly, the guards at the gate smiled at them as they left.

'Salaam alaikum,' Vikrant said to the tiny, bespectacled man in a crisp white shirt. 'I am Nasiruddin Rafique. This is my friend Mushfiq Mirza.'

'Hello, I am Adnan Ghuman. The UNESCO people tell me the two of you run an NGO somewhere in Bangladesh?'

'Yes,' Vikrant said, in his affected Bangladeshi accent. 'That's correct.'

The three men were sitting in the lobby of their hotel and Vikrant and Brijesh sat opposite Ghuman. It was still early in the morning. After a quick breakfast, they were to leave in the Innova along with Hafeez bhai. Ghuman had brought his own hired car and was going to lead the way.

'So,' Ghuman continued, 'I have seen your project proposal. Why don't you tell me the details now?'

Vikrant looked at Brijesh, who was smoothing his Maulana-like beard. Brijesh quickly put his hand into his pocket and took his cell phone out.

'I believe we've sent you a presentation,' Vikrant continued. 'Mushfiqur will show you the same.'

'Ah, all right. So the 3D technology, how much will it cost us?'

'Around ninety lakh rupees,' Brijesh said. 'Roughly, hundred thousand dollars.'

Vikrant looked at Brijesh and said, '*Aamra parun to?*'

Ghuman gave them a puzzled look. Brijesh tried to explain, 'He is from the interiors of Bangladesh and likes to speak in his mother tongue; he is asking me if we can manage within this amount?'

Ghuman sat silently for a moment. The waiter walked up to the table and served each man a thick, reddish omelette and a glass of tea. He placed a basket of dry bread between them, then tossed a few sachets of butter beside it and walked away.

'That's quite an amount,' Ghuman replied. 'We had a Singaporean firm willing to do it for much less.'

Vikrant again lapsed into Bengali. '*Ae ki hoitase re?*'

Brijesh again acted as interpreter. 'He means, what is happening here? Why are you renegotiating after bringing us so far from our country?'

'The price you are quoting is too steep. The Singapore firm gave us a reasonable offer,' Ghuman said.

'Sir,' Vikrant said, 'with all due respect, we aren't making a profit on this either. However, if you feel the Singaporeans are better, let them do it.'

'They've asked us to wait,' Ghuman said matter-of-factly. 'Some kind of delay. The owner of the firm, a fine lady, fell ill at the last moment. That's why we negotiated with you.'

'Well, since you're being so blunt about it,' Vikrant said, playing with his omelette, 'we will too. We can't do it for anything less than this. In fact, we were afraid it would run into a higher amount. So, take it or leave it. You can wait for the fine Singaporean lady to get over her common cold and let her do it.'

Ghuman looked deeply insulted. He was clearly taken aback by Vikrant's outburst. He wiped his mouth with a tissue and got up without finishing his omelette.

'I'll stay in touch. I need to call the head office before taking any decisions.'

Vikrant smiled and nodded his head in approval. 'We do what we have to do, sir.'

Ghuman walked away.

'Well,' Brijesh said. 'There could've been better ways of handling that.'

'Why waste time around those edicts if we aren't mapping them, anyway? We'll come during the vacation for a picture with them if that's what you want. Besides, this buys us more time for a recce. The hills with the edicts are more than two kilometres away from the ground where Azhar is going to speak. We have to find a closer vantage point.'

'I know,' Brijesh said. 'This saved us a trip. His boss will want him to wait for the Singaporeans after he reports how you behaved with him. But I'm sure you're happy for another reason as well.'

'And what is that?' Vikrant asked with an enigmatic smile.

'Nicole gets to do what she always wanted.'

27

Chattar plain, Mansehra, 5 p.m.

'So, Azhar is going to speak at a rally in the northwestern part of Mansehra,' Vikrant said, as he changed his T-shirt. 'It's the same place where Nawaz Sharif spoke in March.'

'Good,' Brijesh replied. 'I called Hafeez from your phone while you were away. We'll be making a trip down there.'

'Sounds good.' Vikrant picked up his phone as it rang. 'It's him, let's get going. Ray showed us these particular hills on the map he sent us, they are about 1800 metres to the right of the stadium. Apparently, there's a roadway as well.'

Brijesh walked out of the door and Vikrant locked it behind him.

'Check the lock again,' Brijesh told him. 'Our equipment is in there, under the bed.'

Vikrant slipped the key into his pocket and walked up alongside Brijesh.

'Why is there a roadway?'

'They plant poppies there,' Vikrant replied. 'Don't you read the emails Ray sends?'

'No,' Brijesh said, as they approached the car. 'Not ones about opium when I have real work to do.'

'Well,' Vikrant replied with a grin. 'It's part of our work now. We tell Hafeez that we want to go and buy some of the stuff there. You know the drill.' They sat in the car and told Hafeez what they wished to do to which he nodded obediently and Brijesh saw a half-smile on his face.

The sun had disappeared, though it was only 6 p.m. They reached an area called the Chattar plain, where some of the rallies were set up. According to the flimsy boards and hoardings and the various pamphlets stuck on the walls, this was where Maulana Mehmood Azhar was going to deliver a speech on Islam and on what God desired from the Islamic youth.

'Mehmood Azhar,' said Brijesh softly. 'I've heard that name before.'

He knew that Hafeez was bound to butt in and tell him about Azhar. As if on cue, he lowered the volume and spoke with a smile. 'Officially, the Pakistani government said he isn't anywhere in our country, just like they did about Osama. But here there are photos plastered all over the walls about him giving a speech.'

'Oh,' Brijesh said. 'Isn't he the guy who has a terrorist organization?'

'Yes, Jaish-e-Mohammad. He was also very close to Osama.'

'Have you ever been to any such speeches, Hafeez?' Vikrant asked casually. 'Any idea what he talks about?'

'He speaks about how we are being oppressed by the other countries in the world. India and America, especially. I have been to one such speech of his.' Vikrant and Brijesh prodded no further. They knew Hafeez well by now. If he kept silent, it was because he felt an obligation to build on the topic at hand.

'I don't know if I should be saying this,' Hafeez said, and paused dramatically.

'Well, we won't tell anyone, if that's what you're afraid of,' Brijesh said.

'I've heard that this seminar of his has been cancelled,' Hafeez said hesitantly. 'Apparently, there is an important visitor at the training camp somewhere in the Chattar plain. He is here to talk to the young militants they've recruited for the organization.'

'Any idea who the visitor is?' Brijesh asked, delicately. Vikrant was still quiet as he tried to process this new piece of information.

Hafeez shook his head vigorously. He continued: 'In fact, after the two of you are done at the plantations, we must head back home immediately. The training camp is around two kilometres away, and we don't want to get into trouble.'

Brijesh and Vikrant had to throw in a smattering of Bengali now, for Hafeez to trust their cover.

'*Aar kotdur zaita hoibo?*' Brijesh asked.

Hafeez looked at Vikrant, totally unfazed.

Vikrant tried to explain eruditely, 'Mushfiq is from the suburbs of Dhaka, he cannot keep himself from breaking into his mother tongue. He is asking, how much farther do we have to go?'

The driver nodded. After a few minutes, they drove past a junction and kept going straight, at the end of which the path diverged into two. One of these led to a T-point, while the other continued towards an upwards slope.

'*Ae toh gobhir bon*,' Brijesh said again, trying to be an authentic Bangladeshi.

Hafeez looked helplessly at Vikrant.

'He is saying, it is such a dense forest,' Vikrant said with a smile.

'The car won't be able to go inside,' Hafeez said, as he parked the SUV neatly.

'So, how did you know that the talk has been cancelled?'

'I have a friend,' Hafeez said. 'He works under Maulana Azhar. They are going to be at the training camp tomorrow night, because of this guest.'

'For what?' Vikrant asked.

'Training the kids for jihad. Azhar and his friend are going to lecture the young militants in the camp.'

'Do you agree with all this, Hafeez?'

'No,' he said. 'Not at all. For the simple reason that my father protected me from it, he didn't want to lose me. And I don't want to lose my son. That's all. For me, it's my family first. I'm beginning to hate these people. They have spoiled our beautiful country.'

Brijesh and Vikrant looked at each other.

'Anyway,' Hafeez said. 'Here we are.' He pointed at a huge field, beside which there was a small hut. It seemed abandoned. The sun was setting and tiny flies were beginning to irritate Vikrant and Brijesh.

'How much do you want, bhai? I'll go and buy it.'

Vikrant shrugged and gave him a thousand-rupee note with a smile. 'You decide.'

Hafeez started walking towards the hut. 'Do you think we can trust him?' Brijesh asked.

'He seems genuine,' Vikrant replied. 'Doesn't betray his emotions. I like the chap.'

'But after the last debacle, where we almost lost Kang, it's hard to trust anyone.'

Vikrant nodded. 'Azhar has cancelled his rally. Something serious is happening. I wonder who this guest is.'

'Do you, really?' Brijesh asked with a sly smile. 'We'll need to make a clean getaway. We have to find out where the camp is and which hill we should use.'

'We need to trick Hafeez into taking us around then,' Vikrant replied. 'He seems pretty disturbed himself.'

'We don't need to trick him. We'll tell him why we're here,' Brijesh replied. 'We are journalists who need to figure out where the training camp is. We need a few pictures, after which we can make our escape.'

Vikrant stood silently, waving away the files. He saw Hafeez walk out of the hut with a plastic bag. 'Do you think we should tell him?' Brijesh said quickly, as Hafeez made his way back.

Vikrant shook his head. 'No. That's a bad idea, we should stick to our cover.'

Hafeez held out the bag.

'Hafeez bhai,' Vikrant said, 'do you smoke this?'

'No, Nasiruddin bhai. I got it for you,' he said, as he started walking towards the car. 'Let's get going. We aren't safe here.'

'You can throw the weed away, we don't smoke either.'

Hafeez turned around, his eyes bulging. 'W-what do you mean?'

'We were just curious. Back in Bangladesh, drugs are an absolute no-no. We just wanted to see what it looks like.'

'You mentioned that there are camps around this place, what are they like? Are they like military camps or religious institutions?'

'They're more like military camps, but it's too dangerous to be around them. You have no idea what will happen, if we get caught.'

'You don't have to worry, Hafeez bhai. All you have to do is drive us out of here as fast as you can. We just want to look from a distance. We are so excited, it's a once-in a-lifetime opportunity to see such a thing,' Vikrant said, placing a hand on Hafeez's shoulder. 'We just want to see these areas once.'

'Ten minutes. Not a second more.' Hafeez sighed. 'After that, we rush out of here and go back to the hotel.'

'No, Hafeez bhai. We go back to Islamabad immediately, as our project has been postponed. We'll check out of the hotel and keep our equipment and bags in the boot.'

'Also,' Brijesh continued, 'we will pay you the price you name, once we are back in Islamabad. You could get your son a worthy education, yourself a good house to live in and not be terrified of the looming threat of him being sacrificed in the name of God.'

Hafeez sighed again and shook his head. He couldn't believe he was agreeing to take them right around the training camp. He got out of the car, then motioned for them to as well. They stepped out obediently.

'Follow me,' he said sternly and walked towards a diversion that led uphill. 'From here you will be able to see the training camp. We are quite a distance away from it, but please make sure the sentries don't spot you with their telescopes.'

'We'll be careful, bhai.'

They trudged up the gentle slope, to where the terrain became rockier and more treacherous. They had to climb very carefully, since it was dark and not much could be seen. Brijesh and Vikrant made an easy task of it, but Hafeez took his time. They walked for five minutes until they reached the top of the hill. It was the lowest one in the area, and Hafeez continued walking through what was now flat land. It was barren and, barring a few shrubs and bushes, there were no major obstacles. They walked for about a hundred metres after which Hafeez stopped at the edge of a cliff. He stretched his arm out and pointed at an enclosed continuation of the Chattar plain. Vikrant and Brijesh followed his pointing finger and saw a fairly large ground, the size of two cricket fields combined.

It was lit up, and there seemed to be some sort of activity going on. They could vaguely see the smoke from a fire, which the young militants must have been using to warm themselves in the November chill.

'Looks like they're preparing for their guest,' Brijesh said, squinting at the camp. 'So Vikrant, where do you reckon we set up the camera, so that we don't miss taking pictures of this?'

'Right here,' Vikrant replied with a satisfied smile.

They looked around and saw that the plain was surrounded on all sides by hills, similar to the one they were standing on.

'What are the chances of us being seen here, Hafeez bhai?'

'Not too high,' Hafeez said. 'But it's still risky. Besides, when they have a rally or a seminar, they tend to beef up security along the valley which they use to enter.'

He then turned and started walking ahead towards a clearing.

'*Ae kothai liya zaitasey re?*' Brijesh asked in a sceptical manner, furrowing his brow.

Hafeez stopped and looked at them both. Vikrant heaved a silent sigh of relief; finally, Brijesh's repertoire of Bengali had been exhausted. He realized that Hafeez was still looking at him curiously.

'He's asking, where are you taking us?' Vikrant said.

Hafeez said, 'Oh, just here, not very far off.'

He pointed towards the narrow valley, then towards the opposite hills.

'Sometimes, there are guys with guns who stand right there. They have these really expensive ones, which can shoot from a far distance, to cover the important person at the rally.'

Vikrant raised an eyebrow at Brijesh who shrugged.

'So we place our camera right here. And we take a shot. Sounds good?' asked Brjesh.

'Yes,' Vikrant said. 'We take the shot and then we run back down to Hafeez bhai.'

'And then we go back to Islamabad. And I never return to Mansehra,' Hafeez concluded.

It was 4 p.m. The stage was set. A hundred young trainees had gathered in front of the approximately ten-foot high wooden stage on which there were four plastic chairs and a standing microphone. The stage had a roof that would shade the honourable guests who would be imparting their ample knowledge about jihad to the newcomers. The new wolves in a never-ending pack. The day was extremely bright because of the sun, but it wasn't too hot. A light November breeze swept huge dunes of sand along the plain. It was the perfect evening to spread Allah's word.

'All set?' Vikrant asked Brijesh, as he unloaded his bag from the car. They had spent a good part of the previous evening assembling the sniper. The trickier parts had been completed by Brijesh, in the confines of their hotel room.

Hafeez tapped on the steering wheel impatiently.

'I'll call you after we take the pictures,' Vikrant said to him, as he began to walk away from the car. 'Keep the engine running.' Hafeez grumbled about 'no amount of money being worth this nonsense', but complied. Clearly the funds that had changed hands had been enough to coerce, if not convince him.

Vikrant and Brijesh began to scale the hillock, going back to the spot that Hafeez had taken them to the previous evening.

Vikrant quickly marked out a tiny 'x' with his toe. He unzipped his bag, pulled out a tiny tripod and set it up.

'I wonder who the guest is,' Vikrant told Brijesh. 'They're making such a big deal of him. Anyway, whoever he is, remember, Azhar is our priority. We have exactly three bullets. And we need to try and do the job in one,' Vikrant said.

'We have no second shot at him, Vikrant. We are approximately 2,000 metres away from him, and we will not get a second chance.'

He shot a glance towards the ongoing rally. Apparently, the three guests had arrived. One of them was speaking animatedly into the microphone. That was all he could see from this distance.

'I could use a hand here,' Brijesh told Vikrant, as he assembled the sniper painstakingly. They worked at it, twisting and turning the screws. Finally, after the six minutes that Vikrant counted off, they were able to screw the last bit on. They placed the scope and Brijesh looked through it at the training camp.

'Fuck,' he said. 'Hafeez was right. They are using two snipers to cover the rally. One just behind the stage, and one on the hill right opposite.'

Vikrant pulled out his binoculars and focused on the stage. He saw the familiar face of Maulana Mehmood Azhar and … his jaw dropped.

'Look at the stage,' was all he could tell Brijesh. Brijesh looked through the scope at the third man standing with the others.

'That's their guest then.'

They sat silently, contemplating what they were to do next. They had three bullets and four targets. They had to take out the 'guest' at the rally as well. They simply had to.

'We need to do this safely,' Brijesh said finally. 'We take out both the snipers, or we risk getting ourselves killed by them. And then, we take him out.'

'Azhar?'

'Of course not,' said Brijesh. 'These are decisions that have to be taken on the field, Vikrant. You, of all people, know that.'

'I agree. Let Azhar get away,' he said through gritted teeth. 'We take that motherfucker out today.'

They looked down at the audience. Then Brijesh got up and switched his position in order to get a better look at the stage.

'Assalaamo Alaikum alaikum warahmatullahe wabarakatoh,' said the slightly pudgy, bearded man on the stage, as he responded to a roaring applause from the young militants who made up his audience. He stroked his beard and grinned from ear to ear at their enthusiam.

'Today, Maulana Azhar has made it possible for me to come to Mansehra and talk to you young guns, the soldiers of Allah's army.'

The militants cheered even louder.

'Today I'm not going to tell you about jihad. I'm quite sure Maulana Azhar has taken care of that. In fact, you may know as much as I do about it. Today, I'm here to talk about the kafirs. The reason Muslims like us are tortured day in and day out. One such country is America.'

'I have said it earlier, while leading the Eid-ul-Fitr prayers in Gaddafi Stadium in Lahore. I am saying it again here. We should stop being patient and declare a war against them.' Saeed was getting into in his stride.

The audience was silent and looked on, wide-eyed in anticipation.

'Americans hate Muslims, my brothers. But they are too powerful a nation for us to mess with at this juncture. When Osama was around, he got them to shit bricks. But then, unfortunately, he got old and he got weak. He didn't prove to be as much of a threat as he had been after the twin tower attacks.'

The crowd nodded in approval. 'But again, I'm not here to talk about America. I'm here to talk about another country that hates not only us Pakistanis, but Muslims as well. Who am I talking about?'

'HINDUSTAN!' the crowd roared in unison. 'Hindustan Murdabad!'

Someone from the audience fired bursts from his AK-47 in the air in jubilation; others followed suit and the crowd cheered frantically.

The man waited for his audience to simmer down. He continued then, in his beautifully modulated voice.

'Calm down. We let them, the Indians, do the slogan shouting. Actions speak louder than words, my friends. We shall let our actions speak for us.'

The crowd of more than a hundred young militants rose to its feet and clapped.

'In November a few years ago, we shook up their country by sending a few boys like you on a boat. The Indians have been planning to get back at us, ever since. But I have a plan.'

Saeed looked at the wide-eyed crowd, playing on their emotions. He was a showman in the way he carried himself, in the way he incited the young blood.

'I have a plan, my friends. To shake the country that has

oppressed us ever since Quaid-e-Azam fought for our existence. They don't believe Muslims should exist but we will show them what we are capable of. First, we get India. Then we get America. And then, the rest of the world. We are on a mission, my friends. Allah's mission.' He paused and raised his arms towards the sky. 'But first, I want to know how many of you will truly support me in my cause, in Allah's cause, to take down this impotent country.'

There was a huge cheer again. Mahmood Azhar rose to his feet and clapped. There were broad smiles all around – an electric air of celebration.

Brijesh looked through his scope, his finger resting gently on the trigger. He saw the bearded mullah mouthing some words and the jubilation that followed. Stunned, he watched the man – one of the main instigators of the 26/11 attacks. He had an urge to run down to the camp with an automatic gun and pump an entire magazine into the man's chest. He racked the bullet into the slot. He had to make it count. It was an all-or-nothing shot. One shot. That's it. One. Damn. Shot.

He adjusted the crosshairs to focus on the Saeed's smiling face. He moved it slightly lower below the nose, so that the bullet's trajectory did not affect the end result, and would still explode upon hitting him. The bullet had a tiny shot of mercury in it, which would cause the explosion upon hitting its target.

Brijesh thought of all those who had lost life and limb in the 26/11 attacks. How had this man, who remained safely ensconced, been able to keep brainwashing and inciting gullible youths with the lure of paradise to go and kill at random without any provocation or previous enmity? They had caused mayhem at the instruction of this man, supposedly a religious leader but actually a merchant of death.

He wished he could tie this man to a chair and make him suffer. The bullet was going to let him get away easily, Brijesh thought. And then he stopped thinking and pulled the trigger.

There was a short, cracker-like explosion and the enemy's head blew up into pieces. Bits of blood, bone and brain flew all over the stage.

Saeed had met his maker in one stroke.

There was pandemonium. Mahmood Azhar scurried off the stage and was soon encircled by a huge entourage of men who shielded him and put him into a jeep.

He had left the day's special guest behind, his face beyond recognition, but there he lay – Haaris Saeed, one of the world's most wanted men, shot through the side of his temple.

Vikrant quickly attached a small piece of explosive plastic with a timer to his gun, and activated it. But they had already been spotted by the counter-snipers who began firing at them.

Brijesh and Vikrant ducked and scampered towards the car under a hail of bullets, filled with fear and excitement—and jubilation.

The drive back to Islamabad was exhausting for Hafeez. He had driven at ridiculously high speeds, passing various police cars on the way. His two Bangladeshi friends hadn't spoken much at all, on the way back. They just sat beside each other, staring out of their respective windows. He had tried to start a conversation now and then, but they just replied in monosyllables. When he asked them if they had managed to get the desired pictures, they each replied with a nod. And when he asked them if something was wrong, they just shrugged. He didn't like the mood, and he was relieved when they reached Islamabad by seven in the evening.

There was an array of police cars and road-checks being set up. Brijesh hoped their car wouldn't be stopped, and as if on cue, that was exactly what happened. A huge man stuck his arm out and motioned for their vehicle to halt. Hafeez cursed under his breath and delicately shifted his foot on the brake. He rolled down his window.

'I need to check your car,' the man with a stern face said. 'Open the boot and all the doors, please.'

They obeyed. Another huge man with an exaggerated moustache came towards their car with an enormous sniffer dog. It looked like it could eat all of them for breakfast, its tongue hanging out and exposing a set of ferocious and revoltingly yellow canines. It sniffed the front seat on the left, and then moved over to the seat right behind it. It sniffed Vikrant's feet and started barking. Vikrant glared at it with equal ferocity. The man looked at him suspiciously, but didn't say anything. He dragged the dog to the boot, where the equipment bags were kept. The dog smelled it and started barking even more furiously. It began to jump at the bag, pawing at it violently. Its handler had to bring his considerable strength into play to hold it back, to keep it from getting out of control.

'I need you to open your bag,' the other man commanded. Vikrant and Brijesh got out of the car and walked to the boot. Brijesh had half a mind to shoot the dog dead with the security guy's holstered gun. Instead, he unzipped the bag and shrugged at the man who sifted through all the material for three full minutes. He didn't find anything of particular interest, except a few pieces of photography equipment here and there alongside what was obviously a camera.

'What is the camera for?' his voice boomed.

'We are on a contract with UNESCO,' Brijesh started, with an obvious Bengali accent.

'Are you Bangladeshi?'

'From Dhaka,' Vikrant said. 'Yes.'

'ID proof?' the man demanded, with a raised eyebrow. 'Driving licence, passport, something that proves you're Bangladeshi.'

Vikrant and Brijesh nodded simultaneously and dug their hands into their pockets. They got out their passports and handed them over to the man without protest. He looked at the passports, then at them, then at the passports again, hoping to catch them out on some pretext or the other.

'You could talk to the man we were here to meet,' Vikrant said finally, as if to put him at ease. He whipped out his cellphone without waiting for the man to respond and dialled Adnan Ghuman's cell phone.

'Ah,' Ghuman replied. 'Yes, my friends, have you changed your minds about the edicts? Decided to do it for less?'

'Actually,' Vikrant replied with a wry smile. 'Quite the opposite. We're leaving Mansehra, and we need you to talk to someone.'

Vikrant handed the phone to the security officer. His partner had moved on to another car, with the dog. The man asked Ghuman all kinds of questions. It took him five minutes to verify that the two Bangladeshis were indeed there as UNESCO volunteers.

'I don't know why your bag smells of something that made our dog bark.' He said, as he prepared to move on.

'Maybe he's allergic to our cameras,' Vikrant said, smiling.

'Mr Ghuman said you were there to meet him,' the man said. 'He also asked me if I could arrest you because you don't know how to speak respectfully.'

Brijesh interrupted. 'We're sorry, sir. But we're in a bit of a hurry. If you have a valid reason, we don't mind staying back. But a sharp tongue sure isn't one.'

The big man scowled at them and then cursed loudly, as he gestured for them to get back into the car and get the hell out of there. Hafeez, who had broken into a sweat, finally seemed relieved. He rolled up the windows and turned the air conditioner on again. He sped off without any further ado, dropping them back at the Marriott hotel, where they took their bags out of the boot. They embraced Hafeez and said goodbye.

'It's been a pleasure, Hafeez bhai.'

'Yes, bhai,' Hafeez smiled. 'For me too. Do let me know if you are back in Islamabad anytime soon.'

'We will,' Vikrant replied with a smile. He took out his wallet and handed Hafeez a thick wad of notes. Brijesh pulled his wallet out and gave him a thinner but still substantial bundle.

'You've worked hard,' he told him. 'You deserve it. Khuda hafiz.'

'Khuda hafiz,' was all Hafeez could reply. He waved goodbye, sat back in his car and drove straight back to the taxi agency.

I'll ask Saahab for a couple of days off, he thought. *I need to spend time with my family*. He pushed open the door of the taxi agency to drop off the car keys.

'You got back from Mansehra safely!' his boss said, with a sigh of relief. 'Allah ka shukr hai.'

'Is there a problem?' Hafeez asked him. The boss looked at

him, his eyes bulging out of his sockets, then motioned to the tiny television that crackled on the table opposite him.

The breaking news read: 'HAARIS SAEED SHOT AT MANSEHRA RALLY.'

And below that: 'The weapon used was destroyed with plastic explosives on the spot.'

Belatedly, Hafeez realized why the dog had barked.

28

The headline read two words but those were the words every citizen of Mumbai had yearned to read for years. Those who read the paper in the morning at home with a hot cup of tea or coffee did not touch their beverages until they had read the whole story, its sub stories and derivative stories. Those rushing to catch trains stopped to buy a newspaper from a vendor, those who were already in the crowded trains strained to read off their co-passengers, shamelessly grabbing the pages when the original reader had finished.

The headline appearing just below the masthead of the *Mumbai Times* screamed, 'Mumbai Avenged'.

The story had been broken that day by Ashish Kumar, one of the finest and most courageous investigative journalists in the country. His investigatory prowess had earned him an impeccable reputation in journalistic circles. He was never seen in the office. He was never seen gossiping with fellow journalists. He never spent the days in coffee shops or the nights in bars. Exposing the big and powerful was his credo. He was regarded as an invisible reporter, the scourge of the high and mighty, and among a handful of reporters who could boast of having contacts in Mumbai and Delhi at every level.

The deadline for stories at the newspaper was usually 6 p.m. and the tabloid went to print at 10 p.m. The front page normally got made by 10.30 p.m. and went for proofreading and final checking at this point. Kumar had walked into the editor's cabin when she was about to clear the front page of the day's edition.

'I have a story,' he said. She was busy reading the last paragraph of the front page and did not lift her head.

'File it for tomorrow's edition,' she said.

'It can't wait until tomorrow. It has to go in today's edition,' he replied.

The editor raised an angry eyebrow at Kumar. She was known to be a despotic with a mercurial temperament and high standards; hers was not an accommodating attitude. Any reporter in Kumar's place would have been subjected to a string of angry adjectives. But she knew that he was no stenographer reporter, as most of the crime reporters of the current generation were; Kumar was different.

She tried to read his face to ascertain if he was joking.

'You know if you file the story now, our page goes way later than the deadline,' she said at last, with a hint of irritation in her voice.

'If you don't like the story, you can sack me,' he fired back. This calmed her fraying temper.

'What's the story?' she finally asked.

He briefed her in two minutes. The almost finalized front page was trashed and a new one was designed.

The next morning, Kumar became the envy of every other journalist.

The story was about Haaris Saeed's killing at the Mansehra training camp. It described the difficult terrain of Mansehra and how a few Indians had managed to penetrate the foolproof security to shoot Saeed dead while he was giving a provocative speech. Normally, such a story would not have seen the light of day, but such were Kumar's levels of persuasion, that he was able to get the home minister's PA to cough up fragments of information that he could assemble into the massive story.

By the next day, the media had gone ballistic. The other papers had caught up, and it was all over the television channels. Social networking sites like Facebook and Twitter were abuzz with stories of Mumbai's Avengers. India's 243 major newspapers and over thirty-nine news channels had space for nothing but the story of revenge.

Every broadsheet had two words in their flyer headlines: 'MUMBAI AVENGERS' and the country was hopeful again. The news reports explained that a team of dedicated officers had risked their lives to ensure that the 26/11 attacks were avenged while the government was still stuck in the rut of diplomacy.

The following day saw more reports, carrying details about the Avengers. The team had been given various names. Some called them Renegade Angels, some called them Rogue Attackers, some The New Vigilantes, Superheroes – however, the Mumbai Avengers caught on best, and was incorporated into the mass hysteria and the broadcast news coverage.

The Avengers were a topic of discussion everywhere. Even the card players in Mumbai's local trains gave up their game for a while to participate in the animated discussions around them. The support was not just verbal or superficial. It had, in a very short span of time, come to the point where people were offering prayers in the Avengers' names at various places of worship. There was an air of celebration and jubilation everywhere.

The government was taken aback by the support for the team and did not know how to react. After all, they were meant to have no knowledge of it. Sky was immediately summoned by the prime minister and questioned about the mission. He was flustered and could not explain the situation to his bosses and political masters. He feigned ignorance about the Avengers' actions.

However, he was happy with the support they were getting. His concern was that now, his best guarded secret was out— and this would have its own repercussions. Now that they were exposed, it would become more difficult to provide the team protection in case they were caught in Pakistan. This was personal now. Beyond that, it was a score that needed settling. Like Brijesh said, it was redemption they sought through the final, most audacious attack that they were planning against the Lashkar terrorists and the ISI.

'Are they planning to attack Muridke?' Sky wondered aloud.

While the frenzy consumed the Indian media, the Pakistanis certainly could not have missed it, as sour as the taste of ignominy might be. Leading media outlets such as *Dawn*, *Jung*, GeoTV and PTV caught on to the Indian fervour and the support the Avengers were being given. The first reactions were of shock and consternation.

The headlines screamed, 'The Mumbai Marauders take lesson from Mossad' in *Jung*. *Dawn* said, 'India at its bulldozing best'. They all portrayed India as the villain that had violated the norms of democracy.

One piece stated that the Indian bloodthirst had never

stopped – now they had sent their soldiers to spill blood in their neighbouring country. Television anchors were worried about how Pakistan would deal with the infiltrating RAW agents along with their own internal issues. The Pakistani government heads immediately summoned the Indian ambassador, who assured them he was completely unaware of the mission. He was sure it had not been commissioned by the government.

The Pakistani rangers, army and ISI were all on the Avengers' trail and hoped to take them out before they could do further damage.

Brigadier Arif Afridi took it as a personal challenge. He knew the Indians were highly motivated by their mission and would stop at nothing till it was accomplished. But they were all that stood in the way of him becoming the chief of ISI. He knew that one wrong move would spell doom for his career, while success could help him achieve more than he had ever dreamed of.

29

Islamabad, 30 June

General Ashfaq Parvez Kayani had been judged the twenty-eighth most powerful man in the world by *Forbes* magazine the previous year. He was the only Pakistani army chief who had been given a three-year extension by a democratically elected government in Pakistan in 2010. Perhaps he was also the only army officer who had held all the sensitive and vital positions in

Pakistan, including chief of X corps, chief of army staff and above all, director of the ISI, prior to his posting as chief of army staff.

In November 2013, following Kayani's retirement, General Raheel Sharif was given the unenviable task of cleaning up his predecessor's mess.

Earlier, they had met at Sharif's brother Shahbaz's New Model Town bungalow. The prime minister was a different man now, much more confident, aggressive, in total command of himself and full of bluster. He had called for a meeting at his office in Islamabad.

He and two other men were present at the meeting who were summoned by Prime Minister Nawaz Sharif: Arif Afridi and the ISI chief, Zaheerul Islam. The atmosphere in the room was grim.

'So you mean to say that those Indian army men just walked into our country and killed Haaris Saeed?' Sharif posed the question to Islam with incredulity.

'Janab Wazire Azamsahab, they entered the country under cover, as archaeologists, with a team of UNESCO officials. The immigration officials swear their documents were genuine. Adnan Ghuman, the UNESCO representative, said their credentials were impeccable,' Islam said, clearing his throat.

'I gather that earlier they were involved in the killing of other Lashkar people like Umavi, Mir and Bradley. I think they had some kind of … er … skirmish with your men, Arif.' Sharif made the last sound more like a question than a statement.

There was silence in the room.

Zaheer looked at Afridi, indicating that he had to explain himself.

Afridi looked ashen-faced, but he mustered up the courage to speak. 'We had laid a trap for them in Jeddah quite successfully and managed to get one of their agents. But he was not willing to speak, despite our attempts to coerce him; we realized that the man would rather die than open up. Then we changed our strategy. We wanted to get to the brain behind the conspiracy, so we let him go and tracked his movements.'

Sharif was listening to every word intently. 'Then what happened? Instead of you zeroing in on their kingpin, you let them sneak into our country and kill another man?'

'I cannot explain exactly how this happened. They are quite cunning and deceptive. They came in with absolutely unexpected techniques. While we were watching their leader Ali Waris and the man who came to Jeddah – a Sikh called Iqbal Kang – as well as their tech experts, they changed tracks and sent two different men,' Afridi said, regaining his composure.

'What did you hope to get by just watching them? Why have you not put any trackers on them?' Sharif was now becoming impatient.

Afridi was ready for this question. He said, 'Sir, my estimate is that it would have taken them less than half an hour to locate the tracking device. It would have been a major waste.' He pulled out a chart with maps and diagrams. Swiftly, he spread everything out on the table and began explaining in detail.

Afterwards, Sharif turned towards Raheel and Zaheer.

'General sahab, I need them dead or alive. I have to expose the hypocritical Indian face to our friend John Kerry. This is how the US can be convinced to bestow new allowances on our country,' Sharif said.

Raheel rose and walked up to where the map lay.

'Sir, we have sealed the border areas of Jammu and Kashmir, Azad Kashmir, Punjab, Rajasthan and even the Gujarat desert areas. There is no way that they can cross the border. I have asked my men to get them alive and not shoot to kill,' Raheel said.

He continued, 'Our border with India stretches over 553 kilometres, of which nearly 450 kilometres are fenced. The unfenced area includes natural river gaps of about 26.6 kilometres, spread over several different places. We are watching these areas and have increased our surveillance, including motor boat patrolling.'

Sharif nodded, affirming his faith in Raheel and his men.

The meeting seemed to have reached its conclusion when Islam decided to pipe up.

'Our intel gathering and collating is at its most sensitive and effective level. We have alerted all our dormant and active assets. Our men are roaming around in most of the villages in the border areas,' he said. 'We suspect that they might try to hide and lie low for a while before they make an attempt to cross over, so we have also started combing those areas where there might be Indian sympathizers. They could be among the Hindus, Sindhis and Hazaras. We are watching the Hindu localities in Jacobabad, Balochistan and the Sind borders where the Bheel tribe lives. Also, we have increased surveillance near the Gilgit-Baltistan mountains, especially near Azad Kashmir.'

He felt better after this long demonstration of intelligence prowess.

Sharif finally smiled and gave his verdict. 'The pride of Pakistan is in your hands. They should not get away.'

Raheel, Zaheer and Afridi stood ramrod straight, saluted Sharif and walked out of the room.

'Who the fuck wants to get away?' Brijesh turned and looked at Vikrant.

'Our orders are clear, Brijesh. We have to make an exit and exfiltrate from Pakistan as and when it's convenient,' Vikrant reminded his senior.

'Yes, as and when it's convenient. Right now, it's not convenient at all. Secondly, we have to leave for India. We cannot do so immediately and it need not be through the Kashmir border. We can go to Wagah or even Afghanistan,' Brijesh retorted.

Vikrant did not look convinced.

'Vikrant, don't you want to be of help to Waris and Laila? Don't you think they may do better with a little bit of backup and help from us?' Brijesh tried to appeal to Vikrant's sense of duty.

Vikrant perked up. 'I guess you are right. It's fair to defy orders if we can save the old man. Otherwise, if we obey his orders and survive, we would have to live with the guilt of leaving him high and dry.'

'Okay, now we have to focus on ensuring that the Pakistani army does not kill or capture us before we reach Muridke in Lahore,' Brijesh said, dryly.

'By now, Hafeez must have started singing like a canary – those men might knock on our door at any moment,' Vikrant reminded him.

Before he could finish his sentence, Brijesh whipped out his Thuraya and was dialling Waris's number.

'I knew you would not go to your mother's house today,' said Waris, in code. 'Quickly now, pay attention. Look good, wear nice sherwanis, clear the kitchen and take a cab to Faisal Masjid. Loiter around there and wait for the next namaaz.' Brijesh turned to Vikrant. 'He has asked us to shave, change our clothes, check out, dump our luggage and rush to Faisal Masjid for namaaz.'

'What? Namaaz? Has the old man forgotten we are not Muslims?'

'Vikrant, where do you hide a tree? In the jungle. Faisal is the biggest mosque in south Asia. It's always crowded; as two men in sherwanis, we will be inconspicuous. They'll never think to look for us there. He also asked us to dump our belongings on the way,' Brijesh instructed. He dialled the reception's number and asked for a taxi to Faisal Masjid while issuing instructions for checkout.

The two men got cracking. They shaved, then sprinkled excessive amounts of attar on their sherwanis and spread rouge on their cheeks.

In the lobby Vikrant ensured that a bellboy took their luggage to the waiting taxi while Brijesh settled the bill in cash.

As the car left the sprawling premises of the Mariott, Brijesh spotted three army vehicles entering the gate of the hotel. They'd left just in time.

Hafeez had finally cracked, from fear of getting booked for complicity. He had haltingly raised his suspicions with his boss, who informed the local police. They had called the ISI and began questioning Hafeez. By the time the Federal Investigation Agency (FIA), ISI and the army got into action, Brijesh and Vikrant had left the hotel for Masjid-e-Faisal.

On A.K.M. Fazal Road, there were rows of taxis at the corner of the intersection. Brijesh asked the driver to halt at a little distance from the cars, but before he could stop, Brijesh cracked him in the neck with a single karate chop. The blow was severe enough for the driver to pass out without a sound. Vikrant threw a thousand-rupee note into his lap and left the car, their luggage still in the boot.

They walked towards the row of taxis without showing any signs of hurry.

'Bhai, will you take us to Lal Masjid?' Vikrant asked, trying sound like a local.

The driver sized him up.

'I'll charge Rs 700 for the trip,' he said.

'Why such a steep price, bhai?' Vikrant asked.

'That's a Deobandi masjid. I don't normally go there,' the driver explained.

'Acha acha, no problem, let's go,' Brijesh said, agreeing to the price.

Their route took them past Parliament House and the ISI headquarters. Vikrant and Brijesh kept their eyes open.

The founder of Lal Masjid, Mohammad Abdullah, had been a friend of former president Pervez Musharraf. After his death, his two sons took over the administration of the mosque. They formed their own vigilance squads, which raided brothels, punished corrupt cops, kidnapped other government servants and established shariat courts. Finally, following a standoff between the students of the seminary in Lal Masjid and government authorities, the army raided the masjid and took control of it, resulting in a situation much like Operation Blue Star at the Golden Temple in Amritsar in 1984.

Brijesh got on his Thuraya again.

'Chacha assalamalaikum, hum aaj shaam ki namaaz Lal Masjid mein ada karenge.'

Waris understood immediately.

'Okay, a van marked Gurdwara Tours will pick you up from outside Lal Masjid. Don't enter the mosque.'

Brijesh was mystified by Waris's level of preparation and organization in hostile territory at such short notice.

They were passing the ISI HQ now and he mouthed an expletive under his breath. So close to the enemy, yet so far.

They paid the driver and pretended to walk towards the masjid gates. Once the cab was out of sight, they turned and stood on the road, waiting for their pickup.

Within a couple of minutes, a van approached them. Brijesh made eye contact with the elderly driver and asked him to stop at a little distance from the gate.

'I have been instructed to take you to Gurdwara Panja Sahib at Hassan Abdal. Take this bag and wear the clothes that are inside it. If we get stopped en route, pretend that you have come for the annual pilgrimage of Nankana Sahib and Panja Sahib. My friend Rajinder here will prepare your documents right now. You must maintain that you have come from New Jersey. These are your American passports. He will click your pictures and put the finishing touches on your documents as we travel,' the driver said.

'What is the distance to Hassan Abdal?'

'We will reach in forty minutes. Now smile,' the assistant said and started clicking their pictures.

As the van sped down the smooth road that led to Hassan Abdal, the calming sounds of the Gurbani playing on the stereo which was accompanied by the humming of the driver did little to quell the sense of uncertainty brewing inside Brijesh and Vikrant. For who knew what might happen next?

30

Muridke, Lahore, 12 November

The whole plan had gone for a toss. Originally Waris, Kang and Laila were to have been left in the country. But with Brijesh's turnaround, they now had two additional soldiers to carry, which greatly increased their chances of being spotted.

Ray and Laila had followed the plan and landed in Karachi, to be admitted to the Sind Institute of Urology and Transplantation (SIUT) at Karachi Civil Hospital. Laila played the part of the concerned wife to perfection, and remained in burqa the whole time. Ray also gave a passable performance as a patient with kidney ailments.

On the day that Ray began undergoing mandatory tests before renal transplant, Laila instructed the nurses to watch him; she had to meet her relatives in Lahore, she told them, and would be back in the evening.

Brijesh and Vikrant had a slightly longer journey by road from Hassan Abdal; four hours in a fifteen-seater minibus, dressed just like the thirteen other Sikhs with them. Their co-passengers immediately took a liking to 'Avtar Singh' and 'Kartar Singh', who throughout the 385-kilometre long journey were most helpful and entertaining.

They were stopped at Bahlol Road, Islamabad–Peshawar motorway point M-1, Islamabad-Lahore motorway M-2, then

Lahore Bypass, Grand Trunk Road N-5 and Shahdara. At every checkpoint, the army men scrutinized every document and every Sikh passenger closely. Even if they had cause to suspect Brijesh and Vikrant, when they saw that Brijesh was a hunchback with one eye, and that Vikrant was using a walking stick as his legs had been weakened due to polio, their suspicions dissipated.

Soon after the sixth checkpoint at Shahdara, the duo alighted from the bus, pretending they had some relatives in the locality. Their instructions were to check in at a guesthouse in Shahdara, which was 25 km from Muridke.

Brijesh kept replaying in his mind the shot that had taken out Saeed and, each time, he felt a surge of pride. Vikrant, on the other hand, tried his best to keep his mind blank. He was no Buddhist monk, but he tried to keep disturbing thoughts at bay, even if temporarily.

Meanwhile, Waris and Kang had travelled on the Samjhauta Express and arrived at the Lahore railway station.

They took a cab to Shahdara, which was barely thirty minutes away from the railway junction, and arrived at the guesthouse where Ray and Laila had reached shortly before them.

They were all together at last, the A-team – and in foreign territory.

Aamir Ajmal Kasab, the lone terrorist who was captured alive in Mumbai after 26/11, was supposed to have studied in an infamous facility in Muridke, according to his interrogators. The others involved had also trained there. Its manicured lawns and immaculately painted walls belied the fact that it was a terror training facility. Jamaat-ud-Dawa claimed to be a charitable organization, but in reality it was a house of terror. The organization, which had been banned by the US in 2005 for being a Lashkar front, drew patronage from the ISI – and though proscribed abroad, it had a free reign in Pakistan. It had branches all over the country and was as famous for the social work it allegedly rendered, as it was for its terror activities. It saw itself as a movement and not as an organization, and had a wide appeal in both rural and urban areas.

Now, the A-Team was stuck next to it. They had relocated to a tiny, crappy hotel just within the borders of Muridke.

'Well, at least we don't need to be subtle any more,' said Waris. 'Makes things easier in some ways, but also trickier.'

They all nodded.

'I've had enough of this Azhar chap,' Waris continued in his raspy voice, his fake wispy grey beard neatly covering his mouth.

'We share the sentiment,' Laila said. 'But sir, it might be unwise to go after him now. He would have doubled his security.'

'I don't think so,' Waris replied. 'He's moved to Muridke, within the JuD HQ. It's their fortress and he is possibly Saeed's successor. He has more than just "doubled" his security.'

'If he's in a damned fortress,' Brijesh said, 'it'll be quite difficult to get in quietly and kill him.'

Waris smacked the glass pane of the window with his right hand impatiently.

Kang said smilingly, 'This is going to be amazing. I know exactly what you plan to do, sir. You want us to go and kill him out in the open.'

'Yes,' Waris said. 'And survive too. I've heard from my sources that a majority of the militants, barring Azhar's personal guards, are on vacation.'

'Brijesh and I,' Vikrant began. 'We'll go in. We don't even have a fucking pistol with us now, but if anyone can handle them right now, it's us.'

Waris raised an eyebrow and walked slowly towards him. Kang cracked his knuckles.

'Did you just call me old?' Waris asked.

'Or me a wuss?' Kang added, as he flexed his biceps. 'Just because of what happened in Jeddah?'

Vikrant looked at Laila. 'Aren't you going to play the part of the feminist?'

'No,' Laila shrugged. 'I just wish I had some popcorn to accompany this matinee show – featuring you getting your ass kicked.'

'Here's the deal, Vikrant. We're going to torch this place. Azhar won't walk out alive. Neither will his men. And if we perish as well, so be it,' said Waris.

At last, it had come to this.

'So who do you want inside the HQ?' Vikrant asked resignedly.

'I'm going in,' Waris said bluntly. He looked at them, challenging them to object. 'With Laila. Just because I'm old and she is a woman doesn't mean we can't wipe that place off the map.'

Brijesh looked on, his face not betraying any emotion. Finally, he nodded.

'What's the plan?'

'I'm glad you asked,' Waris said, with a smile. He settled down on the bed and cleared his throat. The team gathered around.

Waris explained the plan, then turned towards Laila.

'Have you told Ray the exact time at which he is supposed to tinker with the mobile networks in the Muridke-Lahore circuit?

He must disable the phone lines in the government offices from his suite in the hospital.'

'Sir, he is prepared and ready; he is only a bit nervous because he is alone. And he has never been on field duty before,' Laila explained.

'There is always a first time,' Brijesh said.

The JuD was the parent organization of the Lashkar-e-Toiba. In 1990, Haaris Saeed had started the LeT, which literally translates to 'army of the good'. He established the headquarters in Muridke, in the Punjab province of Pakistan, thirty kilometres from Lahore. The headquarters were nothing short of a fortress and stretched over acres of land. But they claimed it was a hospital and an educational centre which included a school and a college.

Mahmood Azhar, India's most wanted person, had sought refuge here after a couple of failed attempts on his life. But Haaris Saeed hadn't been so lucky. Azhar still saw Saeed's head being blown up every time he tried to sleep, though it had been a couple of weeks since it had happened. It was not like he hadn't seen gore before. But the very thought of it being *his* head that could have been blown up sent a chill down his spine. Suddenly, there was an urgent knock on his door.

'Maulana,' a young man spoke from outside the door. 'There is a call for you.'

'Who is it?'

'Sir,' the boy replied, 'it's a lady from some magazine. She wants to talk to you about your cause, apparently. What should I tell her?'

Azhar hesitated. Then he picked up the receiver on a small table an arm's length away from him.

'Salaam alaikum,' he said, in a careful, calculated tone. 'Maulana Azhar here.'

'Alaikum salaam,' replied the lady from the other end. 'I would like to take a minute of your time, sir.'

'Your time starts now,' he said.

'I'm Tasneem Khan, and I've done a journalism course from London. I'm back in Pakistan to start a new magazine. We're still at a very nascent stage and based in Lahore. We want to write a piece on you and project the survivor that you are to the people so they know their fate lies in good hands.' She said all this without stopping to breathe, then continued, 'We want to track your journey right from your getting freed in Kandahar to the last attempt on your life. Besides, you are a good writer and we want you to be a guest editor for the first edition.'

Laila was speaking in Urdu, reading off her laptop screen.

'Your minute is up,' Azhar said. 'Will it be in English or Urdu?'

'Both,' she replied promptly. 'We want a wide reach. Everyone should know what the message is.'

Azhar waited for a moment. The lady seemed harmless, if over enthusiastic. This could help him, and he had a lot to say, about how a few people trying to kill him would not deter his cause. But he had to be careful.

'Fine,' Azhar said. 'Come to the Jamaat school.'

'You mean the headquarters?'

'In other words.'

'Fine, sir,' she replied earnestly. 'I'll come with my cameraman.'

'No,' Azhar said sternly. 'Just you.'

'But sir,' she protested. 'We need a picture for the cover page.'

'Use one from the archives,' he said.

'That won't be an exclusive picture, sir. This is our first issue and we need a photograph. Nobody will buy a magazine if it can't live up to the promise of exclusivity in the first issue itself. I'll just need one camera man, sir, please. Just a few pictures.'

She was literally begging him in her soft, silky voice. And Azhar liked women – especially when they were pleading with him.

'Fine. Just the two of you,' he said softly. 'One camera. No equipment, no stands. Nothing. One simple camera, a pen and a notepad.'

'Thank you, sir.'

'Tomorrow at 4 p.m.,' he said.

'Khuda hafiz, Maulana.'

He did not reply.

About an hour after the journalist had called, the telephone roused the same unassuming and half-asleep boy who had answered the previous time.

'Hello, sir,' a voice said from the other end. 'I'm calling from cylinder engineering. We are going to be short on gas for the next few days.'

'So? You decided to call me to produce gas for you?' the young man replied rudely, scratching his beard.

'No, sir,' the man answered, his tone unchanged. 'I suggest you stock up. We are allotting a maximum of two cylinders per card. We can drop them by tomorrow.'

The young boy liked the fact that he was being called 'sir'. This didn't seem like an emergency and he was at liberty to take such calls. But he asked the man on the line to hold anyway and called the supervisor who handled technicalities such as cooking gas. He seemed to be sleeping too, and when he answered, he was gruff. He didn't want to be disturbed by such a stupid thing. *Of course we need gas, you fool. Order it.* The boy told the man from the gas company that he quite obviously needed it, his tone curt again.

'Sure sir, we'll deliver it to you tomorrow.'

Why tomorrow? He thought. *Fuck it, who cares?*

'Fine,' he then replied and slammed down the receiver. Within five minutes he had fallen back to sleep in his comfortable chair.

Vikrant waited until lunchtime to enter the premises of Pak Gas, Pakistan's leading gas supply chain. He had been waiting in a rented Toyota Corolla with Brijesh for half an hour now. Some of the workers were leaving the premises and he saw this as his chance and got out of the car. He put on a cap to conceal most of his face, then walked in through the neglected gates. A scrawny watchman appeared out of nowhere and called out at him.

'I have to place an order,' Vikrant said, and continued walking. 'I'm from Hotel Regency.'

The guard nodded vaguely and Vikrant strutted in confidently. He saw a number of parked mini-truck carriers that were loaded with gas cylinders. He would need to hotwire one of them and then speed off with it. The area seemed deserted.

He was wearing a black T-shirt, and the uniform of the delivery boys was a dark green, he realized. He needed to steal a shirt if he had to exit the premises without the guard getting suspicious. He searched each vehicle, because it was common practice even back in India for people to leave their shirts in their car to eat or rest wearing their vests. He finally found one that reeked of body odour and cigarette smoke, held his breath and put it on. It took him only a minute to hotwire the ignition and in no time, the delivery truck was making its typical rickety sound. He turned around and counted the number of cylinders. More than enough, he thought. Then he sped out towards the exit. The guard looked half asleep and scanned him superficially. He saw the green shirt, nothing seemed wrong. He had seen that cap before though. He couldn't remember where.

Meanwhile, at the JuD headquarters, Laila and Waris had just arrived in another rented Toyota Corolla. They were stopped by two rather large guards. The guards in Pakistan all looked awfully similar, the Indians thought.

They were verified at the gate. Female reporter: check. Cameraman: check. Camera: check. The guard motioned the car to a parking spot right outside the gate. No, he shook his head at the beautiful lady, who had her head covered with a red dupatta. They weren't allowed to bring a vehicle in.

Tasneem Khan, or Laila, got out of her vehicle and the elderly cameraman parked it rather shabbily in the place the guard motioned to. It was three minutes past four and the harsh afternoon sun was beating down on them. They walked hurriedly through the gates and into the confines of the fortress. Waris put his hand in his pocket and fidgeted with his phone. He pressed the 'send' button of a message he had previously typed out to Vikrant, Brijesh and Kang – saying that they were inside the headquarters. He couldn't believe that they were. Never in his life had he imagined he would be walking through these corridors.

The campus was squeaky clean. The architecture was well executed, the walkways neat and tidy; the entire place was rather pleasing to the eye. Like a college that a student would strive to get into, a college with a ninety-five per cent cut-off and associated medical facilities people vied for. Except that it wasn't really a college. Nor a hospital. A student had never graduated from here, nor had an old man with a heart attack been rushed into it.

Strangely, barring a few guards scattered around, there was little security. Maybe it was their time to rest? Afternoons usually were. They trained vigorously at midnight, stretching into the wee hours of the morning, according to the intelligence Ray had gathered.

'Salaam alaikum,' Waris said to a young bearded man, who wore a rather tight skullcap that barely contained his unruly hair. 'We are here to meet Amir Azhar.'

'Yes,' the man replied. 'He isn't here yet, but he asked you to wait in the third room on the left.'

Laila and Waris nodded and walked towards the room. It was rather surprising that Azhar wasn't around. Where else could he be in Muridke? Waris fidgeted with his camera bag uneasily.

Waris twisted the knob, opened the door and they entered. It was the size of an average classroom. There were a couple of wooden chairs, clearly meant for them. There was no window, and the room smelled musty. Why were there only two chairs? Of course. Azhar wasn't coming here. They had been played.

They rushed back to the door – only to hear the sound of it being latched from the outside.

It had been over an hour since the door had been locked. The room was claustrophobic and the electricity had been cut off. They were roasting in there.

Waris and Laila didn't even bother trying to open the door. Waris had pulled his phone out immediately, but there was no network to support it so they could not call Vikrant, Brijesh or Kang. What could they do?

Waris looked at Laila, whose expression hadn't changed in the past hour. They knew the room was bugged, so they didn't talk. There were no visible cameras, though. Laila looked back at him and shrugged.

Suddenly, they heard the door click open. They sat up straight and saw a man enter. He looked less like a man, more like an animal. He had a huge, greasy beard, fierce eyes, and short cropped hair. He was clearly a mercenary – maybe one of the strongest Azhar had at hand. He was about six feet five. And there was not an ounce of fat on his body.

'So, it's quite apparent Azhar doesn't want to look pretty for our magazine cover,' Waris said sardonically.

The man drew out a Smith and Wesson's pistol and said, 'Shut up, old man. I'm going to be doing the talking. You'll talk when I ask you a question.'

'We're not going to say a thing,' Laila spat out. 'Go fuck yourself.'

The man raised an eyebrow at her and smiled. He walked towards her and tugged at her hair, pulling her head backwards, bringing his face very close to hers.

'Leave her alone,' Waris said stoically. 'Now.'

'Otherwise what, old man?' he said. 'You think we don't know who you are? The ISI has a record of all of you. What can an old fuck like you do to me, if those pretty boys of yours can't touch me.'

He pulled Laila's hair harder. Waris looked at him.

'Remember,' Waris said, 'you asked for this.'

In one swift motion, he raised his knee into the man's crotch. Then he punched him with all his might on the bridge of his nose. The man staggered backwards, his eyes trying to regain normal vision. Laila flew at him and dug her nails into his eyes. She tore at them until they bled and the man bellowed in pain. Waris aimed another blow to his solar plexus, which winded him and left him unable to speak. He ended it by picking up the gun from the floor and shooting him through his temple.

'His backup will come rushing in at any moment,' Laila said, as she frisked the man's pockets for another weapon. She found nothing but his phone, which she pocketed. Apparently the man had thought he had everything in control with just a pistol.

They heard footsteps heading towards the room and rushed to stand on either side of the door. Waris looked at Laila and nodded silently.

The door burst open with a kick and, almost immediately, Waris fired blindly at the man who came in. He needed just one shot. The young man who had been at the reception earlier collapsed in front of them. He held an AK-47 but he didn't have a chance to use it. Waris stuck his head out and heard the sounds of chaos in the making. He lifted the AK-47 and tossed his handgun to Laila.

'Call Brijesh and Kang,' he said. 'I'll buy us some time.'

Laila nodded and dialled their number using the dead man's phone. Waris took aim and fired at the five militants who were running towards him. He fired to scare, more than to maim or

kill. He knew the show of recklessness would keep them at bay
for a few more moments while Laila made the call.

Kang raced towards the Lashkar HQ in the hijacked delivery
truck as soon as he got Laila's call.

'We can't hold out too long,' she panted. 'Get here ASAP,
every second is crucial. It was an ambush. Azhar isn't here.'

'Hold on,' Kang yelled into the phone. 'Stay on the line.'

'No,' she shouted back. 'I have to cover Waris sir.'

The phone line went dead.

Brijesh was in the storage compartment behind Kang,
attaching generous blocks of C4 to the bottom of the gas
cylinders. There were a total of eight cylinders, two of which
Brijesh and Kang were going to plant within the premises.
According to the plan, the other cylinders would remain in the
delivery truck, parked against the foundation wall of the HQ. It
would bring the entire structure to the ground.

Kang hit the upper limit to which the mini-truck could go;
120 km per hour. It grew increasingly hard to manoeuvre it and
he was at the receiving end of plenty of cuss words. Brijesh,
who was unaware of the situation brewing over at the HQ, was
perplexed at Kang's sudden recklessness. He had attached the
detonation cord to the explosives and checked to see if everything
was in place. Then he slipped the remote into his back pocket.

Kang brought the truck to a screeching halt outside the
fortress, at the planned spot. He jumped out and the guards
came running towards him, aiming their AK-47 rifles at him.

'Azhar isn't inside,' Kang informed Brijesh calmly, as the
guards approached them. He put his hands up to show he had

come unarmed. 'It was a set-up. There's a gun battle going on inside.'

'That means the ISI had already tipped him off,' Brijesh said.

'But where is the army? The Lahore Police? Have they got so confident that they can handle us on their own?' Kang said.

Brijesh fingered the Beretta 9 mm at his hip surreptitiously. The guards approached them and looked at the gas cylinders.

'You can leave them here,' one of the two said. Brijesh nodded and lifted one from the back. Kang joined him and picked up another.

'That's good enough. We'll take them inside,' the other man said. 'You aren't allowed in.'

Brijesh and Kang nodded subserviently, turned around and hopped back into the truck. As soon as the guards turned around and started dragging the cylinders towards the gate, they collapsed on the ground. One bullet each through the head had been enough. The third guard began to turn around, looking astonished. Before he could raise his rifle, Brijesh ran towards him, peppering him with bullets. They picked up the rifles that lay next to the dead bodies and dragged the cylinders inside by themselves.

They entered the building stealthily and found that the area was deserted. Then they heard gunshots. Plenty of them, coming from the right.

'Kang,' Brijesh said, 'you plant the cylinders. You know where. We have five minutes at the most.'

Kang nodded and brought his immense strength into play. He lifted both cylinders a few inches above the ground and slung the gun over his shoulder so that it was easier to move, and then walked as quickly as he could towards the innards of the building.

Kang knew he had to unload the rest of the cylinders before somebody charged in. There was a huge iron gate which could not be climbed. It was locked and the sight of the two dead guards outside would have surely raised an alarm. Soon there would be hostile gunmen swarming all over the place.

Brijesh walked back quickly with Kang and helped him drop the cylinders out of the truck in the pattern they thought would be most effective. Then Brijesh climbed into the driver's seat and revved the engine.

'We are going to need Vikrant here soon, Kang. Call him and ask him to come ASAP.

Kang immediately got on the phone with Vikrant. Brijesh shifted the stubborn gear stick into reverse and, after Kang was done, he slammed his foot down on the accelerator. He shifted into first gear, then second, then third and then, just about a metre away from the wall, into fourth. The front of the truck rammed into the wall and shards of glass, metal and brick flew dangerously all over the place. Brijesh and Kang quickly dug their heads into their shoulders to avoid any debris. Half the delivery truck had gone headfirst into the wall and the other half still stuck out. Luckily, it was enough for them to get into the premises.

Brijesh ran in the direction of the gunshots. He saw a total of fourteen armed guards rushing towards the room Waris and Laila were obviously in. He sneaked up behind them and began firing blindly in their direction. He saw at least five falling to the ground instantly, and ran in.

Waris and Laila, who had almost exhausted their ammunition, swiftly stepped out in the open and fired at a few more militants. Laila somersaulted forward and lifted an extra rifle off the ground, and together she and Brijesh targeted another two.

The remaining men were firing blindly and Brijesh had to dive for cover behind a pillar. A bullet had grazed his arm. Laila kept her finger on the trigger. Within eight seconds, all the guards lay on the floor. Dead.

'Follow me, quickly,' Waris said, as he ran ahead of the other two. Brijesh held his bleeding right arm. It was stinging and burning and he couldn't think of anything else. Waris held him by the other arm and pulled him towards the gate, outside which their Corolla was parked. *As long as the signal is jammed, the police and army will not be able to hear from the men in Markaz.*

But they would get here soon enough and so would backup from the other sections of the training facility. Ray could not keep the network jammed for more than fifteen or twenty minutes; the cellular companies would notice the jamming and set it right.

They had to make their getaway now. Brijesh handed his Thuraya to Laila, who connected with Kang.

'I've placed the cylinders. I'm running out,' he said. 'There are a few guys at the entrance, prepared to fire. You'll be outnumbered.'

'We'll scale the wall,' Laila replied. 'You get into the car and start it. Break the window, the key is still in the car.'

Kang replied in the affirmative and ran towards the exit. He pulled out his rifle and fired at the men he saw, killing one and forcing the others to take cover. Laila, Brijesh and Kang ran towards a wall. It was too high to climb and the only way to get out was to gain some elevation. Brijesh sat on his haunches and Laila climbed on to his shoulders, then leapt to the top of the wall. She perched herself there while Waris climbed on to Brijesh. She pulled him up as well. But there was no way Brijesh could climb alone.

'Go to the car,' he shouted. 'I'll come through the main entrance.'

'You'll take heavy fire out there,' she yelled.

'There's no other way,' he shouted back, beginning to run towards the entrance, holding up his rifle. He saw Kang running on the opposite side, firing at three gunmen. He took cover behind a pillar that was pockmarked by bullets. Then he fired exactly one round to distract them and immediately ran out of ammunition.

This was it. Brijesh had two choices. To escape and let them kill Kang. Or to try and rescue him and get himself killed in the process. He took shelter by lying prone behind a raised flower bed. The three gunmen split up. One of them walked towards Kang, the other two towards Brijesh who looked up and saw the gunmen raising their rifles from a distance of about fifteen feet. Game over.

Suddenly, there was a loud rattle of gunshots. Brijesh thought he had been shot. He looked down at his body, wondering how he could be so numb to the pain. But he was intact; he hadn't been shot. He looked up and saw the men collapse. Through blurry eyes, he could make out another figure rushing towards them with a rifle. Then he saw the man shoot Kang's assailant down as well. He raised himself onto his haunches, and tried to regain his senses, staring at the man who had saved him. It was Vikrant.

Vikrant lifted Brijesh off the ground and got him to put his bloody arm around his shoulder for support. Kang pulled his other arm around his neck. They began to run towards the exit, shooting at stragglers as they exited. Waris was waiting outside in the Corolla, Laila beside him.

Brijesh collapsed when they were almost there, but Vikrant dragged him and with all his force hurled him into the car, then jumped in himself. He pulled out the remote control device from Brijesh's back pocket and set off the bomb, without a pause. The plan was back on track.

The explosion within the premises set the ground rumbling. It was like an earthquake. Kang activated the other remote that would set off the cylinders in the truck, but nothing happened.

'Something is wrong. The detonation cord must have fallen off,' Vikrant gasped. 'Sir, stop the car.'

'You'll get yourself killed,' Waris said, as he began to speed away.

'No, sir, I'll manage,' Vikrant insisted. 'If they don't explode, the operation remains incomplete.' He jumped out of the car with his rifle and ran towards the cylinders. A few of the gunmen were emerging from inside, having survived the blast within the premises. He ran towards them and aimed for the cylinder in the middle. With one clinical shot, he hit it.

The result was deafening. The earth shook with the shockwave and there was a blinding explosion. Vikrant was thrown off his feet and Waris reversed the car wildly to reach him. Vikrant had been completely blinded and couldn't see from where to get in.

Laila got out of the car and pulled him in. By this point, Brijesh had lost consciousness. Waris hit the accelerator with all his might and fled the scene, leaving the house of terror in ruins.

31

Lahore

The sound of police sirens was audible even after Muridke was at least a kilometre or so behind them. Navigating the narrow roads took time and it seemed that the cellular company had overridden the jamming signal, which had resulted in a distress call being sent out. The JuD HQ would soon be swarming with police and army personnel.

Brijesh was unconscious and Vikrant was still in a daze. Waris drove the Corolla as though his life depended on breaking every high-speed record there was. They had to get out now.

Kang kept a watchful eye on Waris from the passenger's seat, while Laila kept a close watch on Vikrant and Brijesh, monitoring their condition and looking back from time to time to see if they were being pursued.

'Will someone please check with Ray?' asked Waris, his eyes glued to the road.

'On it,' said Laila, as she reached for the satellite phone.

'Ray,' she said, 'the coast is ninety-nine per cent clear, but I can't be hundred per cent sure. We can't predict what the army and cops are going to do next.'

She listened, then continued, 'Right, so I need you to tell me the quickest route to the nearest hospital … I know, a local hospital might be a bad idea, but we don't have time.'

'Ask him about hospitals in Lahore,' said Waris, from the driver's seat.

Laila relayed the message and waited a few seconds for Ray to respond. 'Jinnah Hospital? How long will that take us? Right … okay, Ray, we'll be in touch.'

She disconnected the call and leaned forward, resting her hands on the back of Waris's seat. 'Jinnah Hospital in Lahore is not the nearest, but it's our best bet. Also, Ray says that while the Lahore-Islamabad Motorway is the quickest route, the Grand Trunk Road will help us stay better concealed.'

'Hang on! You want to go to a hospital called Jinnah Hospital and not expect to be caught the second you enter?' asked Kang incredulously.

'It's our best bet,' she fired back. 'We can make some excuse and get them the medical attention they need or we can go to some small hospital and watch them bleed to death. Or we could carry some infection back with us and die slowly and painfully.'

'What a pleasant image,' said Waris. 'I agree with Laila.'

'Thank you, sir.'

'And that is why you and Kang will take the first flight to Karachi,' he said with an air of finality.

'Sir—' protested Laila.

'That's final, Borges,' said Waris. He used her last name only when he was serious.

She sulked briefly and stared glumly out of the window. 'Besides,' said Waris in a gentler voice, 'I'll be able to take care of these guys and we need to keep a low profile. I would be much happier if you were in Karachi with Ray. Poor chap, God only knows how many times he must have soiled his trousers with anxiety by now.' She smiled, placated by this last bit. If the boss was still making jokes, things weren't all that bad.

Kang cleared his throat and turned to face Waris.

'If it's all right with you, sir, having come all this way, I'd like to pay a visit to Nankana Sahib,' he said. 'Who knows if I'll ever get the chance again?'

Waris mulled this over as he drove past an oncoming unit of army vehicles.

'I see no problem with that. But you will provide regular updates.'

'No problem.'

'No problem indeed,' said Waris thoughtfully, the wrinkles around his eyes seeming to deepen by the minute as he stared out at the road.

For nearly forty minutes, the Corolla bounced along the Grand Trunk Road which, like most highways in the subcontinent, was littered with potholes. Up ahead was the Ravi bridge, their gateway into Lahore.

Brijesh was stirring and Vikrant was slowly getting over his disorientation as they crossed the river and made their way into the heart of Lahore.

'Look sharp, everyone,' said Waris. 'We'll drop Kang and Laila off at a reasonably inconspicuous area and then make our way to the hospital. Kang, you will drop Laila off to the airport and then go to Nankana Sahib.'

Kang nodded, as Laila protested once more.

'I'll be fine, you know.'

'All right then, for my satisfaction, you protect Kang on the way to the airport. Is that acceptable?' asked Waris, as Laila crossed her arms and sat back in her seat.

Progress was slow through the city traffic. The eagle-eyed Waris saw an empty side lane and pulled over. Kang hopped out and walked around to the side of the vehicle to have a look at Vikrant and Brijesh. They seemed all right.

'According to my understanding and Ray's directions, we aren't far from the hospital. Check with Ray once you get to the airport, Laila, and once you find a means of transport to take you to Nankana Sahib, Kang,' said Waris.

Kang and Laila nodded.

'I'll check with Ray when we are relatively safe and get updates on the two of you from him. I do not wish for either of you to directly contact me unless it is a life-or-death situation. Is that clear?'

They nodded again and were soon on their way.

Waris watched them head out on to the main road and hail a taxi. As soon as they got in, he stepped on the accelerator. 'Now, let's get you gentleman some medical attention,' he said. Vikrant blinked, turned his head left and right, and stretched his arms. 'What's our plan, sir?' he asked clearly, sounding quite unlike someone who had just had gas cylinders exploding in his face.

'The plan is to make sure Brijesh gets stitched up and that you don't have a concussion or anything. So just sit back and don't fall asleep,' said Waris, as he drove towards the hospital.

32

All four walls of the office were covered with various kinds of maps – physical, topographical and thematic. Despite having spent a major part of his life in Islamabad, Afridi was quite familiar with Karachi. However, Lahore and its outskirts were virtually unknown to him. Afridi belonged to the Pashtun tribe but his ancestors had spent considerable time in Lahore. He had never thought that he would one day return to the city, not for nostalgic reasons but for vengeance.

The attack on Muridke, the destruction of Markaz, was to his mind, an insult to Pakistan. The earful that he received from the director had left him seething with fury. The words were still ringing in his ears.

'For Pakistan, the attack on Muridke is nothing less than the collapse of the World Trade Centre in New York. Those men entered our lair and we were left gawking at them like bloody spectators. Tamasha bana diya hai inhone Pakistani waqar ka,' Zaheer had screamed at him.

Afridi had immediately flown to Lahore by a special jet. He realized that he could not control the investigation and the chase with a remote. He would have to get down and dirty and work like a field operative.

He had scoured the area to start with. The witnesses had clearly said that there were three Sikh men and one bearded man wearing a polo cap. They also mentioned an extremely good-looking girl; they felt she was possibly an actress or something.

First things first, he had to understand the Lahore landscape. Afridi had asked for maps so that he could examine the possible hideouts of the fugitives. He had to find all the nooks and corners of Lahore and its surrounding villages.

He took turns studying the topographical and thematic maps. There were a large number of Sikhs in Lahore for the Indians to lose themselves amongst. They could also have taken refuge among the tribals and some Hindus sympathetic to India. He knew that the trail of these killers would probably grow cold soon.

And he was just one man. How could he dig them out single-handedly? Lahore is one of the most densely populated cities in the world with a population of nearly a crore. To track down four men and a woman amidst the dense sea of humanity would be like hunting for a black ant on a dark night. But Afridi was determined.

He gathered his team in the office and issued instructions. All cars leaving Lahore should be thoroughly checked. All exit points should be sealed from the Walled City to the outer areas. All groups of Sikhs were to be screened, any anomaly in their documents or failure to explain their presence in the area was to be investigated. All Indian and Pakistani passports were to be examined for their authenticity.

'In fact, anyone who fails to provide proper identification documents is to be detained and have his or her antecedents verified,' Afridi said.

'Set up a control room and keep giving me updates of any suspicious sightings. Ensure that the whole of Lahore is swarming with police, military, para-military and intelligence persons in civil clothes.

'I want so many of our men on the streets of Lahore that it becomes suffocating for these Indians. No one should dare to give them refuge. I want them arrested in less then twelve hours. They should not be able to leave the city limits.'

After his men had been dismissed, Afridi began pacing up and down. Could the Indians be thinking of going towards the Wagah border? Did it seem sensible for them to imagine an escape plan across into India? What if they left through China?

Or Afghanistan? This was a make or break situation. He simply could not afford to lose any more time.

It suddenly occurred to him to speak to his friend Wang. Afridi whipped out his cellphone and started to dial his friend's number. He waited while the phone started ringing.

33

New Delhi, 13 November, 7.30 a.m.

The shrill ringing of his phone shattered Sky's sleep. He extended his hand and picked up the cordless phone, hoping it was not a wrong number. He was still groggy and half-asleep when the caller said, 'Good morning, sir, this is Dixit. Sorry to disturb your sleep. The prime minister has urgently called for a meeting and he wants you to be present.'

Sky was at once alert and awake. The call was not from the home secretary or the home minister. It was directly from the PMO. 'What shall I tell him, sir?' Dixit asked. 'The meeting is at 8 a.m. at the PM's residence.'

'I'm on my way,' Sky said.

He had not been able to sleep the whole night, and had only managed to catch an hour's nap prior to the call. Since the previous afternoon, he had been fielding calls and talking to ministers, bureaucrats, colleagues, agency chiefs. The whole country had erupted into a tumultous outpouring of opinion.

People only wanted to talk about the Muridke operation. The newspapers, the TV channels, Facebook, Twitter, it was all about Muridke.

The only other news which had received more coverage on international news channels recently had been the killing of Osama bin Laden in May 2011. The channels attributed the explosion to anything and everything. From terror groups infighting between Lashkar-e-Toiba and Jaish-e-Mohammad to the Pakistani army's renegade groups' initiative, even the possibility of a rebel group of Taliban asserting their supremacy in this manner.

But Pakistani channels were clear that it was a terror attack by Indian agents. The place was known to be a terror training hub, yet the Pakistani news anchors described it as a terror attack on the Jamaat-ud-Daawa office. A cleverly omitted bit was that JuD was an organization banned by the United States and the Pakistani government, and that their accounts were frozen.

The Indian media lionized the attackers. 'A Rambo-like operation' was what they were calling it. Soon they started showing graphics and outlining the systematic manner in which the operation had been executed. 'They only attacked the terror training school and spared the adjoining masjid and hospital' was the refrain of most of the news readers.

The Indian government, was relieved to know that no direct connections on its part, had been established as yet. Beyond the baseless allegations, the Pakistani media had nothing to substantiate their claims. No one had been detained or arrested.

Although Pakistani channels had begun flashing old sketches of Brijesh and Vikrant in their Muslim avatars of Nasiruddin and Mushfiq Mirza, they could not make any headway. When they claimed that the assailants could be Indians, the TV panelists, the Ministry of Home Affairs representative all clearly denied Indian involvement in the attack.

'Ours is a democratic nation. We believe in diplomatic channels and do not resort to guerilla tactics. We will not even say that these were non-state actors' was the sum and substance of most of the statements issued by the government spokesperson.

The Pakistanis were certain that it was the same team that had killed Haaris Saeed and his cronies in an earlier operation. Sky was the only one who knew that it was Waris and his team who had struck again. He was beginning to feel proud of his friend. But he was not happy about this sudden summons for a meeting.

Also, for a meeting at the PM's residence, this was unusually early.

Just before stepping out, Sky carefully drafted a simple two-line resignation, placed it in an envelope and put it in his shirt pocket. There was a legend in the corridors of power that no one could match the level of Sky's mental preparation. 'Only Sky is the limit' was the joke.

As Sky's car turned towards 10 Janpath, he saw something that lifted his mood. An old couple were riding by on a scooter, which had a pole attached to the spare tyre. A banner was attached to the top of the pole with a message saying: 'May God be with you, Avengers.'

Sky smiled to himself.

Almost immediately after, the car drew to a halt. A motley crowd of some two hundred people carrying placards and boards in their hands were standing outside their destination. Obviously they wanted the prime minister to see them when he came out for a walk or if he was on his way to a meeting.

'Hail Avengers', 'Our salute to you, oh heroes', 'India loves Mumbai Avengers', the placards read.

In the portico he could see several bigwigs' cars. Stepping into the meeting room, he saw that the defence minister, the home minister, the army and navy chiefs and the heads of IB and NSA were all present.

He was the last one to enter. He spotted a vacant chair and sat down.

The prime minister turned to him and said, 'We have reasons to believe that these … these Avengers, are your boys and they have your blessings.'

'Sir, Ali Waris is my friend, I will admit that, but he is a crazy guy. This rag tag team is his. I have no role to play in it. Right from team selection to planning, it is Waris's brainchild.'

'This could have serious repercussions. We could face international embarrassment.'

Sky realized this was the moment of truth.

'I beg to differ. From America to Israel, whoever has punished their enemies on foreign soil has never faced any embarrassment. We should start thinking unconventionally. It's high time. Even the public has come out in support of them.'

'I think now that they have served their purpose. We should just liquidate them, it will be for the common good,' suggested the home secretary.

Sky glared at him. 'They are not paper napkins that can be used and discarded.'

The IB chief was looking at his phone; he was getting text message alerts. He looked up and said, 'I have just received reports that people have come out openly in support of these Avengers and victory rallies have been planned in Mumbai,

Delhi, Bengaluru, Kolkata, Pune, Nagpur and also other places. They say a huge turnout is expected ...'

The PM turned towards his defence minister. 'How feasible is the possibility of extraction?'

'We cannot wage a war with our neighbours on this issue, especially when we have caused a disturbance in their country,' he declared.

'With due respect, sir, they don't think like that when they kill our soldiers at the LoC,' Sky replied.

'Assembly elections are around the corner, we cannot afford to abandon them and have people lose faith in us,' said Sumit Shah, the PM's trusted adviser.

'It will be impossible to mount a full-scale operation inside a hostile country,' said the NSA.

'If I know Waris well, he does not need full-scale operational support. He is a man who can remove a screw with a sledgehammer. He might just need a little support and help and he will find a way back,' Sky said, with a sense of pride.

The prime minister looked at Sky and said, 'Mr Yadav, you seem to be quite proud of his achievements. Give him that small support and help. I would request all of you present here to chip in with your suggestions and ideas. Let's bring them back.'

The finality in his tone put an end to any room for debate or counter-suggestions. He looked at the army and navy chiefs, both of whom nodded.

The meeting was over. Sky removed the envelope from his protect, tore it into pieces and threw it in the dustbin. It was not personal any more. He would not quit until he got the team back.

34

Jinnah Hospital, Lahore

The next few minutes seemed like a bizarre hallucination to Vikrant; he saw familiar shapes and colours fly past, outside the car window, but he was unable to connect them to known objects until a few moments after they had passed. Involuntarily swaying from side to side, he stretched his limbs and shook his head to keep the blood flowing through his body, occasionally checking on Brijesh, whose threshold of pain was being tested to the limit.

The Corolla soon pulled into the main foyer of the Jinnah Hospital and, to Waris's relief, the beefed-up police cordon he was expecting to see was non-existent. After pulling over in one of the waiting bays, he stepped out of the vehicle and approached a ward boy standing nearby.

'Salaam alaikum, I need to get these two admitted immediately,' he said, pointing to the men in the backseat of the vehicle.

The ward boy seemed to prefer life at a slower pace and his speech reflected as much.

'Oh. So … what happened … where did the … uhh … What happened to them?' he asked disinterestedly.

'Car accident,' said Waris, falling back on the tried and tested formula that Brijesh had relied on in Jeddah.

'Oh,' the boy said and began wandering off.

'Look,' said Waris, a little more assertively as he held the ward boy by the wrist. 'Will you please get a couple of wheelchairs to take these men in so they can be admitted?'

Startled by this breach of personal space, the boy went into bureaucratic mode.

'You will have to fill a form and wait for a doctor to examine them. If he decides to have them admitted, then you will have to register and provide—'

'I don't have time for all that, son. I'll fill all the forms you need once you give them some medical attention. They are American pilgrims and if they succumb to their injuries, you will have a major international incident on your hands!'

The boy blinked. Waris could see the cogs turning in his head, slowly but surely.

'They don't look American,' he offered.

'Do you want to see their passports? Do you know what will happen if American citizens die here?'

A doctor passing by happened to overhear the last part of this exchange and stopped in his tracks. Hurrying over to Waris, he asked, 'Who are the American citizens?' Waris pointed to the backseat of his vehicle.

'What happened to them?' asked the doctor, with a sense of urgency in his voice.

Here we go again, thought Waris.

'They were in a car accident,' he said.

'What are you waiting for?' the doctor scolded the ward boy. 'Get these men inside at once!'

The ward boy scuttled off to find a couple of wheelchairs and the doctor sighed in disdain.

Waris opened the car door and let the doctor have a look at his wounded cohorts. After a few preliminary checks, the doctor decided he would have to examine them in a better-lit environment. He turned to Waris. 'American citizens?'

'Yes, doctor. They were here on a pilgrimage.'

Seeing that the doctor was unmoved, Waris dove into the Corolla to produce the fake passports that had been made for Brijesh and Vikrant. He flashed them and the doctor nodded, getting into top gear as he hustled the ward boy over and helped Vikrant and Brijesh into wheelchairs. They were promptly wheeled into the hospital.

'I am Dr Suleiman Baig,' the doctor said, pointing to his nametag. 'You'll need to know that when you fill the form. I'll admit these men and let you fill out all the paperwork.'

Waris nodded and Dr Baig went off to diagnose his new patients' injuries. At the reception, Waris found that the forms were ready and neatly collated on a clipboard bearing the hospital's name and logo. *This Baig seems like quite a useful fellow*, thought Waris to himself, as he began filling out the forms.

'Well, the good news is that you don't appear to have a concussion. Since you're not in any major pain, I don't think we'll need to prescribe any painkillers,' said Dr Baig chirpily, switching off the little flashlight that he had been shining in Vikrant's eyes. As the doctor walked over to his table to note down his observations, there was a knock on the door of his office. Vikrant hopped off the observation table on which he had been sitting.

'Come in,' said Dr Baig, and in walked Waris with a peon who was carrying a photocopy of the forms that had just been filled.

'Take a seat,' the doctor said to Waris as he took the photocopies from the peon, who left at once.

'How bad is it?' asked Waris.

'Your friend here has suffered some trauma, but there's no concussion and there doesn't seem to be any internal bleeding. But his companion, Mr Kartar Singh, has lost a lot of blood and I've sent him to the ER.'

Waris nodded.

'I've encountered a lot of car accident victims and their injuries usually reflect the unpredictable effects of the accident,' said Dr Baig, 'But these injuries seem … how should I put this? They seem inconsistent.'

'They were hit by a passing vehicle,' said Waris calmly.

'Right, that's the part I don't get. There are no neck injuries, no whiplash, all that you'd normally see in an accident. There are no grazes or bruises.'

'So what are you saying?'

'Nothing. It just seems inconsistent, that's all. Car accident victims suffer different kind of injuries,' said Dr Baig, with a smile. 'I should probably go and check on your companion. You are welcome to wait here.'

Waris and Vikrant exchanged grim glances once the doctor left.

'Any thoughts about an exit plan?' asked Vikrant, as he looked at the solitary door that led into the doctor's windowless office.

Dr Baig returned to find Waris and Vikrant standing outside his office. Experience and intuition had taught them never to expose themselves to a situation in which they might be cornered. The doctor flashed them a gentle, disarming smile as he approached them.

'Back on your feet, I see?' he asked Vikrant.

'Yes, doctor. Any updates?'

'Well, your friend's wounds have been stitched up and he's been given medication. There wasn't the need for a blood transfusion, since he hadn't lost as much as I had feared.'

'Thank you, doctor,' said Waris. He quickly added, 'When will he be ready to move?'

'He should be up and about shortly, but I would recommend that both patients take it easy for a day or two. We don't have to hospitalize them but I recommend they get accommodation nearby, perhaps in the sarai. Just in case,' he said.

'Are you saying we can't leave for Nankana Sahib?' frowned Vikrant.

'It's a recommendation, that's all,' smiled Dr Baig.

'Can we see our friend now?'

'Sure. I'll have someone take you to him, while I submit my report and sort out the paperwork.'

A trainee doctor accompanied them to the room in which Brijesh was recovering. Waris was the first to enter.

Brijesh was flipping channels on the television and scanning the news. The Muridke attack dominated almost all the news channels. It was prime time news. The anchors were talking to panelists — experts, former army men and authors — and discussing the fallout of such a brazen attack by RAW agents.

'Ready to roll?' asked Waris, getting straight to the point.

'Just say the word,' smiled Brijesh weakly, as Vikrant took a seat next to the bed and picked up an apple from the fruit basket set on a side table. He wiped it against his shirt and was about to take a bite when he noticed two pairs of eyes on him.

'Is there a problem?' he asked Waris and Brijesh.

'No, no. Make yourself at home,' laughed Waris, as Vikrant sunk his teeth into the apple.

'I'm hungry,' he said between bites.

'The doctor said we should spend the next couple of days nearby, "just in case",' said Waris.

'I think they're required to say things like that,' said Brijesh cynically, as he ran a finger over the bandages on his arm. 'I'm sure I can get the stitches removed somewhere else.'

'Regardless, lying low for a while might not be such a bad idea,' reasoned Waris, 'After all, Ray and Laila need to get back to us with some intel and Kang is going to take a couple of days anyway.'

In the background, the news anchor's voice rose and a breaking news tag started to flash.

'Maulana Azhar *ka khula challenge, jumma namaz ke baad* Jinnah ground *mein khetaab karenge.*'

'What the fuck?' said Vikrant.

'We should kill him in Jinnah ground. Friday is a good day to die anyway. He will be despatched to hell directly,' Brijesh said, sipping from his glass of juice.

'This could be another bait planted by the ISI. You never know, they might think that we will try and eliminate him at Jinnah ground and they can ambush us,' Waris said.

'There must be a way to verify this breaking news,' Brijesh said, finishing his glass of juice.

'I'll have to check with Sky if he is keeping a tab on Azhar's movements,' Waris said, 'and I also have to notify him about our change of exit plans – we have to get out of here fast.'

'Sir, can we ask Laila to look around in Azizabad area and see if these Lashkar men have already started setting up security barricades around Jinnah ground?' Brijesh asked Waris.

'I think she is supposed to check out of the hospital tomorrow morning and take a flight to Dubai,' Vikrant said.

One of the news channels was showing a bearded Mulla Umar Farooq, the right-hand man of Mahmood Azhar, addressing the media outside a masjid. 'After Jumma prayers, Maulana sahib will give a speech on the hypocrisy of India. We could have done it tomorrow or the day after tomorrow, but because of Ashoora (Moharram) on Thursday, we have postponed it to Friday, which is the most sacred day according to Islam. He has also thrown a challenge at those Indian agents who are making unsuccessful attempts to kill him. If they want, they can come to Jinnah ground, we would love to make a kheema of them.'

Vikrant looked around for a dustbin to dispose the core of the apple he had just devoured, when a knock on the door diverted his attention. He dropped it on the floor and positioned himself on the side of the door at Waris's signal. Once Vikrant was in place, Waris called out, 'Come in.'

A man in his forties stood outside the door in a brown kurta worn over a conspicuous pair of green track pants with bright yellow piping. 'Excuse me, but you need to—' Before he had a chance to explain himself, Vikrant had pulled him in and kicked the door shut with his heel.

'Who are you?' he demanded.

'Sir, please …' the man gasped. 'I can't … I can't breathe.'

Vikrant retracted his forearm by a few millimetres to keep the man firmly in place, while allowing him breathing room.

'You are in grave danger and you need to leave now,' said the man without beating about the bush.

'What kind of danger?'

'I can't explain right now, but we have to leave immediately. If you don't, you'll be trapped, and you know it.'

'Who is this "we"?' asked Waris, as he rose to his feet.

'Sir, I can't explain right now, but I promise I'll explain everything once we are safe.'

'What do you think?' Vikrant asked Waris and Brijesh.

'Are you ready to move?' Waris turned to ask Brijesh, who sat up and ripped off the intravenous saline tube that was stuck in his arm.

'Follow me, please,' said the man, as Brijesh sat up and looked around for a shirt.

The surgeons who had stitched up Brijesh's arm must have disposed of his shirt, they realized, so he had to make do with his hospital robe. Vikrant eased his arm off the intruder's throat at last and opened the door an inch to take a look outside. All seemed quiet, so he turned to face the man again.

'Are you sure?' he asked sceptically.

'Positive,' replied the man in green trackpants. 'We must leave now.'

'Lead the way.'

The man opened the door, looked left and right, and motioned for the trio to follow. They did so stealthily, careful to avoid attracting attention. He led them down a corridor to the fire escape. They followed him, unable to shake off the suspicion that in this exposed state, they were sitting ducks for an ambush. They soon found themselves in the basement, looking at a sign on a door that read 'Medical Supplies'. The man pushed the door open and led them to the end of the room, where the basement window looked out at the hospital's foyer. Peering out at the assortment of police vehicles that had assembled outside the hospital's entrance, the man turned to Waris.

'My name is Chandra Prakash and those men are here for you.'

'How do you know they are here for us?' asked Waris.

'I don't imagine there are many groups of three Indians who have been injured while escaping the authorities and come for treatment to this hospital.'

'Who told you we are Indian?'

'I'll tell you everything just as soon as we get out of here.'

'Why should we listen to a damn word you have to say?' asked Vikrant, bristling, as Waris placed a hand on his shoulder to calm him down.

'I don't blame you for being suspicious, sir. Suspicion has followed me through life, either because of my religion or like today, because of my sympathies.'

Waris pursed his lips.

'But now is not the time to discuss my life. We need to move,' he said, motioning to a door on the other side of the room.

With his hand on the door handle, the man turned to find Waris, Vikrant and Brijesh still rooted to their spot near the window. 'You won't find Mahmood Azhar by just standing there,' he said and turned to open the door carefully, without setting off the fire alarm. He didn't need eyes in the back of his head to know that all three of them were picking their respective jaws up off the floor.

The four men left the building through the fire exit and discreetly made their way out of the compound and into an alley nearby, where a van emblazoned with the Lahore Police emblem was parked. Vikrant froze when he saw the van, but seeing that Waris and Brijesh seemed to trust the man, he reluctantly followed. They didn't have much of a choice, really.

Chandra pulled the sliding door open and reached inside, rummaging for something. *He's looking for a gun,* Vikrant thought to himself as he balled his fists and prepared for a counter-attack.

'Here,' said Chandra, as he began unzipping a green tracksuit top with bright yellow piping that ran from the neck all the way down to the sleeves. 'Get rid of that,' he told Brijesh, pointing to his hospital robes and handing him the top. Brijesh gingerly slipped his arms into it and zipped it halfway up his chest.

'A perfect fit,' smiled Chandra as he hopped into the driver's seat. Brijesh and Waris climbed into the back, while Vikrant sat in the front.

'Speak,' he said gruffly.

'Not yet,' said Chandra as he started the van. 'We're not out of the woods. Get rid of your Sikh attire, the roads are swarming with cops and army men. Three Sikhs in a van will arouse curiosity and then, even I will not be able to protect you.'

As they made their way past a solitary police barricade, Chandra drove silently through a maze of inside lanes and alleyways. 'That should be the last of them,' he said as a police van passed them.

'Now speak,' said Vikrant.

'It's a long story so I won't gloss over the details. After all, we have plenty of time now,' said Chandra.

'Why plenty of time?' Waris asked.

'I assume you want to make a trip to Karachi by Friday. I believe I am the only person who can safely transport you to Azizabad without any hurdles.'

Vikrant looked at Waris, unsure of whether to go along with the extremely unsettling information possessed by Chandra or to snap his neck there and then. Waris nodded and gently gestured to Vikrant to calm down.

'Chandra, I'm very grateful for your help so far and so are my associates, I'm sure,' said Waris politely, lapsing into Hindi. 'And since you seem to know so much, you probably know that I'm a man who enjoys the seaside, I enjoy brisk morning walks in the rain and I really enjoy Lebanese food.'

Vikrant furrowed his brow, unsure of exactly where his boss was going with this.

'What I don't enjoy,' said Waris, this time with a bit more aggression in his voice, 'is the idea of someone fucking with me. So I'm willing to be patient with you as long as you stop the mindgames at once.'

'I'm sorry,' said Chandra. 'That was not my intention at all. Let me start from the beginning.'

'Please do.'

'As I've told you already, my name is Chandra Prakash and yes, I am a Pakistani and a Hindu. There aren't many of us left, as you know. Those of us who weren't killed, converted or forced to flee the country were marginalized through other means. I was born with a gift. Well, two gifts really. Natural athleticism and supportive parents.'

'Modesty too,' said Vikrant dryly. 'But what's your point?'

'I'm getting to it, sir,' Chandra said politely. They began to leave the bright lights of Lahore behind, as he continued. 'As a child, I participated in every sport you could think of, with the exception of squash. I hated squash. My dream was to represent my country on the national stage. Islahuddin Siddique and Hanif

Mohammad were just two of my heroes. Would you believe I played five sports at the domestic level?'

'Five? Impressive,' said Vikrant, warming to him finally.

'Indeed, but when the time came to focus my energy on one spent, I picked football and signed up for national selection. Needless to say, I was not selected.' His tone suddenly turned darker. 'According to the Pakistan Football Federation, "disciplinary and miscellaneous issues" prevented me from being a part of the team. What they meant, of course, was that I wasn't Muslim.Even Yusuf Youhanna had to convert to Islam and when Danish Kaneria did not, he was eased out of the cricket team. In a placatory gesture, they waited until I was past my prime and offered me the job of national coach,' Chandra said.

Waris, Vikrant and Brijesh were listening intently by this point.

'National coach? I could have taken Pakistan to the World Cup with my on-field abilities. Instead, they consigned me to a safer role, where there was no danger of a Hindu stealing the limelight from their "purer" players. Can you believe that? And through it all, I had to silently suffer things that no other national coach would or should have to put up with. Insubordination, death threats for substituting players, the list is endless. And all of this was reinforced by a very narrow-minded management.'

'Must have been tough,' offered Vikrant.

'It was, sir. It most definitely was,' said Chandra grimly. Then he regained his cheery demeanour. 'But it wasn't all bad. The commissioner of police in Lahore at the time was something of a football aficionado. During the off-season for the national team, he invited me to his office and told me he believed the Pakistani Pelé was waiting to be unearthed from within the Lahore Police football team, and that I would be the man to do that. He said that if I agreed to coach the Lahore Police team during the off-season, a number of my day-to-day problems would disappear.'

'Like what?' asked Brijesh, as he noticed the series of police checkpoints that had been set up on the way. The police personnel manning these checkpoints simply waved the van through. Very unlike any nakabandi he had ever seen – but this was a police van.

'Oh, the usual stuff. Being randomly rounded up and harassed by the police, not being allowed to buy a house, being followed, having my phone tapped … Unexplained detention of my Hindu relatives. Things like that. It was too good an offer to refuse and so I took up the job. Over the years, I found that job more fulfilling than the national-level one. With the revolving door of footballers coming into and leaving the team, I hardly saw most players for more than a couple of seasons. With the Lahore Police team, it was different.' He smiled, as he pulled over to the side of a fairly deserted stretch of the highway.

Chandra made his apologies and went to relieve himself behind the trees. Waris, Vikrant and Brijesh didn't say a word for fear of being overheard, but the furtive glances they shared indicated that they believed Chandra to be genuine. But what did his story have to do with Karachi and Mahmood Azhar, they wondered. Well, they had the best part of a thirteen-hour-journey ahead of them and it seemed they would have no option but to trust this man—for now.

35

Lahore, outskirts

'Seems like there's only one way out,' Waris said, taking a deep breath. 'But I need to make a call first.'

He picked up his Thuraya and activated the speaker phone.

Within two seconds an unfamiliar voice could be heard at the other end.

'Hello Mukesh, kaise ho? Saab ghar main hain?'

'Jee haan,' a puzzled Mukesh replied.

'Unhe phone dena,' Waris said.

'Jee kaun bol rahae hain?'

'Main unki sasuraal se bol raha hoon.'

'Lekin sahib toh shaadi …'

'Phone do saab ko jaldi!'

Waris's bark was enough to send the man into action. He immediately rushed to Sky's study and handed the phone over – telling him it was his sasuraal, though he was sure Sir had never got married.

'It's okay, he must be my baap,' Sky replied.

'Hello, Sayed saab, you're calling on my driver's cell. How did you get his number?'

'The power of reserve knowledge, it's always handy.'

'So you and your friends have kicked up a major storm, miyan. It's damaging the TRPs of *Big Boss*.'

'Well, then we've killed two birds with one stone. I never really enjoyed that show.'

'Who knows, maybe after you come back, you can enter as a contestant,' Sky said, with a chuckle.

'From one stressful environment to another, eh? Listen Aakash, carefully, I'll be quick now,' Waris said, using the Hindi term for Sky.

'I'm all ears, Sayed saab, go on.'

'We are on our way to Ihcarak,' Waris said, reversing the name of Karachi.

'I knew the moment I saw this on TV that you would be unstoppable. But they will be swarming like ants all over the place, how will you—'

'We will go as Mr India. Don't worry. If we can bring one of their most secure structures to the ground, we can easily take down a less secure one.'

Waris looked at the rest of the team, who were trying to stifle their laughter.

'So how can I help you?' Sky asked

'We are planning to return to our native village and we need you to send the transport.'

'I have just emerged from a talkathon with the PM.'

'What does he want?'

'You'll have to return sooner. "Right away" were the exact words.'

'Well, he can wait for the photo ops. We have work to do.'

There was a brief silence. Waris heard a sigh from Sky.

The team looked on in rapt attention, observing Waris's reddened face.

Then, finally the phone crackled on the other side. 'How much time do you all need for the Friday prayers?'

'We can leave around dinner,' Waris told him.

'Fine,' Sky said. 'I'll tell him. But after that, we extract you.'

'That's exactly why we called.'

'Yes,' Sky replied. 'But do you have any idea how we can do that?'

'The same way those boys came in,' Waris said.

'Through water?'

'Yes, water. Except, with some style. After all, we aren't some gun-toting teenagers.'

'So what do you expect?

'Send us a fish,' Waris demanded, going cryptic again.

'What the fuck? You want to start a war?' Sky said

'Well, you have to put them to use sooner or later. Now seems like a good time.'

'Okay, I guess I can organize that, but I can't get into their territorial waters.'

'Then you catch us in international waters. Leave a speed boat at a fishing village, along with scuba gear.'

'I will send you coordinates before Friday,' Sky said and cut the call.

36

14 November
En Route to Karachi

'You've been driving non-stop for a few hours now. Let's pull over and get some tea. What do you say, Chandu?' asked Waris, who had warmed up to the football coach enough to start bestowing terms of endearment upon him.

'Excellent idea, we'll stop at the nearest dhaba,' Chandra replied jovially.

'Good, I could do with stretching my legs for a while,' said Vikrant lazily.

'Self-centred as always, eh, Vikrant?' joked Brijesh.

'You know it,' replied Vikrant, with a smile. He sat up and spoke to Chandra. 'You know, you have yet to complete your story.'

'We'll get to it as soon as we're back on the road, I assure you,' smiled the football coach, as he spotted a row of parked trucks in the distance, on the side of the road.

Chandra switched on the left indicator and switched lanes to reposition the van, so as to be able to turn off further up the road. He followed the parked trucks until he arrived at a small shack surrounded by charpoys, and pulled over. All four climbed out of the van. Vikrant was the first to drop into the comfort of a charpoy and stretch lazily. They asked the little boy in a browning white vest and blue shorts with a kitchen towel slung over his shoulder for four cups of tea.

'How much longer till we get to Karachi, Chandu?' asked Waris, as he looked around at the serene surroundings.

'Not too long. I would say anywhere between nine and ten hours.'

'That seems like "not too long" to you?' asked Vikrant in shock.

'Well, when you live in Pakistan, you get used to waiting. From waiting for the government to collapse to waiting for some religious group to come after you to waiting for your sports teams to make you proud and, of course, waiting to get your due. Waiting, in this country of ours, is something of a regular occurrence.'

'I suppose it's something you have experience with too,' said Chandra, as Brijesh looked at him. He continued light-heartedly, 'Like waiting for those damn Hindi movies to finally get over. Am I right?'

Vikrant chuckled, as Waris burst into laughter.

'So, you watch a lot of Hindi movies, Chandu?' asked Waris.

'I used to watch one as soon as it was released. Not so much any more.'

'Why's that?' asked Brijesh.

'Well, I can't remember the last time I saw a memorable Hindi movie,' said Chandra ruefully. Then he changed his mind: 'Actually, I can.'

The little boy in the vest arrived just then with a tray bearing four cups of steaming tea, and the men focused on taking tiny sips of the rejuvenating brew.

'So what was it?' asked Vikrant.

'*Chak De India,*' Chandra said, with a straight face. 'As strange as that may sound.'

'It doesn't sound strange at all. It was a good film,' said Vikrant.

'I guess I could relate to certain aspects of the film – the beleaguered coach who used to be a player. The only difference was that he actually got to represent his country,' simmered Chandra.

Eager to bring back the relaxed atmosphere that had accompanied them into the dhaba, Vikrant quickly changed the subject.

'And since then, you haven't seen a single decent Hindi movie?' he asked.

'Not that I can remember,' said Chandra, looking off into the distance.

'There was a time,' he said, 'when there was a point to watching movies. There was a story to be told. There were directors who decided how the story would be told and there were actors who brought the story to life. Watching a film like that was a treat. It was worth the hassle of procuring illegal prints and watching it secretly with a few friends.'

He stopped and blew over the top of his fragrant tea, sending a cloud of steam rolling off it.

'As you probably know, only a small number of Hindi films are released in Pakistan these days. Between 1965 and 2008, there was a total ban on Hindi films. But I digress. As I was saying, watching a film was an experience that left you happy or sad, pensive or buzzed, smouldering with anger or smiling with a song in your heart. Today, there's none of that,' said Chandra.

He took a quick sip, which must have burnt the insides of his mouth. But such was the vitriol brewing inside him that it hardly seemed to matter. He put his glass down, and signalled that it was time to leave.

Brijesh and Chandra reached forward at the same time with the money to settle their bill and shared a laugh. The situation seemed to have been defused, and Waris smiled in relief. There was enough turmoil afoot.

'Shall we continue with your story now?' asked Vikrant, as they settled back for the long drive ahead.

'Certainly,' said Chandra, and cleared his throat. 'As I mentioned earlier, I was appointed the coach of the Lahore

Police football team and my professional life began to improve with players who wanted to learn and grow. But when I wasn't in my coach's tracksuit, things were the same. I was still being harassed and discriminated against. The final straw came when an offer to train in England was shot down by the local authorities, who refused to process my visa application. It wasn't the English who rejected my application. It was my own people.'

'For no reason apart from your—' began Vikrant.

'For no reason apart from my religion,' confirmed Chandra. He continued, 'Hadn't I proved my skill and loyalty? Did I not deserve that opportunity?'

'Anyway, how does all of this concern you, gentlemen? Let me tell you. One of the benefits of being the coach for the Lahore Police team was that I was able to make a few very close friends – the sort of policemen who see the worth of a person as more than just which God he prays to. When explaining the heightened security these days, one of my friends in the Police told me about the Indians who were causing all this havoc across Pakistan and I was intrigued.'

Vikrant shifted uneasily in his seat.

'And then, when all of them ran out of a practice session to change their clothes and head to Muridke, I knew something unusual was afoot. When I had finished in the changing room and packed away all the equipment, I went to the control room, as I always do after practice. While there, I learned that not only had the Indians fled Muridke, but also that they were suspected of being holed up in Lahore. This was an opportunity I was not going to miss and so I made my way to Jinnah Hospital as soon as the control room received a call from Dr Baig,' he said.

'That son of a bitch,' fumed Vikrant.

'We can't thank you enough for this, Chandu,' said Waris.

'The time will come, I assure you,' Chandra smiled. 'But there is more to come – this network of friends in the police also let me in on a few other things, which I can use for the benefit of my Indian friends.'

'You really are a godsend!' Waris said. They would have been trapped without this unlikely little man.

'Well, then,' smiled Chandra, as he looked back at Waris through the rearview mirror. 'You can thank me by taking me back to India with you. I have no family left in Pakistan. I know I'll have better opportunities there.'

'Certainly, Chandu. But since you know so much already, I'm guessing you also know that we can't go back to India yet,' Waris said calmly.

'But you will,' said Chandra. 'Soon!'

It was roughly five in the evening after a gruelling twelve-and-a-half-hour drive, when the van pulled off the Karachi Northern Bypass and on to the Karachi–Hyderabad Motorway. Waris touched Vikrant's arm to make sure he was awake, and saw that he was.

It had been a surprisingly relaxed day considering just how harrowing the previous twenty-four-hours had been. The company had been pleasant, the conversation engaging and the time seemed to have just flown past. Most unexpectedly, they had made a useful ally. But there was one catch: he wanted a safe passage to India. Knowing Sky's meticulous attention to detail, the presence of one extra person could screw up their escape plans.

That bridge can be crossed when we get there, thought Waris, as he began to mentally prepare for the rally that was set to take place after Friday prayers the next day. He had less than twenty-seven hours to coordinate with Ray, Laila and Kang. Karachi wasn't too far now, but it was crowded and complicated. The city's Bagh-e-Jinnah or Jinnah Ground would be hosting Mahmood Azhar's rally, and his Waris and team would have to ensure that this opportunity was not lost.

Chandra turned off the Karachi–Hyderabad Motorway, causing Waris to lean forward and place his hand on the back of the driver's seat.

'We are going to Karachi, right?' he asked as he saw the road signs.

'We are,' replied Chandra, 'but not today. I suggest we spend the night in Gadap Town, to the north of Karachi.'

'It'll definitely keep us off the radar,' agreed Waris.

Gadap Town in the northwestern part of Karachi was less densely packed as compared to other parts of Pakistan's commercial capital and Waris was grateful for this. As the final rays of sunlight faded from the sky, Chandra pulled his van into the driveway of a small, vacant looking house.

'This property was owned at some point by my family. I can never remember them living here, but they owned it,' Chandu said.

'Well, as long as it has a place where we can lie down and a toilet, it's fine by me,' said Waris.

The door opened creakily and the men walked in. The spider-infested front room was not a comforting sight, but it would be far safer here than staying in a clean and luxurious hotel in the middle of Karachi. Chandra made his way into the inside room and opened the dusty cupboard to extract a few moth-eaten bedsheets.

'These are all we have left, I'm afraid. Make yourselves comfortable,' he said.

The trio nodded at him.

'I'm going to go out and get some bottles of water and some food for us. The tank on the roof should fill up in twenty minutes or so,' said Chandra, as he headed for the door.

'Thank you, Chandu,' said Waris, making himself comfortable on the dusty and probably bug-infested sofa.

As soon as Chandu left, Brijesh got on to the Thuraya to touch base with Kang and Ray. Kang would need more time to mobilize, he reasoned. Waris decided to risk a visit to the toilet meanwhile and returned to find Brijesh reclining on the sofa, looking relaxed.

'I assume our boys and girl are doing all right,' said Waris.

'Ray and Laila have been in touch with Sky and Kang and have covered their tracks. They'll meet us at the Jinnah Ground tomorrow. As for Kang, we suspect it'll be a close call, but he'll join us there at some point during the rally or just after,' said Brijesh.

'As long as he doesn't miss the boat out of Karachi,' said Waris.

'He won't.'

At that point, Chandra returned with greasy packages of food and bottles of mineral water.

'That was quick,' remarked Brijesh, as Chandra set about emptying the bags of their contents. Kebabs, rotis, salad and a couple of packets of dry fruit tumbled out. The football coach stood up and walked over to Brijesh and Waris.

'I'm not sure if I'm overstepping here, but since you're going to meet Azhar tomorrow, I figured you might need this,' he said, as he pulled a country-made handgun from his pocket.

Brijesh's eyes widened.

'It's completely untraceable,' said Chandra, 'Easy to dispose of, easier to use and it's loud, so it will disperse crowds and allow you … allow us to escape.'

'That's right. Us,' said Brijesh. 'Once again, you've shown some very good thinking, Chandu. I have no idea where we'd be had you not come to the hospital. But I think you should get rid of it; we'll be fine.'

'I've been working with the Lahore police for a couple of years. I understand weapons and have made the right kinds of contacts, which can be useful in such times.'

'Many thanks, Chandu. But we will be fine …'

'You could thank me by eating the food while its hot,' said Chandra, a twinkle in his eye as he took a seat.

Vikrant stirred awake a little before dawn and sat up. He noticed that Waris and Brijesh were asleep in different parts of the room. But the bedsheets that had been used by Chandra lay in a crumpled heap. Vikrant went to the washroom to freshen up and returned shortly to find Brijesh and Waris still asleep. Chandra was nowhere to be found.

Unperturbed, he went about his daily routine of stretches, sit-ups, push-ups and squats. He was on his seventeenth squat in the third set when the front door opened and in walked Chandra. In a white T-shirt covered with patches of sweat and his green track pants, the football coach smiled from the doorway.

'Good morning.'

Vikrant grunted a response.

'I respect a man with discipline,' said Chandra, sounding just like a coach.

'Thank you,' said Vikrant. 'Where have you been?'

'It's something of a malaise really. I feel incomplete without a morning run. My whole day begins to feel like a waste unless I get that run in,' he replied.

'When do you think we should start making our way to Jinnah Grounds?'

'We've got time.'

Vikrant nodded and returned to his workout. It was time to prepare for the last and final stand.

37

Jinnah Grounds, Karachi, 16 November, 3 p.m.

Waris sat with a map of Karachi laid out in front of him. Vikrant and Brijesh sat across the table from him. The three men had their eyes fixed on the layout of Jinnah Grounds, absorbing every detail.

The area looked like Raj Ghat in Delhi.

Sprawled over half a kilometre, the park held the grave of Mohammad Ali Jinnah and the Botanical Gardens. It was regarded as a major landmark in Karachi and was abuzz with visitors every day of the week.

But it had rarely seen political rallies. Musharraf had once called a rally there but had to cancel it.

This rally, coming so soon after major Moharram processions across the city, had put a strain on the overburdened Karachi Police and the Pakistani rangers.

Exit plans were discussed for the nth time, and Waris briefed Brijesh and Vikrant about diversionary tactics. They could not get this wrong. There would be no second chance.

Waris stood up and began to roll up the map.

'I think we're ready,' he announced. He motioned for Chandra to come closer.

The three of them walked up to Waris.

'Vikrant and you will take the lead on this one,' Waris told Brijesh.

'Laila, Ray and Kang will enter the rally behind you and serve as back-up. Chandu, you will stay put in your van. We'll need a getaway car. You know the terrain like the back of your hand and are our best bet to exit when the job is done.'

'Got it,' Chandra nodded. 'We'll be inconspicuous.'

'Good,' Waris said.

'I assume you will be waiting for us in the vehicle and providing updates?' said Brijesh, looking straight at Waris.

Waris got up and unrolled the map out again in front of the other three.

'You assume wrong,' he said. He jabbed a finger at Jinnah Grounds, then circled a structure next to the park. 'This is Frere Hall. After a terror attack on the U.S. consulate, this building was shut to the public. Frere Hall provides the best overhead view of the grounds – a fact that is invaluable to us. The hall was reopened two years ago and that is where I shall be, watching everything.'

Brijesh nodded and looked over at Chandra.

'Do we have enough diesel in the van?'

'I was on my way to refuel.'

'We'll meet you outside and leave as soon as you're back.'

'Check.'

Brijesh watched as Chandra stepped out of his family home. He watched as Chandra turned for one last wistful look and then hopped into his van and drove off.

Vikrant ambled away to wash his face, while Brijesh laced up his boots. Waris continued to stare at the map until the others got ready.

When Chandra drove up in his van a few minutes later, they piled in, solemn in the awareness that this was another step forward, drawing them closer to the end.

It was nearly 3.15 p.m. by the time Chandra parked at the designated spot.

'I'll be waiting here,' he told the men, watching as they strode away. 'Good luck!' he said, so softly that they almost missed it.

He watched as they blended into the crowd. Three men in Pathanis and skullcaps, their eyes lined with surma.

Waris broke away from the group, veering to his left, 300 metres after they left Chandra's van. He was going to sneak his way as high up the gothic structure of Frere Hall as possible. Brijesh and Vikrant walked into the crowd that was milling in front of an empty stage that had been erected for Mahmood Azhar.

Brijesh touched his leg subconsciously The country-made gun was concealed in his trousers. He was lucky he hadn't been frisked properly on the way in. Vikrant stayed close behind as Brijesh tried to weave his way to the front.

Waris, meanwhile, had managed to make his way to the second floor of Frere Hall, but this was nowhere near high enough. He wondered fleetingly about the threadbare security, but didn't dwell on it. Climbing up so many flights of stairs at his age was going to be challenging.

Brijesh and Vikrant were ten or eleven rows from the stage when a voice on the public address system came through, requesting patience from the audience. Azhar was running late.

Vikrant and Brijesh looked at each other, their irritation evident at the delay.

But Waris was pleased. The delay meant he would have enough time to find a vantage point and it would give Ray, Kang and Laila a little more time too.

The minutes ticked by. Waris was finally where he wanted to be. He pulled out a pair of binoculars and scanned the crowd. *Vikrant and Brijesh are in position*, he thought to himself, *but where are Laila, Ray and Kang?*

Just then, a convoy arrived behind the stage. *Azhar had to be in one of those cars*, thought Waris, *but which one? And where in the name of God are those three?*

Waris stopped mid-scan, swinging the binoculars back a few rows. He had spotted a burqa-clad woman alighting from a cab, along with a man. The two could not be mistaken for anything but a Pakistani Muslim couple on their way to the rally. But he knew them for who they really were.

As Laila walked through the car park, she suddenly stopped and bent down as if to pick something up. Her purse had fallen and the contents were strewn on the ground. She squatted and began to collect her things. Ray joined her. Deftly, she picked up a compact-like case, flipped the catch and stuck it under the petrol tank of the car closest to her. Ray had finished retrieving the rest of the contents of the purse, taking a quick look around to see if anyone had noticed Laila's handiwork. Satisfied that they were not being watched, the couple began to walk towards the crowd again.

Waris smiled.

Vikrant and Brijesh had started to sweat by now as the crowd milled and pushed around them. Anti-India and anti-US slogans rang out, but that did not affect the two men as much as the rising mercury levels. Up at Frere Hall, Waris was beginning to grow frustrated as his Thuraya battery seemed to have run out and Kang was still missing.

Suddenly, a loud roar went up as Azhar and his cronies took the stage. Waris was furious. Where *was* Kang?

The first speaker thanked the Lord for all His blessings and began his talk, eulogizing Mahmood Azhar's unwavering faith and devotion to their cause: the fact that Azhar was back after the man who had shared the stage with him last had had his brains blown into smithereens, not long ago, was proof of his conviction and commitment.

Brijesh and Vikrant started to inch forward. Waris peered through his binoculars, alternating between the stage and the back of the crowd. Everyone was in position except Kang.

Brijesh had spotted Azhar sitting to one side of the stage and knew that it would soon be time to strike.

He nudged Vikrant, signalling that he should follow him, and they made their way further, until they were no more than five rows from the front of the stage. *This it it*, thought Waris, as he watched his men press forward. The muffled sound of the public address system wasn't enough to drown out the sound of the wind blowing through Frere Hall. Nor was it loud enough to drown out the sound of approaching footsteps.

Using Vikrant as a shield, Brijesh leaned against his shoulder, ready to draw his gun.

Suddenly, a loud explosion rang through the car park. An SUV had erupted in flames, shattering the windshields of other cars around it.

The first salvo had been fired.

It was enough for the Pakistani rangers, the Karachi Police and the army to rush towards the site of the explosion. The crowd, wondering what had happened, began to mill around the car park.

It was time for the next step.

Vikrant, who had hidden a knife in his scarf, brought it out and swiftly stabbed one of the security supervisors, before lithely moving ahead. The man screamed in agony and turned to his neighbour, grabbing him by the collar, convinced it was he who had stabbed him. They started punching each other.

The crowd was getting increasingly restive, pushing and shoving.

The men around Azhar sensed this could be the moment the assassins hidden in the crowd would strike. They drew their guns and formed a wall around him, scanning the crowd with narrowed eyes.

We are so close, thought Brijesh, *we just have to get Azhar away from the stage.*

While the pushing and jostling was at its peak, Vikrant moved ahead a few rows and softly said, 'bomb'.

Within seconds, there was bedlam. The security forces had to jump in to stop a stampede. The crowd had gone berserk.

In a moment, soldiers had quickly scrambled onto the stage and formed a protective cordon around Azhar and his men so that a hidden sniper in the crowd could not aim his gun at them.

Brijesh cursed himself for losing focus for a brief moment. He couldn't let that hate-monger get away another time. He charged forward with Vikrant in tow and jumped over the barricade, knocking down two security guards. Laila and Ray had been pushed back by the crowd. Vikrant set off around the stage, hoping to ambush Azhar, while Brijesh followed the route taken by the fleeing men on the stage.

The footsteps were very soft but very clear to Waris's trained ear.

All senses on alert, Waris focused on the sound. Hidden behind the shadows of a pillar, he could make out the form of three men in grey combat uniforms. One of them was armed with a sniper rifle and the others carried automatic rifles.

Waris saw the man with the sniper rifle take aim. But he wasn't pointing it in the direction of the stage. He was aiming at the back of the crowd. Was he aiming at Laila or Ray?

Adrenalin coursed through his body, giving him inhuman strength, as Waris leapt out of the shadows and shoulder-charged one of the assailants, pushing him over the banister and grabbing his rifle as he fell to his death, screaming.

The other two men jumped back, caught unawares. Waris aimed a killer kick at one gunman's jaw and got the other in the groin. Reeling in pain, one of the men fired a stray shot that hit a member of the crowd. The restive crowd had now turned hysterical.

Waris snatched the automatic from the second gunman, jumped over him and wrestled with the third, who was starting to stand up. The man launched two jabs at Waris, who retaliated with a flurry of jabs, hooks and another deadly kick to the head and groin that had the attacker out cold on the ground. Waris turned to see the other sniper fleeing and ran after him. He got him on the head with his elbow, and the gunman collapsed without a sound while Waris picked up the fallen rifles.

Vikrant and Brijesh, meanwhile, had parted, deciding to attack Azhar from different directions.

However, Azhar was shielded from both the front and back, as the other speakers onstage remained near him.

It seemed impossible for them to break the human shield – they needed divine intervention now.

At that point Waris trained his gun on Azhar and took a shot but missed. The man standing next to Azhar was hit. Waris cursed under his breath and fired again. He missed again.

When Azhar saw two men next to him falling like nine pins, he charged out of the shield and got off the stage, hoping to disappear.

In the narrow bylanes, choc-a-bloc with men and vehicles, rows of cars were stuck. Azhar covered his face with his headgear and walked swiftly past, with one of his aides close on his heels.

Brijesh and Vikrant jogged after him on the sidewalk and slowed to a walk as they got closer. They watched as he turned into a bylane that was nearly deserted.

Suddenly a jeep screeched into the bylane and the driver said, '*Huzoor aaiyye, yeh gaadi aap ke liye hai.*'

The jeep door opened for Azhar, who looked at the driver, quickly taking in the Pathani outfit and the beard. He hesitated for just a moment before getting into the jeep.

The driver backed up in the direction he had come from, tyres and brakes screeching in protest.

Brijesh and Vikrant looked at each other in consternation. Not again. Azhar could not have escaped them again!

They looked around for a bike or a car to go after the jeep – when they saw a bullet-proof car bearing the Karachi police emblem speeding towards them. Chandra was at the wheel, Laila and Ray behind him.

The car stopped with a jerk, and Vikrant and Brijesh scrambled into it. Chandra seemed agitated and in a hurry. *'Kis taraf gaye maulana sahib?'* he asked urgently, almost shouting.

'We saw the jeep turn left,' Vikrant replied, momentarily puzzled by Chandra having referred to Azhar as 'sahib'. Chandu shifted gears and sped in that direction. Hope soared again.

After driving half a kilometre, the driver stopped the jeep under a nondescript and deserted structure.

'Why did you stop here? We must get to the office,' Azhar demanded.

'Janab, this is where you leave this world and start the journey to hell,' Kang said calmly, pulling out a gun from the pocket of his kurta.

'Dhokha diya hai Hindustani kafir ne …' the now sweating Azhar screamed.

'Jinhone plane kidnap karke tumhe riha karwaya woh wafadar the kya?' Kang retorted, referring to the IC 814 hijacking and subsequent release of Azhar in exchange for the passengers.

Out of the corner of his eye, Kang saw a vehicle approaching at full speed.

He aimed the gun at Azhar's face and shot him in the forehead. Twice. He was taking no chances.

The police car screeched to a halt and Chandra, Vikrant and Brijesh leaped out. Chandra was the first to reach Azhar. He turned to Kang, his eyes filling with pure hatred.

Kang looked at Chandra's face and froze.

Vikrant and Brijesh were puzzled by the instant hostility between the two.

'Kang, this is Chandu. He's helping us escape.'

'This is not Chandu,' said Kang coldly. 'Yeh to ISI ka kutta Afridi hai.'

Their rage and elation had momentarily blinded the men to the approaching army vehicles. Four cars suddenly screeched to a halt, cornering the trio. *'Maulana shaheed ho gaye,'* someone cried.

In one of the army vehicles was Waris. He was staring straight ahead, his hands tied behind his back.

Afridi then turned and slapped Kang.

The army men pushed all of them into the waiting vehicles. It was over now.

38

Korangi Warehouse, Karachi

Waris was seething with fury and frustration. He had been checkmated for the second time by his nemesis. How could the enemy have been so smart as to predict their every move and then decide to join them as a meek, subjugated Hindu – a perfect cover that none of them had seen through?

How could they have known that his heartrending story would be so convincing that Waris's team would feel sorry for him and even think of taking him back to India with them?

The ISI man had outsmarted him. The man who had got so close to them was virtually number two in the hierarchy, Waris reminded himself, and they had slipped up by not recognizing him.

Waris's eyes were blazing; his hands were tied to a rod that ran the length of the roof. His legs were chained to a peg on the floor.

He looked around and saw six men in army fatigues with Heckler and Koch MP5 submachine guns. They all looked alert and capable of causing real damage. Waris estimated that several hours must have passed since he was tied up. These men had only arrived a couple of hours ago, which probably meant that it was time to either cut him down for interrogation or shift him somewhere else. But where were the others? Had they already been killed? Or were they also strung up like a Bombay Duck left out to dry? And what fate had befallen Laila and Ray? They were not field agents and did not have the training for this sort of thing. Or maybe, Waris thought to himself, he was being overly pessimistic. What if his team had actually managed to escape and was on its way to free him? The door would fly open any minute and he would see Brijesh's familiar face.

Almost immediately, the door did indeed fly open – but the man who entered was not Brijesh. However, he did look awfully familiar. He was dressed in army uniform, but bore an unsettling resemblance to someone Waris knew. Someone Waris had seen and spoken to very recently. Then it struck him that the man standing in front of him was none other than their travelling companion and newfound friend.

He walked up to Waris, looked into his eyes and said, 'Such a shame that a Muslim would perpetrate such senseless violence against his Muslim brethren.'

'And you! Masquerading as a Muslim and violating every precept of Islam!'

'What the fuck do you know about Islam?'

'The list of your inhuman and un-Islamic acts is too long. And you cannot expect to have this conversation with me when I am hanging from the roof, Chandu,' said Waris, emphasizing the name.

Afridi looked at his men and barked an order. 'Untie his hands and give him a chair, but keep his legs tied.'

Then he turned towards Waris and said, 'My name is Arif Afridi, not Chandu.'

Brijesh, Vikrant, Kang, Ray and Laila were tied to a steel handrail that ran along the wall of what looked like the inside of a warehouse. There were bloodstains on the wall and suffocating stench of urine hung in the air. The place seemed to have witnessed many painful deaths.

'Sir, I did not even say goodbye to my wife in Kolkata. I didn't write an email to my son in the States before coming here. Now I'll die in this rotten place and they won't even know where I am,' Ray said despairingly.

'As I see it, there is one main door and there is a back door. Most of their personnel are deployed towards the front, with only two men at the smaller exit. If we put up a fight now and engage them in such a way that we keep them from coming towards the back door, we can make a getaway,' Vikrant said in a whisper to Kang.

'I can buy you guys some time to exit,' Kang said, tugging at the ropes that bound his wrists to see if he could break them.

'It would be wonderful if you could buy us some time,' said Vikrant wryly. 'And what will you do if they open fire?'

'They didn't take away my vest. It can take some hits,' Kang said.

'I have my karambit knife in the heel of my left shoe. Wait for my signal, then make a move for it,' Vikrant said.

'As I suspected, these ropes aren't very strong. I'll be able to break them in no time,' Kang said confidently.

Waris was cuffed and tied to the chair.

'I understand you are an army man with a track record of malicious and hostile overtures towards Pakistan,' Afridi said, as he took a seat in front of Waris.

'I am a proud soldier of the Indian army and would like to die with my boots on,' Waris said, looking straight into Afridi's eyes.

'No one needs to die here. I can get you amnesty if you are willing to use your strategic and defence knowledge to help your Muslim brothers,' Afridi said, with an encouraging smile.

The two men looked at each other for a long moment, wordlessly.

To onlookers, it might have seemed as though Waris was contemplating taking up Afridi's offer. But only Afridi could see the raging fire in Waris's eyes. The lines across his brow were only deepening.

Then Waris spoke, in a calm voice that belied the anger in his eyes.

'Even if you were to cut me into pieces and burn those pieces and then bring me back to life and repeat the whole process for all eternity, I would still not betray my country, Chandu.'

Afridi smiled sardonically.

'Pride comes before a fall, my friend. This is the land of Islam. And anyway, what kind of Muslim are you? You betray your religion for your country!' Afridi tried another tactic.

'No true Muslim would wish ill on India,' Waris said matter-of-factly.

'What kind of fucking logic is that? Is it in the Quran or hadith?'

'It's in the conduct of Imam Husain, the grandson of the Holy Prophet. You need to catch up on your reading, Afridi. When he was besieged by the Muslim army, he said, "Let me go to India, a Hindu country, when not a single Muslim lived here". This is the country to which Imam Husain preferred to migrate, giving it preference over the whole glut of Islamic states in that era,' Waris explained.

Afridi was speechless.

'Either you should come out and say Imam Husain was mistaken. Or say that his conduct is worth emulating for all the Muslims of the world. Respect the country where even the family of the Holy Prophet wanted to settle down, leaving their homeland,' Waris continued.

'Stop this nonsense, Waris,' Afridi barked.

'Lt Gen. Sayed Ali Waris,' his prisoner corrected him.

The blinding brightness of flashlights in their faces briefly disoriented the team. A senior army man walked up to them and then turned towards his entourage to say, 'Listen up, I want you to take good care of them.'

'Janaab, I will take such good care of them that I will make surma of their bones and use it to line my eyes,' said an officer.

'No, Major, don't be impatient. Wait until tomorrow's press conference is over. These guys have caused enough damage to us by parading one young boy in front of the world – a boy who was common riff-raff. His exhibition caused a major embarrassment to Pakistan in front of the US and other countries. Now the shoe is on the other foot,' said a senior officer with the name 'Ayaz Ahsan' embossed on his name tag.

'They captured one boy. We have an entire army unit. Shouldn't we expose India's heinous designs? This is exactly what the world needs to know to destroy the illusion of Indians being peace-loving people. We will finally expose them for the bloodthirsty and murderous animals that they are,' he continued authoritatively.

The thought of the impending press conference and the international embarrassment for their country as a result of a mission that was not even officially sanctioned unsettled the whole team.

'Ji janaab,' the major said.

'For now, give them some food and water, but not all at once. One by one, so that they do not try and act smart,' the leader said.

'Janaab, are you sure about the food and water? I wanted to starve them for some time and you are being so generous to them,' the major said.

'I want them to look well fed and robust. I don't want them to look pitiable. The media should not accuse us of bringing out some tired old captives,' the senior man said.

'You know, we plan to showcase you to the world. Half-a-dozen of you mercenaries from the Indian army were sent here, to Pakistan, to spread terror and your group included serving army men of the ranks of lieutenant general and major. You have not brought glory to your country, but eternal disgrace and condemnation, and the world will pick you apart, piece by piece,' laughed Afridi.

The laugh sent shivers down Waris's spine. He was numb with premonition. The team had always thought of death as failure. They had never anticipated arrest and subsequent embarrassment. He had to find a way out of this. He simply could not let his country be shamed this way.

We all are serving army men, it would take a real moron to think the Indian top brass had not sanctioned this mission, he thought. He had to think of something immediately to keep the ISI from claiming another victory.

'Where are the others? Are they alive?' Waris asked calmly.

'They are quite well and being treated like royalty. After all, we cannot afford to hurt these special guests of ours until we make them international heroes on prime-time television. They are very much here, you will be reunited tomorrow before the press conference,' said Afridi, enjoying every second.

It dawned upon Waris that the team was better off dead than alive. If they were killed in such a way that their bodies could not be recognized, the ISI would have no evidence to back their claims. This would also give India some much needed reprieve.

To be killed in a manner that involved mutilation, he would have to provoke Afridi.

'I know that by now you are probably remorseful about this mission and are deeply worried as you foresee the reputation of your country in tatters. You see, I am feeling bad too. I hate the idea of not being able to show mercy to my Muslim brother,' Afridi said, breaking the silence and disrupting Waris's chain of thoughts.

His Muslim brother had something altogether different on his mind.

Food and water were wheeled in on a cart. Surprisingly, the captors were quite hospitable. The cart held several bowls of meaty biryani made of basmati rice, platters of tender and succulent kebabs and a mound of Karachi sheermal, that delicious paratha served only at gatherings of the most affluent. The meal seemed to be a far grander affair than any of them could have predicted.

'Pakistani hospitality is known across the world,' the army

officer said, with a smile. 'Who wants to eat first? Only one person will be untied at a time,' he added.

Vikrant made eye contact with Kang and whispered, 'Are you ready? We have to act at once.'

Kang nodded and began pulling at the ropes. They were stronger than he had anticipated. For a moment, panic began to set in. If Vikrant were to give the signal and Kang failed to respond, everyone's lives would be in danger. Significantly more danger, that is. He summoned all his strength and began struggling again.

Vikrant noticed Kang's swollen tendons and strained expression even though he was trying his best to disguise the effort, for fear of alerting the enemy. The soldiers unfastened Ray's hands. Unaware of Vikrant and Kang's plans, Ray began walking towards the food cart.

Folded and concealed in his shoe heel, Vikrant's karambit knife was meant for such just an emergency. He managed to flip it open and began cutting Kang's ropes. Just then, Kang's immense reserves of strength managed to make a breakthrough and the ropes began giving way.

Ray was hungry and had settled down to his meal, when he was startled by a loud war cry that emanated from behind him. He turned around in time to see Kang lifting a soldier above his head and throwing him against a wall like a gunny bag.

'*Waheguru da khalsa Waheguru di fateh!*' he shouted.

Vikrant had cut his own ropes and jumped on a couple of soldiers in front of him.

The captors were taken by surprise as Kang began crushing and pummelling them while Vikrant used his knife to slit their throats. To make things simpler, he eventually put away his knife and picked up a machine gun dropped by one of his victims.

'Kang! Go to Brijesh and Laila, I'll cover you,' Vikrant said, as he unleashed a burst of fire from his MP5 machine gun.

For a man of Kang's size, he moved with amazing agility – he rushed over and freed Brijesh and Laila.

The Indian quintet had now ducked behind a heap of debris and were exchanging fire with the soldiers on the other side.

'Chandu, you should be more concerned about your country being a failed state, rather than devoting so much energy to India. After Afghanistan, Pakistan will be the new terror state,' Waris taunted Afridi. 'Filled with terrorists in Pathani suits with flowing beards and many in army uniforms.'

'Shut up! It is the Indian army that terrorizes the weak and helpless Kashmiris,' Afridi said, bristling.

'The Indian army's record is not as bad as Pakistan's excesses in Waziristan and FATA. The Indian army does not organize training camps for terrorists and arrange to have them sent across the border,' Waris said.

'And how do you justify your team's antics? Going across the world to kill people,' said Afridi bitterly.

'Not people, we have only killed terrorists. If we were so indiscriminate, we could have planted bombs across Pakistan and killed hundreds and maimed thousands. Our actions stem from your country's inaction,' Waris said.

Afridi glared at Waris, as the fury in him reached critical mass.

'Chandu, Pakistan was a cancer. The politicians thought surgical removal would prevent malignancy from spreading across India. You guys begged for a separate nation on the basis of religion. You begged, your forefathers did, your leaders did, and now that cancer has become self-perpetuating,' Waris explained.

'Watch your words, you hypocritical Muslim,' Afridi screamed.

'Do you know the man who created Pakistan was not even a strict Muslim? He ate pork, drank wine and never observed namaaz in his lifetime. He who tried writing the destiny of millions of Muslims across the border was a member of the Khoja Jamaat from Samuel Street in Mumbai. Why is he Quaid-e-Azam and not a hypocrite?' Waris retorted.

Afridi pulled out his revolver and made as if to kill Waris, when he heard gunshots at the lower level.

Waris laughed out loud. 'You cannot finish them off. They will finish you instead.'

Afridi immediately ran out to issue instructions to his men.

Kang, Brijesh and Vikrant were trying to work out their next step. They knew they could not continue to sit there and exchange volley for volley.

'Kang, all of you move towards the rear. I'll hold them here,' Vikrant said.

'How can you handle them alone?' Ray asked, worry lining his forehead.

'Kang is a one-man army. Now move,' Brijesh said, as he started inching towards the rear.

The first one to move was Kang. He ran towards the huge wooden door and used his boulder-like shoulder to smash it.

Flying bullets grazed Kang, injuring him in the arms and legs, but he kept running, slashing at the oncoming enemy soldiers with his kirpaan.

He spotted an army van in the distance, and turned and began frantically waving at the others. Brijesh sprayed bullets at random in an effort to give Laila and Ray cover, so they could run towards Kang.

That's when Afridi stepped out into the first-floor corridor and saw them. When Kang noticed the man who had once brutally tortured him, he saw red. 'You are next, you motherfucker,' he shouted. Afridi retreated and whipped out his walkie-talkie, issuing a barrage of instructions.

Brijesh was on the move and searching for Waris, while Kang began advancing towards Afridi, focused on the prospect of settling scores with him.

'Kang, you need to take them to the van and reach the boat. I can trust only you to take them out. Their safe exit from Pakistan is more important than your revenge,' Brijesh said cripply.

Kang nodded reluctantly and began moving towards the van, with Laila and Ray in his wake.

As he ran up the stairs, Brijesh realized that the firing had become more sporadic. This meant that Vikrant had either killed them all or had been taken out. He ran upstairs with an MP5 gun in hand, firing at whoever crossed his path.

He entered a long corridor with several rooms on either side and realized that checking each room would take forever, and that Afridi would soon call in reinforcements. Time was of the essence.

'Waris sir!' he called out loudly, doing away with protocol and the rules of this engagement.

'I'm in here,' came the response from down the corridor.

As he charged into the room, Brijesh was met with a volley of bullets. He saw the gunman lurking behind a wall, but turned towards him and went for a headshot. Quickly untying Waris as the gunman's body hit the ground, Brijesh saw that Waris had lost a lot of blood.

'We cannot die here, we cannot die in Pakistan, we should leave …' Waris was slurring, partly due to the disorienting loss of blood and partly because he was going into shock.

'I know, sir,' Brijesh said, as he lifted Waris onto his shoulder and ran towards the ground floor.

'Chalo chalo, I can see them coming,' said Kang, as he got the van started.

Brijesh and Waris climbed into the van. At the last moment, Vikrant dashed in too, and the tyres squealed as Kang slammed the accelerator hard.

39

Post Midnight
Khayabane Ittehaad, Karachi

'Do we know where we're going?' asked Vikrant from the backseat, as he mopped beads of sweat from Waris's brow.

'Yes,' replied Laila quickly, as she held on to the dashboard with one hand and tried deciphering an old map she had found in the glove compartment with the other. Kang was never one for cautious driving and his penchant for cutting across lanes and driving off the road served the team well now. Also, at midnight, the roads were considerably emptier than they could have hoped for, which made his dangerous game at the wheel relatively safe.

'So where *are* we going?' asked Vikrant as they bounced around in the speeding van, while Brijesh put pressure on Waris's wounds.

'We are going to the harbour, Vikrant,' Laila snapped. 'That's where Sky has told us to – right! You missed the turn, Kang!'

'Don't worry,' he replied. 'I'll take the next one.'

Vikrant realized it was probably best not to try Laila's patience at this point and decided to leave her to her own devices. True to his word, Kang took the next right turn and as luck would have it, the road happened to be a dead-end. Before anyone had a chance to panic, Kang had already begun to swing the van around and bring it back on to the main road.

'Once you take the turn we were originally supposed to take, you need to keep going straight past three … four … four! You need to go past four traffic lights,' said Laila, having finally decrypted the old map. Meanwhile, Waris, who was slipping in and out of consciousness, spoke audibly and clearly for the first time in a while. 'Are we sure we aren't being followed?' he asked, his words slow and carefully measured.

'No tails so far, sir,' Kang replied promptly. 'I've been keeping an eye on the mirrors and there's been no suspicious activity.' Reasonably satisfied with Waris's condition, Brijesh also spoke for the first time in a while. 'I don't like the idea of going to the harbour in a straight line. Drive around to throw anyone who may be following us off our tail,' he told Kang. Then he turned to Vikrant and asked, 'How much ammo do we have left?'

Vikrant pursed his lips. 'Not very much, I'm afraid. One MP5 is out of ammo, the other has six rounds, and the pistol I picked up on the way out has two rounds.'

'I've got four,' said Laila, referring to her pistol – which had been instrumental in saving Kang from a number of attackers at the warehouse.

'So, twelve rounds,' said Brijesh. 'We have twelve rounds and they're probably mobilizing a small army to hunt us down. I don't like the odds. Have we checked the van for any weapons?' Vikrant chose not to respond and instead, clambered into the storage section of the van to hunt for anything resembling a gun. 'Nothing in the glove compartment or around the front seat,' said Laila.

'Where did you stash the spare weapons you guys bought?' Brijesh asked Ray, who fumbled for an answer before offering, 'The thing with that is, sir … Well, we didn't really stash anything anywhere. And the guns and rounds we were carrying were either used up or taken away when we were apprehended.'

'We were captured, Ray. Not apprehended. Never use "apprehend" in this context,' corrected Brijesh.

'Yes, captured,' repeated Ray.

'Guys, you are not going to believe this,' came Vikrant's voice from the storage area. Ray and Brijesh turned to find Vikrant cracking open a case. It revealed a dusty rocket-propelled grenade launcher with two rounds. 'Is that a—' began Ray. Ever the pragmatist, Brijesh interrupted and said, 'Only two rounds. That's not very reassuring. Also, an RPG is going to attract far too much attention.'

The glee on Vikrant's face dissolved. His expression seemed to say, 'At this point, I don't care.'

'Set it up anyway,' said Brijesh. Whether or not to use it, we shall figure when we get there.'

Meanwhile, Afridi was sitting in the front passenger seat of an armoured jeep in a convoy of five vehicles, barking orders into a walkie-talkie. He had often been compared to a shark in ISI circles – now, he had the taste of blood and was moving in for the kill.

'Do we know which way they went?' he yelled into the walkie-talkie.

'Heading south, sir,' came the crackling response.

'Get the Karachi Port Trust on to it and put out a description of the van and those bastards immediately!'

'Yes, sir. One more thing. HQ wants a report about how they were able to escape after being captured.'

'CAPTURED?' shot back Afridi. 'Those people are criminals. We apprehended them. As for the report, I'd rather hand HQ their sorry carcasses than some dumb report.'

Afridi dropped the walkie-talkie between his feet and turned to the driver. 'If we lose these … these … criminals,' he blurted out, failing to find a profanity vile enough to suit the occasion, 'if we lose them, you will be out of a job, we will all be out of a job, so pull your thumb out and DRIVE FASTER!'

For the next ten minutes, Afridi sat in silence, mulling the consequences of letting the team escape and the glory in which he would be bathed once he finally got them by their necks. The primary target of his aggression and anger would be that gormless lackey, he thought, as he visualized himself using every instrument at his disposal to make Ray squeal for mercy.

Just then, his walkie-talkie crackled to life.

'Sir, KPT has been alerted and we've had a sighting four kilometres from your location.'

'Finally! Some good news! Where exactly?'

'Keep travelling southeast, sir. It's 12.45 a.m. and the roads are emptying out. You'll catch them on the emptier roads.'

'Keep me posted,' said Afridi with a wide grin, as he reached into the glove compartment for his trusty sidearm.

'He's fading,' said a concerned Brijesh, as he watched Waris slip back into an unconscious state after mumbling deliriously for five minutes.

'We'll be at the harbour soon,' said Kang reassuringly. 'Once we hit the Lyari Expressway, it's a straight stretch and we'll be in harbour territory. After that, it'll be a case of finding the right jetty.'

'And if we run into any trouble …' said Vikrant, as he patted the locked and loaded RPG that sat on his lap, 'we can deal with it.'

'Let's try and leave Karachi intact when we leave, if it's all right with you, Vikrant,' said Brijesh.

'Of course, it's a last resort, that—'

At that moment, a vehicle slammed right into Kang's side of the van and they were propelled across two lanes as a result of it. The van stalled, the door and frame caved in on the driver's seat, and Kang was stuck.

'Oh my God!' screamed Laila, as the vehicle prepared to smash into their van again.

'Shoot out its tyres!' yelled Kang, trying to get the engine running again.

Brijesh leaned out of the window with a pistol and shot out the front tyre, causing the army jeep to veer off the road and slam into a tree. 'DRIVE!' he yelled. The engine seemed to oblige as the van started up again and accelerated, leaving the driver of the jeep behind as he stumbled out of the vehicle, bloodied and disoriented.

'This is the first of many vehicles and soldiers we are probably going to encounter, so everyone, stay alert,' said Brijesh. Waris stirred and said clearly, 'I want a status update'. Brijesh placed a hand on his shoulder gently and said, 'Just a little hiccup, nothing to worry about, sir.'

Waris shrugged Brijesh's hand off his shoulder almost dismissively. 'I'm fine,' he said gruffly. Unfortunately, the same could not be said of Kang, who was struggling to keep his focus on the road while concealing the injuries he had suffered when the jeep had rammed straight into him.

He bit down on his lower lip and grimaced as every movement of his shattered right leg and arm sent a shockwave of pain through his body. While his left arm and leg tried to take over the steering wheel and the pedals respectively, it was easier said than done, particularly when driving at such a high speed. Vikrant leaned over.

'Are you all right?' he asked, as he tried to see the damage for himself.

'I'm fine,' said Kang hurriedly. 'Totally fine.'

Kang wasn't one to complain about his injuries generally, but this was unlike him, Laila noticed. That was when she saw his splintered ulna sticking out of his forearm – and more damage below. Her eyes widened in shock and she was milliseconds away from letting out a scream, when Kang shot her a look. The mission was at far too critical a stage for him to jeopardize it by panicking everyone else, he reasoned. He looked over at Laila and blinked and she seemed to get the signal, despite her horror at the sight of his mangled arm and leg.

She turned back to see if anyone else had noticed, but seeing Ray peering nervously out of the window, Vikrant busy prepping the RPG after the collision and Brijesh taking care of Waris, she knew she had to keep quiet. But for how long? She didn't have too much time to ponder – her attention was diverted by the screech of tyres and the approach of two motorcycle-riding, gun-toting men in grey uniforms. They didn't seem to be army uniform, or of any other forces for that matter. Judging by their finesse with an automatic rifle while hitting incredible speeds on a motorcycle, they were from some special unit.

A flurry of bullets ricocheted off the van and Waris flinched.

'Get them off our tail, Kang!' yelled Vikrant, as he grabbed the only MP5 with ammo and fired one of its last six rounds at the motorcyclist. Brijesh held his breath, knowing the value of those precious few rounds and their potential to come in handy later on. Negative impact, he thought to himself as he watched the bullet deflected by the handlebar of the motorcycle. The motorcyclist returned fire with a volley of bullets that broke the rear window and punctured the roof of the van.

'That was too close,' said Vikrant, reaching for the RPG. 'Vikrant, no!' said Brijesh. He took the MP5 from Vikrant and took aim, as enemy bullets bounced harmlessly off the side of the van.

'Bull's eye,' said Brijesh under his breath, as he saw the motorcyclist's limbs flailing – he flew off the bike and hit the road like a ragdoll, with a smoking hole in his forehead. The motorcycle flipped a number of times before coming to rest in the middle of the street, its front wheel still spinning.

There was still one more motorcyclist to deal with.

Afridi gnashed his teeth as he heard his motorcycle-riding assassin confirm that his partner had been taken out. The surviving assassin had apparently dropped back a few metres and was tailing the van.

'Don't you fucking dare lose them or I swear I'll destroy your entire family,' he growled, thinking of what he would do to Laila after Ray was disposed of.

Just look at the way she dresses and behaves around men, he thought to himself. *The best thing to do to her would be to put a bullet through her head and dispose her of like the pile of garbage she is. And that pretty boy*, he thought, *needs to be put in his place. I'll probably have him publicly whipped before rolling him in some salt and broken glass and then hang him for all of Pakistan to see what happens to anyone who decides to wage war on our country.*

He stirred out of his vision to the news that the motorcyclist was closing in on the van again, and that his own convoy had finally arrived at Lyari Expressway. Catching up with the van wouldn't be a problem now.

'Step on it,' he said to the driver. 'I want first crack at them.'

'Yes, sir,' said the driver, as he pushed the vehicle into top gear.

'Update,' said Afridi into his walkie-talkie. He hoped the motorcyclist had managed to kill at least one of them. He just hoped it wasn't Waris. That pleasure was to be all his.

No response.

'Update,' he repeated, the impatience palpable in his voice.

No response.

'Where is this moron?' he said to no one in particular before slamming the walkie-talkie on the floor between his feet. He scrunched his eyes shut and massaged his temples. It felt as though everyone had 'ruining Afridi's day' as the number one priority on their agendas.

The motorcyclist had caught up with the van but did not expect Brijesh's arm to reach out and grab him around the neck before he could so much as fire one solitary shot. Brijesh took hold of the gun – another MP5 – and tightened his grip around the hapless man's throat.

'Shoot him!' said Vikrant, but Brijesh staunchly refused.

'We ... need to save ... ammo,' he said through gritted teeth, struggling to snap the assassin's neck.

'Brijesh! You can spare one bullet. Do it or I will,' said Vikrant, growing increasingly concerned with the motorcyclist's resilience.

'Kang! HIT THE BRAKES!' yelled Brijesh, and a startled Kang did as ordered.

Laila was sensibly secured by her seatbelt, but Ray and Waris slammed into the front seats. Ray helped his boss sit back and looked over to find Brijesh calmly sitting back down. 'Drive on,' he said matter-of-factly.

'Did you get him?' asked Waris, back in his senses.

'He did. He really did,' said Vikrant, as he watched the van speed away from the disjointed-looking body across two lanes of the freeway. The sudden brake applied by Kang had caused his neck to snap but the violent whiplash effect might have even cracked his spine in half, he realized – not that any of the team members were remotely interested in finding out. Aside from dispatching the assailant sent for them, they had just doubled their ammo count.

'Nine rounds,' grinned Vikrant, as he checked their latest acquisition. 'So we have eighteen in total. Good enough for now, I think.'

'How much longer till we reach the dock?' piped up a voice no one had heard for a long time.

'I don't know, Ray,' said Brijesh. Then, sensing the young techie's anxiety and trying to lighten the mood, he told him, 'But it's good to hear your voice after such a long time.' Ray smiled nervously and opened his mouth to say something, but was interrupted by Laila. 'Roadblock, guys, all the lanes are blocked,' she said, anxiety in her voice.

'Can you go through them?' asked Brijesh.

'I don't know,' replied a groggy Kang.

'Do they look strong enough to stop us?' persisted Brijesh.

'I don't know,' repeated Kang, dreading the jarring jolt that would go through his body upon impact.

'Punch through,' said Brijesh.

The team braced for impact as the police unit that had assembled the road block began waving their sticks furiously, ordering the van to stop. A senior policeman seemed to be reaching into his holster for a revolver. He took aim. Laila began to slide down in her seat, trying to make as little of herself visible. The policeman fired and the bullet ricocheted harmlessly off the bonnet of the van, as Kang accelerated – with the impact only milliseconds away.

Fortunately, the barricade seemed to have been set up in a very ad hoc fashion and the van was able to cut right through it. Sections of the roadblock flew left and right as the van powered forward and the sound of the collision masked the pained grunt that emanated from Kang's mouth. The broken bones in his leg were now unaligned. The slightest movement caused excruciating pain to surge up and down his body. Not long to go now, he said to himself.

As the convoy arrived at the spot where the body of one of the two motorbike assailants lay prone, Afridi got on the radio with the last car in the group. 'Don't leave this man lying out here like this,' he said. 'He died for a noble cause and I want to see him given a burial with the dignity he deserves. I will personally write a letter to his family.'

'Yes, sir,' came the response.

'WITH THE BLOOD OF THOSE BASTARDS!' raged Afridi, as he exhorted the driver. 'How many more of our people do you want to see killed by those Indians? DRIVE FASTER!' His thoughts returned to revenge again. The sardar, he thought, there's some unfinished business. He would get that drill and make holes all over his body and let him bleed slowly to death.

Along the way, the last vehicle in the convoy picked up the second fallen assassin with the same dignified burial in mind.

Afridi glared at the incompetent policemen as they drove past the remains of the barricade they had assembled. The morons, he thought, why must he be surrounded by such buffoons? It was almost as if they wanted the Indians to escape.

'We have visual, sir,' announced the driver triumphantly. Afridi finally had his eyes on his prey.

40

Kiamari Village, Karachi

'Patience,' said Brijesh soothingly to Waris. 'We'll be there soon.'

The calm in his voice belied his tension, which was written clearly on his face as he looked back through the rear window and a cavalcade of Pakistani armed forces vehicles was gathering on the horizon a few kilometres down the Lyari Expressway. The team was only a short distance from the turnoff that would take them straight to the harbour but before that, they had to outrun a fast approaching army of very pissed-off Pakistanis. *This*, thought Brijesh, *is going to be a tight photo finish.*

'Guys, just give me the word,' said Vikrant, crouched on one knee with the RPG over his shoulder. Shaking his head at his colleague's impetuosity, Brijesh leaned forward and asked Kang and Laila, 'How are we holding up?'

'Okay,' said Laila. Kang merely nodded.

'ETA?' Brijesh persisted.

'Soon,' muttered Kang.

Kang's mood had been deteriorating ever since they had left the warehouse, thought Brijesh. He leaned back and allowed the man at the wheel his space.

In fact, the only person who knew exactly how Kang was doing was Kang himself. All Laila could see was that his movements had become more economical; his face was frozen in a contorted mask of pain and agony and his skin had gone very pale. She dreaded to imagine the pool of blood collecting below his seat. She looked over at him in concern and he blinked. That was her signal to back off.

The reality was that Kang would probably need to be cut from the vehicle. Chunks of metal had devastated his right arm and leg, and entered his thorax from the right. He kept gulping down the blood that came gurgling up into his throat as a result of the internal bleeding, but he had no way of knowing just how badly his organs were skewered. It was probably not too useful to dwell on that, particularly in light of the fact that Afridi's bloodthirsty hordes were descending on the team.

He used his left hand to apply pressure to his ribs – when his hand returned to the steering wheel, it was covered with blood. Blood was trickling down his body to his ankles and collecting in a little puddle below the accelerator. He tried to focus on the road signs for the port and its various jetties.

The only thing that stood between the team and home was five kilometres – and a crew of angry Pakistanis.

Afridi grinned for the first time in a long while. He thumped the driver's shoulder.

'Well done, my son,' he said effusively. In his darkest moments, Afridi hadn't completely ruled out the possibility of not catching up with his prey at all. He would lose credibility, the ISI would lose its fear factor, Pakistan would lose face and, of course, the media would take a gigantic bite out of him for this goof-up. He could not let that happen.

He leaned out of the side of his vehicle and took aim with his trusty sidearm. The bullet ricocheted off the side of the van, causing it to swerve. *A few more shots and I'll have them for sure*, he thought. The cavalcade began closing the gap between themselves and the van when his car suddenly swerved. An irritated Afridi glared at his driver, who said hesitantly, 'They seem to be throwing luggage at us to slow us down, sir.'

'Luggage? What luggage?'

'There were some bags, I couldn't see them properly, and I just avoided what looked like the outer casing for an assault weapon,' the driver said.

Afridi's eyes narrowed as he turned to face the driver. 'What assault weapon are we talking about here?'

The driver mumbled something under his breath.

'No,' said Afridi, 'I asked you to tell me what assault weapon you saw the casing for. I do not recall asking you to mumble incoherently.'

'It was an RPG case, sir,' the flustered driver conceded. 'I don't know where they got it, but maybe they just had the box.'

Afridi's eyes looked like pale saucers with olives in the middle. But he curbed the burning urge to smack the driver over the head and reached for his walkie-talkie instead. He clicked the broadcast switch on his handset and began speaking into it.

'Be advised, the suspects are in possession of an RPG,' he said.

'Do you have visual confirmation, sir?' came a firm but respectful voice.

'They threw its outer case at us two minutes ago,' said Afridi, slightly annoyed that he had to explain himself.

'But sir, it's possible that they just had the case in the van and threw the–'

Afridi's patience had reached its limit and he flew off the handle in trademark style.

'Why on God's green earth would anyone carry around the casing of an RPG without the actual projectile launcher inside? Are you being intentionally difficult or are you really that daft?' he asked the hapless soldier at the other end of the walkie-talkie.

'No, sir,' the man fumbled.

'Do you think people like collecting gun case–' began Afridi, as his eyes focussed on the van, 'All right, I've got your fucking visual confirmation for you. I see one of those cockroaches holding an RPG aimed at us!' He turned to his driver and screamed: 'RAM THAT VAN AS HARD AS YOU CAN!'

'Steady, Vikrant. Collateral damage must be avoided at all costs,' said Brijesh.

'Okay,' said Vikrant, with a hint of a catch in his voice. 'The jeep is closing in fast. If I need to shoot this at him, it's got to be now or they'll be too close.'

Ray turned and looked with horror at the jeep speeding down the expressway – having almost caught up with them. It was when he saw the whites of Afridi's eyes that he turned around and took cover.

'Too late,' said Vikrant to himself as he swivelled around, placed the RPG at his feet and picked up an MP5. Before he could turn and discharge a few rounds at Afridi's head, the jeep had rammed into the van.

Kang tried to swerve and avoid the full impact of the jeep, but, he only succeeded in sending it sliding across the road. The shock took its toll on the broken Kang and he grunted loudly as he steered the van back into the middle of the road and drove on. 'Are you all right?' asked a very concerned Laila, but this time

Kang had no response for her. He feared his time was nigh and he just had to get the van to the right jetty. *And then everything will be all right*, he thought, as he turned quickly off the expressway.

Vikrant had managed to regain his composure and he stood back up with the MP5, waiting for Afridi's jeep to get within range. But it didn't. Another vehicle from the convoy charged at the van and Vikrant fired at its tyres. After Brijesh's strict 'no collateral damage' instructions, he had to take a non-lethal shot. The first shot was a negative impact. The second hit the jeep's grille harmlessly. This was proving to be a more difficult task than he had imagined.

It was with the third shot that Vikrant registered a hit and blew out the front left tyre. The vehicle seemed to wobble, but nothing more.

'That was a waste,' grumbled Vikrant, as Brijesh grabbed his wrist.

'Don't you understand what he's doing? He's sending out cannon fodder to deplete our ammo,' said Brijesh. 'Then, when we're out of ammo, he'll come in and kill us all … or worse.' Just then, the wobbling jeep somersaulted and crashed upside down in the middle of the road that led off the expressway towards the port. A cloud of smoke rose from it, as its occupants struggled to pull themselves out of the wreckage.

'Good work,' said Brijesh. 'You've blocked the road and bought us some time.'

The jeep had skidded to a halt on the narrow road, making it impossible for any sort of vehicle, barring a scooter or a motorcycle, to get past. They watched the soldiers, crushed under the weight of the jeep, desperately trying to claw their way out. Brijesh turned back around and thought to himself, *what's the difference between them and this group of people in the van? Both are fighting for their country. How is it the soldier's fault if his political leadership is wrong? A soldier's job is to follow orders and protect his country and its people. Isn't it?*

He heard a loud crash and screams. In a bid to catch the enemy, Afridi's jeep had ploughed straight at the upside-down jeep, sending it flying and crushing its occupants. If they hadn't already suffered serious injuries, this was sure to have smashed all their bones. Afridi was a man possessed. Vikrant was frozen as he watched him standing up on his seat with what looked curiously like an RPG on his shoulder.

Vikrant leapt for his own RPG. It was already loaded and was just a matter of placing it on his shoulder and aiming – but it was too late. That tell-tale hissing sound of a rocket flying in their direction meant that there was to be only one course of action.

'Take cover!' he yelled, as he threw himself to the floor.

'DIRECT HIT!' yelled a triumphant Afridi, as the hissing rocket-propelled grenade smashed into the rear left tyre of the van, making it fly sideways. It landed on its side and slid along the road towards the grassy bank before coming to a rest. Ray was the first to emerge, climbing out of the door that opened skywards. He climbed out and offered a hand to Brijesh, who was busy securing Waris.

As Vikrant crawled out of the rear window of the van, he noticed Afridi's jeep rolling slowly towards them. He knew the man was toying with them. He opened fire with the MP5 to buy some time for the rest to get out of the van. Unsurprisingly, Afridi's jeep pulled over to the side and his co-passengers began returning fire from behind the vehicle.

By the time Vikrant had fired another volley and worked out that he only had a couple of rounds left, he turned around to see Brijesh slowly climbing out of the van with Waris on his back. Laila too was out and seemed unscathed, save for a cut across her forehead. 'Where's Kang?' he asked, just as a shot rang out.

Vikrant reeled and fell behind the van, clutching at his right arm, from which blood gushed. He had been careless and turned away from the enemy, leaving himself open to attack. Laila returned fire with her pistol, sending the attackers scurrying back behind their vehicle. That, however, did not stop them from firing rounds at the van. Most bounced off harmlessly, but there was the ever-present danger that six of those bullets had the team members' names on them.

Brijesh yelled out to Vikrant. 'Do it! This is your time!'

Vikrant turned to find Brijesh diving back into the van to extract Kang, and picked up the RPG that had fallen out of the van when it toppled over. He got on one knee and heard Kang scream as Brijesh tried to free him. With the RPG propped on his shoulder, Vikrant moved out from behind cover, took a deep breath and pulled the trigger.

Everything seemed to happen in slow motion.

Ray looked on wide-eyed. Laila was helping Waris stand up as he pointed at the trajectory of the grenade. Brijesh was inside the van trying desperately to help Kang out.

The grenade hissed, leaving a white trail as it swerved and crashed headfirst into the bonnet of the jeep, causing it to jump a few feet in the air and explode in a ball of yellow and white flames. Afridi was flung from the jeep into the trees that lined the road. The others were tossed around in different directions.

One man came flying and landed closer to Vikrant than the rest. He hit the ground with a splat and as he rolled over, Vikrant had to keep his gag reflexes in check – the man's stomach and chest were split open and blood, guts and intestines were gurgled out of the gash and spilled out onto the black tarred road.

The man lay on his back, breathing heavily. As Vikrant walked over to him, he saw the anger blazing in his eyes despite his obvious pain. Amid the sounds of Kang screaming in pain, the police sirens in the distance and the crackling sound of the fire emanating from the bombed jeep, Vikrant clearly heard the man mouthing expletives, accusing him of being a kaafir, among other things.

But it was nothing Vikrant hadn't heard before. The thought of letting the man suffer crossed his mind, but that wouldn't be the right thing to do, he decided, and reached for the MP5 and took aim. He fired a shot clean through the forehead of the wounded man, who stopped twitching at once.

Meanwhile, Kang was still struggling. They heard a crack and a loud, animal-like roar of pain, and knew he'd been extracted from the van – but at what cost?

As the team would soon discover, that had just been the sound of Kang's leg breaking in another place. Brijesh slid out and said, 'Guys, gather around. Leave me one gun and the RPG and make your way to the dock. We'll follow. Vikrant, take the lead and make your way to the jetty. To Sky's speedboat!'

'Bullshit!' said Vikrant. 'We're going nowhere till we get Kang out.'

'I appreciate that but this place will soon be swarming with soldiers and the ISI. And when that happens, we'll hold them off to buy you guys time to get out of this goddamn country,' said Brijesh.

'But Bri–' began Laila.

'GO! NOW!!' said Brijesh, as he dived back into the van.

'There's no time,' said Vikrant, as he placed one of Waris's arms over his shoulder and with Laila and Ray covering them, made his way towards the jetty.

'Remember,' Brijesh called from inside the van, 'when you get to the boat – reach for the sky!'

Afridi held his head and sat up in a muddy patch covered with leaves. Aside from a few grazes and bruises, the awful ringing in his ear and the disorientation associated with being near an explosion, he was in relatively fine shape. He dusted himself off as he stood up and made his way towards the road. He allowed himself a little laugh at just how far he'd been flung from the jeep as he walked briskly towards it and picked up a pistol from the ground.

He craned his neck as he walked out of the foliage. *Had they been killed? Were his men parading the streets with their carcasses?* Not for the first time, his thoughts were interrupted by reality. The remaining members of his convoy and three armoured assault vehicles had turned up alongside the smouldering remains of his jeep.

'What the fuck is going on?' he asked.

'The road was blocked, sir. It took us time to get here,' offered one of the policemen.

'Do you have them?'

'No, sir.'

'Of course you don't,' laughed Afridi, 'why would you? Why would anyone think it is important to save this country's honour?'

He lifted his hand and slapped the policeman in the face with all his strength. His nose and mouth imploded microseconds before blood spurted all over his face. 'Now,' said Afridi angrily, 'who wants to join this Indian sympathizer without a face and who wants to join me in nailing their balls to the wall!' The men grunted their approval and boarded their respective vehicles.

'Get out,' said Afridi to a policeman who was entering one of the armoured vehicles. Snatching the keys from the cop, he jumped into the driver's seat and sped off in the direction of the port.

Using the RPG's body as a splint attached to his shattered leg, with what seemed like kilometres of insulation tape, Kang limped along the road with a rather unorthodox prosthetic limb and Brijesh for support. 'All good?' asked Brijesh, as Kang struggled to keep moving.

'No, this thing weighs a ton!' fired back Kang, who was still bleeding although most of the blood flow had been suppressed by the amount of insulating tape—a rare surplus commodity found in the van—that had been wrapped around his wounds. As strong as Kang was, it took Brijesh's grip on the RPG handle to keep the new 'leg' moving.

'Not long to go now,' said Brijesh, pointing to the lights along the harbour. 'We're almost there.' The sound of police sirens was coming closer every second. 'Come on, we have to move faster,' he said.

Suddenly, the duo was caught in a flash of headlights. Without thinking, Brijesh placed his hands on the sedan's bonnet as it braked, shocked at the sight of the two men.

'Sir, we need your vehicle, please,' said Brijesh humbly, desperation in his voice.

'I can give you a lift,' said the gentleman behind the wheel. He seemed to be in his late fifties, with a head of finely coiffured hair and an accent to go with it.

'You don't understand, sir, we need your car.'

'Young man, this "car" as you put it, is no ordinary car. It is a finely engineered German vehicle with five thousand three hund—' said the man before he was interrupted by a raging Kang.

'It's just a fucking car! Now if you would be so kind as to PLEASE GET THE FUCK OUT OF IT? Thank you,' he said, before resting on his RPG launcher leg again.

The startled gentleman climbed out of the vehicle as Brijesh helped Kang into the backseat and took the wheel, gun in hand.

'Thank you, sir,' said Brijesh as he started the engine, 'Your vehicle is insured, I hope?'

'Well, of course it is. What kind of—'

For the second time, the man was interrupted. This time the interruption came in the form of Brijesh flooring the accelerator and zooming off towards the port. As Brijesh followed the road signs, Kang sat quietly looking at the state of his arm and leg, and thinking about the electric drill. He was still haunted by the sound of it, the way his skin had flecked off his body as it entered and the burning wound it had left.

'Kang, I need to ask a major favour of you,' said Brijesh gravely.

'What?'

'I want you to ready that RPG,' said Brijesh.

'I guess this won't entail cutting it off my leg.'

'Cutting it off you will take too long, so it will need to be fired from your leg. But the recoil could take your leg off completely.'

Kang began to lift his leg out of the window and position himself behind it. The pain was so great, he was now numb. Once Brijesh was content with the arrangements and had loaded up the last grenade, he sped towards the phalanx of Pakistani security agency vehicles and then made an audacious handbrake turn – to line the mouth of the RPG launcher with the vehicles.

'Fire!' yelled Brijesh as he turned to put his hands on the gun and hold it in place, trying to secure Kang's leg.

Kang pulled the trigger and the hissing grenade began its flight to destruction.

Brijesh felt a spray of blood on his face as the RPG launcher blew out of the opposite window of the car – with Kang's leg still attached to it.

Brijesh turned and drove swiftly down Beach Avenue towards Clifton Beach.

An anticipated volley of bullets pulverized the German automobile, but failed to slow it down. Brijesh was hit, taking bullets in the collar bone, shoulder and tricep as he drove towards the jetty.

Meanwhile, the team had arrived at the boat marked 'BMW' at Kiamari village, but were unable to enter, mainly due to the presence of a mysterious miniature aircraft on top of the boat. 'That's a Hornet I,' said Ray. 'A light unmanned combat aerial vehicle.'

'That's marvellous, Ray!' said Laila, with more than a tinge of sarcasm. 'Any idea how we get it off the boat?'

'I don't see a control panel or an ignition slot of any sort. Do you see any remote controls around?' he asked, missing her sarcasm entirely.

'Guys, hurry up, I hear gunfire. We have to be prepared to leave without Kang and Brijesh,' said Vikrant, as he placed his hand on the unconscious Waris's shoulder. The senior officer sat propped up against a crate.

'No, there's nothing here,' said Ray. 'There's no device.'

'Maybe it doesn't need a device,' said Laila.

'Yes, there's always the chance it could be voice-operated,' replied Ray.

'Stop bickering, you two!' snapped Vikrant. 'We need to get this off the boat at once. Sky would never knowingly place a defective—'

And the penny dropped.

'Remember, when you get to the boat, reach for the sky' had been Brijesh's words to them. *What a strange thing to say, unless ...*

'Here goes nothing,' said Vikrant, and said the words clearly: 'Reach for the sky!'

The drone powered to life and an array of lights flashed, as a small engine within it came to life. It slowly ascended and hovered in the air above them. 'You're a genius,' said Ray in awe. 'No, Ray,' replied Vikrant, 'You and Laila are the geniuses.'

He lifted Waris and carried him into the boat, adding, 'If it hadn't been for your bickering, we never would have worked it out.'

The drone seemed to be controlled by something or someone else, because it suddenly zoomed back towards the city. They watched as it rained down a flurry of bullets and heard the explosions it was causing. 'Death from above,' said Vikrant softly, to no one in particular, as a white sedan appeared at the end of the jetty. It seemed to be hurtling towards them.

'Guys, take cover,' said Vikrant as he propped himself up with the MP5, one final bullet in the magazine.

The sedan braked suddenly and Brijesh's face appeared.

'Get Kang into the boat,' he said, sombrely. 'He hasn't got much time.'

'But you're bleeding too,' said Ray.

'I'm fine.'

Afridi stood at the end of the jetty and watched the boat leaving the shore. He hopped into a speedboat with two of his men and began to give chase. What he needed was some air support. His speedboat was doing thirty-five knots per hour, which was about as fast as the Indians' boat and it would be difficult to overtake them or even intercept them, given their headstart. He decided to call Raheel Sharif.

'Janaab General sir, assalam alaikum, this is Afridi, special operations, ISI speaking.'

'Haan, waalaikum salaam. Arif, bolo.' Raheel didn't seem happy to be disturbed.

'It's an emergency, sir, and that's why I had to disturb you. Those Indians are getting away. They have just got on to a speedboat at Kiamari and may be heading for the Gujarat coast. We need to stop them or destroy them before they manage to leave Pakistani waters,' Afridi said, the panic mounting in his voice.

'I'll get the air chief to scramble the jets,' Raheel said, ready to sign off.

'General sir, since we have some frigates and warships at Manora, can we press them into service? They would be the closest and can intercept them,' Afridi suggested.

'Do you want to put the entire might of Pakistan behind a bunch of riff-raff? I'll see what I can do,' Raheel said and disconnected, without waiting for an answer.

Meanwhile, Vikrant was at the wheel, fully focused on the way ahead. He manoeuvred the speedboat past several dhows, trawlers and fishing nets parked near the coast.

He turned around and saw Brijesh lying face down, clothes drenched with blood. Next to him was a far bloodier Kang, one leg missing. Waris was still weak, reclining against a sack. They had been hit hard, but they had survived.

Laila and Ray were taking turns on the GPS equipment. 'Turn right, Vikrant, turn right. A wrong turn will take us towards the Chinna Creek mangroves, where we'd be trapped.'

'Sir, they are closing in on us. There are three or four boats and their numbers seem to be increasing. They may have received assistance from the Manora cantonment,' Ray yelled over the noise of the engine.

Forty knots was the best they could do. The boat had begun to wobble; any increase in speed would cause it to overturn.

Waris gestured to Laila to come closer and said something in her ear. She nodded and rushed towards Vikrant.

'He says that once you cross twenty nautical miles, you have crossed Pakistani territorial waters. Sky is sending a submarine for us. But once we are in the submarine, they will not be able to lay their hands on us in international waters,' Laila said.

Vikrant nodded. He could see a huge dark shadow moving towards them at a steady speed.

'What is that?' Ray asked, scared out of his wits.

Afridi now had seven boats chasing the Indians. He instructed them to open fire.

'Sir, they are out of range, there's no point in firing,' said an officer.

'Fuck you, I said fire at them! Any stray bullet could hit them,' Afridi shouted.

One of the officers piped up. 'Sir, I can see a destroyer moving towards them.'

Even before the Indian speedboat was in range, the Tariq class destroyer had opened fire on it.

Laila and Ray fell flat on the floor.

'How much further?' yelled Vikrant at the top of his voice

Laila turned on her stomach, looked at her GPS instrument and replied, 'Only two nautical miles and my coordinates state that soon after we cross it, we will turn east and jump into the water to get into Shalki.'

Vikrant turned back to look. A destroyer class vessel was leading the band of boats that was attacking them, and the distance between them was reducing rapidly.

Just then he heard the sound of a whirring chopper over his head and a volley of bullets.

'Laila, get everyone the scuba gear and snorkels. Ray, help Brijesh, Kang and Waris get theirs on. We have no time,' Vikrant ordered.

The chopper had gone ahead and was turning back now.

Vikrant knew how to handle fire from a chopper. Although it had the advantage of altitude, it wasn't the most accurate. As the chopper came closer, Vikrant pulled the boat into a zigzag movement. He could only see a huge, daunting body of water

– nothing but darkness and water. But he kept going doggedly.

'Vikrant, we are out of Pakistani waters,' Laila said.

'But they are still chasing us,' said Ray.

'They can claim hot pursuit,' Vikrant explained. He saw that his entire team had strapped on their snorkels. He asked Laila to grab the wheel, while he picked up a snorkel and put it on.

The destroyer had begun firing at them again.

Just then, he saw a fighter aircraft flying dangerously low towards them.

'This is it,' Vikrant said.

Afridi was livid when he was told that the Indians had left Pakistani waters. 'I can see an airforce plane. Ask the pilot to shoot them,' he said into his radio.

'Sir, they have crossed our boundary. Any fire could provoke a war,' the pilot replied.

'Shoot at them! It will be my responsibility.'

'Sir, I also see an Indian warship in the distance. It would not be advisable. There could be war.'

'Shut the fuck up and shoot!' Afridi screamed, his eyes red hot with anger.

Vikrant turned towards Laila. Brijesh would go with her. He instructed Ray to take Waris. 'I will handle Kang,' he said.

He looked up at the fighter plane and urged Laila to jump before they were bombed. Laila tried to lift Brijesh up, with Vikrant and Ray supporting her, and together they slipped into the water. Then Vikrant helped Waris, who was just about conscious and slowly joined Kang, who summoned the last reserves of his strength and entered the water with them.

Just in time, behind him, a rocket blew up the speedboat. It had served its purpose.

The celebrations aboard the submarine were muted. In their hurry to get out of Pakistan and ensure that no one was left behind, they had failed to put the adequate amount of pressure on Kang's volcanic bleeding. Somewhere between the time they finally got out of their speedboat and the time that Ray went to share a joke with Kang, he had bled to death.

It was only a short while ago that he had asked Vikrant to keep slapping him to make sure he didn't die in Pakistani waters. 'You're not going to die out here,' Vikrant had said. 'You're far too tough for that.'

Brijesh placed a hand on his face and gently closed the eyelids of one of the most courageous men he had had the privilege to work with.

Brijesh fell to his knees and took Kang's dead body in his embrace. With his head resting on Kang's chest, he seemed to breathe his last too.

They sat in silence for the remainder of the journey. *The last few days have scarred us all*, thought Vikrant. *Some more than others, but the price of freedom isn't cheap and the cost of vengeance is very high*. He accepted that someday he would have to pay this cost. But for now, their mission had been accomplished.

The submarine took what was left of the team to a speedboat just off the coast of Mumbai and they slowly climbed into it. Brijesh and Kang would be buried at sea with all the honours the Indian Navy could bestow.

The first person aboard the speedboat was Waris.

'Is that—? Have we—? Gateway?' he asked, confused.

Laila looked over at him and Ray leaned in to listen.

'What was that?' Ray asked.

'Is that the Gateway of … of India?'

Ray and Laila turned and peered into the distance. Sure enough, it was the Gateway of India, with the iconic Taj Mahal Palace Hotel in the backdrop.

'Take some time to look at that sight and let it sink in,' said Waris, softly but clearly. 'Let it remind you of what we fought for.

Laila stroked his back, as he began to cough.

'What I'm trying to say is that your victories are India's victories. But your names will never be known. If they are known, it will be by those who want to hunt you down and kill you. That is the price we pay for our vengeance. I hope you are all at peace with that. I know I am,' he said. Those were the last works he spoke

Epilogue

Islamabad, ISI HQ.

'No, I will not take the call,' said Afridi, softly but sternly to his PA, as he ran his fingers through his hair. The PA nodded and quietly retreated from his boss's office, shutting the door softly behind him.

Under normal circumstances, the chief of army staff wasn't a man whose calls could be ignored, but these circumstances were far from normal.

A man of discipline, Arif Afridi had never been one to disrespect his equipment or the facilities of his office, but today he sat on the leather chair with his feet on the table. He stared into blank nothingness in his office, which was usually lit by an array of energy-saving light bulbs. One solitary table lamp provided context to the bleak despondence that had taken over the man who was widely considered to be one of ISI's most competent officers.

He reached for the television remote control and pressed the standby button. The black LED screen reflected his mood briefly, before flickering to life in an orgy of colours. He skipped past the sports channels. The trials and tribulations of cricketers held little interest for him any more.

'In an audacious attack on Pakistani soil, militants believed to be of Indian origin destroyed government property and—' said the anchor of a Pakistani television channel.

He clicked the little plus button on his remote control to change the channel.

'... unidentified attack on the Pakistani city of Karachi. Authorities are linking this to a series of attacks over the course of—' said the stoic anchor of a British news channel.

Click.

'Where is the justice for the innocents killed by these Indian militants? Why is the LoC not being patrolled more carefully and where is—' came the voice of another Pakistani news anchor.

Click.

'If you ask me, this is a case of the chickens coming home to roost. By being a terror haven, they effectively set themselves up for the—' opined a right-wing analyst on an American news channel.

Click.

'... the anniversary of 26/11. The country wants to know what is happening across the border. Is every Indian man, woman and child entitled to celebrate or should this be a moment of reflection? We will debate this on—' shrieked a shrill Indian television anchor.

Such was the effect of his voice that Afridi switched off the television set.

He looked across his table at the display cabinet behind it. The medals, trophies, plaques and other memorabilia paid tribute to his sparkling career, but much like the JuD headquarters, that bright, sparkling career lay in ruins. A section of the cabinet that contained a little trophy for a marathon in which he had participated and been placed third, caught his eye.

Beside the trophy were commendations for archery, horseriding and squash, but these didn't matter much to him now. What did matter was the framed photograph of an army officer with a gigantic collage of medals across his proud chest: Lt Gen. Yusuf Jan Afridi, his father.

He wondered how things had turned out like this. After all, it had been his life's mission to avenge his father's humiliation. He had set about his life and career to right all the wrongs that had been committed by India against his father and by association, his country. And at the end of it all, he had let those bastards slip away. It wasn't even the fact that he had lost so many people who were vital to the ISI's cause. That he had let his country down hurt, but even that wasn't the lowest point for him.

The fact was, he had grown up to be a failure, just like his father before him.

Afridi took out a little key from his breast pocket and unlocked a drawer that contained some of his father's possessions. A little pocket watch that was stuck at ten minutes past eight. A few medals. A letter. And of course, General Abbu's service revolver. The one with which he had ended his life.

Afridi allowed himself a wry smile despite himself, at the clichéd nature of what he was about to do.

He cocked the revolver, rested the mouth of the barrel on his temple, and closed his eyes.